The Knitter's Heartwish

Heartwishes, Volume 4

Daisy Dexter Dobbs

Published by Department of Daydreams, 2022.

THE KNITTER'S HEARTWISH

First edition. September 13, 2022.

ISBN: 978-1587850868

Written by Daisy Dexter Dobbs.

Also by Daisy Dexter Dobbs

Watch for more at www.DaisyDexterDobbs.com.

Dedication

My daughter, Jen, and I are best friends. She's loving, kind, caring, brave and adventurous. She's absolutely brimming with creativity, skills, imagination, and curiosity. Happily, Jen shares my love of shopping at garage sales and thrift shops and making great finds. She also has a fabulous sense of humor, which means much of the time we spend together is enveloped in laughter. Most of the close female characters in my books (friends, siblings, mothers and daughters) are at least partially based on the wonderful relationship my daughter and I enjoy. She's brought so much joy into my life, just by being herself. I'm proud of her. I admire and respect her. And, seriously, how fortunate am I to have a daughter with a passion for reading who provides me with great insight, an eagle-eye, and excellent suggestions for my manuscripts? I can't begin to tell you how much I cherish the precious gift of being Jen's mom—and that's why this book is dedicated to her...even though neither of us can knit worth a darn.

Book Description

~<>~

Maureen Malone loves knitting unique items for the kids at the children's hospital where she volunteers. Hoping to brighten their day, Reen even wears her quirky knitted hats with the long yarn braids in the children's ward. The kids giggle, the nurses grin, and some people pretend not to see her.

Reen's happy to provide a little laughter, even if it means looking silly. While some people are multi-degreed or have high-profile jobs, she believes humor is as important as being proficient in calculus, or well-read in Shakespeare.

Leaving the house to deliver more hats, Reen slips on an icy step, breaking her ankle and tailbone. Her neighbor, Professor Drake Slattery, witnesses her fall and, ignoring her protests, takes her to the hospital.

With dark, wavy hair and blue-gray eyes, the brilliant single dad can easily pass for Clark Kent...maybe Superman. But it doesn't matter. She and Drake are only good friends—buddies with very little in common.

Maureen makes Drake crazy. She's stubborn, lacks common sense, acts before thinking, and has all the self-confidence of a peanut. She's a packrat, filling her house with other people's castoffs and endless skeins of yarn. Sometimes it seems she has yarn for brains.

That said, Drake wouldn't change a thing about her. He's watched her knit until her fingers bleed so she can finish her special projects for the sick kids in the hospital. There's no better person he knows than Reen Malone. His twins love her...and so does he.

Of course, none of that matters because, that time he tried to kiss her, Reen made it clear she thinks of him like a brother.

The Knitter's Heartwish is book 4 of the Heartwishes series. This original full-length contemporary romance novel is full of warmth and humor—with a very special touch of magic. While all Heartwishes books are part of a standalone series, you'll enjoy them more if you read them in order. These are small town romances with happily-ever-afters, and no cliffhangers.

Chapter One

Early January: Glassfloat Bay, Oregon

~<>~

"AFTER SPENDING a few days with him, I've decided he looks like a Mortimer." Maureen Malone texted a photo to her sister as they spoke. "Morty for short. What do you think, Laila?"

A moment later, gentle laughter came over the phone. "Oh my gosh, Reen, he's darling. And look at those soulful eyes! You're right, that's the perfect name for him."

"Good, then Mortimer the Dragon it is."

"Which kid requested a dragon hat with orange hair?"

"Lucas Carmody. He's got pale skin with a flock of freckles, and had thick orangey-red hair before he lost it. I think the green and orange yarn will look good on him." Reen gave a satisfied smile as she affixed a small cellophane-wrapped piece of marzipan candy to the hat she'd knitted. The tiny marzipan dragon with a replica of the little boy's freckled face that she and Laila had created complemented the hat's whimsical visage.

"Instead of using safety pins I'm tying the packets of candy with ribbon, looping it through the knitted fabric. I thought that would be safer for children's fingers." Reen packed the hat and matching candy in the box along with the other knitted and crocheted hats and corresponding molded marzipan treats.

"Good thinking. With all the needle pokes those poor kids must get, I'm sure the last thing they'd want is to prick a finger on a pin."

Among her yarn creations keeping the dragon company in the shirt-size box was a baby blue aviator cap with pink knitted goggles on top; a purple Viking hat with a curly, crocheted red beard

3

attached; a happy, tongue-lolling Dalmatian hat; a lion mane cap; a teddy bear hat; and some Valentine-themed hats for next month's holiday.

Reen smiled as she looped tiny marzipan princess likenesses through the yarn on a pair of bejeweled princess crown hats. One child's face was tinted a light beige color, while the other was tinted the same soft copper shade as the little girl who'd receive it.

"I'm proud of the job I did on these hats," she said, snapping a side-by-side photo of the identical princess hats and sending it to Laila. "It's my first attempt at creating coily hair. What do you think?"

"Look at those adorable halos of corkscrew curls!" Laila said. "They match the pink squiggles we made on the marzipan princesses. How did you manage to get yarn to hold a tight spiral like that?"

Gently bouncing the springy hair, Reen said, "Ruthie Brone from the yarn shop gave me instructions. I wrapped yarn around skinny wood dowel rods, tying the ends so they wouldn't unravel. I soaked them in water, put them on a cookie sheet, and baked them in a 200-degree oven until dry, about fifteen minutes. Once everything was cool, I carefully unwrapped the yarn from the dowels to keep the coils nice and tight and, *voila*! It was time consuming but really easy. I'm very happy with the results."

"They're perfect. So who requested the pink coily hair?"

"Cute story," Reen told her, smiling at the memory. "The light colored marzipan princess is for Ava Mitchell, whose hair was blonde before it fell out, and the darker toned princess is for Shannon Brone, whose hair was dark auburn. The last—"

"Brone? Any relation to Ruthie?"

"Her great-granddaughter. Poor thing's been ill a long time. The last time I volunteered, Ava told me she and Shannie want to be twins, and asked if I could make them matching hats with super curly pink hair so they could look the same. Isn't that sweet?"

"It really is. They're going to love the hats, Reen."

"I hope so. I'm getting excited imagining the smiles on the faces of the kids when I deliver all of these," she told Laila. "Your idea to include matching candies with their likenesses was pure genius. The miniature candy versions turned out adorable. I know how busy you've been at the bakery, so I really appreciate you taking the time to do this with me."

"You've already thanked me seven billion times," Laila teased. "Believe me, helping you with this project was my pleasure. Whatever we can do for those precious kids at the hospital is a top priority as far as I'm concerned. Honestly, your talent with yarn still amazes me, Reen. Those character hats you make are incredible...like cartoons come to life. It's no wonder the kids are crazy about them. I wish I wasn't such a giant dork when it comes to knitting."

"Don't be silly, Laila, you're not a giant dork. You're just...um..."

With Reen's phone on speakerphone, Laila's laughter rang through the room.

"See? You can't even come up with a semi-plausible compliment about my sorry knitting attempts. I can almost hear the gears grinding in your head as you try like hell to come up with a synonym for *knitting challenged*."

"No, I was about to say that your...your crocheting is really coming along nicely," Reen hurried, as images of her sister's atrocious knitting and crocheting efforts flitted across her mind. "Anyway, your special set of skills are baking-related. We both know I'm as much a dork in the kitchen as you are with a pair of knitting needles."

"No you're not." Laila's tone was unconvincing.

"Ha! Without your magical kitchen wizardry I never would have been able to create a batch of marzipan. Heck, I didn't even know what the stuff was before, and now it's one of my favorite things to eat! And then coloring the individual portions with the all-natural food colorings you came up with? Sheesh, Laila, I mean, I was right there in the kitchen making them with you and I still can't quite figure out how we did it," Reen admitted.

"It was fun. I enjoyed it. Don't forget the nut-free cookie versions and the sugar-free marzipan versions."

"I've got them labeled with the children's names to keep them separate." Reen nodded to herself as she spoke. "I'm so glad you suggested checking with the nurses to see if any of the kids have food allergies, sensitivities, or possible food interactions with their medication before passing out the marzipan. It never even crossed my mind."

"That's why I'm the older, smarter sister," Laila quipped.

"Nope, forget about it, Hazelnut," Reen addressed her dog with a tsk. "I already told you marzipan isn't healthy for you. Hazel's been exceedingly attentive and affectionate," she told Laila, chuckling as she tousled the dog's fur. "That nose of hers has been going a mile a minute since we made the marzipan."

"I can imagine. Your little rescue dog certainly is a charmer."

"Little?" Eyeing Hazelnut, Reen laughed. "She's grown into more of a rescue pony. But I love my cutie pie." Wrapping an arm around Hazelnut, Reen drew her in for a hug, speaking to her in baby talk. "She's my baby, aren't you, Hazel?" The dog's tail twirled like a whirlwind. "That's why I have to take care of you and make sure you don't eat foods that are bad for you."

"So which hat are you wearing now?"

"My responsible dog owner hat, of course."

"Ha! Good one." Laila chirped a laugh. "You know what I mean."

Reen's smile stretched wide. "What makes you think I'm even wearing one?" she asked, tugging on the pair of thick, long, buttery-yellow yarn braids framing her cheeks.

"Because I know you, Maureen."

"Hmm, too well, it seems. Okay, smarty pants, I'm wearing the knitted pink Viking hat with two ivory-colored horns stuffed with pillow filling," she patted one as she spoke, "and yellow braids hanging down. It turned out cute. I look just like that woman in the opera."

"What opera?"

"Oh...you know..." Folding two layers of tissue paper over the hats in the box, Reen struggled to recall the opera or character's name.

"Nope. I don't"

"Remember the Bugs Bunny cartoon where Elmer Fudd sings 'Kill da wabbit, kill da wabbit!' in a loud opera voice and there's this rotund Viking diva wearing a horned helmet?" Reen motioned to her knitted cap. "That opera."

Laughing, Laila replied, "Yeah, I think I know the one you mean."

A diehard knitter, Reen loved creating themed hats for the kids at the children's hospital in Wisdom Harbor, just down the coast from Glassfloat Bay. She volunteered there and had a shift this morning. After seeing those brave children who'd lost their hair from chemotherapy and other treatments she was determined to do whatever she could to help make them smile.

"I heard the kids loved the hand puppets you made them for Christmas," Laila said.

"I'm so glad. When I delivered them I asked what else they'd like me to create. Honest to God, Laila, my heart nearly broke when one sweet little girl smiled shyly while patting her bald head, asking, 'Maybe you could knit me some hair?'"

"Aw...poor little thing." Laila offered a sympathetic sigh.

"Several of the kids made similar requests. One asked if I could make her a bunch of purple braids, and one of the boys wanted to know if I could make him a hat that looks like a skunk." Reen chuckled at the memory. "One by one they offered their creative suggestions and I was delighted to take on the challenge."

"Just how many hats and caps have you made over the past few months?"

With an inadvertent shrug, Reen answered, "Probably more than a hundred."

"Yikes, you're a veritable knitting machine!"

On her last volunteer shift Reen encouraged the children to draw colorful crayon pictures of the hats they'd like to have, promising she'd do her best to bring their artwork to life. This morning she'd be picking up the drawings and couldn't wait to see what their youthful imaginations had conjured.

Today's delivery included her most creative attempts so far. Seeing her wear one of the hats when she arrived at the children's ward made the kids giggle and the nurses grin, so Reen happily donned a different one each time she made the trip. Not surprisingly the quirky hats made other drivers laugh or give her curious looks on the road, which is why she chose to wear a hat in the car as well.

She believed everyone could benefit from a dose of unexpected laughter now and then, and was happy to provide it. While some people boasted college degrees and were academics, Reen thought making people smile was every bit as important as being proficient in calculus, or being well read in Shakespeare.

The one element her hats had in common was attached yarn hair that had been braided, knitted, crocheted, or left flowing in colorful strings, even if it was just a small amount peeking out the bottom of the caps.

"Hold on a minute while I pick up these boxes," Reen told her sister. After tucking her blonde curls behind her ears, she wedged the phone between her ear and shoulder, then lifted a stack of the boxes from the living room coffee table with an *ooph*.

"I really should make two trips instead," she muttered.

"That would be too easy," Laila chided.

Discarding her own chastising inner wisdom, Reen struggled, adding the last sizeable box to the pile. The large, rectangular, shallow boxes weren't heavy, just awkward.

Peeking around the lidded boxes in her arms, she spotted the look Hazelnut gave her. "Hazel's giving me her typical forlorn, guilt-inducing *You're just going to go out and leave me here all alone again, aren't you?* expression."

"She must have learned it from Friday," Laila said. "He does that to me every time I pick up my purse."

"Be a good girl, Hazel. I'll be back later...I promise." Still looking mopey, Hazelnut gave a soft, reciprocating bark. Reen couldn't imagine what she'd do without her friendly, often goofy, oversized mutt.

Opening the front door, Reen was greeted with a brisk chill. "Whoa, it's cold outside."

"Yup, we've got one of those unusually cold Pacific Northwest winters," Laila agreed. "If you'd let me help you organize your garage like I keep offering, you could park your car in there instead of outside."

"I know, I know." Reen wished she'd listened to her sister. The garage was stacked with clear plastic storage bins holding countless skeins of yarn, assorted knitting needles, crochet hooks, and endless projects in various stages of completion.

To make matters worse, she was a card-carrying packrat, evidenced by her factual *Warning: I brake for garage sales* bumper sticker.

"One day I'll get everything neat and organized," she vowed to Laila as well as herself as she stepped outside. "I'll actually be able to use the garage for the purpose it was intended." At least that's what she kept promising herself. It was an ambitious goal for a woman who'd saved every scrap of artistically crayoned paper any child had ever given her.

Laila mumbled something inaudible in response.

"What was that? You're not making fun of your poor packrat sister again, are you?"

"Nope, just snickering because we're like two peas in a pod...messy, overpacked pods."

Reen's pie in the sky dream list also included owning her own yarn shop one day. Two things stood in her way—finances, and the fact that String Me Along, the long-established store where she got most of her knitting and crochet supplies, had been a treasured fixture in Glassfloat Bay for decades. Ruthie Brone opened the shop fifty years ago.

After Reen's mom, Astrid, failed in her attempts to teach Reen to knit and crochet, Astrid suggested she take a class at String Me Along. It was in sweet old Ruthie Brone's classes just a few years ago where Reen became almost as addicted to knitting as she was to chocolate.

Ruthie had the patience of a saint. The Brones were good people and Reen couldn't imagine opening a competing shop in the same town. Since moving away from Glassfloat Bay and people she'd grown to love since relocating from Chicago wasn't an option, bye-bye yarn shop ownership.

"After I deliver the hats to the kids I'll come to the bakery to work on those Valentine's Day flyers. You've come up with a mouthwatering assortment of sugar-free and gluten-free treats this year, Laila. So far the scones with the hazelnut paste in the center are my favorite."

"I knew they would be. Drive carefully. It's icy out there and we're not used to driving on icy roads like we were when we lived in Chicago."

"Okay, Mom," Reen teased. "Seriously, Laila, sometimes I think you worry about me almost as much as you worry about the twins." She laughed. "I'm a big girl now who can take care of herself."

Making sure her phone was securely lodged in place before pulling the front door closed behind her, Reen smiled over her shoulder at her mopey dog. "Quit your sulking, Hazelnut. You know I always come ba—"

In the blink of an eye, Reen slipped on the icy concrete step, going down with a mighty thud, and startled yelp. Her arms flailed while her phone and the boxes she carried flew into the air before sprawling around her.

Stunned, she sat there with one leg folded beneath her in an awkward position. It all happened so fast she wasn't sure if she was injured or merely surprised.

"Reen? Maureen? What happened? Are you all right?" Laila's alarmed voice sounded far away.

"Yeah...I think so." Reen was surprised to see the phone was no longer at her shoulder. She had no idea where it was. "I fell on the step. Practically knocked myself out."

"Maureen, I can't hear you. Reenie, what's happening?"

"I'm all right, Laila, don't worry," she called out. "I guess the phone fell when I did."

"What?"

"Aw, I'm okay, Hazel," Reen assured the concerned dog who'd come outside, whimpering while nuzzling and licking her. But as soon as she tried moving, both her tailbone and her ankle told her she hadn't come away from her fall unscathed. From the amount of pain, she suspected a bad sprain.

"Maureen!"

Reen blinked in confusion. That was odd...Laila's voice had lowered a few octaves.

Still dazed, she turned to see Drake Slattery bolting out of his car and running toward her. "Drake?"

"You're bleeding," he noted.

"Bleeding?" Laila yelled. "Reen is bleeding? Drake is that you? What the hell happened? Drake? Reen...? Will somebody please talk to me?"

When she looked down at her legs Reen was surprised to see so much blood coming through the thin, torn slacks of her pink volunteer uniform.

"I didn't realize," she said.

Drake looked left and right. "Where's your phone?"

"I have no idea."

"It's okay, Laila," Drake said after retrieving Reen's phone, which had slid across the icy lawn, landing almost at the sidewalk. "Reen slipped and fell hard. I saw it happen. It might be a sprain or a break. I'm taking her to the ER. I'll call you from there."

Reen grabbed her phone from Drake. "I'm fine, Laila, just a little banged up, that's all. I don't need a doctor. I just..." she took in a deep breath as a wave of pain hit, "...I just need to relax for a minute before I get up."

"I'm taking you," Drake said.

"No, you're not."

"Maureen Malone," Laila all but screamed in her sister's ear, "either you let Drake take you to the hospital or I swear, I'm calling an ambulance."

"Okay, okay! Sheesh, Laila, tone down that mom voice of yours, okay?" Reen managed a sickly little laugh. "I'm fine. I'll see you later, after I go to the doctor and get the hats delivered." She ended the call.

Her fingers ran across the edge of the step she sat on. It was rough as well as icy. "That damned stone step has jagged edges. I should have had it fixed long ago." Those were the things her late fiancé, Bob Brechler, used to do for her before he was killed falling from the slick, moss-covered roof trying to repair loose shingles of the fixer-upper house they'd bought together.

"I should have noticed that and fixed it myself," Drake said. "I'll get to that this weekend."

Reen winced. Not from pain but because, as book-smart as Drake was, his comically bad handyman projects were almost legendary.

"There's really no need, Drake. You're busy enough as it is and I don't want to impose on you."

"You're not—"

"I'll give Hudson a call to come over and take care of it." Noting his slightly dejected expression as she smiled up at him, Reen quickly added, "You already do more than enough for me. You're a great friend." The last thing she wanted to do was make him feel bad.

For some reason he looked even more disappointed and she wasn't sure why.

Both professors at Wisdom Harbor University, her late fiancé, Bob, and Drake had been close friends. The same year Bob died, Drake's wife, Janet, walked out on him and their two children, leaving Drake for another man. Reen adored his kids, watching them often for Drake when he had a scheduling conflict. The guy was a great dad.

Returning his attention to her injury, Drake frowned. "You need to get this looked at right away."

"No need. I'm fine, Drake."

"Should I call your sister back?" he threatened.

That had Reen laughing. "Oh my God, no!" Smoothing her fingers over Hazelnut's fur, she leaned in to hug her angsty dog. "Shhh, don't cry, Hazel, sweetie, I'm okay."

"I saw it happen as I was pulling out of my garage." He nodded a few doors down. Drake was the one who'd suggested the house for sale to Reen and Bob when they got engaged, making the two friendly couples neighbors.

"What's happening, Dad?" his son, Kevin, called from the car. "Is Miss Reen okay?" He opened the car door and he and his sister, Lilly, got out.

"Hey, remember I told you that I need you two to stay in the car," Drake told his six-year-old twins. "Miss Reen is going to be fine." He returned his attention to her while the curious and concerned kids ignored his instructions and came to Reen's side. Drake tsked at them but didn't press the matter.

"Maureen, you fell hard. Your legs are all cut up, and I don't like the look of the way that leg is bent. Can you move it?"

"Sure..."

Hearing her moan at the attempt, Drake gently helped untangle her leg from beneath her.

His hands were all over her legs, examining them as he rolled her pant legs up to her knees. "Look at that ankle," he said, his eyebrows arrowing down as he removed her shoe and sock. His touch was warm, gentle, tender. If she wasn't in agony, she'd enjoy all the attention.

As Drake's fingers gingerly explored her flesh, he frowned. "It's swelling fast. I'm getting you to the emergency room."

"No, really, Drake," she rested her hand on his shoulder, "I'm just a little stunned and scuffed up. I'll be fine in a minute." She tried to be cavalier but when she shifted position her attempted laugh came out sounding more like a sick moose. "I fell on my tailbone," she said, wincing. "If you could just help me get to my feet, I can—" Clinging to the arm of his tweed sport coat with the suede elbow patches, she tried pulling herself up, giving up quickly as pain and dizziness took hold.

"Huh..." she blinked fast, "looks like I did a number on myself."

"I think your ankle might be broken."

"How is that possible? All I did is fall off a step. I haven't had a single broken bone in all my life. I'm sure it's just a bad twist."

"Kevin, Lilly," Drake said, "you two get in the front seat of the car. I'm going to put Miss Reen in the back so she can stretch out her leg." Looking around him he asked, "What are all these boxes?"

"Hats I made for the kids in the hospital," Reen explained. Amazingly none of the box lids had come off. It would have been a shame for the hats to get soiled, or the marzipan candies smashed, before delivering them to the children. "Like this one," she flipped her yarn braids.

When Drake looked at Reen, she could swear his eyes twinkled as he smiled and happy crinkles bracketed his blue-gray eyes. "Well you make a spectacular Brynhildr. All you're missing is the spear."

"Bryn who?" Reen asked, her eyebrows scrunching.

"In Germanic mythology," Drake explained, "Brynhildr, more commonly known as Brunhilde, was a shieldmaiden and a Valkyrie. Have you ever heard the expression, *It's not over until the fat lady sings?*"

Lilly gave a thoughtful frown. "Are you saying Miss Reen looks fat, Daddy?"

He stopped in the midst of planting one box on top of another, a minor look of alarm crossing his features and he gave his lips a nervous lick. "Oh...no, no, of course not, Lilly. It's a reference to Brunhilde's famous scene of sacrifice in *Götterdämmerung.*"

Her head tilted, birdlike, Lilly looked up at her dad. "Gotter..."

While Reen imagined the average man was clueless about Brunhilde, who she guessed must have been the Viking diva in the Bugs Bunny cartoon, Drake, a professor of ancient history and classical archaeology, was most definitely not your average man. He was like a walking, talking encyclopedia. He could probably rival Google.

They'd become good friends since Bob died and Janet left. During that time Reen learned Drake was as fanatical about opera, classic literature and Masterpiece Theater as most guys were about football or baseball. Once locked onto a subject of interest, he could go on at length about things that were usually way over Reen's head...and often fairly boring, at least to her. But she liked hearing him talk anyway, and was getting better all the time at suppressing her natural yawn response.

In this case, his operatic facts were happily distracting her from focusing too much on her pain.

"It's *Der Ring des Nibelungen*, the last in Richard Wagner's cycle of four music dramas," he explained to Lilly, who looked like she was suppressing a yawn herself. "When Brunhilde learns of Siegfried's death she's overcome with grief and commits suicide by throwing herself on his funeral pyre so she could join him in death."

His daughter's previously bored expression morphed as her eyes flew wide, her bottom lip trembled, and tears sprouted.

"Don't cry, sweetie, it's just a scary old made-up story," Reen assured Lilly, drawing the girl into a hug. "It never happened." Patting Lilly's head, she glanced at Drake and rolled her eyes. Although brainy as hell, sometimes the facts and figures professor could be a real dope when it came to suitable dialogue with children.

Reen would never forget the conversation one evening when she and Laila ran into Drake and his kids at Larker's Fish and Seafood for Thursday night fish and chips. They sat at a communal table where the kids were watching a funny Dracula cartoon on the large flat-screen TV. When Lilly and Kevin debated each other about whether or not Dracula was real, Drake helpfully supplied historical details about the grisly, gory deeds of Vlad the Impaler.

The complimentary-for-kids dessert of vanilla ice cream with thick, red strawberry sauce went untouched. Reen imagined there were plenty of nightmares that night.

Taking in Reen's comforting words to Lilly now, after his daughter's reaction to his tidbit of opera enlightenment, Drake looked unsettled. "Too much information again?"

"Mmm-hmm. Don't forget, Lilly thinks what happened to Sleeping Beauty is traumatic, Drake." The poor guy was so clueless and apologetic Reen had to keep herself from laughing.

"Sorry, Lilly," he told his daughter. "Sometimes Daddy gets a little carried away."

"I know." Lilly sighed, patting her father with patient understanding that belied her years. "It's okay, Daddy. I'm used to it." She fingered the yellow braids on Reen's hat. "I really like your hat, Miss Reen. Could you make one for me? I could pay you from my allowance."

"It's not polite to ask, Lilly," Drake chastised.

"I'd be happy to Lilly," Reen told her. "And it would be my gift to you for Valentine's Day, How about that?"

Her face lit up with excitement, then she turned to Drake. "Is it okay, Daddy?"

"As if you're not busy enough already," he muttered to Reen before giving a shrug. "Yes, okay, but I want you to make sure to do some chores for Miss Reen in exchange for her generosity."

"I will. I promise. I can take care of her and make her hot cocoa after school when she comes home from the doctor."

"That sounds fair to me," Reen said with a smile. "Do you like to draw, Lilly?" The girl nodded. "Good, then I want you to draw a picture of the hat you'd like me to create for you and I'll try to make one just like it."

Lilly's grin was ear to ear. "You could do that?" Reen offered a confirming nod. "Yay!" Lilly clapped. "Thank you, Miss Reen." She bent to give her a hug.

Drake glanced at the gold watch on his wrist. Rather than relying on his phone for time checks, he'd worn his dad's prized retirement watch since his father died the year before. With Drake being somewhat old school, it was fitting.

"We still have time to get you kids to school before you're late."

"I don't want to leave Miss Reen," Lilly said. "I want to go to the doctor too."

"You don't have to worry, honey, I'll be fine. After the doctor gives me a quick checkup I'll deliver the hats and then maybe I'll call Laila to tell her I need to take the afternoon off at the bakery. Then I'll just plop in front of the TV and relax until it's time to go to bed."

"You're not delivering any hats today," Drake informed her, gathering the boxes into a neat stack.

"Yes I am. I'm volunteering at the children's hospital this morning and bringing the hats. The kids are expecting me, Drake. I'm not going to disappoint them. You know what a letdown it can be right after the holidays and I thought the cute hats would brighten their—"

"Sorry, there's no way you're volunteering, making hat deliveries, or doing anything else today, Reen. The hats are going back inside your house. You can deliver them when you're better. In fact, I'll help you deliver them...but not today Ms. Brunhilde." He tugged on one of her yarn braids, making the hat sit crooked on Reen's head.

After righting her hat, she gestured toward the strewn boxes. "But—"

"But nothing," Drake insisted. "I think we'll leave this here," he told her, plucking the Viking cap from her head.

"Hey! I need that," Reen protested, unsuccessfully reaching for her hat. "I probably have hat hair now. My hair's a mess." She finger-combed it.

"Well I guess that means your messy hair will match the rest of you this morning, Ms. Malone," Drake kidded. Picking up the boxes, he opened Reen's front door and Hazelnut followed him inside. "The only activity you'll have today is me driving you to the hospital."

"Oh my gosh...I can't drive." The realization hadn't really hit Reen until that moment. Craning her neck to look up at him, she said, "I feel terrible imposing on you like this, Drake. You have an early morning class today, don't you?"

"It's no imposition, besides," he called from the living room where he set down the boxes, "I'm sure my students won't miss their crusty old professor. I'll call and have a sub cover for me." Before Reen knew what was happening, Drake was outside again, scooping her up into his arms.

She uttered an audible gasp. "Oh my God, Drake, what are you doing?"

Giving her a curious look, he laughed. "Well, definitely not the tango."

"I'm too heavy for you to carry. You'll hurt your back."

He offered a probing look that had her squirming. "Maybe you're right. I can just drop you in the mud and drag you along the icy sidewalk by your hair. Would that make you feel more comfortable?"

Caught off guard, she didn't know if she should laugh or hit him. "No, this is fine. Thank you."

"That's better." A self-satisfied smile turned up the corners of his mouth.

A hopeless romantic, Maureen Malone had been waiting her entire life for a handsome man to gather her up into his arms, gazing lovingly—or she'd take lustfully—into her hazel eyes before whisking her off for a romantic rendezvous. Lord knows she'd daydreamed about it often enough. In those scenarios she was often Lois Lane and the man was Superman.

With his dark, wavy hair and black, horn rimmed glasses—which he alternated with contacts—Drake Slattery could easily pass for Clark Kent...maybe even Superman. But it didn't matter. They were nothing more than good friends. Besides, Reen had never imagined the long-awaited romantic scene with Lois Lane having messy hat-hair, or blood-spattered legs peeking through a torn hospital volunteer uniform—or nursing an aching ankle and butt as Superman transported her to his Fortress of Solitude for a romance-saturated rendezvous.

Her ears perked. Did she just hear Drake grunt?

It made her self-conscious as hell. In her fantasies, she was effortlessly thin and beautiful. While she'd never be truly slender, not with her penchant for chocolate, at least she *usually* managed to stay within the normal weight spectrum.

Or at least she thought so until she heard that grunt.

"Jeez, Maureen, look at you. You're a real mess."

Reen sighed at his decidedly un-Superman-ish statement.

"You say something?" Drake asked with a somewhat pained expression.

"No, no...just sighing a little about the pain."

"Don't worry, we'll get you fixed up soon."

~<>~

After dropping Lilly and Kevin at school for their first grade class, Drake drove Reen to the hospital where, under her blatantly ignored protests, he carried her into the emergency room.

A thorough checkup and series of x-rays verified her injuries. She couldn't believe it. She'd gone thirty-some years without breaking any bones and now, with one abrupt slip on the ice, she'd managed to break both her left ankle and her tailbone. And, holy mackerel, it hurt like hell.

"Why am I not surprised?" Drake said, eyeing the cast on her leg as Reen struggled to find a semi-comfortable position.

Her head cocked. "You mean that it's broken?"

"Nope, I figured it was. I mean that your cast is purple."

"Oh that." Her fingers smoothed along the nearly knee-high cast. "They gave me a choice."

"And purple's your favorite color," he stated rather than asked. He'd probably heard her say it a thousand times.

"It's much more chic and less boring than white, don't you think?" She lifted her leg a few inches off the hospital gurney, showing off her stylish cast. "A white one would get gray and dirty-looking over time. Purple makes me feel cheerful, and I'll feel even better after I get one of my sisters to paint my toenails to match." She beamed a smile at him.

"Purple toenails?" His lip curling in distaste, Drake looked uncertain.

"Lighter." She studied her toes. "Just the right shade of lavender."

"The doc said you can go home as soon as they bring you the donut pillow...you know, for your *broken butt*." A big old grin split his face as he emphasized those words.

Her eyebrows knitting, Reen mirrored his earlier question. "Why am I not surprised?"

"You mean about you having to use a donut pillow for your *broken butt*?"

"No, that you wouldn't be able to resist overusing that particular term once you learned I'd fractured my cossack." She folded her arms across her chest, wincing as the slight movement jostled her enough to make her bottom ache even worse.

"You mean coccyx," Drake corrected. "Which is your tailbone." He gave a mischievous smile. "Which, in layman's terms, means you broke your butt."

"Whatever, Professor Know-it-all." She gave a dismissive wave. "You know, if you acted this un-professor-ish at the university they'd have you disbarred. Speaking of the university, why don't you go? You don't have to stay here and babysit me." Elevating her chin, she looked away.

"Attorneys are disbarred. Professors are fired or can have their tenure stripped but they can't be disbarred. And I'm not leaving you here all by yourself, Maureen. I already told you, they've got an assistant subbing for me so—"

Engaging in a dramatic faux yawn, Reen made a chattering motion with her fingers. "Blah, blah, blah..." After rolling her eyes, she looked up at Drake, immediately regretting her uncommonly cranky attitude when she saw his taken aback expression. The man had gone out of his way to help her this morning, bringing her to the hospital and staying with her through the long battery of tests. She should be thanking him instead of grousing at him.

"I'm sorry, Drake. You didn't deserve that. I'm just," her hands flew up, "I don't know...out of sorts and cranky for some reason." Involved in her apology and forgetting to watch the way she sat, Reen put too much pressure on her tailbone, and the punch of pain had her feeling dizzy again.

Wrapping an arm around her back and shoulders, Drake smiled. "The reason you're giving a stellar Ms. Cranky-Butt performance is because you're in a lot of pain. I can see it etched all across your face." His fingers traced from her temple to her jaw. "As soon as that injection the nurse gave you takes effect you'll feel a lot better."

"Thanks." She leaned her head against his arm. "And thanks for staying with me. Thanks especially for calling Laila back and convincing her she doesn't have to worry about me. The last thing I want is my mom and sisters dropping everything to rush over here and baby me." Treated to a duo throbbing effect at both points of injury, Reen moaned. "You know, I had no idea broken bones could hurt so much."

"The doctor said a fractured coccyx is one of the most painful breaks, and it takes a long time to heal. You're dealing not only with a broken tailbone but a broken ankle too, Reen. Plus the older we get, the tougher it is to deal with fractures. At your advanced age it's no wonder you're feeling a tad on the grouchy side." He winked at her and Reen laughed out loud.

"Oh, Drake, you do know how to make me feel better...or maybe the shot's starting to work. I'm feeling kind of nice and..." she closed her eyes and sighed, "floaty."

"Probably the meds since I doubt I have a floaty effect on you." The deep sound of his laughter was rich and masculine.

Studying his chiseled Clark Kent features, Reen smiled up at him. Little did Professor Slattery know that he was having more of a floaty effect on her than he could imagine. The lusty way he looked at her made her feel like grabbing him into a lip-lock. Maybe breaking a couple of bones wasn't so bad. After all, it gave her Drake's full attention for hours. It had been eons since the two of them spent this much time together alone.

Whoa! Reen blinked. What in the world was she thinking? She and Drake were friends, pals, buddies. Nothing more. The only reason she was having these mushy thoughts about him was because of the drugs they'd given her.

Sure, her mom and sisters were convinced Drake had a thing for her but they didn't understand that a man and a woman could be good platonic friends. Just because they're the opposite sex doesn't mean they have to get all gooey-eyed with each other or hop in the sack together.

Not that the thought had never crossed Reen's mind. But aside from the fact that Drake and her late fiancé were both professors and close friends, he and Reen had little in common, other than a good sense of humor. Drake was a cat person, she was a dog person. The multi-degreed professor was just this side of being a genius while college dropout Reen was more captivated by binging on Netflix comedy shows and rom-coms than being intrigued by the academic documentaries he found so fascinating.

Drake relished doing challenging crossword puzzles. For fun. His favorite games were word or trivia-based. He enjoyed sitting through endless lectures as much as Reen loved digging through other people's junk at garage sales.

Then there was Reen's unfortunate habit of tangling words or common idioms, and forgetting to think before she spoke, which frequently resulted in something dopey popping out of her mouth...like blurting out *cossack* when she knew damn well the word was coccyx. It was frustrating because, while she might not be the brainiest girl on the block, she certainly wasn't an idiot...even if she gave a good impression of a birdbrain when flustered.

"Anything I can do to help make you more comfortable?" Drake asked. "Hungry? You haven't had anything to eat. I can get you something from the cafeteria. Something...chocolate?" His eyebrows jiggled playfully. "You've always said that's the best medicine."

Normally it was but, as shocking as it was to Reen, she had no desire for chocolate. All she wanted was her good buddy Drake, her tall, dark and handsome pal, there at her side, looking at her the way he was now, all caring and concerned...as if she was the most important woman in the world to him.

Catching the melodious sigh about to escape her lips, she shook her head, trying to clear the ridiculous drug-induced thoughts. No, the man who made her heart do flipflops, Reen reminded herself, wasn't Drake, it was Hudson Griffin, Glassfloat Bay's resident contractor and handyman. How could she possibly forget that? She was crazy about Hud. Adored him.

She frowned. Stupid drugs were addling her brain.

"Something wrong?"

"Hmm?" She blinked a couple times. "Oh...no, I'm fine. Everything's hunky-dorky. Thanks." She caught Drake trying to conceal a chuckle. "What's so funny?"

"You said hunky-dorky instead of hunky-dory, that's all. The medication must be blurring your thoughts."

Startled that she'd said that aloud, Reen sucked in a breath. "Oops, you're probably right. Slip of the tongue." She gave him a casual smile. *Hunky-dory* was a phrase her mother often used. With Drake in mind, Reen had altered the saying to *hunky-dorky* because it so perfectly described the tall, dark and handsome bookworm. Trouble was, no one else was supposed to hear her private coined phrase.

"Oddly enough," Reen continued, "I'm not hungry for chocolate, or anything else. But go ahead and get something for yourself."

Sitting on the chair beside her, Drake took her hand and squeezed it. "Naw, I'm good."

Yes indeed...every woman should have a hunky-dorky pal like Professor Drake Slattery.

Drake's phone rang. Looking up from the display he said, "Sorry, Reen, I've got to take this."

She thought her ears were playing tricks on her when she heard him say *Saffron* into the phone. She couldn't imagine why her snooty Realtor cousin was calling Drake.

As he strode out of the room she caught herself thinking he had a great looking butt.

Squeezing her eyes closed, Reen was determined to deflate her pain-killer-induced bubble of Drake-related fantasies.

Chapter Two

~<>~

PROPPING HER elbow on the small kitchen table, Reen rested her chin on her fist. She looked exhausted and uncomfortable sitting atop her inflatable donut pillow on the hard oak kitchen chair. She'd painted its back spindles white with little purple flowers and green leaves. The chair was one of numerous garage sale finds Reen had *rescued* in the midst of her house's artsy refurbishment.

Drake was tired himself after sitting around the hospital for hours, then going directly from the ER to the orthopedist's office where they spent another two hours. It was no wonder poor Reen was so beat.

Clapping his thigh, he said, "Come on, Hazelnut, you've waited so long to go out I'll bet you're about to burst." Whimpering, the dog raced to the door to be let outside.

"Oh my poor Hazel," Reen muttered wearily, her eyelids closed. "Thank you, Drake. Sit down and make yourself comfortable." Her hand flitted aimlessly through the air. Her being exhausted, combined with the pain medication, had her coming across as happy, sleepy, and woozy.

Turning her head, she opened her eyes, watching Hazelnut sniffing and inspecting the postage-stamp-sized yard before doing her business. "Want to guess why I named my dog Hazelnut?"

"Hmm...could it be because you love chocolate with hazelnuts?" Drake answered easily, since he'd heard the information repeatedly.

"Bingo! Great guess, Professor."

"Thanks. So why didn't you just name her Nutella?" He already knew the answer to this too.

"Are you kidding?" Reen made a sour face, accompanied by a raspberry sound. "Where's the imagination in that? Hey, Drake, did I ever tell you Hazelnut is a rescue dog? We fell madly in love with each other as soon as our gazes connected at the shelter."

"I think you may have mentioned it once or twice." He chuckled, having heard everything anyone could ever possibly want to know about Reen's beloved mutt at least a dozen times.

"It was the same day Annalise found her rescue dog, Choo-Choo Lavern. I'll bet you don't know who Choo-Choo Lavern was." Reen gave him a drowsy smile.

Of course he did. After all, both Reen and Annalise had told him the story ad nauseam.

"You know why you don't know? Because you," she waved a finger in his general direction, "rarely watch classic old movies. You just watch all those looong, boring academic documentaries."

"I see." He did his best not to laugh. "Sounds interesting." It was a mercy lie for a friend in pain. "Why don't you tell me all about Choo-Choo Lavern?" He prepared himself for another lengthy explanation of the tie-in with one of Reen and Annalise Griffin's favorite Danny Kaye movies from the 1940s, *Wonder Man*. If rambling on about mindless movie trivia helped Reen feel better, he was willing to listen for the umpteenth time. Well, maybe not listen exactly, but do his best to feign paying attention while he effectively tuned her out.

Once Reen finished regaling him with her mind-numbing film details, she just kept right on going. "And did you know that my cutie-pie Hazel looks so much like Laila's dog, Friday, Delaney's dog, Thursday, and my brother Gard's dog, Tundra, that they could be long lost siblings?" Reen capped her question with a sizeable, vociferous yawn. "They're all so big they almost look like ponies, or donkeys, or," her hands flew into the air, "I dunno, some other big furry creature. Like a hyena or a wolf...like that."

"You don't say."

"I do say. You know what else I say?"

"What?"

"I'm soooo pooped, Drake." She made an exaggerated pouty frown. "I mean really, really, really, really tired. Super tired to the power of infinity tired." Her eyelids fluttered closed. "Guess how Gard's dog, Tundra, got his name." Without waiting for his reply, her eyes still closed, she went on, retelling the story. Then, for the thousandth time, he heard how Thursday and Friday got their names. Finally she repeated her reasoning for naming her dog Hazelnut.

"Hey..." Her eyebrows arrowed down and she frowned. "Does it seem like I'm talking a lot?"

"I hadn't noticed," Drake valiantly lied.

"Oh good, cuz I hate rambling on and on and on, you know?"

"Uh-huh." He decided he deserved a medal for swallowing all the laughter striving to make its way out. The woman did love to talk, with or without pain medication. She was pretty damn adorable and a regular ratchet jaw when she relaxed and let her guard down.

"I mean, I like to be a little chatty, just enough to be sociable, but babbling on and on isn't very attractive." Her expression turned dreamy. "Do you think I'm attractive, Drake?"

Whoa...danger ahead.

Reen would never ask him a question like this unless under the influence of medication. If he leveled with her, telling her she was more than simply attractive, she was stunning, beautiful inside and out, he'd risk destroying the chummy friendship they'd cultivated.

His reply had to be as vague, evasive and generic as possible. "Yeah, sure." He added a nonchalant shrug. "As friends go, I'd say you're an attractive friend."

"Good...that's good. You're an attractive friend too."

After letting Hazelnut in again, Drake's gaze scanned the family room, which was right off the kitchen, noting her furnishings were sparse. He'd never really paid much attention to that before. Reen's furniture reminded him of what you might find in a dumpy little frat house—if the frat boys were into arts and crafts.

Reen's sofa was a pullout bed she'd found at one of those garage sales she loved to pick through. A good thirty-years old, it was too stiff and unyielding to be comfortable. She'd knitted an afghan for it, which dressed it up some, but the colorful purple-y throw was like putting spats on a pig. It couldn't disguise the fact that the upholstered arms had lost their cushioning, leaving not much more than hard wood beneath the old olive green brocade fabric.

The sofa bed's springs made themselves known wherever you sat. Even Hazelnut preferred lying on the rug to that dilapidated sofa.

The sound of Reen's light buzzing made him smile. He'd learned never to refer to it as snoring because she insisted she never snored. He begged to differ after watching some of those academic documentaries with her.

There weren't any soft armchairs in the room either. Reen was always jabbering about her great secondhand furniture finds and her plans to reupholster, refinish, and otherwise heal the ailing old objects that may have once been appealing and utilitarian. Where he saw somebody's worn castoffs, she saw a potential treasure awaiting a little TLC. He had to give her credit. The furniture and household items she'd fixed up looked great. Drake didn't have a creative bone in his body and envied Maureen's uncanny eye for design.

The trouble was, each time she finished a project, she usually ended up giving it away to someone who needed it more than she did.

Noticing her eyes were open again, he said, "I see you created another garden scene," carefully handling the four-foot-long wall-hanging. It was suspended from a white painted tree branch against the pale lavender wall of the dining area. She came up with ideas he'd never think of, and they worked. Reen's talent for making something beautiful out of yarn and scraps of material amazed him.

"I think I like this one even better than the last one you made."

"Aw, thanks, Drake. You never know when another plumber-in-need might come along, right?" She gave a sluggish laugh.

Reen was talking about the day a plumber spotted a wall-hanging she'd recently completed, a three-dimensional outdoor scene using different yarn techniques she'd described to Drake that went right over his head. The plumber was there because Drake had flubbed fixing the kitchen sink, only making things worse. The plumber told her it was uncanny how much the wall-hanging reminded him of his mother's beloved flower garden when he was a child.

Once Reen learned the woman was in a hospice for end stage Alzheimer's, she took the wall-hanging down, rolling it, then wrapping it with twine. "Here, Charlie, hang this in your mother's room. It might spark a pleasant memory for her," she told the plumber, presenting him with the intricate art she'd spent months creating for herself. The guy had tears in his eyes, refusing to accept any payment for his work.

Reen confided in Drake later that, although the garden scene probably wouldn't help his mother at this point, she hoped it brought the plumber some peace and comfort when he gazed at it.

Forever thoughtful, she was always doing nice things like that for people.

Drake's gaze traveled over the conglomeration of battered furniture around him. He'd never forget the time he'd suggested she just chuck the ratty old furniture and buy something new...as in from the current century. Reen's horrified expression told him she'd rather spend God knows how much money, not to mention hours and effort, fixing her precious rescued finds than abandon them to the Salvation Army or, God forbid, the city dump.

"This isn't going to work," he said, scratching the back of his head.

"What do you mean?" Reen followed his gaze.

"There's no comfortable place to sit." He watched as the dog twirled in place a few times before taking a spot at Reen's feet. It was probably the most comfortable place in the room.

"Oh, sorry. Try sitting on those oversized floor pillows propped in the corner," she pointed. "I picked them up at the church rummage sale last week. They're from Morocco. Aren't they cute? They're more cushy than the sofa."

Looking at her in disbelief, Drake clapped his chest. "I'm not talking about me, Reen, I'm talking about you. There's no place comfortable for *you* to sit."

"Oh." He watched as she looked around the room as if seeing the all but useless, ragtag furniture for the first time. "I've been searching for a used recliner and some cushy armchairs but haven't had any luck yet. Maybe I'll try Goodwill after my ankle is better and I can drive."

"Or you could always do what most people do and go to an actual retail furniture store to find a few brand new comfortable pieces," Drake suggested, knowing all too well the reaction he'd get.

"Are you serious?" The aghast look she gave him didn't disappoint. "And spend a small fortune when I can find fabulous pieces full of charm and character for a fraction of the cost? I don't think so. I just need to find the time to do some serious furniture hunting. I spend most of my time working at Laila's bakery, at the children's hospital, or in my office here at home."

"Office?" His eyebrows pinching, Drake looked left and right. "What office?" Reen's two-bedroom handyman-special house was tiny and he didn't remember any home office. "You mean in the second bedroom?"

"Oh no, I use that room for my knitting and crocheting. It's filled top to bottom with plastic bins full of yarn and other needlework supplies." Her mouth screwed to the side. "Next time I buy bins I need to make sure I can see through them. The blue ones I got on sale are all opaque, and the content descriptions I taped on them keep falling off. Makes things a little hard to find."

"Uh...that sounds just like your garage." Drake did his best not to snicker.

"Yeah...I know..." her nose crinkled in acknowledgement, "I'm planning to get everything logically organized as soon as I'm up and around again. Everything neatly stacked in covered clear plastic bins." She pantomimed with slicing motions as she spoke. "And I'll get one of those label makers so my descriptions will stick."

"You've been saying all that since we first met."

"Have I?" She blinked a few times before yawning twice. "Oh...well anyway, I made that little corner nook in my bedroom into a sort of office area for myself. I found a great secondhand desk at a garage sale. It's small enough to fit next to the dresser without taking up too much space. I got the chair secondhand too. What a terrific find! It's a fabulous old schoolhouse chair and it's—"

"All wood with a wood seat," Drake surmised.

Reen's gaze went blank. "Well...normally it's very comfortable." He watched as she shifted on the handy donut pillow strategically placed beneath her butt.

"I can drive you around to the garage sales this weekend if you want," Drake offered with a half-hearted shrug. "If you think you'd be up to hobbling around on your crutches." As far as he was concerned, rummaging around garage sales or thrift shops was comparable to dumpster diving. There weren't many pastimes he enjoyed less, but he'd do just about anything for Maureen if it made her happy.

"You?" Reen laughed at what he considered his incredibly kindhearted offer. "Thanks, but the last time we stopped at an estate sale together you tsked, sighed and rolled your eyes every two minutes."

"I did not." Drake folded his arms across his chest, recalling she may be right.

"Ha! In order to take full advantage of thrift shopping, you have to be willing to spend the time digging through lots of discards." She made a motion like a dog digging for a bone. "And you, Professor Impatient, were fidgeting like a child after only an hour. As a matter of fact, your kids fidgeted less than you did."

"*Only* an hour. Do you hear yourself, Reen? That's not an hour of doing normal-people shopping, it's an hour of climbing over dirty old furniture and crawling through passages full of dust and mites and God knows what else, trying to find that elusive needle in a haystack that doesn't exist. That's an hour that, in real time, is equivalent to six hours of manual labor."

As her chin elevated, Reen's expression morphed into a self-satisfied smile. "You of all people know that's not true," she accused, mirroring his crossed arms position.

She'd lost him there. "What's not true?"

"The needle in a haystack," she informed with a curt wave, as if he should immediately know what she was talking about. "They most certainly do exist. Laila found one, if you recall." She looked plenty smug now—and he had to admit she had reason to be.

"Okay, yes, you're right," Drake grudgingly admitted, "but how many bona-fide genies do you think there are lurking in ancient perfume bottles in the basements of old mansions? I'm pretty sure your sister found the one and only."

"Oh ye of little faith. For all you know—" Reen's expression pinched and she moaned. Hazelnut's ears immediately perked and she gazed up at her mistress.

"Are you okay? Are you in pain? When's the last time you took your pain medication?" He should have been paying better attention, realizing it was probably time for her next dose when she started talking less dreamily and more lucidly.

Glancing at the time display on her phone, Reen winced. "I was supposed to take it almost an hour ago. I forgot." She grimaced again. "Whew, that pain comes on like gangbusters."

"You can't do that, Reen." Drake headed for the kitchen to fill a glass with water. The counter was full of old-timey ceramic salt and pepper shakers she'd found at garage sales and the only drinking glasses in her cupboards were ones with retro cartoon characters on them. He smiled when he chose the Sleeping Beauty glass for her.

"You have to take care of yourself, do what the orthopedist said and take your medication when you're supposed to. Both of those breaks are serious. The doc said you need to stay on top of the pain for the first few days so it doesn't escalate and become too difficult to manage." He gave her the water as she dug in her purse for the right pill bottle.

"Thanks, Drake," she said after taking her pill and making a note of the time. "I know you're right, I need to be more cognizant when it comes to taking care of myself. I swear, I'd be the world's worst drug addict...or alcoholic for that matter."

Drake lifted an eyebrow in question. "Aaannd, you came to that conclusion how?" He took a seat across from her at the kitchen table, sipping water from a Dudley Do-Right glass. His chair was painted opposite of the one Reen sat in, with purple spindles and tiny white flowers.

"Well," her shoulders hiked in a shrug, "look at me." She picked up the pill bottle, turning it left and right. "Here I've got a hefty supply of pain medication, the sort people break into houses to steal, and I forget to take it—even when I've got broken bones."

"You said the pills make you feel loopy."

Reen's head bobbed. "I really don't like feeling that way. It's worse than the way I feel after getting tipsy from alcohol."

Drake couldn't help barking a laugh and Reen's head whipped toward him.

"What's so funny?"

"I wouldn't classify what you drink as alcohol," he teased, knowing Reen's penchant for mixing a smidgen of sweet flavored liqueurs like Bailey's, Kahlua and Frangelico into her coffee now and then. "It's more like flavored sugar syrup with a hint of a kick. I'd get indigestion from all that sweetness long before I ever got close to feeling inebriated."

After a lengthy stall, during which Drake was sure she was trying to come up with an appropriate retort, Reen's shoulders slumped. "I suppose that's true."

"Whoa." Drake's glanced at her with surprise. "Well it's got to be either the pain or the pills."

"What do you mean?"

"You agreed with me just like that." He snapped his fingers. "That never happens."

"Never say never."

She gifted him with one of her big, genuine smiles. That's when she was her most beautiful. Funny, she'd been doing that more today than usual, even through the obvious pain. And the way he'd caught Reen looking at him several times today, it was almost as if she had some interest in him, other than considering him merely a good buddy. But he knew damn well that wasn't the case.

To his regret, she'd made it abundantly clear she thought of him as nothing more than a friend. Just what a guy loves to hear. On top of that, Reen was solidly hooked on Annalise's brother, Hud Griffin, the contractor-owner of Griffin of all Trades who, unlike Drake, wasn't a dull academic. Much like Reen, he was a creative guy, proficient in working with his hands. Anytime Drake attempted something handy he inevitably screwed up, making a mess of things.

Hud was that brawny outdoorsy type women seemed to go for. He could run circles around Drake when it came to sports, videogames, or knowing the best place to go for a brisk morning hike. The worst part? As much as Drake wished Hud was an SOB, he was actually a hell of a nice guy, a true friend and undeniably likeable. Even Drake could see that Hud and Reen were an ideal match.

Drake was pretty sure her agreeable mood and rush to smile today had more to do with the medication than any sudden interest in him. He'd already resigned himself to the fact that he and Reen would never be more than pals. It was better than not having her in his life at all.

"I still have addictive tendencies. It's been a real battle at times," Reen confessed, snapping Drake out of his daydreaming. He hadn't a clue that she'd ever had a problem with drugs or alcohol.

"I didn't know you had an addiction problem. You never mentioned it before."

"Mmm-hmm. Number one would be chocolate," she counted on her fingers, "then all things yarn-related, and then going thrift shopping."

"*Ohhhh.*" He forced himself not to laugh. Addict Indeed. "So I guess that makes you a chocoholic yarnaholic shopaholic." Drake lifted an eyebrow.

"I almost forgot," Reen added. "I'm a Hudaholic too." This time she giggled. Clapping her hand over her mouth she giggled again, which told Drake the pain meds were taking effect. "Oops, I shouldn't mention that. No one's supposed to know." She made a shushing motion over her lips with her finger. "It's a secret."

Listening to Reen spout her enthusiastic affection for Hud, Drake felt his bright mood wane. A secret? Half the town knew she was crazy about the guy.

"I won't tell a soul," he promised with an affable wink.

"Thanks, Drake. I can always count on you to be my BFF." Reen gave him an irrefutably loopy smile. "Can't I?"

"Always," Drake assured.

"Hey, I have a question for you."

"Shoot."

"How come my cousin, Saffron, called you before, when we were still in the hospital? Is she trying to sell you a house or something?"

"No, we were just coordinating our plans for tomorrow."

"Plans?" Reen frowned. "What plans?"

Funny...he had the briefest instinct that Reen was jealous. But that was ridiculous.

"We're attending a lecture at the university on 'Politics, Religion and Society under the Tudors and Stuarts.'" Reen yawned and Drake chuckled. "I'm putting you to sleep already, hmm?" He'd taken her to several lectures over the past couple of years, hoping there'd be one she enjoyed but, although she politely feigned interest, it was obvious they weren't her cup of tea.

"No, no," she gave a dismissive wave, "it sounds fascinating." Another yawn. "I'm just tired from the pills. So, um, Saffron likes that sort of stuff, lectures at the university?"

"Very much." Drake nodded. They'd shared some stimulating discussions following university lectures. "She subscribes to WHU's lecture series and gave me a call when she saw this one on the schedule. Saffron said she remembered my interest in early modern England and thought we might enjoy taking it in together and then discussing it over dinner afterwards."

"Dinner and discussion, huh? Hmmm...I see." Now she was pouting and Drake couldn't help laughing.

"Why are you laughing at me?"

"Because it sounds like you're jealous," he said, because it sure as hell did seem that way.

"Jealous?!" Breathing in an audible gasp, Reen nailed him with an accusatory look. "I am not! Why would I be jealous?" In the next instant she'd apparently forgotten their discussion as her attention turned to Hazelnut. Visibly relaxed, Reen rested her head on her arm across the table while speaking undecipherable baby talk to her dog.

So much for her being jealous. Drake chuckled to himself. He knew she and Saffron had an antagonistic relationship and supposed Reen simply wasn't keen on the idea of Saffron and Drake developing a friendship. He wondered what Reen would think if she knew Saffron had more than friendship in mind—and that Drake considered exploring the option.

She might make a fuss about their pairing initially but once she got used to it he felt sure Reen would be on board. Drake had to admit he enjoyed having Saffron Devington coming on to him, clearly making her intent known. It didn't hurt that she was an attractive brunette either. He was tired of hanging around, putting his love life on hold, waiting an eternity to see if Reen would ever have an epiphany about him.

If he kept waiting he'd be collecting social security before Reen might start seeing him in a different light.

He watched as Reen's expression shifted from tired to goofy to loopy. She was cute as can be. His pal. His buddy. His BFF. Maureen Malone. The woman he loved...but could never have.

"I need to pick up Lilly and Kevin from school soon," he told her. "Why don't I take you over to your family's house until you're not so...sore." He avoided saying loopy. "Your sister Kady's staying there now, right?"

"Mmm-hmm. I'm glad my little sister is back." She gave a long blink and lazy smile. "I really miss her when she's gone."

Maureen and her youngest sister, Kathleen Doolan Malone, aka Kady, were close. The entire Malone family was happy to have Kady back home after the couple of years she'd spent backpacking overseas.

"Bekka House is plenty big enough to accommodate both of you," Drake noted. "That way you won't be all alone if you need something."

"Soft furniture," the half-asleep Reen muttered. "Comfy couch. Comfy bed...and friendly ghosts..."

After experiencing a number of encounters of his own with the inviting trio of friendly ghosts at Bekka House, Drake wasn't about to poke fun at Reen's impromptu mention.

"Yes," he chuckled, "friendly ghosts, and a bedroom for you on the first floor," Drake reminded her, hopping up from his chair. "Come on, let's go to your room so I can help you gather the clothes and other things you'll need while you stay there." He suspected he needed to act fast before Reen fell asleep but by the time he brought her crutches around, she was already buzzing.

Standing in place, Drake mulled over his options. He could bring Reen just as she was to Bekka House or he could go through her drawers and closet trying to find what she might need. Nope, not a good idea. He didn't want to rifle through her personal stuff...bras, panties, and whatever. He looked toward her bedroom and back at Reen before getting her coat and slipping it on her, which wasn't all that easy since she was pretty much deadweight.

Once he had her sufficiently bundled, he gathered her in his arms and carried her to his car, slipping her into the passenger seat atop her donut pillow, and buckling her seatbelt, where she kept up her light snoring. Back in the house, he grabbed Hazelnut, Reen's crutches, and her purse, depositing the dog and everything else in the back seat.

He was about to lock the door when he thought of Reen's insistence on delivering her knitted hats to the kids at the children's hospital. She often told him about how much she loved seeing the sick children smile when she gave them her imaginative knitted creations. The recollection of Reen's impassioned expression when she talked about those kids made Drake smile himself. He went back into the house one last time to get the boxes of hats. Those went into the car's trunk. After locking her place up, he headed for Bekka House.

Chapter Three

~<>~

"MISS REEN! How are you feeling?" Lilly asked, running to give her a hug. "Is your butt feeling better yet?"

"You're not supposed to say butt," Kevin chastised in a superior tone. "Dad said we're supposed to say backside."

"Oh yeah." Lilly blushed and offered a shrug. "Sorry."

"I'm hanging in there," Reen said. "From what I hear it's going to be quite a while until I get back to normal."

"Ahh, I see Sleeping Beauty's awake," Drake teased, following his children into Bekka House and setting two plastic bags of Chinese takeout on the kitchen counter.

Hazelnut instantly became his best friend as the dog nuzzled up against his leg while sniffing the newly fragrant kitchen.

"Bright eyed and bushy tailed." Reen gave a salute. "I can't believe I conked out like that. That's twice in one day you've had to carry my, um, *ample* body to and from the car."

A grin took hold as he teased her. "Three times, actually, but who's counting?"

He could almost see the gears work in her head as she mentally counted. Cringing, she said, "Ooh, that's right. Your poor back is really going to be sore by tomorrow. You might need those crutches more than me. Sorry."

"You have nothing to be sorry about. Don't forget, I've been doing your brother-in-law's workouts at his Sumerian Fitness classes at the university twice a week. You know firsthand how rigorous Zak's classes are."

"Do I ever." Reen nodded readily. "He's the master of torture."

41

"Show Miss Reen your muscle, Daddy," Lilly encouraged, flexing her own biceps. "Daddy's just like a cartoon muscleman now," she said with a proud smile before bending to drape her arms around Hazelnut for a hug.

Going along with his daughter's request, he made a muscle, showing it off to Reen. "See? Just like Lilly said. Totally musclebound." He cracked a smile that was mirrored by Reen's.

"Very Schwarzenegger-esque," Reen agreed.

"What's that?" Lilly asked while she and her brother offered clueless expressions.

"He's a little before your time," Drake told them before returning his attention to Reen. "You need to stop talking about yourself as if you'd never lost all that weight a few years ago, Maureen. You're not...eh..." he stumbled, trying to find the right word, deciding it was safe to go with the one she'd used, "...*ample* anymore."

"Go ahead, Drake, you can say fat." She offered a crooked smile.

"Well you're not," he emphasized. "You haven't been overweight for a long time."

"Right. I'm positively svelte now." She made a goofy face and fluffed her hair. "Heck, Drake, with your new buff body I'll bet you could pick my willowy self up and carry me around for hours without the slightest effort." Affecting a model-like pose, she rolled her eyes in a self-mocking gesture.

Her posing had Drake's eyes glued to her enticingly curvy body. Rather than lavish her with the compliments he wished he could, Drake kept their exchange limited to the teasing good buddy dialogue they most often used.

Giving Reen a wary look, he elevated an eyebrow. "Well...maybe not for hours."

He couldn't understand why Reen couldn't see herself the way he saw her. The way everyone else saw her. Since they'd met he'd seen her at her best and at her worst; with makeup and without;

overweight and at her goal weight. It didn't matter. Maureen Malone was a beautiful woman, inside and out.

She and her sister, Laila, who'd dieted together and later became counselors at the now defunct Tuned by Turner weight loss clinic, explained to him some time ago that it can be difficult after you lose a large amount of weight to see yourself as someone who's not overweight anymore. They'd told him of incidents where they'd caught their reflections in a store window when walking by, wondering who that slender woman was.

"Hey, I thought you were supposed to be giving me a pep talk," Reen joked. Once she focused on the bags Drake brought, her eyes widened. "Xiang Symphony! Oh my gosh, you got take out from my favorite Chinese restaurant? I haven't had anything from there in at least a year. Oh Drake, I love you. What would I ever do without you?" She held out her hands, wiggling her fingers in entreaty.

Drake gladly obliged, walking into Reen's arms for a thank-you buddy-hug. He'd take closeness with her anyway he could get it. He was rewarded with a kiss on the cheek too.

"So what did you get?" She rubbed her hands in anticipation, then made the mistake of forgetting her injury and bouncing in her seat. She nearly howled as her face turned an angry shade of crimson.

"Whoa, careful there," Drake cautioned. "You may not be fat anymore but I guess you'll always be a foodie." He couldn't help the genuine laughter that emerged. Maureen became mesmerized with food the way other people got excited about found money.

Always amused by her gusto when they went out to eat, he couldn't help wonder if that extraordinary passion of hers extended to the bedroom. Alas, that was something he'd never know. That's what fantasizing was for.

"Guilty as charged," she readily admitted, trying to get comfortable after irritating her tailbone.

"Plates in the cabinets?" he asked.

She nodded. "Third from the left. Silverware's in the drawer just below that."

"I chose foods I've seen you order in the past," Drake told her as he took plates for her and her sister Kady from the cabinet, pairing them with forks and a couple paper towels from the roll on the counter.

"I got potstickers, eggrolls, wontons..." He withdrew each cardboard carton as he spoke, placing them on the counter. While getting the dinner ready he dodged Hazelnut's eager nudging as the dog wound in and out of Drake's legs. "I remembered you like shrimp so there's butterflied shrimp and kung pao shrimp." He smiled as he took another carton from the bag, holding it aloft. "This is vegetable fried rice for your vegan sister, Kady." After taking out small cellophane bags he added, "And some almond cookies and fortune cookies."

"I love almond cookies." She closed her eyes and mmmm-ed.

"Me too!" Lilly echoed.

Drake pointed a warning finger at Reen. "Don't bounce," he reminded.

"I won't."

"Can we have almond cookies too?" Kevin asked.

"Yes, I got enough for all of us," Drake answered.

"Tell Kevin not to eat my fortune cookie and steal my fortune this time," Lilly said.

"Kevin's not going to do that, are you, Kevin?"

"No, Dad," his son said with the innocence of an angel.

"Wow," Reen's eyes grew wide, "you brought a veritable feast. What fun!"

"It's going to be hard for you to get around the kitchen or cook trying to manage the cast and your crutches so I thought I'd help make things a little easier for your first night at least." He looked over all the cartons. "You'll probably have enough leftovers for lunch and dinner tomorrow." Moving closer he cupped his hand over his mouth. In a conspiratorial whisper, he said, "Plus I know you're not the biggest fan of Kady's vegan cooking." Drake followed that with a wink.

The look Reen gave him was wholly agreeable as well as thankful. "I still shudder when I think of that vegan tofu-kale scramble she made for her bon voyage dinner before leaving for her trip," she recalled.

"Or the spinach sweet potato thing with..." his eyebrows furrowed, "what was it again?"

Reen's expression soured. "Beets."

"How could I forget that?" His memory of the single bite he took kicking in, Drake shuddered. "Is Kady here?"

"No, she's working a shift at Bubble Tide Books this evening. But I know she'll really appreciate the vegetable fried rice. It's a favorite of hers. It was thoughtful of you to remember she's vegan, Drake."

"No problem." He offered a nonchalant shrug. "Listen Reen, I've got to get going. The kids are hungry. I've got sweet and sour chicken for Lilly and Kevin and Mongolian beef for me." He lifted one of the bags with a few cartons still inside. "I want to get it home before it gets cold."

"Aren't you going to tell Miss Reen about what we did after school today at the hosibul?" Lilly said, stumbling over the word while playing pattycake all over the very patient Hazelnut.

"It's *hopistal*," Kevin corrected with a tsk, butchering the word as much as his sister had. "Yeah, Dad, tell her what we did." Much to Lilly's annoyance, he wedged himself between his sister and the dog, doing his own sort of cupped clapping along Hazelnut's body.

"*I* was playing with her!" Lilly heatedly insisted.

"Children, behave, and it's *hospital*," Drake informed them. "I'll tell Miss Reen all about it later."

"Why were you at the hospital?" Reen asked. "Did you or one of the kids get hurt?"

"No, no, everything's fine." Turning back to his kids, Drake told them, "Let me just get everything on the table for Miss Reen before we go so she doesn't have to get up and hobble around on those crutches."

"Why go? Stay here and eat with me. I'd love the company and unlike my place, Bekka House is plenty roomy enough for all of us to sit together at the table."

Drake glanced at the kitchen clock. "It's getting late. I should get them home before they get C-R-A-N-K-Y," he spelled.

"You spell that all the time, Dad," Kevin informed with an exaggerated tsk. "We know it spells cranky."

"We won't get cranky, Daddy," Lilly promised, hugging Drake's leg and looking up at him with her adorable smile. "Can we stay and eat dinner with Miss Reen? Please, please, please?" The little stinker even batted her eyelashes at him. God knows where she picked up that tactic.

"It's Friday. They don't have school tomorrow," Reen reminded him. Clearly catching Lilly's ploy, she batted her eyelashes too.

No doubt about it, both females knew exactly how to wrap him around their little fingers.

"You're not feeling your best, Reen, are sure you wouldn't rather relax all by yourself where it's nice and quiet...and sane?"

"Positive. You three are like family. Lilly and Kevin may not be sane or quiet," she winked at the two of them, "but they're awfully nice. Aren't you, kids?"

"Yes, Miss Reen," they chorused, looking like a couple of guiltless cherubs.

She turned back to Drake. "There, you see? And you're kinda nice too, Professor Slattery," she beamed a playful smile, "so that's that. We're all eating Chinese food together. Okay?"

He needed little persuasion to spend more time with Reen. "Okay. But don't say I didn't warn you."

"Miss Reen?"

"Yes, Lilly?"

"Can me and Kevin go—"

"Kevin and I," Drake corrected.

Lilly grinned. "Sure, Daddy, you can come too." She covered her mouth and giggled. She'd pulled that one on Drake before when he'd corrected her. "Anyway, can we go look at the silver Christmas tree?"

"Can we?" Kevin chimed in.

"Of course you can," Reen told them. "Drake, would you mind plugging in the rotating color wheel for them? That way you kids can watch the metal branches change from blue to red, green, yellow and back again. Just like sparkling jewels."

Lilly clapped at that.

"Sure." Drake headed into the expansive family room, which was filled with cushy seating and plenty of furniture, much of which was older but none that gave any indications of potential collapse like the seating at Reen's house. "You two can stay in here while I get the food ready but remember, *look* doesn't mean *touch*, okay?"

"Yes, Daddy," Lilly said, folding her hands in front of her. "Thank you, Miss Reen!" Slapping her thighs, she used baby talk to call out, "Come on Hazelnut, let's look at the tree together." The dog looked to Reen, who nodded and made a shooing motion with her hand, before Hazelnut followed Lilly.

The aluminum tree was a year-round fixture at Bekka House. Before Reen's oldest sister, Delaney, moved to Glassfloat Bay from Chicago, she was married to a stodgy English professor who loathed Christmas, Delaney's favorite holiday. He wouldn't allow a Christmas tree in the house.

After he'd cheated on her with a student, they were divorced and Delaney found the tarnished, decades-old tree discarded by a neighbor, outside at the curb. She dragged the sixties relic into the house, fixed it up, and adopted it as her own. She hadn't taken it down since, except for the cross-country move to Oregon.

Delaney and her husband, Varik, insist there's something magical about the tree, with its eccentric collection of ornaments. It was somehow connected to their heartwish ring experience. Drake imagined there must be something special about the tree because everyone, including him, enjoyed being around it.

Returning to the kitchen and dining area, Drake lined the cartons of food on the table, putting large serving spoons in each. Knowing his kids were only interested in the sweet and sour chicken, he dished out their portions, giving them each half an eggroll and a scoop of rice before calling them to the table.

As they enjoyed the abundant array of Chinese food, it soon became apparent Reen would have more than just another dinner from the leftovers.

"This works out great," she said. "All I'll have to do is reheat in the microwave tomorrow." Taking a forkful of food, she gave a contented smile. "Mmm, they make the best kung pao shrimp." Sitting back in her chair, she patted her stomach. "It's not full of celery like some places. This one's loaded with shrimp and peanuts. I'm tempted to gobble it all down but I can't eat another bite." She took a sip of the hot tea Drake made for them. "So what's all this about the hospital?"

"Can I tell her, Daddy?" Lilly asked.

"Sure, schnickelfritz." Drake reached over and tweaked Lilly's nose.

Reen's expression brightened. "That's what Grandma Bekka used to call me," she said. "I've never heard anyone else use that word before. Nice memory."

"My grandfather would call us that," Drake said. "And when we were cranky he'd call us picklepuss. Isn't that right, Kevin?" He gave his son a lopsided smile.

Folding his arms across his chest, Kevin frowned. "I'm not cranky, and I'm not a picklepuss," he crankily insisted.

Drake watched Reen cover her mouth in a vain attempt not to laugh.

"Picklepuss," Lilly taunted him beneath her breath before giggling.

"Schnickelfritz," Kevin retorted, with a generous pout.

"Hmph." Sticking her chin high in the air, Lilly looked down her nose at her brother. "I'd rather be a schnickelfritz than a picklepuss."

Kevin's pout morphed into an angry scowl. "Oh yeah? Well—"

"Uh-oh...looks like we have a case of nickname wars," Reen said with mock alarm.

His eyebrow hiking in warning, Drake addressed his children. "What we're going to have is a case of schnickelfritz and picklepuss going home without getting any fortune or almond cookies unless they behave." Drake knew parents weren't supposed to bribe their children with sweets but sometimes, particularly when both he and his kids were overtired, it was the only way he could insure they'd listen.

Both kids slunk down in their chairs, chorusing "Sorry, Daddy," and proving to Drake once again that there were worse things in this world than occasionally bribing your kids with food.

With an absolving smile, Drake told his twins, "That's better. Now if you two are finished annoying each other, Lilly, you can tell Miss Reen about our visit to the pediatric cancer ward at the hospital this afternoon."

Sitting up straight in her chair, Lilly's expression grew animated. "After Daddy picked us up from school we took all the hats you made to the children, Miss Reen."

Registering obvious surprise, Reen's face lit with a smile. "You did? I had no idea." She turned to Drake. "How did you get all the boxes?"

"After I carried you to the car when you fell asleep this afternoon I went back in for them before I locked everything up."

"Aw, Drake, that's so sweet. I really wanted the children to have them today because I'd promised them. Obviously," she eyed her cast and crutches, "I had no way to get there myself, so I truly appreciate it. I had all the hats labeled with the names of the kids and their room numbers. I hope that made it easier."

"Are you kidding? We'd still be there searching if you hadn't. The three of us were glad to do it. Kevin and Lilly made a great delivery team, and the kids at the hospital were crazy about your hats and the little candy things you'd attached. I took a photo of each child wearing their new hat for you." He took out his phone and opened his pictures so Reen could scroll through them.

"How thoughtful! Oh, Drake, these are fabulous!" Tears welled in her eyes as she gazed at each photo. "Look at little Bobby Tarkle, he looks just like a Viking...and Marci Levine makes such a cute aviator. Aw, what a cute princess Rosa Martinez makes." She oohed and aahed through all the pictures, making comments about each of the children. Drake was amazed she knew each of the more than two-dozen kids by name. "Thank you so much."

"It was fun," Lilly said. "I really liked talking to the other kids and they were so happy to get the cute hats and fancy candies you made. They really loved them. All the kids said to tell you they hope you get better real soon."

"Aw, that's really nice."

"Shannie was so, so, *so* happy about her new hat," Lilly told Reen. "Oh boy, you should have seen how excited she was. She wanted me to tell you thank you, and that it's perfect."

"I'm really glad to hear that, Lilly. She's in your class at school, right?"

"Uh-huh. She's one of my best friends." Lilly's face fell. "She's been sick from cancer for a long time now."

Reen took Lilly's hand, giving it a squeeze. "I know, sweetie. It's always hard when someone we care a lot about gets very sick and we don't know what to do to help make them better. It makes you feel kind of lost and helpless, doesn't it Lilly?"

Nodding, Lilly's chin trembled and she wiped tears from her cheek. "I just talk to her, and when she looks sad, I try to make her laugh. But I don't know if that helps anything."

"I'm sure it does. I'm certain Shannie really appreciates the time you spend with her," Reen assured Lilly, finger-combing her hair away from her forehead. "Just being there for your friend when she feels sick or in pain makes a big difference. And if you can bring a smile to Shannie's face, or make her laugh, that's extra good medicine for her."

"Which one was Shannie again?" Drake asked, impressed as always by Reen's innate acumen with children. She'd been more of a mother-figure to his children than their own mother ever had.

It seemed Reen always knew the right thing to say to his kids, where Drake often struggled to relate to youngsters—his own or anyone else's. It wasn't that he didn't like kids, he adored them. He just had trouble interacting or connecting with them. Reen loved to tease him for being a giant teacher nerd who couldn't get his head out of his books long enough to know how to hold a normal-person conversation, much less a discussion between an adult and child.

She was probably right.

"Shannon Brone," Reen answered. "She's the great-granddaughter of Ruthie Brone, owner of the String Me Along yarn shop. Such a sweet little girl. Very brave too. She's been through a lot the past year with one treatment after the other."

"Do you know what type of cancer she has?" Drake asked softly and Reen gave a confirming nod. Being as caring and concerned as she was about those kids, he wasn't at all surprised Reen knew the answer.

"She has..." Reen's eyes closed in a long blink as she let out a wobbly breath, "an aggressive form of childhood leukemia that puts her in a higher risk group."

God how Drake hated to hear that. It made him extra thankful his twins were strong and healthy. He couldn't imagine either of them becoming that ill or having to endure cancer treatments.

"The medicine made all of Shannie's hair fall out," Lilly said. "Even her eyebrows and eyelashes." Turning to her Dad, she reminded him, "She got one of the princess crown hats with the matching curly pink yarn hair." She made spiral motions around her head with her fingers. "The other one went to Ava Mitchell. When we came into Shannie's room she was wearing the cute puppy dog hat Miss Reen made for her before, the one with the long floppy ears made out of all those circles of yarn, remember?" Lilly made a descriptive motion over her own ears. "You can't hardly even tell she doesn't have any hair left when she wears it."

"Ah yes, the rust-colored cocker spaniel hat." Drake smiled in recollection, remembering the way the little girl loved it, and how her eyes lit up at the sight of her new princess crown hat with the cluster of pink springs.

Turning to Reen, Lilly told her, "Shannie and Ava are so excited to wear their new princess crown hats together so everyone at the hospital will think they're twins."

That made Drake smile. Their different skin color evidently presented no problem whatsoever to the girls when it came to pretending they were twins. Clearly, Lilly, saw no difficulty with it either.

"I had fun making both of those hats," Reen said. "I remember going loopy making all the little yarn loops for the puppy dog ears." Making a squiggly motion with her fingers, similar to Lilly's, she laughed.

"Shannie said it looks just like her puppy, Lulu," Kevin added. "I saw her dog a couple times and she's right. You did a real good job, Miss Reen. You're a great yarner."

"What a nice compliment. Thank you, Kevin."

Drake and Reen exchanged smiles before he corrected his son. "You mean knitter, Kev." Drake snapped his fingers. "I almost forgot. Be right back." He left the house and returned soon after with a wad of rolled up papers in his hand. Setting them in front of Reen, he told her, "These are the pictures you asked the kids to draw, you know, of the sorts of hats they'd like you to make for them."

"Oh that's wonderful!" Reen paged through them, smiling and muttering appreciative comments as she eyed each child's imaginative sketch. "Aren't they delightful? Thank you for collecting these. It'll give me something to do while I'm recovering." She put them in a neat stack.

"There's a thank-you and get-well card from Shannie there too," Lilly said. "She drew you looking like a princess with a cast on one leg and a puffy pillow strapped to your butt—oops, sorry, I mean backside." She gave an impish look of apology.

"That was very thoughtful of Shannie," Reen said.

"Shannie said all the yarn stuff you make for her always makes her feel a thousand times better," Lilly said. "Do you think you could teach me how to make yarn hats and stuff, Miss Reen?"

"I'd be happy to show you how to knit and crochet. You'd be my first official student." The corners of her eyes crinkled with her smile.

"We'll pay you, of course," Drake said and he watched Reen's expression become incredulous.

"Oh please, don't be silly. Heck, I don't even know if I'll be a good teacher or not." She focused on Lilly again. "If Lilly doesn't mind being a guinea pig," Reen gave a playful smile, "I'd love to have the opportunity to see if I can successfully teach her to knit and crochet."

"You can teach me how to make a guinea pig hat!" Lilly suggested through a round of giggles. And Reen gave her a thumbs up.

"Dad wore a hat too while we delivered them to the kids," Kevin said as Lilly nodded in agreement.

"You didn't...did you really?" Reen's eyes sparkled as she smiled. He could tell she was close to giggling at the thought of him wearing one of the hats.

"What can I say? The kids insisted."

"Which hat? The bearded Viking? The clown? The sheik's turban?"

"Eh...no. It was the Brunhilde hat you had on this morning."

Reen clapped her hand over her mouth when a bubble of surprised laughter popped out. Her giggles were in full force now.

"I didn't want to wear one meant for one of the children." He shrugged. "Kevin and Lilly assured me I looked cool with the horns."

"Not to mention the blonde braids." Giggling, Reen covered her mouth with her hand. "Oh Drake, I would have loved to see that."

"Don't worry, you didn't miss a thing. The twins asked one of the volunteers to take pictures of us together. They want me to post it online. Which, of course, is never, *ever* going to happen."

"I didn't see that one. Ooh, show me, show me! I have to see it." Reen's backside rose from the donut pillow and Drake caught her by the elbows, mid-bounce, preventing her from another painful butt-related episode.

Her eyes grew wide and her cheeks flushed. "Oops! I almost did it again, didn't I?"

"You most certainly did. I swear, you're worse than my six-year-olds, Maureen." He was still holding her arms. She looked so adorable gazing up at him with self-reproach in her eyes. So soft, sweet...kissable. It would have been so easy to bend forward, just a little, and plant a kiss on her lips.

The chance thought triggered a demoralizing memory of what had happened the one time he'd attempted to act on that urge. It was a year ago, the night he'd taken her to the opera, and the memory still stung. In attempting to kiss her, he'd embarrassed himself as well as Reen that evening, making things awkward between them. She'd gone out of her way since then to ensure he understood their relationship was one of friendship and nothing more. He got the message, loud and clear, and he wasn't about to forget it now when Reen was in a vulnerable state.

Drake straightened, setting her back on her pillow before letting go of her.

"Why were you looking at Miss Reen all funny like that, Dad?" Kevin asked with a distinct sneer.

The kid was far too observant. "Eh...just making sure she's feeling all right, Kev." Without skipping a beat, Drake turned back to Reen. "You either need an in-home caregiver to watch your every move," he admonished a bit more harsh than he intended, "or you need to act like a responsible adult who has a broken butt and stop bouncing when you get excited. Otherwise it'll take you a lot longer to recover."

While Reen looked suitably remorseful, Kevin and Lilly covered their mouths, snickering. "Daddy said butt," Lilly said, pointing her finger at their father.

"Never mind about that," Drake admonished them, doing his best not to laugh. He reached for his phone and took a moment to study the photo he'd just told Reen about. Wincing, he groaned, imagining all the raised eyebrows if the faculty of Wisdom Harbor

University caught sight of the pictures of the supposedly revered Professor Slattery.

"Oh my gosh, look at you! How adorable. I love it!" Reen said. "You have to post this, Drake. It would definitely go viral."

"That's exactly what I'm afraid of." He glanced at the silly image again. "Esteemed professor indeed," he muttered beneath his breath before taking his phone back and pocketing it.

"Drake?"

"Hmm?"

"You're the best." She touched his sleeve, smiling up at him. "Thank you for being such a good sport...and such a great friend."

"No problem, glad I could help. Seeing the big smile it put on your face, as well as the kids at the hospital, was worth the abject humiliation," he joked. The fleeting look of adoration he spotted across Reen's features was the icing on the cake.

Chapter Four

A Few Days before Valentine's Day

~<>~

PERCHING HER FACE in her hands as she stared at her iPad, Reen sighed. Her gaze skittered across post after post online. "These memes everyone shares are designed to induce guilt," she grumbled. "The end of this one says 'Ninety-seven percent will ignore this post—I think I know which of you are in the three percent who'll share it and which of you won't.' Oh brother."

"What on earth are you babbling about?" Laila asked.

"I don't get it," Reen complained. "Do people really believe this stuff? If we were at lunch with friends and someone passed around a picture of a sad-eyed puppy, saying she knew which of us would share it and which wouldn't, I'd feel insulted. Nobody talks that way in real life."

"Somebody's spending *way* too much time online." Glancing at what Reen was griping about, Laila tsked. "Those memes are created to manipulate the reader. If you don't take a break from social media, Reen, it'll numb your brain...and you won't go to heaven."

Reen shot her sister an incredulous look before letting out a yelp of surprised laughter. "What?"

"My meme says if you don't put down that damn iPad once in a while you have a ninety-seven percent chance of not going to heaven...and I know whether you will or won't." Giving her sister a sideways glance, Laila smiled.

"Very funny. Getting offline is easier said than done, especially when you have broken bones. I can't do anything except sit here in Griffin's Café's padded booth or on a big poofy pillow, or on my—"

"Fat doughy fanny cushion?" Laila offered helpfully, hiding a grin behind her mug of coffee.

"I don't have a fat doughy fanny." Reen fought the urge to laugh, remembering a time when that description of her backside might have been accurate.

"I mean the cushion with the big booty hole where your broken caboose is supposed to go," Laila clarified, doing a great job keeping a straight face.

"Your clarification and sincere sympathy are greatly appreciated," Reen said, sarcasm evident in her voice just before she winced with discomfort while attempting to shift in her seat.

"Shame on you, Laila," their sister-in-law, Sabrina, teased. "How would you like it if you were the one with the fractured keister and Reen taunted you about your unfortunate heinie situation?"

Sabrina and Laila worked ineffectively to swallow their laughter.

"You guys are hilarious," Reen said with a deadpan expression. "How long did you spend Googling to come with all those butt synonyms?"

"Until my gluteus maximus was too sore to sit anymore," Laila answered.

"And until my derriere was numb," Sabrina offered, mirroring Laila's mischievous expression.

"Until our badonkadonks were smarting," Laila tacked on.

Unable to keep from laughing any longer, Reen gave in. "Okay, okay, I know you're right about me spending too much time online." Her extended sigh sounded more like a groan.

"I spend hours sitting on this donut pillow looking at one post after another warning me about what a horrible person I am if I don't share. It's like being in grade school, passing around those awful chain letters full of doom and gloom." She scowled at the memory. "I hated them. Never followed through. Then everyone would get mad at me because I broke the chain. So stupid."

"Ah, so you're the one who broke all those chains," Laila said. "I wonder how many poor unfortunate people had their arms and legs fall off because of your unwillingness to follow through with those chain letters."

Reen stared at her sister for a solid ten seconds. "You're in the wrong business," she finally said. "You should close your bakery and go on the road as a stand-up comedian."

"You two crack me up." Adding a teaspoon of sugar and dash of cream before sipping from her coffee, Sabrina chuckled. "You're just like me and Annalise. Just ignore those silly memes that have you so ticked off and get back to your knitting."

"I know you're right. I'm in danger of losing brain cells as I sit like a lump on a log trying to recover from these damn fractures." Her sigh was a low, mournful sound. "But I can only knit so many hats. I've got enough now to outfit the entire population of Glassfloat Bay several times over."

"Perfect! Save them for when you start your own business," Laila suggested. She was always encouraging Reen to follow her dream.

Normally Reen would brighten at the mention of the pleasing idea, but the near constant throbbing at her fracture sites gnawed away at her usual upbeat attitude. She hated being a wimp, but fighting the pain for so long had evidently made her negative and cantankerous.

When she felt the unpleasant side of herself eclipsing her positive side, Reen recalled the smiling faces and sweet attitudes of the sick children at the hospital. They were so brave. Painful butt and ankle aside, Reen reminded herself she was a fortunate woman who had no business steeping herself in a vat of self-pity over temporary aches.

"Harry loves his fireman hat," Sabrina said. "He shows everybody. You made it look so real, Reen. How did you get the brim shaped like that?"

"I'm so glad he likes it. I knitted the top and bottom of the brim over a piece of hard plastic I'd cut out. It was an experiment that worked well." Reen smiled, recalling the joy she'd had creating that hat.

"Definitely. Harry says he looks just like his daddy now. And Drake's daughter, Lilly, told Harry she adores her sparkly golden princess crown hat. She said you made it look exactly like the drawing she gave you."

"Wonderful! I combined metallic gold yarn with the regular yarn to help make it look like all the glittery stars she drew all around the crown. I think it worked really well."

"Speaking of Drake, where's he been lately?" Laila asked. "I haven't seen him here at the café in at least two weeks."

"House hunting with our dear cousin, Saffy." Reen rolled her eyes at the thought of their rich, pompous cousin, Saffron Devington. The two of them had never really clicked. Unfortunately, they'd developed the juvenile habit of sniping at each other.

"What do you mean?" Laila's smile evaporated. "Drake loves that house. That's why he moved back into it after his parents died last year. His kids love it there too."

"It's a great old house. Much better than the cold, industrial-style loft apartment they lived in before." Reen shuddered. "Of course, that ritzy, antiseptic condo was his ex-wife Janet's idea, not Drake's."

"Yeah, then she dumped him for somebody else," Laila reminded them, "and walked out on her kids too."

"Bitch," the three said in unison.

"Did you see the awesome playground set Drake erected for Lilly and Kevin?" Sabrina asked. "It's Harry's favorite place to visit now."

"I was shocked at what a great job he did building it," Reen admitted, absently stirring her coffee. "He had Hud come over to inspect it and make sure it was safe for the kids."

"My brother said he was really impressed with Drake's work," Sabrina said.

"Drake's made some wonderful improvements to the house recently too," Laila said, "which is surprising for a man who's not naturally handy with tools."

"And who used to muck up every one of his DIY projects," Reen added.

"He must have studied so hard to learn how to do each project," Laila said. "I honestly can't imagine him ever wanting to move."

"How-to books and the internet are the professor's best friends," Reen told her. "It seems he's got his mind set on becoming more of a do-it-yourselfer." She thought about her jagged concrete step, recalling it was shortly after she told Drake that she'd ask Hud come over to fix it that Drake got serious about improving his DIY skills.

"He might be giving in to our cousin's lofty plans for him to move up in the world," Laila said with a sneer. "Apparently Saffy doesn't think his current house is prestigious enough for a professor of Drake's stature."

"Bingo." Reen's expression mirrored her sister's. "After all, the Devingtons live up there in the clouds," Reen flicked her wrist upward, "in that mansion on Beauregard Hill."

"Do you think Saffron's interested in Drake?" Sabrina asked, bringing the last of her chocolate chip pancake to her mouth. "In a non-real-estate way, I mean."

"I've wondered the same thing," Laila said. "Saffron's had that goo-goo eyed look lately whenever Drake's around."

Reen tossed a dismissive wave at the ludicrous idea. Recalling her cousin's phone call to Drake the day Reen fell, and later learning about their lecture and dinner date, made her seethe. It soured her stomach to think of the two of them as anything more than real estate agent and client.

"Dollar signs. That's all our cousin sees when she looks at Drake," Reen said, trying to convince herself. "The only thing Saffron's interested in is her next commission. I can't think of two people with less in common. She collects money the way Drake does degrees."

"That's not entirely true," Laila pointed out. "Saffron's multi-degreed too."

"All I know," Sabrina said, "is that they've been spending a lot of time together lately and looking pretty cozy."

"I can't imagine anything about Saffron that would attract Drake." Reen knew what she said was absurd even before the words left her mouth.

"You mean aside from her being rich, beautiful, intelligent, a theater and opera aficionado, being well read, and having a master's degree?" Laila asked through a thinly veiled smirk.

Reen blinked. "Why are you sticking up for Saffy all of a sudden? Since when did you sign on as one of her cheerleaders?" Reen sipped from her coffee, hiding behind her mug to conceal the pink cheeks she knew were there from being embarrassed at her own childishness.

"Don't get snippy, Maureen," Laila chastised. "All I meant is—"

"Oh good grief," Reen interrupted, "you make it sound like Saffron and Drake are an ideal match, Laila." Her stomach grumbled in response. "You forgot to add self-centered, mean, and arrogant to her list of attributes," she reminded her sister.

Reen wasn't sure why she was trying so hard to defame Saffron. Her cousin wasn't really *that* bad. If she and Drake were attracted to each other, so what? Why should Reen care?

"True." Laila shrugged. "Look, I'm no more a fan of our stuck-up cousin than you are, Reen, but you've got to admit they have plenty in common."

Before Reen could fully process Laila's comment and respond, Sabrina asked, "How many degrees does Drake have now anyway?"

Reen started counting on her fingers. "God only knows...six, seven? I can't keep track. Drake's the epitome of a renaissance man. He's got a working knowledge of just about any subject thrown at him."

"He should go on Jeopardy," Sabrina suggested.

"The only problem," Laila pointed out, "is that he'd be answering question after question and winning *until* he came to any category having to do with—"

"Sports," Reen interjected with a resolute nod, her brief discord with Laila already dissipated. "Poor Drake would choke. He's the only guy I know who gets football and baseball mixed up."

"True." Laila laughed. "Our sports-oblivious Professor Slattery is Glassfloat Bay's handsomest, hunkiest geek."

Reen smiled at the spot-on observation. "He loves learning like we love hot fudge sundaes. Aside from being super brainy, he's truly a good man. He's going to make some lucky woman a wonderful husband someday." Giving a near imperceptible shrug, she added in a tiny voice, "Who knows? Maybe that woman will be Saffron."

"By the way he looks at you," Laila said in that observant tone Reen knew so well, "that lucky woman could be you." She wiggled her eyebrows.

"Oh puhleez, Drake looks at me like I'm his sister." A chuckle tangled in Reen's throat as she recalled fleeting moments when she'd caught the hunky-dorky professor looking at her in a decidedly non-sister-ish way. "We're just good friends. Neighbors. That's all." She wondered at times who she was trying to convince more—Laila or herself.

"He's a great guy," Reen continued, "but I have far less in common with Drake than Saffron does." She hated to admit it but it was true. "The professor is a bona fide intellectual, while it took me practically two years to learn how to knit one, purl two." Screwing her face, she mimicked a bumbling knitting scene.

"You make yourself sound like a dolt," Laila noted. "You were engaged to an English professor. You had no trouble keeping up with Bob."

"That's because Bob was smart, but not intimidating-smart. Sure, he knew all about English but he wasn't an expert in every subject under the sun, like Drake." Reen leaned closer to the table, speaking in hushed tones. "Besides, you know who I'm interested in."

"But Reen..." Sabrina started, her expression etched with pity.

"I know, I know." Reen gave an indifferent wave. "Your brother and Monica Sharp are currently an item." Her shoulders slumped at the thought. "Emphasis on the word *currently*. Things can change. As far as I know they're not exclusive. They both still see other people, right?"

"I...I don't think so." Sabrina touched Reen's hand in a sympathetic gesture. "They really seem taken with each other. I'm only telling you so you don't get your hopes up too much."

"I understand. But we'll see how long their attraction lasts," Reen said, trying to be optimistic.

"Reen's got a point," Laila said. "Monica doesn't strike me as the type who'll stick around for too long." After the less than cordial real estate transaction she'd had with Monica regarding the building that housed her bakery, Laila wasn't much of a fan.

"Exactly," Reen said with an ear-to-ear smile. "And guess who'll be there to pick up the pieces when she dumps Hudson?" Thumbing her chest, she grinned. At Sabrina's still uncertain expression, Reen sighed. "Okay, maybe I can't compete with Monica in the looks department but—"

"Oh, Reen," concern was written all over Sabrina's face, "I didn't mean that at all. You're a beautiful woman. I only meant—"

"That's okay, I know you didn't mean it that way." Reen gave Sabrina's hand a reassuring squeeze. "Thanks for the compliment. I was just going to say that I know your brother likes me...and liking can turn into loving, right?"

"In the movies, yeah," Laila offered, earning a giant tsk from Reen.

"Thanks for your support," Reen tossed at her. It wasn't easy being positive about her chances with Hud. Monica Sharp was sexy, sophisticated, oozing with confidence, and model-thin with what appeared to be ample surgical enhancements in the right places. She worked at the same real estate agency as Saffron where they teamed up together on the exclusive, pricier listings.

"For heaven's sake, Reen," Laila said, "you're your own worst enemy. Monica has nothing on you, except for a few augmentations." Laila cupped her hands in front of her chest. "If you're really that hooked on Hud," she shrugged, "go after him."

Reen rolled her eyes at that. "This isn't high school, Laila. What am I supposed to do, put on my old cheerleading outfit and challenge Monica to a cheer-off?"

"Now that's something my brother would enjoy watching." Sabrina laughed. "But, seriously, I know something you *could* do that might work." Her expression grew impish.

Folding her arms across her chest, Reen readied herself for being teased again and replied with minimal enthusiasm, "What?"

"Plant a big lip-smack on Hud Saturday night."

"What?!" Reen's face scrunched in disbelief.

"The city council has approved a kissing booth for the Valentine's Day Fling," Sabrina explained. "Could anything be more perfect?"

"Sabrina's right." Laila gave a nod. "I forgot to tell you about it, Reen. It's a great idea—right out of the 1950s. I bet it'll bring in a good amount for the cause we're supporting."

"It's for Wisdom Harbor Children's Hospital," Sabrina added.

"Really?" That caught Reen's attention. "I thought the city council was going to nix the kissing booth idea because some people in town are anxious about germs. Mildred Fophamer, who's had a seat on the city council since dinosaurs roamed the earth, put up a big stink about how unsanitary kissing is."

"Sounds just like Mildred," Sabrina said with a knowing smile. "She caused all sorts of trouble years ago when Annalise, Hud and I were kids. Always calling our parents to rat on us about something or other. Like playing catch in her yard or something." She tsked. "Busy body."

"Millie also believes kissing booths contribute to the delinquency of minors...as well as their parents and grandparents," Laila said.

"Of course she does." Sabrina's eyes closed in a long blink as she shook her head. "Smooching her cats is probably her only kissing experience. She's so ridiculous. We argued for the kissing booth, telling the city council that anyone afraid of germs didn't have to get kissed or be a kisser." Sabrina brushed her hands together. "Simple."

"I already bought special lipstick for it," Laila told them. "It's supposedly kissable so it won't leave an imprint after you plant one on the guy's kisser. The color is Mango Go Deep."

"Mango go..." Giving her a strange look, Reen asked, "What does that even mean?"

"Hell if I know, but it sounds deliciously naughty, doesn't it?" Laila's eyebrows bounced.

"So are we all participating?" Sabrina asked. "You can borrow Laila's sexy lipstick and lure my brother with your mango lips." Her grin was contagious.

"Oh...I don't know," Reen hesitated. She was full of false bravado when talking about winning over Hud but got cold feet when it came to actually doing something about her attraction. The idea of kissing him gave her butterflies. Scratch that. It was more like hornets buzzing around, especially when picturing Monica standing there watching. "I don't think I can...not with my broken tailbone and ankle."

"Of course you'll do it, Reen. We all will," Laila said and Sabrina nodded in agreement. "I sincerely doubt your broken butt will inhibit your ability to kiss." Her face lit with an impish smile. "Remember, it's for charity. For the kids."

With possible kissing booth scenarios on her mind, Reen sipped from her coffee, wrinkling her nose. "Oh...this is cold."

"Maybe because it's been sitting there ignored for the last twenty minutes while you were daydreaming about Hud," Laila noted.

"I was *not* daydreaming about him," Reen claimed, "I was merely—"

"Merely checking the photos on his social media pages." Lifting an eyebrow, Laila gave her a knowing look.

"I told you, I was looking at memes!" Reen gave her iPad a sideways glance, casually closing the site where she'd been checking out the handsome contractor.

"I'll get you two a fresh cup," Sabrina offered. Scooting out of the booth, she headed behind the café's counter with their mugs. She returned a moment later with steamy hot coffee. "I've got a couple of tables ready to leave. I'll take care of them and be back in a few minutes."

"She must really enjoy working here." Reen stirred a packet of stevia into her coffee, watching Sabrina scurry off to one of the tables, displaying a ready smile for her customers. "She's making good money with her artwork and Gard makes more than enough money for her to stay home to concentrate on her art, so she's not working because she needs to financially."

"I think a lot of it has to do with the way Stuart practically kept Sabrina a prisoner during their marriage," Laila said. "Working here for Annalise gives her a sense of independence, plus she obviously enjoys interacting with the customers."

"The customers were all so wonderful, standing by her when Sabrina and little Harry had that terrible crisis." Reen shivered at the recollection. "Sabrina's been through so much."

"I don't like to think about what would have happened if Gard hadn't received the heartwish ring from Varik when he did," Laila said with a tremor that must have been contagious because Reen found herself shuddering as well.

"Delaney said Varik had an inner sense of knowing one morning," Reen said. "Something told him it was time to pass his ring to Gard. Fortunately, Sabrina and Harry got their well-deserved happy ending with our brother."

"I've never seen Gard so happy," Laila said. "They really are perfect for each other."

"Absolutely." Reen's gaze dropped to Laila's finger. "What about *your* heartwish ring?" She smoothed her finger over the multihued blue stone on her sister's hand. "Any idea who gets it next?"

"Not a clue." Laila held out her hand, turning it back and forth. "Mom says I'll know without question when the time is right."

"Look what I have for us." Sabrina returned to the booth. Setting a plate of white-frosted scones dotted with tiny red heart-shaped sprinkles on the table, she informed them, "The Great Pretender's maple bacon walnut scones."

Enthusiasm written across her face, Laila sat up straighter in her seat briskly rubbing her hands. "I'm dying to see what you two think. Be honest. I don't want to offer them to my customers, or yours, Sabrina, unless they're topnotch."

"Bacon?" Reen's eyes grew wide. "They sound scrumptious. I remember when you got the idea for these." She smiled at her sister. "If you made them, Laila, I know they're fabulous."

"I couldn't resist trying one earlier. Mmm." Sabrina licked her lips. "They're amazing."

"I'm so glad to hear that. If you think they're worthy I plan on making several dozen mini-scones for the Fling Saturday night. You two are the first to sample them."

Reen broke off a corner of a scone, popping it into her mouth. Her eyelids fluttered closed at the burst of deliciousness baptizing her taste buds. "So good. Sweet, smoky and nutty." She gave Laila a sidelong glance. "This couldn't possibly be one of your reduced calorie recipes...could it? Please say yes."

"It is. Sugar-free, gluten-free and about a third less calories." Her expression was optimistic. "So you think it's a success? Do you think anyone will know it's a *pretender*?" She hung air quotes around the word.

"Are you kidding? No way." Reen took another bite, closing her eyes in pleasure. "Outrageously good, and good *for* me too? I'm in bacon heaven, Laila. Great job. I think these might be my favorite so far." She bit off a larger piece.

Sabrina gave a thumbs up as she finished a bite and broke off another piece. "Reen's right. This is a major success, Laila. No one would ever guess these are relatively guilt-free."

"Exactly what I wanted to hear. Thanks." Looking relieved, Laila asked Sabrina, "Where's your sister? I want to see what Annalise thinks too. She's usually working at this time."

"She'll be here soon. She's picking up Valentine supplies for decorating the café and the community center. But don't worry, I guarantee she'll be crazy about the scones." She squeezed Laila's hand. "So what were we talking about when I left? Drake, or was it my brother?" Sitting on the edge of the booth's seat, she nibbled on a scone, looking toward the front of the café when the door opened. "Well speak of the devil. Look who just came in."

Facing away from the front of the café, Laila turned to get a look, while Reen offered a pained moan, rubbing her backside as she attempted to turn.

"Ouch. I keep forgetting about the donut pillow." She shifted her position to get comfortable.

"Aw, your poor widdle broken butt." Laila offered a mock pout.

By now Reen was used to the frequent cutesy mentions of her broken tailbone. "I'm ignoring you," she teased. "I can't see...which one is it, Drake or Hud?"

"Hud." Sabrina waved at her brother.

Fluffing her hair, Reen whispered, "How do I look?"

"Ravishing." Laila patted her sister's hand.

Finally turning enough to spot Monica intertwining arms with Hud as they walked in, Reen's bright mood soured. "What's *she* doing here? I thought Monica and Saffron hated this place. They call it a greasy spoon."

"While Griffin's Café may not be highbrow enough for them," Laila said, "Monica's no dummy. She knows this is one of Hud's favorite places. I mean, hell, one sister owns it and the other works here."

"Mmm-hmm." Reen nodded. "If Hud comes here, Monica's sticking like glue so she can keep her eye on him and keep him away from female predators."

"Like you?" At the sight of Reen's stunned expression, Laila laughed. "God you're easy."

"Shhh, they're heading this way." Sabrina looked up and smiled as they approached. "Hey, Hud. Nice to see you, Monica."

Hud greeted each of them with a smile while Monica gave a queenly wave. "I haven't been here in a while and missed getting my cuppa joe and a scone to start the day." Giving Laila a curious look, he leaned forward, then side to side.

"What are you doing?" Laila followed his gaze. "Am I full of crumbs or something?"

"Nope. I'm looking for Abby and Gus. I thought they were attached." Hud grinned. "This is the first time I've seen you without the babies this early in the morning."

"Oh!" Laila laughed. "It's a nice break," she admitted. "Zak doesn't have an exercise class to teach until this afternoon so he's watching the twins this morning. I love it when his schedule allows me some free time."

Clutching Hud's arm in a possessive gesture, Monica flashed a smile and cooed, "Morning. Sorry to hear about your fall, Reen. Having a fractured ankle and rectum must hurt terribly."

Reen's jaw dropped, landing somewhere on the café's floor.

Monica glanced from Reen to Laila and Sabrina. "Uh-oh, didn't I get that right? Fractured anus...is that it?"

The shrill sound of a train whistle blustered inside Reen's head as steam shot out of her ears. She'd never balk at the term *broken butt* again. It was almost endearing compared to Monica's cringe-worthy alternatives.

"It's her tailbone, remember?" Hud said, seemingly charmed by Monica's clearly bogus inanity act.

"Ouch." Monica wrinkled her perfect little nose. "In any case, it sounds painful." Reen could almost believe Monica's sympathetic look was genuine.

"Any word on when the cast comes off?" Hud asked.

"The orthopedist is taking x-rays this afternoon. If they look good, he'll swap the cast for a walking boot that I'll wear until the ankle heals." Reen crossed her fingers. "I'll be so happy to ditch the cast and crutches."

"I can imagine," Monica said. "It's all so clunky and unattractive, including that godawful purple color. They must have been all out of white casts that day."

"Nope." Ignoring the twitch starting at her lip, Reen did her best to smile. "I chose the purple on purpose."

Making a silent "O" with her lips, Monica telegraphed a look of surprise. "Too bad you'll have to wear one of those Frankenstein-ish boots." She bent to the side, checking out Reen's posterior. "Hud said you have to sit on a special cushion for your cracked rump." She studied Reen's butt situation as she spoke.

One eye twitched along with her lip. Twitchy fought the scowl threatening to hijack her face. Cracked rump indeed. She wasn't a beef roast.

"It's a donut pillow," Laila jumped in, spotting Reen's escalating twitchiness. "A cushion with a hole in the center to take pressure off her tailbone."

"You have to carry that whoopee cushion thing wherever you go?" Monica looked revolted. "How embarrassing."

As Reen seethed, Sabrina said, "Um, you two are free to sit anywhere you like." Her arm gestured wide.

"This booth's plenty big for all of us." Hud double-slapped the tabletop of the oversized half-circle booth. "We can all squeeze in here." He got ready to slide into the red vinyl booth seat. "We haven't all had a chance to talk in quite a while."

"I see the perfect spot by the front window." Monica tugged Hud's arm before he could sit. "We have so many details to talk over before we head out to look at houses."

"Houses?" Sabrina's smile morphed into a surprised frown. "You mean for Drake or for you, Hud?"

"Both of us, actually," Hud told her. "Monica talked me into it after she told me about the great places Saffron's been showing Drake."

As if orchestrated, as soon as Drake's name left Hud's lips, the café door opened and in walked Drake and Saffron.

"Saffron," Monica called, twiddling her fingers in way of a greeting. "We're over here."

"Hey there, how's your ankle and broken butt?" was the first thing out of Drake's mouth as he walked toward them.

Reen could hear him snicker while she playfully sneered at him.

When he and Saffron arrived at their booth, he said, "Without Lilly and Kevin around I can get away with calling it your butt instead of your backside."

"Oh goodie," Reen said.

"You look awful," Saffron told Reen.

Reen expelled a sigh born of frustration. "Hello to you too, Saffy," she answered her nemesis cousin, using the nickname Saffron despised.

"So? How are you doing?" Drake asked Reen again. "She's actually looking much better than the last time I saw her," he told Saffron. "Poor thing was in so much pain. Maureen's a real trooper."

"Thanks." She felt her expression brighten at Drake's supportive words. "Everything still hurts but the pain pills help."

"Still making you loopy?"

"Not too bad. I've learned how much I can take without that happening and stick to that, unless it's in the middle of the night and I don't care about getting loopy."

"You have to hobble around on those crutches to get around, huh?" Hud angled his head toward the pair of crutches propped in the corner.

Reen loved it when Hud talked to her without her talking to him first. She just wished it didn't have to do with her ankle and butt.

"Yup," she said, wiggling one of the crutches leaning against the wall at her side. She wasn't at her most eloquent when in Hud's presence.

"I had to use crutches once during high school," he told her, "when I got a broken leg playing football. They're not easy to maneuver. I was clumsy and awkward the whole time."

"Oh I'll bet you managed just fine." Monica said, briefly leaning her head on Hud's arm.

"*Grace* is definitely not my middle name," Reen said, eyeing Monica's cuddly ways with Hud. "It seems I've lost any sense of coordination the way I keep banging into people and inanimate objects."

"That doesn't sound all that unusual for you," Saffron said. Focusing on Reen's disagreeable expression, she added, "Oh don't give me that look, Maureen, you know I was just teasing."

"It's so sad," Monica said to Saffron, "your cousin has to sit on a special hotdog pillow."

"Donut pillow," Drake and Laila corrected in unison.

"Oh. I knew it was something food related," Monica said.

"She has to cart around the crutches and pillow wherever she goes," Sabrina told them.

"Fortunately...or maybe not," Reen said with a chuckle, "I've got a gargantuan canvas tote bag Kady let me borrow. It's peppermint pink and covered with rainbows, daisies and peace signs. If that weren't enough, both sides have big block letters spelling out, *make love, not war.*"

"The saying was used primarily by those opposed to the Vietnam War," Saffron explained, as always, relishing an opportunity to show everyone how brainy she was. Rubbing her arms as if she had goosebumps, she added, "Ugh, Kady has such horrendous taste."

"Our little sister has her own unconventional style," Laila said, defending the youngest Malone sibling. "She does Bohemian well."

Saffron mumbled something inaudible beneath her breath.

"I'd be horrified if I had to carry something like that around." Monica gave an accompanying shudder. "I'm sorry for you, Reen."

"I'm betting Kady found that bag in a thrift shop," Drake surmised. He elbowed Hud. "The Malone women are infamous for their love of garage sales and secondhand stores."

"So I've heard." Hud's smile tempted Reen to let out a dreamy sigh. It was like the entire room brightened when he turned his smile on her.

"You know us well." Laila laughed. "Kady found the tote while we still lived in Chicago, at one of her favorite thrift stores."

"I look like a reject from the hippie movement. But," Reen shrugged, "it's the only bag big enough for my handy-dandy butt pillow."

"I look forward to seeing it...the tote bag, not your butt." Hud chuckled.

Reen picked up the folded tote on the seat between her and the wall, opening it so everyone could get a look.

"Oh...well...that really is unique, isn't it?" Clearly doing his best not to laugh, Hud tilted his head, studying the colorful bag. "It's not really so bad. After all, it does the job, right?"

Before Reen could say anything, Saffron got in her two cents.

"It's hideous." One corner of Saffron's lip lifted in a sneer. "I'm sure you could find something more suitable if you tried."

Reen's eyelid twitched again as frustration coursed through her veins.

"Aw, go easy on her, Saffron." Monica telegraphed a sympathetic expression. "Maureen must be mortified carrying that loud, decades-old thing around."

"I think it's kind of cute," Drake said. "It looks...happy. Matches Reen's personality."

"Thank you." Reen boasted a vindicated smile. She could always count on her buddy, Drake, to stand up for her.

"Just like her purple cast," Saffron agreed with a muffled chuckle as her hand smoothed up and down Drake's sleeve. "With all her many quirks, Maureen has never been one for trying to fit in."

"Oh for—" Reen's shoulders slumped and she took a deep breath. "I'm tired of our relationship being so combative, Saffron. Is it really that difficult to be civil to me? To find maybe one miniscule nice thing to say?"

Saffron's spine stiffened. "Well, I—" she began in a snotty tone, and then stopped cold, staring at Reen for a moment before dropping her gaze. "You're right. I apologize, Maureen. I shouldn't be picking on you, especially when you're injured. I...I guess I've grown used to our verbal jousting. I'm sorry you're in so much discomfort. Really." She looked genuinely contrite.

Maureen nearly did a cartoon doubletake at her cousin's kind apology—words she'd swear she'd never hear spilling from Saffron's lips. A fleeting glance at Laila told her Laila was just as surprised.

"Thank you, Saffron. I appreciate that." Reen shifted carefully in her seat. "Okay, time to get the conversation off me and my bones. So, Drake, I hear you're looking for a new house."

Dropping his gaze to his feet, Drake said, "I thought I might look at a few places Saffron picked out for me."

"He thinks I have great taste." Saffron rubbed his sleeve again, "Don't you, Drake?"

"Definitely. You're up on all the latest trends." Drake draped his arm around Saffron's shoulder.

"You're not selling your family house, are you?" Laila said.

"Well..."

"You love that house, Drake," Reen reminded him. "You've always said it's full of so many wonderful memories."

"As well as creaky floors, old tile and plumbing, a sadly outdated kitchen and bathroom, and have you seen that hideous wallpaper?" Saffron shuddered. "But it'll make an adequate rental property." She smiled up at Drake. "With Drake's standing in the community, it's time for him to liberate himself from sentimentality and move up from that weathered cottage to a more suitable residence."

As far as Reen was concerned, Saffron's criticisms about the Slattery house were mostly unfounded. It was cozy and welcoming.

With the exception of a few areas Drake was still improving, what Saffron considered *outdated* was what Reen would call period charm. It was exactly the type of house she loved.

"Nothing's definite," Drake said. "Just something I'm thinking about."

"A residence on Beauregard Hill would be more appropriate for someone with Drake's stature," Saffron said, "a man who's been awarded the prestigious designation of Distinguished Professor of Ancient History and Classical Archeology at Wisdom Harbor University."

"Beauregard Hill?" Laila muttered beneath her breath. Her surprise was mirrored in Sabrina's expression.

"If that's what Drake wants," was Reen's noncommittal answer. Gazing up at him, she asked, "Is it, Drake?"

"Oh it will be," a self-assured smile spread across Saffron's face, "once he sees the amazing properties I've selected for him today."

Tugging on Hud's arm, Monica said, "Let's go sit down. I need a cup of coffee."

"Sure," Hud patted Monica's hand, "in a minute. I just want to catch up with Reen and—"

Monica's knees buckled and she clutched the top of the booth's back. A tiny moan escaped her lips.

"Monica! Are you okay?" Hud's face was full of concern as he supported her. "You look white as a ghost. Should we leave?"

Monica fluttered a touch at her forehead, kind of the way Lana Turner might do in one of those old movies Reen liked to watch on TCM. "No, I...I'm all right. But I *would* like to sit down...at the front of the café near a window so I can feel the sun on me."

"Of course, whatever you like," Hud said, just the way a perfect, gallant boyfriend should.

It was obvious to Reen that Monica was faking, just to keep Hud all to herself. She was such a good actress, Reen was tempted to applaud. Biting her lip, she kept herself from muttering *And the Oscar goes to...* aloud.

"You sure you're okay?" Saffron asked.

"Yes...I'm fine." Her eyes closed, Monica still clutched the booth's back as if she were woozy. Nice touch, Reen thought.

"Hud's right," Saffron told her, "you look pale, and that's the second time you nearly fainted today."

"Saffron...I'm fine," Monica repeated, opening her eyes to nail Saffron with a blunt look.

Saffron's responding smile was instant. "Of course you are." Transforming her expression from concerned to carefree, she draped her arm around Monica, gently tugging her close. "You're probably just hungry, that's all."

"Right, that's it," Monica agreed, returning Saffron's blithe expression and prompting Reen's curiosity as to what exactly was going on because her cousin and Monica were acting weirder than usual.

"Well I'm glad you're hungry," Sabrina told the group of four. "You're among the lucky ones this morning. Laila's created the most mouthwatering new scones for the Valentine's Day Fling. Maple bacon walnut."

"Bacon?" Drake's eyes popped wide. "That's all I need to hear."

"I've got to agree," Saffron said. "Sounds good to me."

"Bring 'em on," Hud agreed.

"According to my expert taste testers," Laila said with a wink toward Sabrina and Reen, "they're just as good as they sound."

"That's no surprise," Drake said. "Everything you make is delicious."

"Well thank you, Professor!"

"One for each of you?" Sabrina asked.

With a feeble chuckle, Monica said, "I'd never keep my size double-zero figure if I allowed myself to indulge in something so fattening."

"That's the beauty of it," Reen pointed out. "These are part of Laila's reduced calorie line."

"Thanks but I I'll just stick with a slice of dry toast." Wincing, Monica added, "I really need to sit down now, Hud." She grabbed his forearm. "Nice to see you again," she said to Reen, Laila and Sabrina. "I hope you're feeling better soon, Reen."

"Thanks." First Saffron apologizes and now Monica is downright cordial. Reen was amazed.

"You're coming to the Fling Saturday, aren't you, Hud?" Sabrina asked her brother.

"Sure." He gave a broad smile. "Looking forward to it, aren't we, Mon—" He was led away before finishing his question.

"Drake and I will be there too. See you then." Saffron gave him an adoring look that had Reen's brain working overtime, wondering what the heck was going on between them. Could Drake really be interested in her cousin? It sure looked that way.

"I'll be back in a minute," Sabrina told Laila and Reen as she followed the foursome to the front of the café.

"How about that apology from Saffron," Laila said.

"I know! Last thing I ever expected." Reen shook her head back and forth in wonder. "It was such a nice apology too."

"It was. She really seemed sincere."

"And Monica was actually pleasant," Reen noted. "Go figure. Of course, right now I'm trying to figure out how, *A*, anyone can actually be a size double-zero and, *B*, how Monica can have bazooms," she bounced clawed hands at her chest, "nearly as big as grapefruits when she's that skinny."

"Maybe she's a breatharian." Laila's shoulder lifted.

Reen screwed her features. "A what?"

"Someone who exists on nothing but air," she explained. "Seriously, it's a thing people claim they do. Google it."

"That might explain her sudden display of weakness." Mocking Monica, Reen fluttered the back of her hand against her forehead, closed her eyes and moaned. "Oh dear me...hurry, Hud, I need to sit where I can feel the sun warming my itty-bitty size double-zero body." The sisters snickered like a couple of gossipy teens.

Glancing at the framed photos of classic silver screen stars lining the wall above their heads, Reen pointed to the moody black and white pose of Lana Turner that she'd spotted earlier.

"Boy are we on the same wavelength," Laila said thumbing toward the 1940s era photo. "She's exactly what I was picturing when Monica put on her performance. I guess Monica must be a fan of Turner Classic Movies too, huh?" The sisters laughed.

A sudden rush of guilt swept over Reen. "Shame on us, acting like a couple of snarky teens. What if Monica really is sick?"

"I sincerely doubt that." Laila wrinkled her nose. "I think it's just dramatics to draw Hud's attention away from us. From *you*."

"Good, they're sitting at Charlene's station," Sabrina said after returning to the table. "Surprising about Drake considering selling his family house, isn't it?"

"Even more surprising to see him and Saffron being so huggy," Laila said. "Looks like she's got the hots for him." She drained the last of the coffee from her cup.

"That's your husband's fault," Reen accused in a bouncy tone. "I thought Drake looked fine before Zak helped him get his new superstar physique. Or, as Lilly calls it, his cartoon muscleman body." She chuckled at the recollection. "But I admit his transformation still amazes me."

She'd never forget the first time she saw him shirtless after he'd been beefed up. She was taking Hazelnut on a walk one summer afternoon and there was Drake, mowing his lawn. It was the first time she remembered being at a loss for words around him.

"My Gard's a hottie too." Sabrina's cheeks tinted pink as she spoke about her newlywed husband.

"Nope, uh-uh." Laila clapped her ears. "You're talking about our brother, Sabrina. The rotten kid who made arm farts while I was on the phone with my boyfriend."

"Newsflash," Sabrina folded her arms across her chest, "your brother never outgrew that particular sport." The three women laughed. "Leaving the subject of arm farts behind," she said, looking toward the front of the café, "I see Annalise unloading her car's trunk. I'm going to give her a hand."

"We're right behind you," Reen and Laila chorused. Laila slipped out of the booth and Reen struggled in vain to follow.

"You just stay put," Laila told her.

Reen had little choice. Unfortunately, her broken ankle and fractured rump roast kept her from joining them. With a monumental sigh, she opened her iPad again, prepared to find a new batch of guilt-inducing memes she'd refuse to share.

Chapter Five

Saturday – Valentine's Day

~<>~

EYEING THE CLOCK on her nightstand, Reen sucked in a sharp breath. Nobody called at five-fifteen in the morning unless something was very wrong. It was Laila's ring. "Laila?" she said into the phone, her voice sounding as sleep fogged as she felt. "What is it? What's wrong?"

"Reen, you need to get over here right away." Laila's voice was high pitched and agitated.

"Oh my God..." Reen flicked on the lamp and sat up in bed. "Sure...of course...what happened?" Struggling to come to full alertness, she shoved away haphazard locks of blonde falling in her eyes and scrubbed her face with her hand.

"Was someone in an accident?"

Concerned by Reen's demeanor, Hazelnut was at her side, licking her face and hand.

"Are you sick, Laila? Is it Zak? One of the kids?" Reen's heart stuttered at the thought of anything happening to those precious babies.

"No, we're okay. But I need to see you. Now."

"Did you and Zak have a fight or something?" Reen sat on the edge of the bed, resting her head in her hand as she graduated into wakeful thinking from her dream-laced sleep. "You're not leaving him are you? You two are perfect for each other, Laila. Whatever it is, you can work it out." Yawning, she patted her nervous dog as she spoke. "Remember what Mom always says, 'Marriage is a marathon, not a sprint.'"

"No, nothing like that. I've just got to see you."

"For God's sake, Laila, you're scaring me. Tell me what's wrong."

"Just come over. You need to come over."

Laila's behavior and attitude were so out of the ordinary. Reen couldn't imagine what had happened but she knew she needed to be at her sister's side, pronto.

"I'll get dressed and be at your place as soon as I can."

Clutching the cane she'd been able to swap for her crutches, she hopped to her dresser where she grabbed clean undies from a drawer, stepping into them as Hazelnut ran circles around her, brushing against her legs.

"No, not my place," Laila told her. "I'm at Mom and Tore's condo."

As Laila's words sank in, Reen stilled and a rush of dread washed over her. "Something's happened to Mom? Or Tore?" The idea was unthinkable. Too horrible to imagine. Their mom and stepdad were two of the greatest people on the planet—the lifeline of their family.

"Oh God...oh God...hang on, Laila, I'll be there right away."

Trying to get into her jeans, Reen bumbled and fell, on her tailbone of course. In an aching heap on the floor, she swallowed a curse at the massive zing of pain at the bottom of her spine. She crawled to her nightstand, dragging her Frankenstein boot close. Thanks to Monica, she'd never be able to think of the boot in any other way. She slipped in her leg and strapped Frankie closed.

"Reen, stop," Laila said. "Take a deep breath and calm down. There's nothing wrong. Nothing for you to worry about. Everybody's fine. I just need to see you, that's all. We need to talk."

Reen cocked her head, frustration quickly replacing trepidation. "You woke me at five-fifteen so we can have a chat?"

"It could be the most important chat of your life, Reen. Get your broken butt over here." Laila ended the call before Reen could get a straight answer.

~<>~

Shrugging out of her coat, Reen turned to her sister. "Okay, what's going on? What's this all about, Laila?"

"Ooh I love that sock with the purple cows on the pink background. Where'd you get them?"

Reen looked down at her good foot. She'd mistakenly pulled on one of the knee socks from her childhood. Why the hell her mother had brought boxes of the childhood clothing of her six children all the way from Chicago when she and Tore moved to Oregon was a mystery. Well, not really. Astrid Malone Thorkelson was a sentimental packrat. She kept all her favorites, whether they were her children's clothes, their artwork, or pretty much anything else.

No wonder Reen had such a hard time yanking the sock on. It was a miracle she'd been able to get dressed at all after Laila's alarming wakeup call.

"Laila!" she said, fists balled at her hips.

"Okay, okay..." With her hands bracketing Reen's shoulders, Laila led her sister into the dining room. "Sit down, Reen. I've got a pot of coffee on. I'll get you a cup." She left Reen and her imaginings alone. "You want a little Kahlua?" she called from the kitchen.

"Don't be ridiculous, it's not even six o'clock." After thinking about it, Reen nibbled her bottom lip. "Why...do you think I'll need it?"

"Since I'm about to change your life, yeah, I'd say so. Probably a shot of Baileys too."

Laila's enigmatic response didn't help loosen the nervous knot twisting in Reen's gut. "Nothing like getting blitzed on spiked coffee before the sun comes up," Reen muttered beneath her breath.

"Oh...is it okay to have that with your pain pills?"

"I only take one if the pain gets really bad, which is usually first thing in the morning when I get out of bed." As if on cue, Reen's butt and ankle throbbed. "I didn't take one this morning because I was rushing to get here, afraid something horrific had happened and I forgot. And since I was in such a hurry, I forgot to take the pills with me." Wincing, she rubbed her backside, and moved her leg around while mumbling to herself about her twin aches.

"Ooh, sorry. Maybe the spiked coffee will help then."

"You're really freaking me out. Seriously, what the hell is going on? What do you mean, change my life? Why am I here getting liquored up before I've even had breakfast?"

Laila returned with a tray holding tall, skinny white coffee mugs dotted with lacy red hearts, and matching dessert plates with an assortment of mini scones from her bakery. "I'll tell you everything as soon as Mom and Delaney get in here from the bedroom."

"Delaney's here too?"

Laila nodded. "They're in there talking while Mom gets dressed."

Reen's thoughts flew to her sister Delaney's family. If anything had happened to her brother-in-law and niece... "Please tell me Varik and little Rebekka are okay."

"They're fine." Laila offered a placid smile.

Reen's features pinched as her thoughts whirled. "It's Valentine's Day. Why would Delaney be here this early on her birthday unless something's wrong?"

"You'll understand soon." Laila's tone was annoying tranquil. After setting the tray down, she lifted one of the pretty mugs. "Remember these? Mom broke out her special Valentine coffee set in your honor."

Surveying the Scandinavian-inspired oval dining table with its beveled tabletop and rich walnut finish, Reen noted it was set with the handcrafted lace-trimmed linen runners and placemats that had been in the family for generations. Eyeing the mug Laila held, Reen remembered well the adorable heart-themed china set she and her sisters had admired as children, but were never allowed to touch. No doubt about it, something of significance was going on.

"Of course I remember. That's Great-Grandma Helga's china, right?" After Laila's confirming nod, Reen asked, "Why?"

"You'll see," Laila said in a singsong voice.

Reen's frustration was almost palpable. "If all you wanted was to have a pre-dawn coffee klatch, you could have come to Bekka House. It would have been a lot easier for me. Do you have any idea how difficult it was," she double-slapped her Frankenstein boot, "getting myself ready so I could get my broken butt in the car and drive over here at the speed of light?"

"Oh my gosh, you're right." Laila's expression became genuinely contrite. "I'm so sorry, Reen. I completely forgot how hard it is for you to get around. One of us should have come to pick you up. I got so excited I wasn't thinking straight...none of us were."

"Excited? Oh my gosh, are you pregnant again? Or is Delaney? Is that what this is all about?"

"No, silly, that would change my life or Delaney's, not yours."

Reen's face grew warm as she gasped aloud. "Holy mackerel, it's not Mom, is it? I mean, at her age she couldn't possibly—"

"No!" Laila said. "Now you're just being ridiculous."

"Then what?!" Reen flapped her arms. "What?!"

Laila smiled up at their mother and sister as Astrid and Delaney walked—no, practically *danced*—into the room. Laila joined them. Arms draped over each other's shoulders, like a trio of cancan dancers, they grinned, staring at Reen.

"Did you spike it?" Astrid asked, nodding at Reen's coffee.

"Yup." Laila nodded.

"Good. She'll need it," Delaney said.

"You're making me crazy!" Reen growled. "What's happening? Why all the urgency, the secrecy, and special china?"

Laila, Delaney and Astrid sat at the table with Reen, exchanging secret smiles and looking at her as if waiting for her to sprout horns.

Suddenly it dawned on Reen. "This is about your books!" she said to Delaney. "It's the only reason why you'd be here this early on your birthday. Happy birthday, by the way."

"Thanks. And what about my books?" Delaney asked, her eyebrows knitting together.

"*Delaney's Diary*," Reen, said excitedly. "They're turning your book series into a movie...or maybe a TV series!" Grabbing her sister's hands, she gushed, "Oh Delaney, I'm so thrilled for you. Best birthday present ever!"

"Whoa, slow down, Maureen." Covering Reen's arm with her hand, Delaney laughed. "While I love the idea, and your never-ending support of my writing...nope."

"Nope?" Reen repeated.

Delaney shook her head back and forth. "No TV or movie deal. The reason you're here is even more important." Glancing at their mother with a conspirator's wink, she added, "Get ready for your Kodak moment, Mom." Everyone but Reen dissolved into gentle laughter as Astrid went to the kitchen, returning a moment later with her vintage Kodak Instamatic.

Completely clueless again, Reen was back to square one. "Why is Mom getting ready to take pictures? I don't understand."

"Give me your hand, Reen," Laila instructed, wiggling her fingers.

Astrid got into place, aiming her camera, which made Reen even more angsty.

"Why? Are we doing a pre-dawn séance? Psychic hocus-pocus is more up Kady's alley than mine." Reen rolled her eyes before placing her hand in Laila's.

"If your little sister wasn't out of town," their mother said while clicking her camera, "she'd be here too."

"Squeeze my hand," Laila instructed.

Click.

Once Reen complied, Laila slipped her hand away.

Click...click...

One glance at the palm of her hand had Reen gasping. "The ring..." Her gaze flew from her hand to Laila and back again. "Your magic heartwish ring!"

Click...click...click...

"Now you know why you're here before the crack of dawn." Laila bounced excitedly in her chair.

"It's yours now, sweetheart," Astrid told her.

"I'm so excited for you." Delaney rubbed her sister's arm. "Even more than if my books were optioned for a movie." The warmth in her eyes and her genuine smile told Reen she meant every word.

"Thank you, Delaney, but..." Reen gazed at the ring. "Me? Really? I...I never expected..." At a loss for words, she simply stared at the striking, mystical piece of jewelry in her hand. "Why," she finally managed. "Why me?"

"Who knows?" Astrid said, motioning with her hands for her daughters to huddle close for another photo. "Maureen you look more like a deer caught in headlights than a happy girl who's just received a magical heartwish ring."

She looked up at her mother. "That's just how I feel."

"Well, try smiling for me, sweetheart. These photos are for posterity." Astrid gave an ear-to-ear grin, perhaps, Reen thought, to demonstrate what she wanted from her daughter. Reen did her best to comply. "Yes, that's perfect! *Click.* "In answer to your *why me* question," Astrid explained, "the rings are meant for whoever needs their magic most at the time. You know it works that way."

"Right, I do, but...wow..." Reen examined the captivating ring she'd admired since she was a child. Guilt washed over her as she thought about her brother, Nevan, who'd been working so hard to gather enough money to restore Nevan's Irish Pub and the historic brick building that housed his popular family eatery. It had been ravaged by fire and lingering smoke damage after the devastating fire in Sabrina's third-floor apartment over a year ago. The minor amount he received from his fire insurance was like a drop in the bucket.

"This should go to Nevan, not me," she told her mother and sisters, turning the ring between her thumb and forefinger. "He's been working so long and hard to restore his building and business. Can we figure a way for him to get it instead? Maybe there's some sort of ritual, or maybe a—"

"I understand how you feel but it isn't meant to be that way," Laila told Reen with a helpless shrug. "At about three o'clock this morning I woke up with the ring growing warm around my finger and the bedroom filling with a radiance that even woke up Zak. I knew immediately that it was meant for you, Reen."

"I almost had a heart attack when I got a call from Laila just after three." Her hand flying to her throat, Astrid laughed.

"Sorry, Mom, but it's not every day something so monumental happens," Laila said. "I wasn't sure what I was supposed to do. I figured you'd have the answers."

"The one thing I do know, sweetheart," Astrid addressed Reen, reaching to clasp her daughter's hand, "is that you have no reason to feel guilty. None. We all love Nevan and know the boy could use a dose of magic but...the ring is meant for you at this time."

"Maybe Nevan will be getting Gard's ring when it's time for him to pass it on," Delaney offered.

"That could be," Astrid agreed. "You just need to accept the decision, Maureen, and go from there. Go ahead, honey, put it on," she urged. "It'll fit like it was custom made for you."

Reen slipped the ring on her finger. Her mother was right, it fit perfectly. As soon as it was in place, the metal band grew warm and the lustrous stone glowed. Keeping her gaze focused on the shimmering ring, she reached for her coffee mug and took a big sip. Then another.

"I told you you'd need your coffee spiked." Laila gave her a teasing elbow nudge.

"My head is reeling." Reen massaged her temples. "What am I supposed to do now? How will I know what to wish for? Will I get some sort of psychic message or something?"

"Something like that." Astrid smiled.

"I know, I'll make the wish for Nevan!"

"You're very sweet to want to help your brother with your wish, sweetheart, but the ring doesn't work that way." Astrid's smile was warm and loving. "When the time is right you'll discover the reason you're the intended recipient. Remember, your Grandma Bekka was very specific about that when she told us about the legend and origin of the twin rings."

Considering her mother's words, Reen gazed at the ring and frowned. "It sounds like the ring makes the wish, not me."

"No, it...it's hard to explain," Astrid said, a line creasing the space between her eyebrows. She sat in quiet contemplation for a moment before continuing. "The ring seems to connect with your heart's innermost desires...maybe even things you're not consciously aware of yourself. Then it makes those desires known to you so you can use the ring to help make them come true. Perhaps," her shoulders lifted in a shrug, "you'll learn that Nevan will be the recipient of your wish after all, but it might be something entirely different."

"Good explanation, Mom," Laila said. "It's this strange inner knowing that comes over you, Reen." She moved her hands through the air like a magician's. "I had no idea either, remember? And then, bam," she tapped the table, "I knew without a doubt."

"Right, it happened for me the same way," Delaney agreed. "It's like you don't choose the wish—it chooses you, just like Grandma told us years ago. But it's still really you making the wish, and you'll be absolutely, perfectly happy with what the ring reveals." Screwing her features, Delaney chuckled. "Oh boy...sorry, I think I just made it even more confusing."

"No," Reen squeezed her sister's hand, "you did just fine." Gazing at the three of them, she smiled. "All of you. Thanks, I think I get it, and have a better understanding of it now."

Although the tale of the rings once belonging to Odin seemed unlikely at best, Reen knew the miraculous power of the twin set of rings firsthand after witnessing what they had done for her sisters and her brother, Gard.

Turning her hand this way and that, admiring the stunning piece of antique jewelry, Reen was gripped by a curious blend of emotions. "Making life changing wishes is a huge responsibility," she muttered, half to herself. "I don't want to screw it up."

"You won't, honey," Astrid assured.

"I bet I know what your heartwish will involve." Following a naughty snicker, Delaney drained her mug.

"Or maybe you should say *who* it will involve." Laila's laughter was as mischievous as the expression on her face.

Reen knew from experience objecting to her sisters' good-natured teasing was futile. She merely gave them an exasperated look.

"You're talking about your sister and that cutie-pie Hudson Griffin?" Astrid asked, referring to the good-looking contractor in her usual manner. "I thought Hud and that real estate agent...what's her name?"

"Monica Sharp." Reen's voice was monotone.

"Right, Monica." Astrid snapped her fingers. "I thought they were a couple."

"They are," Reen confirmed. "For the moment. Things could change."

"Oh hell yes they can," Laila said, "now that you've got the heartwish ring you can have Hud eating out of your hand."

"You know better than that, Laila. The ring doesn't work that way. Besides, I doubt Reen's prepared to make that wish." Astrid's gaze fell to the heartwish ring. "Even if she had the power to guarantee Hudson would follow her around like an adoring puppy forever. Am I right, dear?"

"Go through the rest of my life knowing I was with someone who didn't want me without magic making it happen?" Reen absently toyed with the salt and pepper shaker figurines. "I couldn't be happy that way."

"Yes but maybe—" Laila began.

"Just the same way," Reen cut her off, pointing an outstretched finger at her both her sisters, "you and Delaney couldn't be happy if you knew in your heart of hearts Zak and Varik weren't genuinely in love with you."

Laila and Delaney shared a long, knowing look before chorusing, "She's right."

"Of course she is." Their mother rose from the table to open the blinds and let the early morning sun in. "Looks like we're in for a beautiful Valentine's Day. What a perfect day for the ring exchange."

"If it meant keeping Hud with her for good, I'll bet Monica would make that wish just like that." Laila snapped her fingers.

"How about using your wish to send Monica far, far away?" Delaney joked. "Like Mongolia, or a nice little community in Iceland."

They all chuckled at the idea, with Reen briefly imagining the satisfying scenario.

"Now girls, you know firsthand the wish must come from the heart," Astrid gently reminded her daughters as she returned to the table, checking everyone's coffee cups and refilling where necessary. Setting down the thermal coffeepot, she turned to Laila, clasping her hand. "You of all people understand the true meaning of making an unselfish heartwish, sweetheart."

"Mom's a thousand percent right," Reen agreed, adding a little splash of Frangelico to her cup and taking a deep whiff of the hazelnut flavored liqueur. "If my wish is half as kind and unselfish as yours was, I'll know I made the right decision."

"Ohhh..." With her cup halfway to her lips, Laila's expression softened to the point where Reen thought she might cry. "Thank you."

"There is one wish I've thought about," Reen said. "I've always wanted to own my own yarn shop, like String Me Along. Maybe the ring will decide that's a good wish for me."

"You've talked about doing that for years," Delaney acknowledged, breaking off a corner of a butterscotch pecan scone. "Now it's possible."

"Of course!" Laila slapped the table, making the salt and pepper shakers hop. "It's the perfect wish for you! Imagine surrounding yourself with all things yarn related and making money at the same time." She sipped her coffee and *ahhhed*. "You'd be in seventh heaven."

"Yes but..." Reen looked into Laila's eyes, then dropped her gaze.

"She won't be making any money if she doesn't stop giving away all of her special knitted creations for free," Delaney said.

Reen's gaze lifted. "Some things are more important than money, Delaney. Charging the families of sick children for the hats and other items that I make for them isn't an option I'm willing to consider."

"I understand," Delaney started, "but—"

"Look," Reen said, "I don't have many skills or talents. God knows I'll never be a brilliant mathematician or business person," she chuckled as she admitted that, "but the one thing I *can* do pretty well is knit and crochet. If my yarn creations can help sick kids and their parents smile, even for a little while, I feel like I'm doing my small part in this world. Something worthwhile."

"Don't you hate it when Reen starts making really good sense and makes the rest of us feel totally selfish and inadequate?" Laila teased.

Reen pinned Laila with a solemn stare. "And what about my commitment to The Great Pretender? We started your bakery together, Laila. I can't just leave to start a yarn shop. I'd feel terrible letting you down when you depend on me."

"The Great Pretender is *my* dream, Reen. It was never yours." Laila's expression was affectionate and appreciative. "I don't expect you to tie yourself to TGP out a sense of obligation."

"I enjoy working there. It's fun helping people discover your delicious and deceptively healthy baked goods." Reen smiled, lifting a marzipan-filled mini-scone topped with flaked almonds and admiring it. She recognized it as one of her sister's popular gluten-free, reduced calorie creations. "It's very satisfying for me." She took a bite. "In a number of tasty ways."

"Listen, Reen," Laila said, clearly not about to give up, "you're a valued and integral part of TGP, but you're not indispensable."

"Oh gee...thanks," Reen teased.

"Knock it off, jokester," Laila gave her sister's hand a playful slap, "you know what I mean. Since we started the bake shop it's grown astronomically. We're staffed with good people, people you helped train, and you know there's often very little left for you and me to do anymore, right?"

"Well..." Reen's shrug was nearly imperceptible as she traced the ceramic bow on the butter dish with her fingertip.

"Right!" Laila answered her own question. "Maureen, I love you for being concerned about me but you don't have to worry about leaving TGP. Yarn is pretty much your life so," her shoulders lifted in a shrug, "use your wish to open a yarn shop." She sat back in her chair, arms folded across her chest. "There's absolutely no reason why you can't—"

Reen held up a finger, as Laila kept on. "Ruthie Brone," was all Reen said.

"Do I really have to keep reminding you girls that you don't consciously pick the wish?" Astrid said. "It might be a yarn shop...and it might not." Giving Reen a clueless look, she asked, "What does Ruthie have to do with any of this?"

"Remember when you tried for months to teach me how to knit and I failed miserably?" Reen asked her mother, and Astrid gave a categorical nod.

Her hands together as if in prayer, Astrid looked skyward. "I had the patience of a saint," she cracked, and they all laughed.

"You won't get any argument from me." Reen cringed as she recalled one yarn fiasco after another. "That's when you suggested I take lessons from Ruthie, remember?" Astrid gave a nod. "Best recommendation ever. That sweet, patient old woman taught me everything I know about working with yarn. Plus she was one of Grandma Bekka's closest friends."

"True," Astrid said. "Aside from that, String Me Along is the first Black owned business in Glassfloat Bay. Your grandma told me that Ruthie met a lot of opposition and had quite a struggle fifty years ago to get her shop open and operating. She was one strong, determined woman."

"Exactly," Reen said. "I could never open a competing shop in the same town. It wouldn't be right. You all know it—and so does the ring, I guarantee it."

"What about Wisdom Harbor, or Jigsaw Landing?" Delaney suggested. "Those towns aren't too far from here."

"Far enough." Reen shook her head. "I love it here. Why would I want to work in another town where I'm away from my family and friends all day, every day? So," she gave a dramatic shrug, "the yarn shop wish is out. It's just not doable."

"Well there *is* another alternative to a knitting shop or Hudson Griffin." Delaney brought a blueberry lemon scone to her lips, licking off the coarse sugar crystals. "I'm thinking of a brainy nerd with killer looks." She chuckled, then bit into the scone, murmuring her satisfaction.

"Drake's crazy about you," Laila agreed. "Have you noticed the way he looks at you?"

Reen's eyebrows knitted. "How many times do I have to tell you we're nothing more than friends? We hang out together with his kids and catch a movie or a bite to eat sometimes. Plus...he was Bob's closest friend." Plucking a few crumbs from the table, she placed then on her plate.

"Does that make you feel guilty?" Astrid asked. "Being attracted to the man who was your fiancé's best friend?"

"No, Mom, and I'm not attracted to Drake in that way." She uttered a mighty sigh. "Besides, we're complete opposites. I know you all want to see me happy and content with a good man at my side," she attempted a patient smile, "but Drake Slattery isn't that man."

"Too bad," Astrid said. "He's a real hottie."

Sipping from her mug, Reen nearly choked on her coffee as laughter bubbled up in her throat.

"Aren't you too old to be noticing Drake's hotness factor, Mom?" Laila snickered.

"Trust me, child, we never get too old to look." She brought her mug to her lips and sipped. "Or appreciate." Astrid winked.

As if on cue, Astrid's husband, the girls' stepfather, Tore, strode into the dining room. His graying blond hair still damp from his shower, Tore was dressed in sweatpants, black turtleneck and a hoodie, ready for his morning jog along the seashore. He was a kind, caring, and very attractive man who made their mother's eyes light up whenever he came into a room.

"We're never too old to appreciate what?" he asked, wrapping his arms around Astrid from behind and kissing her cheek.

"Fine art," Astrid said without skipping a beat. "We were just saying we can't wait to see Sabrina's exhibit at the Glimmer Hope Art Gallery next week. I'm not sure who's more excited, Sabrina or our son."

Pouring himself some coffee, Tore frowned, examining the mug's decidedly feminine heart design. "Where's my regular Viking coffee mug?" he asked in the Norwegian accent they all loved. "What's with the hearts and flowers china? You ladies having an early morning Valentine's party? Or maybe it's a birthday celebration." He kissed Delaney on the cheek. "Happy birthday, Delaney."

"No but it *is* a special occasion," Astrid answered. "Check out Maureen's hand." Reen held it up, spreading her fingers to show Tore the ring.

"Ahhh! So you're next in line for Odin's heartwish ring. That's great!" He glanced at his mug again. "No wonder Astrid set out the good stuff." His gaze fell on the bottles of sweet liqueurs. "And her favorite coffee accompaniments." A corner of his lip hiked into a half-smile. "Congratulations, Reen. Do you know what wish the ring has in mind for you yet?"

"Thanks, Tore. I haven't got a clue. Mom says it'll come to me when the time is right. But my sisters are full of ideas." She glanced at them and laughed.

"Listen to your mother, she's right." He rubbed Reen's back. "As she always says—"

"Everything's going to be hunky-dory," Reen and her sisters chorused through laughter. It had to be their mother's favorite saying.

"*Ja*, exactly." Tore nodded in confirmation.

Astrid held her hand out, squeezing Tore's hand when he took it. After kissing his wife's cheek, he downed his coffee and smiled at them. "And now I'll let you lovely ladies get back to your talk about hotties." Laughing, Tore grabbed a scone and headed out the door.

"Busted!" Laila barked a laugh and Astrid's cheeks colored a guilty shade of pink.

"And that, girls," Astrid said with a smirk, "is what's called an example of selective hearing." Getting to her feet, she gathered the empty mugs and plates. "So are you three ready for the Valentine's Day Fling tonight? Everyone's excited about it."

"Yup. We've all signed up for the kissing booth," Delaney told her as she helped clear the table. "Sabrina and Annalise too. It should be a lot of fun." She turned to Reen. "Hey, have you and Drake ever kissed?"

Reen wrinkled her nose. Recollections she'd rather forget flooded her thoughts. "We came close once but...no."

"You did? When?" Delaney pressed.

"It doesn't matter. It's nothing interesting," Reen said, eager to change the subject and sorry she said anything in the first place. "Laila, could you pass me a date-nut scone? I haven't tried those yet."

"Sure." Dropping a scone on her sister's plate, Laila gave a secretive smile. "I'll bet it's when Drake took you to the opera last year. Right? I swear, you two looked like a fairytale couple. It was sooo romantic."

"A fancy, romantic dress-up date at the opera?" Delaney said with surprise. "And you say it was nothing interesting? Hey, come on now," she beckoned with her fingers, "don't leave me hanging."

With a dramatic sigh, Reen gave in. "It's when Drake took me to the premiere of *Carmen* at the Keller Auditorium in downtown Portland. And it was *not* romantic. We just went as friends," she added quickly. "It was a last minute thing. He didn't have anyone else to go with at the time, that's all."

An avid opera fan, Astrid sighed. "How I envied you for going. Those tickets were near impossible to get. Tore tried for weeks."

"Really? Just for an opera?" Reen was genuinely surprised, remembering that she thought the opera was okay but nothing spectacular. She didn't understand most of what was going on.

"I wish you could have seen them together," Laila said. "Like Prince Charming and Cinderella."

"The only reason I looked good is because of you." Reen offered her sister an appreciative smile. Having spent all afternoon helping her get ready for the event, Laila knew how uncertain and out of place Reen felt that evening. The two of them spent all afternoon choosing the right outfit, hairstyle and makeup until Reen ended up looking better than she'd ever imagined possible. She barely recognized herself. A small smile tugged at her lips as Reen recalled their day of preparation together.

"One of Drake's colleagues, another professor, gave him a pair of tickets he couldn't use because his wife was scheduled for a C-section that day. Drake loves opera." Reen tossed up her hands in a *go figure* gesture. "He knows I'm not an opera fan but asked me to go so he didn't have to go alone."

"Saffy's an opera fanatic," Laila pointed out. "It's good this happened a year ago because he'd probably ask her to go with him now."

"Your cousin?" Astrid looked dumbfounded.

"Uh-huh," Laila confirmed. "They've been all snuggly together lately."

"Hmm, I suppose Drake and Saffron do have a great deal in common," Astrid noted, tipping the bottle and dripping the last of the Kahlua into her cup. "Anyone want more? I just happen to have another bottle." She winked.

"Not me." Reen could sense giggles on the horizon. It didn't take much alcohol to get her giggling for no reason. "I'm as liquored up as I want to be at this time of the morning."

"Did you like *Carmen*?" Delaney asked after she and Laila also declined more of the coffee liqueur.

Thankful for the change in subject from the unsavory idea of Saffron and Drake as a couple, Reen said, "It was really long, over dramatic, and all in Italian. Or Spanish or something," her fingers flit through the air, "so I didn't understand much. Except that it had a sad ending and you know how I hate those. Drake quietly tried to explain things as we watched. I did like some of the songs, like the toreador one."

"The opera takes place in Spain but it's usually sung in French," Astrid explained, lifting the crystal dome on a plate of her homemade swiss cheese, bacon, and leek quiche tartlets that everyone loved. A chorus of *mmmms* sounded around the table. She passed them around as her daughters protested she was going to make them fat—and then helped themselves anyway.

"The Toreador song is one of my favorites too," Astrid agreed. "It's so dynamic and passionate." Her eyelids fluttering shut, she hummed a bit of it.

"Yes," Reen pointed to her mother, "that's the one. Probably the best part of the evening, with Portland being so laid back and casual, was having the opportunity to get dressed up for a change. I finally got to use some of my fancy Chicago clothes and jewelry that have just been sitting around collecting dust since we moved to Oregon. But I couldn't have put it all together without Laila's help."

"Reen wore a floor-length dress in a pale, whispery shade of aquamarine, pairing it with a long flowy chiffon scarf with pastel flowers." Laila paused to sigh. "We found a pair of Grandma Bekka's earrings, small clusters of pearls with a tiny aquamarine stone at the center. So perfect! Drake's eyes popped when he saw her." She slanted a glance at Reen. "He didn't look too bad himself that night."

The image of hunky-dorky Drake decked out and handsome as hell darted into Reen's mind. "Uh-huh, he looked good."

"Just good?" Delaney asked in a teasing tone.

"Okay, *really* good," Reen said with a chuckle, recalling how distinguished he looked in his dark charcoal-gray suit, black, white and gray striped tie, and circle motif pocket handkerchief in the same colors as the tie. He was the epitome of tall, dark and handsome that night. She remembered feeling uncomfortable having her buddy eyeball her like she was a hot fudge sundae...maybe because she'd caught herself looking at him in the same way. Friends don't usually do that.

"I took lots of pictures and have them saved," Laila told them. "I'll send them when I find them."

"I'd love to see them," Astrid said. "So what happened as far as the almost kiss?"

"Oh, that..."

"Yes," Astrid's eyebrow angled up, "that."

Reen's sigh came out more of a grumble. "When he took me home and we were at my door I told him I had a great time. He said he was proud of me for not falling asleep from boredom during the performance."

Astrid's burst of laughter had her covering her mouth with her fingers. "Sorry."

"*Anyway*," Reen drew the word out, "Drake's hand was on the doorjamb and he sort of leaned in, and I knew, you know? I could tell he was going to try to kiss me and I didn't know what to do because part of me wanted him to, and part of me was like, *no way is this a good idea*. He whispered to me then...said I was beautiful, and he was this close," she held her thumb and forefinger a few inches apart, "when I ducked."

"Ducked? You ducked?" Laila winced. "You never told me that. Oh poor Drake." She covered her face with her hand, peeking out of her fingers.

"Yeah." Reen nodded, still ashamed at the appalling way she'd handled it. "It didn't go too well. I never meant to embarrass him or hurt his feelings but I could tell he felt wounded when I reminded him we were just friends and it would be weird for us to kiss. Like kissing one of my brothers."

"You actually told him that?" Delaney asked. "Ouch," she added when Reen confirmed it.

"What a stomach punch," Astrid noted. "That poor boy."

"And now you know why I didn't want to tell you guys about it," Reen said. "I felt terrible as soon as I said it. I never intended for it to come out sounding so—"

"Tactless and insensitive?" Laila asked, making Reen cringe.

"Exactly." Reen offered a helpless shrug. "I was afraid if we kissed it would make things awkward and ruin our friendship, and that's something I don't want to lose. Needless to say, Drake's never made another attempt to kiss me...or any other sort of romantic gesture. Neither of us mentioned the incident again. I guess we figured it was best to pretend it never happened. So, yeah, I was an idiot. If I had the chance to do it over again, I'd handle things differently."

"You mean you'd kiss him this time?" Delaney asked.

"I-I'm not really sure." Reen had asked herself that same question dozens of times. She still didn't know the answer. "But I'd do everything in my power not to hurt Drake's feelings again because he didn't deserve that."

"You must have been at least a little curious about kissing him," her mother said. "Let's face it, the professor's not hard on the eyes, dear."

"I suppose so." The day Drake took her to the emergency room for her broken bones came to mind. When she'd been loopy on the drugs they gave her, her inhibitions were low and her mind raced with what-ifs concerning Drake. She'd been so busy being his pal, she may have missed noticing that he could very well be her Clark Kent. Her Superman. Her feelings that day were decidedly more romantic than buddy-ish.

"But after I made a complete fool of myself and totally humiliated the man when he tried to kiss me, I'll never find out how I'd feel because Drake would never put himself in that position again. And I don't blame him."

Reen sucked in a deep breath. Yes, she'd always wonder. Had she made a mistake keeping Drake at arm's length, mostly because she was afraid she couldn't measure up to him? Because she felt dimwitted next to his braininess? Because she feared he'd grow bored with her and her limited range of knowledge compared to his broad spectrum of interests?

It really didn't matter. It was too late. She'd handled things badly and that ship had sailed...right over to her cousin Saffron Devington's port of call.

"Besides," Reen reminded them with a luckless sigh, "it's Hudson Griffin that I have my sights on, not Drake, remember?" She wasn't sure if she was trying to convince them or herself.

"Which brings us back to tonight's kissing booth," Laila said with a warm smile and squeeze of her sister's hand that Reen suspected was designed to make her feel better. "I can't think of a more perfect excuse for kissing Hud."

"That's *if* he buys a kiss from me," Reen said. "That's a big if, especially if Monica is there attached to him like a sheet of plastic cling wrap." Picturing Hud's face drawing near, she chuckled. "Maybe I'll plant a kiss on his lips...then watch as Hud's eyes pop open with the realization that, *Holy cow, Reen's the one, the woman of my dreams!*" A dreamy sigh escaped her lips. "It could happen..."

She studied her hand as she mused. Between the microscopic likelihood of Hud falling for her, and Reen trying to guess what in the world she'd ultimately be wishing for, it felt like her brain was tap dancing inside her head.

Chapter Six

~<>~

REEN WAS BUSY pressing Valentine stickers all over her Frankenstein boot, trying to dress it up for the Fling, when the doorbell rang. Just in case she hadn't heard it, Hazelnut made sure she knew they had a visitor. Glancing at her phone Reen saw it was just after ten a.m. Having been up since before dawn it felt more like two in the afternoon.

"Shh, it's okay, Hazelnut," she called to her trusty companion as she slipped back into the boot and strapped it tight. "Be there in a minute!" she yelled, wondering who might be there on a Saturday morning. "Hey, Hazel, maybe it's someone delivering a big heart-shaped box of Valentine's Day chocolates. What do you think?" She snickered at the silly idea while her dog gazed at her in wonder before racing back to the door and barking again.

Cane in hand, Reen hobble-clumped her way to the door, her eyes wide in wonder when she spotted her cousin, dressed in one of her omnipresent dark business suits, through the glass side panels. Saffron Devington was the last person Reen expected to see, especially considering her visitor came bearing a sizeable heart-shaped box covered in lavender satin that she held out to Reen.

"Saffron?" was all Reen could manage as she opened the door, accepted the box and motioned for her cousin to step inside.

"Happy Valentine's Day, Maureen. I remembered you used to like nuts, caramel and nougat. I hope that's still the case."

Reen was dumbfounded. "Yes...yes it is. But—"

"Oh," Saffron went on, offering a smile Reen rarely saw on her cousin, "and, see? The box is your favorite color too."

"Thank you, Saffron, I really appreciate it but I don't understand. Why are you bringing me a box of my favorite chocolates?"

"Because it's Valentine's Day and you, dear cousin, are a chocoholic. Is there any better reason?" Affecting a cute pose, Saffron tacked on a wink and she smiled, which was so unlike her it made Reen's jaw drop.

"How are your bones?"

Her composure rebounding, Reen said, "I'm no baby when it comes to pain but I wouldn't wish broken bones on anyone." She rubbed her backside. "It's better each day though." She led her cousin into the sizeable family room, gesturing for her to take a seat, her mind struggling to conjure a reason for Saffron's cheery visit.

The shiny metal Christmas tree in the corner caught Saffron's attention. Maureen had plugged in the rotating color wheel earlier when she came into the room. Watching the changing jewel-toned color hues relaxed her.

"I see you still have Delaney's vintage aluminum tree up...with all the Christmas ornaments."

Ready for a dose of sarcasm-laced criticism, Reen folded her arms across her chest. "Yes, everyone seems to enjoy it and it makes Delaney happy to see it when she comes over."

"Well it's...unusual," Saffron said, studying the eclectic mix of ornaments. "Nice...colorful and very calming." She smiled then. "A great conversation piece."

Reen let her arms relax. "Saffron..." Her head tilted to the left while she stared at her cousin. "Are you all right?"

Her cousin's genuine, non-acerbic, laughter was an infrequent sound. "I'm fine. Don't worry, I haven't lost my mind, and I'm not ill. Although I'll admit to being more tired than usual." She pinched the bridge of her nose, blinking a few times. "We've had several closings the past two weeks and since Monica's missed a lot of work I've had to put in some long hours."

"Has she been sick?" Monica Sharp wasn't one of Reen's favorite people and she wasn't all that interested, but figured it would be polite to ask since she and Saffron were good friends.

"Oh, uh, yes, I think she's had a bad, um, cold or maybe the flu. I'm not really sure. She brushes it off when I ask her." Reen noticed her cousin's cheeks coloring, and she seemed somewhat edgy as she spoke about Monica. "You know Monica," Saffron went on, and Reen just smiled because she hardly knew her at all. "She's not a complainer. Poor thing seems pretty blue because of what happened with Hud though."

"Hud?" Reen's head zeroed in on Saffron like a pointer dog. "What happened? Was he in an accident?"

"No, they broke up."

Saffron's newsflash shocked Reen into a drop-jawed expression again.

"Actually, Monica broke up with him," she added.

"I didn't know they were having problems." Tamping down the ear to ear grin threatening to reveal itself, Reen told herself she should feel ashamed for getting excited about the newly unattached Hud, and sympathizing about poor Hud-less Monica.

"As far as I know, they weren't. Monica told me a couple weeks ago she was in love with Hudson...that he was definitely *the one*. That's what makes this so hard to understand." Looking nowhere in particular, Saffron heaved a sigh "So sad."

"You don't think Hud was cheating on Monica, do you?" Reen's thoughts raced. Hud didn't seem like the type who would cheat on his girlfriend but then men can be strange creatures, being led around by the tiny brainless commander in their pants.

"I don't have the faintest idea. His attention always seemed riveted on Monica when they were together but..." Saffron looked baffled. "All Monica told me is that she felt it was time they go their separate ways."

Reen's capricious thoughts turned to tonight's kissing booth. There was a whole new game in town now, which made her feel inappropriately giddy.

"Anyway, Maureen," Saffron's hand flit through the air, "I've been thinking about what you said at the café—about trying to make peace with each other. You're right. We should." Her expression grew solemn as she held Reen's gaze. "Life is too short and precious to spend it being adversaries."

Saffron kept right on amazing her this morning. "I wholeheartedly agree," Reen said.

"I know I'm not the easiest person to get along with," Saffron admitted. "I can be a bit of a know-it-all and perhaps somewhat judgmental." Her laughter this time was gentle and self-effacing.

When Saffron was quiet for a long moment, seeming to search for something else to say, Reen smiled at her. "If you're waiting for me to agree with you, I'm not going to be that impolite." Reen chuckled. "It seems we've always been at odds, Saffron. I'd love for us to change that."

"Good because, like I said, life is short..." The sudden sadness veiling her features concerned Reen. "I'd really like to work on mending fences with your sisters too. We're all family, after all."

Reen wondered if her cousin had received some alarming medical news, causing her to want to make amends with people before something happened.

"Saffron..." Reen clasped her cousin's forearm, "is anything wrong? I mean, you're not seriously ill, are you?"

"Me?" Saffron almost seemed on the verge of tears when she dragged in a deep breath, shifted in her seat, and changed her countenance until she was smiling again. "No, I'm fine. Just overtired." Jovial now, she patted the large heart-shaped box. "Aren't you going to open your candy?"

"You don't have to ask twice." Reen smoothed her fingers over the box before removing the cover. "The purple is really a nice touch." Her favorite color and her favorite types of chocolate, and Saffron remembered them both. With a sudden wash of shame, Reen realized she had little idea of Saffron's likes or dislikes.

Lifting the cover released the sweet smell of chocolate, which had Hazelnut deciding now was a perfect time to look all cute and adorable, and get chummy with them.

"No, go away, Hazel," Reen admonished. "You know chocolate's poisonous for dogs. I don't want to lose my furry best buddy." She kissed the top of her head then shooed her away. Hazelnut wasn't happy about it but she dutifully strode about ten feet away, screwing herself into the carpet in what she considered the best spot to watch the selfish chocolate eaters.

Reen and Saffron studied the sheet inside the box, detailing the makeup of each chocolate, before making their selections. Reen chose a milk chocolate hazelnut ganache, while Saffron selected a dark chocolate. Their second choices again had Saffron choosing dark chocolate. Reen made a mental note of her cousin's preference, vowing to start a list in her phone later, noting some of Saffron's favorites.

"Want some coffee?" Reen asked, feeling like she had a hangover from the far too early start to her day.

Saffron held up her hand as Reen grabbed her cane and started to rise. "I'd love some but only if you let me make it. You just sit and relax." She got up, heading for the kitchen. "I think I remember where everything is."

"Great, thanks." Thankful she didn't have to get up, Reen yawned. Her thinking became sluggish when she was this tired. From receiving the heartwish ring at the crack of dawn, to Saffron's unexpected personality transformation, to the stunning news about Hud and Monica, there was so much new to absorb. She was about to take a nap when her cousin showed up on the doorstep. Looks like she'd have to postpone that for a while. She yawned again.

"Uh-oh, I heard those yawns," Saffron called from the kitchen. "Am I tiring you out too much?"

"Oops, sorry. No, not at all. I guess my yawns were a little louder than I'd anticipated."

"Think Lion King," Saffron said and they both laughed.

"I was up really early this morning for a Valentine breakfast with my mom and sisters. It's catching up with me."

"With your bones still mending you should rest before tonight. I'll leave right after we have our coffee so you can relax."

"No, really, that's not necessary, Saffron," Reen insisted. "I'm enjoying our visit." She really was.

"Me too." She came back into the family room, tray in hand with coffee and fixings. "It's been far too long since we had a nice chat over coffee."

Searching her memory, Reen couldn't remember any instance where they'd gotten together to have a friendly discussion. What a shame.

"I heard through the grapevine that the Maythorne brothers might be at the Fling tonight," Saffron said after setting steaming mugs in front of herself and Reen. Her eyebrows danced as she spoke.

"I've never met them," Reen said. "But from the look on your face it seems you may have." She laughed. "Each time they've visited Glassfloat Bay I was still living in Chicago. I hear they're a trio of bona fide hunks."

"You heard right. Calder, Axel, and Westford." Saffron's smile spread. "All gorgeous. I first met them years ago, when I was a sophomore in high school and they came to stay at Maythorne Manor over the summer, visiting with their uncle, Franklin." Her cheeks reddened. "I had such a crush on Calder."

"I've never seen you blush like that, Saffron!" Reen grinned at her cousin. She was familiar with the mansion. It was at the Maythorne Manor estate sale where she and Laila had spent a couple hours foraging through the grand old house, resulting in Laila finding the ancient box containing a genie's bottle.

"I blame it on those teen heartthrob memories." Chuckling, Saffron pressed her hands against her flushed cheeks. "Calder, who's a couple years older than me, was always nice but he barely even knew I was alive."

"Someone at the café mentioned they may be moving here to live in their family house." Reen had also heard rumors about it at the estate sale. News traveled fast in Glassfloat Bay, especially when the news focused on members of the Maythorne family, the town's founders.

"That's what I heard too." Covering her mouth as she chewed, Saffron tittered a girlish laugh.

"Are the brothers still single?"

"I'm not sure." Saffron's smile expanded. "I hope so."

"Interesting. It looks like the women of Glassfloat Bay are in store for a treat tonight."

"It almost makes me wish I'd signed up for a turn at the kissing booth." Saffron's cheeks pinked even more.

"There's still time."

"No." She shook her head back and forth. "I couldn't." She stared at Reen for a long moment, looking like she wanted to say something. "I have a confession to make," she said finally, just above a whisper.

Reen had no idea what to expect. "Does it involve you and Calder Maythorne and some teenage hanky-panky?"

"Oh my goodness..." Gasping aloud, Saffron nearly choked on her coffee before laughing. "No!"

"All righty then." Reen joined in her cousin's contagious laughter. "I'm all ears." She sipped from her cup and *aahhed*. "Mmm...so good. Thanks for making the coffee. You made it good and strong, just the way I like it."

"I like it strong too." Saffron looked down at her hands for a moment. "I've always envied you, Maureen," she admitted, instantly rendering Reen more awake and attentive.

"You have a natural easy way with people. You're warm, have a great sense of humor, and people automatically like you. Then there's all your artistic talent on top of it. I think I sometimes get upset with you because, well...because you make me feel inadequate." Her gaze dropped to her hands again. "And that's why I get out of sorts and snarky with you."

Another milk chocolate was halfway to Reen's mouth before she stopped, suspending her fingers and the candy in midair. Gobsmacked, she gazed at her cousin as if Saffron had suddenly morphed into an alien.

"You envy *me*?" Reen's voice came out like a sick, squawking bird. Saffron nodded in confirmation. "It's always been the other way around for me, Saffron. Talk about feeling inadequate. You're super smart, multi-degreed, chic and sophisticated. You know all about opera and ballet and classic literature. Sheesh, all I can do is knit. And I'm lucky if I can put an outfit together without looking like I'm still in eighth grade." A spurt of laughter escaped her throat. "When I grow up I want to be just like you," she teased.

"Really?" Saffron looked just as dazed as Reen felt. "Wow...I never knew you felt that way about me."

"Ditto."

"Chic?" Saffron's lip quirked into a half-smile. "I remember you and Laila telling me I look like a mortician because I wear nothing but dark colors."

"Oh...well..." Reen's embarrassed grin was frank as her gaze swept over her cousin's conservative navy suit. "I meant a very *chic* mortician." A moment after Saffron appraised her own severe outfit, the women fell into easy laughter, something they hadn't done together since they were kids, and maybe not even then.

"I-I need some advice, Reen, and you're the best one to ask."

Reen's fingers rested against her chest. "Me?" It was going to take a long while to get used to the new Saffron.

"Mmm-hmm. I know you and Drake Slattery are very good friends," Saffron started.

At the sound of his name, Reen popped the candy in her mouth, chewing like mad, clueless to where this could be leading.

"Since he's so fond of you and you two have so much in common, I hoped you could give me some insight."

"Insight? You mean what sort of properties or neighborhoods he might be interested in for him and the kids?" Even as she asked the question, Reen knew it had nothing to do with what Saffron wanted.

"No, I can handle that." Saffron offered a trivial laugh. "I mean, well you see, Maureen...it seems I've developed feelings for Drake."

The candy sank to the pit of Reen's stomach where it sat like a clump of tar. She wasn't sure why, since she'd already suspected her cousin was attracted to Drake.

"Rather strong feelings."

"Oh...I see." It was the only thing that came to mind while Reen searched her brain for a suitable response.

"I want to make a good impression," Saffron continued and Reen forced herself to listen objectively. "To find out what he does and doesn't like. Things he enjoys doing. Places he likes to go. Tidbits about his children. I've haven't been around children much and don't honestly know the best way to relate to them. Do they like going to the zoo? The library? Out for ice cream? Things like that."

"Uh-huh." Sipping from her coffee, Reen swallowed hard as chaotic thoughts caused an electrical malfunction in her brain, making it flash and spark as it bounced around in her skull. "Being neighbors, I've come to know Drake and his kids pretty well. I'd be glad to offer some suggestions." She was amazed at the calmness in her voice...considering the brain thing.

"There's just one problem," Saffron noted.

Only one? Reen thought. "What's that?" she asked, aware of her pulse thumping in her ears now.

"Before I do my best to impress Drake, I want to make sure you and he and just friends, that you don't have more serious feelings for him." She took Reen's hand in hers. "We may not have always gotten along but you're my cousin, Maureen, and I wouldn't want to do anything to cause you heartache. If you have feelings for Drake, I'll forget about all this and step aside. Just say the word," she waved her hands to the sides, "and I'm out of the picture."

Caught off-guard, Reen didn't know what to say. Drake and Saffron. How did she feel about them together? As a couple. Romantically. Kissing. Arms and legs tangling...hands everywhere...tongues dancing...

She blinked a few times, sweeping a rush of unsavory, intimate images from her mind.

Did she have feelings for Drake?

Well, did she?!

After striving to squelch any possible romantic interest in Drake, it wasn't an easy question for her to answer. Something deep inside kept her from an immediate and unquestionable denial of the foolish notion which, she figured, probably meant the honest answer must be a big fat...MAYBE.

The conscious awareness of her *maybe* feelings made her groan.

"Maureen?" Saffron asked, nervousness evident in her expression.

Reen forced a smile. It was now or never. If she did indeed have romantic feelings for Drake she'd be in danger of losing any chance she might have with him one day. And by *one day* she meant the day she'd have completed all the necessary classic literature reading, opera listening, ballet watching, lecture attending, and numerous self-improvement courses she'd need to approach the same level as the professor.

She wanted to think she could achieve all that in, say, two months, but realistically it would take closer to two years.

No, logically it would never happen at all because Reen was the world's worst procrastinator and would keep putting her daily self-education goals off until she woke up one day to the news that Drake and the beautiful, well-read Saffron were celebrating their tenth wedding anniversary.

Having lost her appetite, Reen removed the substantial box of chocolates from her lap, setting it on the coffee table, staring at it for a long moment. She looked up from the table to Saffron, who gazed at her with rapt attention. With anticipation. With unveiled hope.

Oh God...

True, they'd been adversaries for years but Reen never doubted Saffron was a good person. Annoying as hell sometimes, but not an inherently bad person. Like Drake, she was refined and educated. An academic. They shared so many interests in things Reen knew very little about. Commonsense and intuition told Reen that Saffron was a far better match for Drake than Reen could ever be.

Saffron's anxious expression, along with the way she sat wringing her folded hands, told Reen she must be taking forever to answer her cousin's simple question.

The sense of hope openly etched across Saffron's features was almost palpable. It was plainly evident she had serious feelings for Drake and was hoping to perhaps build a future with him and his children. Of all the times in her life, this was one where Reen needed to be completely fair and objective. It was important for her to tuck her own feelings deep inside and, instead, think about what would be best for both Drake and her cousin.

Reen drew in a measured breath, expelling it with a mild whoosh.

"Drake and I are very good friends," Reen told Saffron with the warmest smile she could muster. "Strictly friends."

"Oh that's wonderful." Saffron brought her hands together, resting her fingers against her chin. "You had me worried there for a while when you didn't answer right away."

"Sorry. I can easily see the two of you as a couple," Reen told her truthfully. "I think you'd be really good for each other. I'm sure Lilly and Kevin will like you once they get to know you. They're wonderful kids, Saffron. I'll be glad to help you with *Project Drake*," Reen made air quotes, "in any way that I can."

"Project Drake...I like that." Letting out a breath she apparently had pent up, Saffron visibly relaxed, resting against the back of the sofa cushions.

Reen noticed for the first time how stunning her cousin was when she smiled.

"Thank you, Maureen. Your help means a lot to me. I'll be happy to repay the favor. Call me anytime you need something and I'll be there. You know, Drake talks about you all the time."

"Always complaining about me, huh?" Reen laughed. "He's forever teasing me. I'm sure he's told you his buddy Reen isn't the brightest crayon in the box, and he's filled you in on some of my countless flubs and mishaps." Feeling her cheeks grow warm, she covered them inadvertently with her hands.

"Are you kidding?" Looking at Reen like she was crazy, Saffron said, "It's Reen and I did this; Reen and I did that; Reen did this for the kids; you should see what Reen made for the children at the hospital; Reen, Reen, Reen." She laughed. "That's almost all I ever hear when we're together, which is why I wanted to make sure there wasn't anything romantic between the two of you before I pursued this any further."

Drake talked about her all the time? In a positive light? Reen had no idea.

"No, we're just neighbors and good friends, that's all," Reen reiterated, telling herself she was perfectly satisfied with maintaining the great friendship she and Drake had developed. It was so much easier thinking of him in those terms, than anything more intimate.

Saffron covered Reen's hand with her own. "I've always wished I could make friends as easily as you. I've never been very good at it, aside from my friendships with Monica and Bunny Turner."

Saffron had just mentioned two of Reen's least favorite people.

"I think it's due to your relaxed, approachable personality, and your ability to laugh at yourself. Another thing I'm not very good at." Saffron followed that with soft laughter. "Drake's easygoing personality is similar. It's no wonder he values your friendship so much. I knew you were the best person to talk to about him and hoped you wouldn't mind."

"I appreciate the compliment and, no, of course I don't mind."

"I also knew, even with our past differences, I could trust you. That you'd keep what I've told you private. Promise me you won't tell your sisters, okay? I know you're all very close—another trait I envy—and I also know I'm not their favorite person. I...I'd hate to be the Malone family joke."

It's good Saffron stipulated that because Reen's first instinct was to call Laila as soon as Saffron left to tell her sister everything she'd just learned, word for word.

Expelling a deep breath, Reen clasped both of Saffron's shoulders. "You have my word that I won't share anything you've told me with my sisters." She meant it. There was no way she could exploit the sincere, almost fragile, look of hope she'd seen in her cousin's eyes just so she and her sisters could laugh about it.

Frowning momentarily, Reen thought about what Saffron said. "I thought you and your sister and brother were close."

Saffron's smile was cheerless this time. "I love them both, of course. Sadly, Lorraine and I are so different it's hard to believe we're sisters sometimes. We're always clashing. We just can't seem to put our differences aside long enough to become friends." Saffron looked from her folded hands up into Reen's eyes. "It's always been that way with me and my parents too. It's almost like my brother and I don't share the same genes with the rest of the family." She added a meager chuckle.

"I'm sorry, Saffron." Being blessed with such a wonderful family, it was hard for Reen to imagine family members being at such odds.

Saffron breathed a prolonged sigh. "I adore my brother though. Redmond and I have always had a great relationship." Her eyebrows knitted and she looked on the verge of tears. "Poor Red."

"What's wrong?" Reen had never had much of a relationship with her cousin, Lorraine, not to say she hadn't tried. Saffron was Little Miss Congeniality compared to her stuck-up sister. The way Lorraine made no qualms about looking down on the Malones as being her *poor relations* rankled Reen. Aunt Colleen and Uncle Walter were the same way. Red, on the other hand, was a breath of fresh air in the midst of the stuffy, snooty, and quite wealthy Devington clan. He was a fabulous guy who was interesting and fun to hang out with.

Saffron's mouth opened and closed. "I...I'm not sure I can talk about it. Sorry."

"That's okay," Reen assured, touching her cousin's wrist. "I'm here if you want to. I've got good listening ears." Patting her ears, she hoped her smile came across as supportive. She also hoped there wasn't a serious problem concerning Red.

After a lengthy silence, Saffron's eyes welled with tears. "My parents disowned him, Reen. Disinherited him," she said so softly Reen had to strain to hear her.

"What?" she asked, not sure if she'd heard Saffron right. "I don't understand. Why? What happened?"

Saffron reached into her purse for a tissue and dabbed her eyes. "My father, was livid that Red left his banking job." Her eyes closed in a long blink as she gave a dismissive wave. "But that's nothing compared to the uproar when Red..." tears streamed down her cheeks, "when he came out to the family, me, Lorraine, Mom and Dad, at dinner the night before he left for his trip to Ireland. Lorraine made no effort to hide her disgust. I'm the only one who offered my poor brother any support or understanding."

"Oh no... I honestly don't know what to say, Saffron, other than poor Red." Reen was afraid her innermost thoughts about how Red's parents and Lorraine had treated him might be too full of vitriol to be appropriate. Her cousin must have been crushed at a time when he needed his family's unconditional love more than ever.

"I'm so sorry." Saffron got a new tissue and mopped her eyes and nose. "I can't believe I just burdened you with my entire, ugly family ordeal. I never intended to come here and heap all of my angst on you when we've never even been close. You must think I'm terrible. Or crazy. Or both."

"How about neither." Instinctively, Reen threw her arms around her cousin, pulling her into a supportive hug. "You and I are family. I care very much about what you and Red are going through. I'm honored that you'd feel comfortable enough to confide in me about something so painful and personal."

Sharing a second pot of coffee, the cousins spent the next thirty minutes discussing what had happened, with Saffron filling in all the blank spots. As each moment passed, Reen felt their connection growing closer, stronger.

Reaching the end of their conversation about Red, Reen looked at her phone. It was time to lighten the mood for both of them so they'd be ready for the evening's upcoming festivities.

"It's almost eleven-thirty," Reen said. "That means we need to have a crash course in the subject of Professor Drake Slattery before you go to the Fling tonight. By the time we're finished, you'll be an expert and tonight just might end up being the best Valentine's Day you've ever had."

When Reen spotted fresh tears shining in Saffron's eyes, she grew teary-eyed herself. Making eye contact, the cousins spontaneously drew each other into another hug, with Saffron softly repeating *thank you* in Reen's ear.

Chapter Seven

~<>~

LESS THAN FIFTEEN minutes after Saffron left, Reen's doorbell rang again, just as she was about to snuggle up on the couch and take that much-needed nap. She was exhausted and, after her cousin's lengthy visit, all talked out. She was usually a motormouth in need of a brake, so this was a rarity.

Just as she had two hours earlier, cane in hand, Reen hobble-clumped her way to the door, with Hazelnut already standing at attention, waiting to see who was on the other side. After her discussion with Saffron, seeing Drake standing across the threshold surprised and unnerved her somewhat.

"What are you doing here?" Reen asked.

"Well nice to see you too." Drake broke into a broad smile as he met Hazelnut's enthusiastic greeting, petting her. He and Reen stood looking at each other for a while until Drake said, "So, are you going to ask me in or what?"

Used to seeing Drake in his usual professor-ish garb, Reen was caught off guard at the sight of him in a plaid flannel shirt with rolled sleeves, a pair of great-fitting indigo jeans, and black leather sneakers. He'd been wearing his contacts most of the time lately and today was the first time in a while she'd seen him in his black-rimmed glasses.

He was so Clark Kent.

Looking him up and down, she felt her mouth go dry.

With the realization she'd been ogling her friend, she shook herself out of her stare, hoping he hadn't noticed her momentary lapse. "Oh!" Embarrassed, she swallowed hard. "Oh, yeah, sure. Sorry, I'm just kind of tired. I was up really early this morning and

I," she gave in to in a cavernous yawn, "was just about to take a little snooze so I can be bright-eyed and bushy-tailed for tonight."

"Ahh, sorry. I promise not to keep you long. I just wanted to ask your help with a couple of things."

Reen frowned. *Please*, she said to herself, *please don't let him be here to ask me advice about Saffron.* "No problem. Come on in. Want some coffee?"

"No thanks. Just sit down and relax." He led the way into the family room where he took a seat on the couch. "Unless you want coffee. I can put on a pot if you want some."

Reen hesitated. Drake made the world's worst coffee. "Ummm..."

He snickered. "Okay, okay, you don't have to spell it out. I know my coffee's not the greatest."

"It's perfect for people who like their hot water with the faint essence of coffee," Reen assured. They shared a chuckle over the too-true assessment of his sorely lacking coffee-making skills. "Sooo...what can I do for you, Professor?" Reen was so beat she hadn't noticed the small bundle in Drake's arms until he sat down...and the little bundle moved.

Eyeing the pale-blue towel-wrapped package, she did a doubletake. "Oh my—Drake, is that a baby?"

"Not exactly." He lifted a corner of the towel to reveal the cutest little kitten Reen had ever seen.

"Oh my gosh, it's adorable. And so tiny." The kitten made a teensy purring sound. "Aw, it's precious."

"It's just a few weeks old. It's for the kids. Lilly's been after me to get a cat for a long time. One of her best friends has one and she loves it."

"I've heard Lilly talking about it," Reen said. "Over and over again." She smiled and noticed Hazelnut keeping her distance, although she sniffed the air from afar..

"One of the professors I work with called me a while ago asking if I'd be interested. His cat had a litter of five and he's only keeping one." Drake stroked the tiny forehead of the mewling kitten as he spoke. "I just came from his place. They were all cute but there was something special about this little guy. My heart melted a little when I first saw him and picked him up. He looks a lot like Mittens, the cat I had when I was a boy."

"Lilly will be so excited. Where are the kids, anyway?"

"They have a playdate with Harold at Gard and Sabrina's place." Drake glanced at his watch. "I need to pick them up in forty minutes so I can get them cleaned up and fed before the babysitter comes tonight. So, what do you think I should name him? Or should I leave it up to Lilly?"

Reen thought for a moment. "The only problem with leaving it up to Lilly is that Kevin might get jealous and they could start fighting over who gets to name the kitten. It might be better if you introduced them to their new pet with a name you've already chosen."

"Good point. I hadn't thought of that. How about Mittens Two, or something like Boots?" His expression twisted. "Nah," he answered his own question. "Not original enough. I'm not all that great coming up with names. Got any ideas?"

Reen took a good look at the adorable fluff ball in shades of gray and white. "He reminds me of the skeins of wool yarn I've been using for one of the hats I'm knitting. See? Over there with my knitting needles." She pointed to the end table. "In fact, I'm working on a kitten hat."

After a quick glance, Drake told her, "You're right. It's the same color as this little guy."

"What do you think about calling him Knitten?" Reen suggested with a big grin. "You know, with a silent K. Knitten the kitten."

"Knitten." Drake looked down at the swathed bundle and smiled. "Knitten," he said again, directly to the kitten, who responded by tapping Drake's chin with his tiny paw. "I like that. I think he does too. See how he responded to the name? It's perfect, Reen. Thanks. I think Lilly and Kevin will definitely approve when I tell them you named our newest family member."

Gesturing again to the end table, Reen said, "I think I'll save the new cat hat for Lilly. Maybe for her birthday. I can make matching kitty slippers for Christmas. What do you think?"

"I think Lilly is one very lucky little girl. She's crazy about you, you know," Drake told her. "So's Kev."

"The feeling's mutual. Your kids are terrific." If Reen ever had children of her own, she'd want them to be just like Lilly and Kevin Slattery. Spending as much time as she did with Drake and his children sometimes gave her the sensation of family. They shared so many good times together it wasn't difficult imagining the four of them as mom, dad, and kids.

A memory flitted across her mind and Reen smiled, recalling a midsummer day last year when Drake and his twins showed up on her doorstep, with Drake looking slightly frazzled. It seemed the kids, who'd been out of school for a week, were getting antsy. So Drake decided to give them a special treat—the joy of listening to some of his favorite opera selections.

According to Drake, during his explanation of the first act of Puccini's La Bohème, when Mimi and Rudolfo realize they are in love and sing about it, Lilly and Kevin squirmed and got whiny. Puzzled by their reaction, Drake decided to switch to another fun activity instead, hoping they'd enjoy it better.

Reen remembered Drake telling her, "So I brought out a set of charts I thought they'd find interesting—the sort of thing I always liked as a kid. But they rolled their eyes and groaned while I explained about atoms being the building blocks of all matter, consisting of three sub-atomic particles, protons, neutrons and electrons." Poor Drake had looked so lost and clueless with his two bored-to-tears children at his side.

It was three strikes and you're out when Drake had confessed to Reen, "Since the kids said they don't want to see my slides showing how archaeologists excavate a dig site using trowels, shovels, and other tools, carefully removing dirt and noting the precise location of any artifacts found," he took a breath and scratched his head, "I'm out of ideas for fun activities. I need your help, Reen."

"We need your help, Miss Reen!" Lilly and Kevin had echoed, their bodies sagging against Drake's legs.

Reen was careful not to laugh at his hilarious choices for a summer afternoon of fun. The last thing she wanted to do was ridicule Drake in front of his children. Aside from his tendency to find fascination where others found endless boredom, he was a great dad and the twins adored him.

"Hmm..." Reen tapped her cheek. "I know." Bending, she placed her hands on her knees and asked the children, "Who wants to go to the seashore to build sand castles and then get ice cream cones?" In an instant Lilly and Kevin were jumping in place shouting, "Me! Me!"

Drake's grin was as wide as the seashore. "I can always count on you, Reen."

The four of them had walked the few blocks hand-in-hand beneath the sunny sky with the soft ocean breeze tickling as they headed for GB Cones, the decades-old ice cream shack on the sand. They had a ball together, with Drake getting all architectural and precise with his sandcastle construction and his kids giggling as he demonstrated how to create a lasting structure...just before a small influx of water collapsed his masterpiece of building ingenuity. It was one of Reen's favorite memories.

Thinking about how much she enjoyed Drake's children reminded Reen of her conversation earlier with Saffron, about how she wanted to get to know Lilly and Kevin better and develop a rapport with them. If all went well, Saffron would be the one going with them to get ice cream and build castles in the sand.

And Reen was perfectly fine with that.

She was. Really.

Distracted by her wandering thoughts, she realized Drake had said something she missed.

"I'm sorry, what did you say?"

"I was asking about tonight. You're going, right?"

"Mmm-hmm. Me and Frankie."

Drake's jaw muscle twitched as he gave her a hard look. "Frankie?"

"How could you forget?" Reen double-slapped her knee-high boot. "It's short for Frankenstein, thanks to Monica's memorable description."

"Oh!" His jolt of laughter disturbed little Knitten, who popped his eyes open, gave a warning glare, then stretched and yawned before going back to sleep. "I remember now. Hey, would you mind helping me out with something for tonight?"

"Sure," Reen answered without hesitation. She wondered if Drake was about to ask her questions about Saffron, which would be okay, just kind of weird. "What do you need?"

"Here, take Knitten for a minute while I go to my car." He deposited the furry little bundle in Reen's arms.

Hazelnut ambled over to the couch, her nose working overtime as she checked out the new kid in town. "This is Knitten," Reen told her dog, opening the towel so Hazelnut could get a better look. "You and he are going to be good friends, isn't that right, Knitten?" She took the cat's little paw, shaking it gently. Hazelnut studied the kitten for a while longer before giving the tiny cat a friendly couple of licks. Knitten responded by batting Hazelnut's head with his paw.

Doing her best Humphrey Bogart impression of Rick in Casablanca, Reen said, "I think this is the beginning of a beautiful friendship."

Drake returned carrying clothing over his arm. "You know I'm not too savvy when it comes to putting clothes together. What do you think would work best for tonight. I want to look appropriate for a Valentine function, but not like a clown."

"A clown?" Reen laughed. "What makes you think you'd look like a clown?"

"The hearts," Drake explained, holding up a black tie peppered with little red hearts, white squiggles, and the word LOVE all over it in peppermint pink. It could easily win an ugly tie contest. "I'm not used to wearing novelty stuff and I don't want to look foolish. But I don't want to look stuffy either. So which one should I wear?" He presented three ties, the one with hearts, one with diagonal gray-toned stripes, and one with diagonal blue-toned stripes. One ugly selection and two lackluster ones.

"I'm guessing you didn't buy the tie with the hearts," Reen surmised.

"My mom gave it to me about ten years ago." He gazed at the tie with affection. "I've never worn it but can't get rid of it."

"Of course." Reen nodded, knowing Drake still grieved for his parents who died the year before. After his mother lost her battle with cancer, his father had a heart attack. "It's a nice keepsake. I think you should keep it always. But I wouldn't wear it unless that wide shape and print style comes back into fashion." Drake's late mom was a sweet, wonderful woman, whose taste in clothing bordered on carnivalesque.

"I'm planning to wear this," he held up a jacket, "my black and gray tweed sport coat, with this white shirt and black slacks. Or maybe I should wear the light gray shirt." He showed that to Reen too. His shoulders slumped. "It's been a long time since I had to make decisions about what to wear to take a woman out. I'm out of practice. I want to look good, you know?"

Ahh, of course, he wanted to look good for Saffron.

So their attraction was definitely mutual.

"Yes," Reen nodded, offering a sympathetic smile, "I know." She decided she'd do all she could to have Drake look his best for her cousin. "First of all, lets nix the ties. Too starchy for the Fling."

"Really?" He glanced at the trio of ties draping from his hand. "I thought the black and gray stripe was pretty cool."

"If we were in Chicago," she shrugged, "it might be a different story, but this is Oregon, land of the informal and laidback. Actually," she stepped back, evaluating him from head to toe as she tapped her chin. "I'd suggest that you wear that nice soft black sweater, the V-neck one I told you I like a lot, remember?" Drake nodded. "With this white shirt underneath it, open collar. Forget the sport coat and black slacks." She eyed him once more. His jeans looked crisp and new. And tight in all the right places. "Wear these jeans, they look great on you."

"Jeans?" He glanced down at his legs as if forgetting what he had on. "Isn't that too casual? I don't want to look like a bum."

Reen laughed at that. "Trust me, Drake, you're not going to look like a bum or a clown. Wear what I told you and you'll look—" Reen stopped herself before the word *hot* popped out of her mouth. "Perfectly appropriate for your date with Saffron." She tacked on a friendly clothing-counselor smile. "If you think about the past Flings, that's what guys your age usually wear."

"This'll be my first Fling," Drake admitted.

"Really? I didn't realize. Why haven't you gone before?"

"For one thing," shoving his hand through his hair, Drake gave an uneasy smile, "Janet never wanted to go. She thought community events like the Fling were corny and beneath her. Remember, my ex-wife was from Manhattan. That's a good deal different from sociable Glassfloat Bay."

Yes indeed, she remembered Janet perfectly. The woman could easily outdo Monica, Saffron, or even Saffron's sister, Lorraine, when it came to being snooty and pretentious.

"I'll admit most of the events are on the corny side," Reen confessed, "but I think they're the most fun. I love the way everybody gets into the spirit of things here. I love Chicago and miss many things about it, like the deep dish pizza, hot dogs with all the trimmings, and Italian beef sandwiches," she licked her lips, "but a big city can't have the charm and close-knit feel of a small town like Glassfloat Bay."

"When I was at Cornell University—"

"In New York, where you met Janet, right?"

"Right. We were both taking classes at the College of Arts and Sciences, Anthropology for me and Medieval Studies for her, so we saw each other nearly every day. Living in New York for those few years I realized there wasn't any comparison to Glassfloat Bay. I really missed this place."

"While your ex couldn't wait to leave and get back to the life she knew in New York," Reen surmised. *And away from her husband and children*, she avoided verbalizing.

"Right. I only know Janet's still in New York because she sends Lilly and Kevin a postcard from there on their birthday and another at Christmas." Grimacing, Drake pinched his nose between his eyebrows. "Sorry, Reen, but the last thing I want to talk about right now is Janet."

"I can't blame you." Taking a deep breath, she said, "Back to tonight's Fling. It's always fun. I'm sure you and Saffron will enjoy it. I think this is her first time going too. I know she's really looking forward to it...to going with you."

"I've got another question for you," Drake said, looking into Reen's eyes.

"Shoot."

"What do you think about me and Saffron? Getting together, I mean." His penetrating gaze didn't waver. Reen felt like he was trying to see deep into her soul.

Needing a break from the intensity of his stare, and feeling the need to shutter her soul from scrutiny, Reen dropped her gaze and fiddled with the kitten still nestled in her lap. She had to remember she only wanted what was best for her friend and also for her cousin. This wasn't the time for her to be juvenile or selfish, wanting to keep Drake's attention and friendship all to herself. There's no reason she and Drake, and his adorable kids, couldn't maintain their solid, sociable connection if he and Saffron became a couple.

Reen reminded herself that any wild thoughts she may have had, like Drake being her Clark Kent, or him looking super-hot in his tight jeans, or about the two of them exploring a romantic relationship, were due entirely to her lack of sleep. Thinking logically wasn't easy when she was overtired.

And this was a time when logic must prevail.

Her thoughts spun like a roulette wheel, with the little marble finally settling on the area labeled *Hud*. The very thought of his name brought a smile to her lips.

Now that Hud was no longer attached, Reen was free to do whatever necessary to attract his attention. After all, he was the man she'd been pining over for the past couple of years, not Drake. Right? Right! It was time for her to set her very own *Project Hudson* plans into motion. If she played her cards right, she and Hud Griffin could be an item before summer.

Reen looked up again. "You and Saffron have a lot in common, Drake. You're both good people and I think you might be perfect for each other." With a resolute nod, she finished, "That's what I think."

Drake's blue-gray eyes looked like the ocean just before dusk. "I guess what I want to know, Maureen, is how do you *feel* about it...about me and Saffron?"

He was looking at her again in that certain way, making Reen damned nervous. Why did he have to stare at her with that solemn expression? Why did he have to make this so serious? Why the hell did he want to talk about feelings? Weren't men supposed to have some sort of allergy when it came to talking about feelings?

"Good! I feel good," she answered with gusto through a chummy grin. "I feel happy that you're getting on with your life and you found a woman who's miles better than your ex-wife. I feel you should go for it!" Reen finished with a big thumbs up gesture before picking up her phone and looking at the time.

"Well look at that, Drake," she continued her speedy babbling, wanting to avoid giving Drake an opportunity to ask her any more uncomfortable questions. "Time's flying. If you don't leave now you'll be late picking up the twins. You and Knitten better get moving!"

For some ridiculous reason, Reen felt the sting of tears approaching. How silly! There was absolutely no reason to cry. Except maybe for happy tears. Yes, that's what they were—happy tears, brimming behind her eyes planning a salty avalanche if she wasn't careful. She certainly couldn't get weepy now in front Drake. Men didn't understand happy tears. He might get the mistaken idea that Reen had feelings for him.

A curious look across his face, Drake gave his watch a quick glance. "You're right. I better get going. Thanks for everything, Reen." He took Knitten from her, gathered his neckties and clothing, and left.

Refusing to succumb to tears, because there was no logical reason for them, Reen waited until Drake was out of sight, then collapsed on the couch for a much-needed nap. Almost as soon as she closed her eyes, she was dreaming of sandcastles.

Chapter Eight

~<>~

THERE WAS A surprisingly good turnout at the Valentine's Day Fling. The unusually warm, sunny day responsible for the evening's dry, mild weather no doubt had something to do with the generous attendance.

As soon as she crossed the community center's threshold, Reen found herself in a celebratory mood. The abundant and imaginative holiday decorations made it impossible not to smile. Wearing a favorite dress, she felt she fit in nicely, right down to her fancied-up Frankenstein boot. She'd found the long-sleeved, tomato-red jersey knit dress at the same estate sale Laila had found her genie bottle. So it had special significance to her, and perhaps even a touch of magic, she liked to believe.

With magic on her mind, Reen surreptitiously lifted her hand waist-high, turning it back and forth, admiring the heartwish ring's attractive stone. She wondered when she'd learn what to wish for. Between the pre-dawn phone call and subsequent ring-passing, followed by Saffron's unexpected visit and confession, the day had been chaotic. Reen was exhausted but excited at the same time.

"I've been looking for Kady, is she here?" Sabrina asked, joining Reen and interrupting her random musings. "I've seen so little of her since she's been home from her overseas backpacking trip. Don't tell me she's off somewhere again."

"The girl does love to travel." Reen laughed. "She's at a seminar in Seattle, learning about what it takes to be a bookstore owner." At Sabrina's raised eyebrows, Reen explained, "Kady's decided to become half owner of Bubble Tide Books."

"Wow, I had no idea! That's great, I'm happy for her. Kady's always loved reading." Her gaze fell across Reen's dress. "That shade of red is perfect for you. Love the dress's great retro vibe." Sabrina fingered the fabric. "So soft too. Where'd you find it?"

Her fingers sweeping over the supple fabric, Reen smiled. "I'll give you three guesses."

"Knowing your expertise at making sensational finds at garage sales, thrift stores, and estate sales, it's gotta be one of those."

"Bingo!" Reen laughed. "Estate sale up on Beauregard Hill. It had a big honkin' set of 1980s-style shoulder pads," she clutched at her shoulders, "that I removed. I love your outfit too," she told Sabrina, who wore a red, white and pink striped dress. "Perfect for Valentine's Day."

"Thank you. Just before the babysitter came, Harry ran up to me, gave me a hug and said, 'Ooh, Mommy, you look just like a pretty circus clown!'"

Covering her mouth, Reen laughed. "Oh dear, kids really do say the darnedest things, don't they? Trust me, Sabrina, you most certainly do *not* look like a clown. Now if he'd said you look like a model, that I would believe. Even after losing all the weight, I still don't think I'd feel confident enough to wear horizontal stripes. You, with that gorgeous slender figure of yours, pull it off beautifully."

"Thanks, but I'll have to stick to vertical stripes if I keep chowing down on Laila's scones. Those things are so delicious and addictive they should come with a *warning—weight gain ahead* label."

"Tell me about it."

Gazing at the garlands of oversized valentines interspersed with puffy red satin hearts and white paper doilies strung on pink satin ribbon overhead, Reen said, "The way you and Annalise used vintage Valentine cards to decorate the community center is so imaginative. Everything looks so festive. Where did you find all the old valentines? There must be hundreds here."

"I'm so glad you like the way it turned out." Sabrina gazed up with a satisfied smile. "I think they're pretty adorable too. You're not the only one who haunts secondhand sales." She elbowed Reen and laughed. "Like you, I found my treasure at an estate sale in one of the mansions on Beauregard Hill. Dozens of the cards were stuffed into old shoe boxes. Some go all the way back to the late 1800s. I got the entire lot of them for only ten dollars, can you believe it?"

"Amazing price! That was some very clever thrift shopping, Sabrina."

"I've learned a valuable thing or two from my mentor."

"Really? Who's that?"

With an exaggerated tsk, Sabrina made a goofy expression. "I'm talking about you, silly! Who else? I scanned and enlarged the cards, then had copies made so we'd keep the originals in good condition for future Valentine projects."

"Excellent idea," Reen told her. "Really unique and creative."

"Oh good...after Annalise and I plastered old Valentines over every empty spot we found, we worried we may have gotten slightly carried away." She spread her arms wide and grinned. "But I think it turned out well."

"It's perfect," Laila said, coming up from behind them. "You can never have too much bling. Did you and Annalise decorate the kissing booths too? They're so cute and festive with the tiny red, white and pink twinkling lights strung up. I didn't expect two booths."

"Those are Christmas lights I found in the clearance aisle at the craft store after the holidays," Sabrina said. "I knew they'd come in handy sooner or later."

"A packrat after my own heart," Reen teased.

Standing at their side, Delaney bounced in place. "I helped decorate the kissing booths. Of course I followed Sabrina's instructions to a T."

"Look at you in your polka dots!" Reen said, holding her sister by the arms as she admired the pink dress adorned with quarter-sized white dots. "Darling dress, Delaney."

"Thanks, I got it at Goodwill. They just don't make dresses like this anymore—at least not that I can afford. Varik, who's usually oblivious to what I wear, even noticed and complimented me, saying I looked like a beautiful Valentine."

"Smart husband." Reen winked. "Love the dotted nails too."

"Aren't they cute?" Delaney asked, fluttering her fingers. "Sabrina did them for me."

"Put a paint brush in my hands and I'll paint anything," Sabrina joked.

"I see your sister, the glitter queen, has been busy too, Sabrina," Reen noted, spotting ample red, pink and white glitter, not only on the booths but decorating the paper tablecloths too. "I love it."

Gesturing toward Annalise, who manned one of the nearby treats tables, Sabrina nodded. "Yup, I'm sure it comes as no surprise that she's the one responsible for all the sparkly residue the community center staff will be cursing us for over the next several months."

Coming closer, Annalise raised her hand. "Guilty as charged. One simply cannot have a celebration without copious amounts of glitter," she informed them.

"You got some on your cheeks." Laila reached to wipe it off but Annalise pulled back.

"Whoa, hold on there, these sparkly cheeks are on purpose." Out came a tiny pink tube from her pocket. "This is dynamite stuff. It goes on like lotion then leaves a shimmer trail when it dries. Anybody want some?" When nobody took her up on her offer, she shrugged, repocketing the iridescent makeup.

"A lot of women must have signed up to staff the kissing booths if we have two of them," Reen noted.

"Actually, it's not all women," Annalise explained. "The booth on that side is for the men. Now nobody can accuse us of being discriminatory or sexist." They all laughed.

"Equal opportunity kissing booths, hmm?" Reen said. "Clever, and so politically correct." She smiled. "How many guys have signed up?"

Sabrina withdrew a sheet of paper from her pocket, chuckling as she glanced at the list containing a solitary name. "Only George Baxnopper so far."

"The flirty eighty-something councilman?" Laila's lip curled in distaste.

"Yup." Shrugging, Sabrina told them, "Seems most of the men aren't interested in selling kisses, only buying them."

"I suppose if someone ties Baxnopper's hands behind his back it might be okay," Delaney mused. "The guy's a bit too, ahem, *handy* for me." She followed that with an eye roll. Glancing at her sister's leg, her expression brightened. "How cute! I love what you did to your boot."

As all eyes traveled to her leg, Reen showed off her heavily decorated boot. "I'm Valentined to the max."

"All it needs is a touch of glitter," Annalise suggested. "I have some jars in the back room." Her eyebrows lifted into an expectant arc.

"Jars?" Delaney said with surprise. "I've only seen glitter come in those skinny little tubes." She held her thumb and forefinger an inch apart.

"They don't call me the glitter queen for nothing." Draping an arm over Delaney's shoulder, Annalise promised, "Someday I'll introduce you to the many wonders of glitter, my friend." Looking into the distance, she spread her hand through the air as if envisioning a glittery marquee. Turning to Reen, she said, "So, what's the verdict? Shall we glitter up that boot?" She rubbed her hands in anticipation, making Reen laugh.

"I think I'll take a pass on the glitter. I'm already worried enough about getting these stickers off so I'm not stuck with all these hearts and cutesy *be mine* sayings for the next couple of months."

"Now there's something I've never seen before," Laila said.

Bending to clap the top of her boot, Reen said, "Oh you can find these stickers everywhere."

"No, I mean over there." Laila nodded toward the entrance. "Saffron. I can't believe she's actually wearing a pop of color instead of her usual dark, drab uniform. And, damn, she looks good too."

Reen followed her sister's gaze and smiled. Saffron had taken her advice and added some red for the festive evening. She still wore a dark business suit but the red and white poppy print blouse beneath it made a big difference. It took a lot of coaxing but once she learned that red is one of Drake's favorite colors, Saffron agreed to wear something *a little more daring*, as she put it. She'd even worn a slash of red across her lips, and let her rich brown hair fall to her shoulders rather than having it tied back.

Reen's gaze shifted to Drake, who looked Fling-perfect wearing the outfit Reen suggested. Actually, the man was handsome regardless of what he wore, whether it was formal wear, one of his professor-ish sport coats, or jeans. Noticing one errant lock of dark hair falling to his forehead, Reen was once again reminded of his Clark Kent-Superman likeness. Yes indeed, her fine-looking neighbor—her hunky good buddy—was quite a catch.

Suddenly aware her thoughts had veered off the main road and traveled into taboo territory, Reen blinked a few times, took a breath, and shifted her mindset, reminding herself that Drake was here with Saffron. And Reen was happy about it. Really happy.

It was clear by the attentive way Drake eyed his date, that he approved of Saffron's attractive new look. Reen felt good that she'd done the right thing. She really did.

"Saffron really does look nice," Reen agreed with Laila, ignoring the slight tug at her heart.

"I almost didn't recognize Saffy," Delaney said. "I wonder what prompted her to drop the conservative mortician look for a change?"

"Who knows?" Reen felt an earnest smile take hold. "Valentine's Day can be magical." As she spoke she spotted Hud coming in the door and walking up to Drake. She noticed Monica wasn't attached. In fact, she didn't see Monica at all until Reen happened to glance across the room, recognizing the attractive blonde with her hair swept up into a stylish chignon, studying some of the artwork for sale. Wearing a figure-hugging rose-pink dress with a deep décolletage, Monica looked beautiful as usual.

Reen saw a quick glance pass between Monica and Hud before he wandered off in the opposite direction.

When Saffron caught Reen's eye, she smiled, lifting her eyebrows and touching her silky blouse as if to ask Reen if she thought it was all right. Smiling in return, Reen gave her cousin a subtle nod of approval. A moment later, when Saffron looked in the other direction, Drake did basically the same thing, looking for Reen's approval of his outfit. Again, she nodded, thinking it was very sweet how the two of them wanted to look good for each other.

The evening progressed so quickly Reen forgot she was dead tired. She nibbled assorted homemade treats, laughed until her jaws hurt, and spent too much time trying to dance in her cumbersome boot, which meant her ankle would be mighty sore tomorrow. But she didn't care because she was thoroughly enjoying herself.

While Drake and Hud stood with Reen's brothers, Gard and Nevan, engrossed in a marine fishing demonstration offered by a representative of the Oregon Department of Fish and Wildlife, a radiant Saffron came up to Reen.

"I wanted to thank you again, Maureen. Our talk was invaluable. I've been following your advice, trying to engage Drake in conversations about his favorite subjects, and it's working perfectly, just like you said it would." She nodded at the fishing demo, where Laila's husband, Zak, and Delaney's husband, Varik, had just joined the other men. "Looks like I'll have to ask him about marine fishing too, hmm?"

"Drake wants to get into fishing so he can fish for lingcod, his favorite fish," Reen told her. "He orders it each time we go to Larker's Fish and Seafood with his kids."

"Larkers...in Jigsaw Landing?" Saffron asked and Reen nodded. "I've never been there. I hear it's one of the best fish houses on the coast."

"It is, definitely." Reen offered her cousin a gentle elbow nudge. "This is a perfect opportunity, Saffron. Tell Drake I recommended Larker's and their lingcod fish and chips, then you can suggest the two of you go there together so you can try it."

"Great idea. I'll do that." Saffron pulled her in for a hug, which Reen reciprocated. "I'm looking forward to us getting to be great friends, Maureen. We've missed so many opportunities and I don't want to miss any more." She glanced up at the clock. "Better keep your eye on the clock. Your thirty-minute stint at the kissing booth is coming up soon, isn't it?"

Reen checked the time. "It is. So far it seems the kissing booth is a success with ticket holders having plenty of fun, even at the pricey cost of five dollars per kiss. Looks like the Fling will be raking in a tidy sum for Wisdom Harbor Children's Hospital from those booths."

"From what I've seen so far, it seems most of the kisses exchanged have been friendly pecks," Saffron noted, "with only a few attempting more intimate exchanges."

"That's probably because the Kissing Police have been keeping a diligent eye on things," Reen confided, snickering.

"Kissing Police?"

"Mmm-hmm, also known as Glassfloat Bay's illustrious councilwoman, Mildred Fophamer," Reen filled her in, and Saffron gave a knowing nod. "See that sign?" Reen pointed at the kissing booth and Saffron's gaze followed. "That's thanks to Millie."

The two of them studied the sign written in big block letters that Mildred tacked on the kissing booths, warning participants: *Keep it Clean! Brief Closed Mouth Kisses Only!!!*

After sharing a chuckle over it, they continued chatting until Drake came to claim his date. Reen could hear Saffron asking him about the fishing demo as they walked off together. Folding her arms across her chest as she watched them, she gave a gratified smile. It might take her a while to get used to them as a couple, but she would eventually.

"I make one hell of a matchmaker," she muttered beneath her breath, watching the couple laughing together, arm in arm.

"I think I must be ill," Laila said into Reen's ear as she came up behind her.

"You're sick?"

"I must be, because I think I've been hallucinating. I could swear I saw Saffy being all chummy with you and giving you a hug." Laila wore a questioning frown. "What gives?"

Reen wanted so much to tell her sister but she'd given Saffron her word. She'd also told her cousin she wasn't going to mention Saffron's visit earlier today because it would entail too much explanation. That meant Reen would have to act surprised when someone told her about Hud and Monica breaking up.

"We just thought it was a good idea to finally bury the hatchet," Reen offered in succinct explanation.

With a hand on Reen's shoulder, Laila examined her sister's back. Reen looked over her shoulder. "What are you doing?"

"Making sure Saffy didn't bury that hatchet in your back." With that, Laila smirked, patted her sister's back, and headed across the aisle to the Hazelnut Growers of Oregon's exhibit, with its table full of brochures and delicious honey-roasted hazelnuts.

Swaying in place as she listened to the band play one love-themed song after another, Reen checked the time again. She had fifteen minutes before her turn at the booth. Movement at the former men's kissing booth drew her attention. By seven-thirty, old Mr. Baxnopper, aka Kissless George, was finally ushered away, and the booth converted to an exhibit from Oregon's Pendleton Woolen Mills featuring their colorful blankets and throws.

Reen and her sisters had an eyepopping surprise earlier as they watched the seven o'clock kissing booth shift change, with their mother stepping up for her turn. Astrid hadn't informed any of them she'd signed up. Tore was first in line, followed by Pastor Bengston, Dr. Shadrik, Mayor Stevens, and several other seasoned gentlemen. The sisters teased their mom plenty but were happy she had a good number of ticket holders buying a kiss from the still attractive sixty-something grandmother.

"I can't wait to dig into that crab," Laila said. "Want to head over there with me?"

With Oregon's Dungeness crab season in full flourish, Reen looked forward to sitting down for the steamed crab dinner she'd purchased. Offering all the crab you can eat, the meal came with an ear of buttered corn, Annalise's delicious potato salad, a little wood hammer for claw cracking, and small containers of melted butter.

"I'm holding off until my stint at the kissing booth is over. I doubt anyone wants to kiss someone who smells and tastes like a fishery."

"Good point." Laila tossed her a wink. "Later." She gave her a finger wave as she headed for the food.

Aside from the popular kissing booth, this year's Fling boasted a variety of stands from local restaurants, and exhibits from businesses, artists and craftspeople. Bakeoffs featuring homemade treats from the town's best cooks and bakers were a favorite, with proceeds benefitting Wisdom Harbor Children's Hospital. One of Reen's favorite exhibits was Glimmer Hope Art Gallery's, displaying a number of imaginative artworks by local Oregon Coast artists. It was the venue where Sabrina's *SabrinArt* creations would soon be shown.

Topping it all off was the live music and dancing, including a dance contest just for seniors, sixty-five and over, twisting to the music of the band playing Chubby Checker's The Twist. The wonderful sight of the town's older citizens recapturing their youth and having a ball warmed Reen's heart. She hoped she could still move that well when she reached that age.

Sidling up to Reen and whispering in her ear, Laila said, "Wait'll you hear this."

Reen chuckled at the enthusiasm in her sister's voice...and the smell of crabmeat on her breath, reinforcing the wisdom of her decision to wait to cash in her crab ticket until she'd finished at the kissing booth.

"Don't tell me," she said to Laila. "You won the framed photo of the sea lions sunning on the dock that you had your eye on."

"Nope, they haven't had the drawing yet. Fingers crossed though." She made the gesture. "I'm here to deliver some very special and unexpected news. Ready?"

"Sure." By her sister's demeanor Reen knew it had to be the news about Hud and Monica.

"Hud just told Sabrina that he and Monica broke up."

"What?" Dropping her jaw, Reen popped her eyes open wide, hoping her attempt at amazement seemed genuine. "You're kidding."

"It's true," Laila assured. "Sabrina wanted me to let you know before your turn in the kissing booth."

"So that's why Hud and Monica haven't been together all evening. Did Sabrina say how it happened?"

"She's in the kitchen," Laila thumbed behind her, "helping Annalise dish up the crab dinners so she didn't have much time to talk. Apparently Monica's the one who broke things off. She told Hud they'd be better off as friends. That's all Sabrina knows so far."

Wincing, Reen remembered her mother saying what a gut punch it is for a guy when a woman he's interested in says she just wants to be friends. Poor Hud.

"I know I joked about wanting it to happen, and even hoped it would, but honestly? I never expected they'd break up."

"Me neither," Laila agreed. "They always looked pretty lovey-dovey together."

Laila was right. As much as Reen was crushing on Hud, she had to admit he and Monica seemed like an ideal couple. It was sad to see both of them looking so blue when everyone else there was celebrating Valentine's Day, the holiday earmarked for love and romance.

"Here." Laila plopped something into Reen's open hand, then closed her fingers around it.

"What's this?"

"My Mango Go Deep lipstick." Laila's eyebrows danced. "It's nearly eight-thirty. Go to the bathroom and fancy yourself up. You've got a smudge on your chin and it looks like some of Annalise's glitter is on the tip of your nose. Fluff your hair, it's a little flat on one side, and put on the lipstick. Once you kiss Hud he'll never know what hit him." She elbowed Reen.

Aware her heart was thudding, Reen clasped the lipstick in her fist. "Have you seen Hud tonight? He doesn't look happy. He's probably feeling gloomy because of Monica. I'll bet he doesn't even use any kiss tickets he bought."

"I checked. He bought two of them," Laila told her. "He used one for Mom, which I thought was super sweet of him. That means he's still got one ticket left. Since there's only you and his sister, Sabrina, left on the schedule it looks like you'll get a chance to knock Hud Griffin's socks off tonight. Make the most of it."

With a glance at the round schoolhouse-style clock on the wall, she gave Reen a hug. "Good luck, sis. I've got to go. I'm due at the brownie bakeoff judging table. Tough job," she shrugged, "but somebody's gotta do it." Tittering a laugh, she was on her way.

Standing in place, thunderstruck at the realization that she might be kissing Hud soon, Reen remembered what her sister said about her soiled face. Her fingers feathering across her chin, she headed for the restroom. Funny, she'd been waiting a small eternity for a chance like this and now that it was here she felt more angsty than excited. Hud had always been off limits so it was fun and easy to daydream about him, imagining all sorts of sexy what-if scenarios.

But since she'd learned from Saffron that Hud was now fair game, Reen wondered if she only wanted what she couldn't have.

Halfway to the restroom she muttered to herself as she hurried along. "Ridiculous." She gave a dismissive wave. "I've been crazy about Hud for, what? Two years? Of course I want him now that he's free."

Her thought process whirled as she tried convincing herself Hud was the man she wanted. Something elusive nagged at her. Something she couldn't quite put her finger on. "You're just being silly," she mumbled beneath her breath. "It's not like there's any other man you want." She blinked, pausing before pushing the swing door to the restroom. There was that vague nagging feeling again.

A few minutes later, Maureen Malone stood silent before the wall-sized mirror in the restroom, studying her reflection. She felt good in this dress, it flattered her figure. Her face was free of smudges or glitter. Her naturally curly blonde hair was evenly fluffed. And her freshly mangoed lips coordinated well with the tomatoey shade of her dress. Convinced she'd done all she could to make the most of her appearance, she headed for the kissing booth.

As Reen took her place, relieving Delaney, who told her she'd had six ticket holders, with two of those being her husband, Varik, Reen wondered what that odd number was that the band was playing...until it dawned on her it was the sound of her own heart reverberating a *thud-boppa-thud* beat.

Looking out onto the crowd and feeling slightly dazed, she kept telling herself it was no big deal...just a kiss.

The booth was located in an optimum position, giving her a beneficial people-watching view of the large room. She noticed Monica, coffee in hand, looking dejected. Trailing her gaze, Reen could tell Monica was eyeing Hud while he laughed along with a group of people near the long stretch of tables featuring the prizes everyone hoped to win. After patting one of the men on the back, he looked up, locking gazes with Reen, and gave her a killer smile before heading in her direction.

Thud-boppa-thud...

Before Hud reached her, Reen glanced straight ahead, wondering what exhibit or activity people were lining up for, until she realized the six men were queued up for their turn at her kissing booth. It was a pleasant surprise. A definite confidence builder, especially when she noted they were all good looking guys who resided on her mental list of possible dating candidates.

Always thoughtful, even though absentminded, Drake had brought over a tall wooden stool so Reen wouldn't have to be on her feet between kisses for the entire thirty minutes. Saffron was with him and when Drake's back was turned, she smiled, giving Reen a subtle thumbs up, indicating her evening was going well. What a pleasant change, seeing her cousin looking so happy. It was amazing to see how a genuine smile could transform a person's countenance. Saffron was positively glowing.

Reen had fun as, one by one, she accepted tickets from the men, exchanging friendly pecks and enjoying their short visits and innocuous small talk. The Maythorne brothers, Axel, Westford, and Calder, were among those in line. As they introduced themselves, turning in their tickets and collecting their chaste kisses, Reen decided they were even more handsome than she expected. Calder, she recalled, was the one Saffron used to have a crush on. Reen could certainly see why.

As the Maythorne trio left, Reen looked up, noticing Hud had joined at the end of the line.

Her hawk-like gaze ever vigilant, Mildred Fophamer stood kitty-corner from the booth, fists planted on her hips. Deep frown lines were engraved into her brow line, as she watched for an opportunity to issue another of her *keep it clean* reminders. Even Reen's own mother and stepfather didn't escape Mildred's scolding as Tore gave his wife an ardent kiss.

Reen suspected Mildred secretly relished her Kissing Police title.

"I've got one ticket left," Hud told Reen when the man in front of him left and Hud reached the kissing booth. "I saved it just for you." His eyebrows bounced playfully as he waved his ticket.

Taking a moment to collect herself and do whatever she could to avoid coming across like a tongue-tied idiot, Reen blinked, swallowed hard and took a deep breath. All the while, her thoughts raced—*OMG...Hudson Griffin...this is it, this is it, this is it!*

"Oh you did, hmm?" she teased, proud of herself for maintaining her calm and not tripping over her words. "Well I'm truly honored." She took his ticket, dropping it into a jar with the others.

"I've thought about doing this for a long time," Hud told her, reaching forward to cup her face.

"You have?" That came out sounding like she was a teensy gerbil. Reen cleared her throat. "You have?" she repeated sounding more blasé. His admission surprised her.

"Yeah." Hud nodded, giving a roguish smile. "The grapevine says you might have been thinking along the same lines as me."

Feeling her cheeks flare hot with embarrassment, Reen said, "Oh good Lord..."

"Hey," he tipped her chin up with his finger, looking into her eyes, "don't be embarrassed. I think it's kind of cute that you wanted to kiss me."

Before she could respond again, Hud leaned in, startling Reen by giving her the type of kiss she'd dreamed of getting from Hud for so long. It hadn't even registered that it was open-mouthed until she heard the chastising screech of the Kissing Police faulting them for their transgression.

When Reen opened her eyes she saw something in Hud's expression she'd never seen there before. It was a look, a certain realization. While it wasn't quite the *Holy cow, Reen's the one, the woman of my dreams!* look she'd yearned to see, it was an expression that revealed Hud's interest in exploring this—*them*—further.

Reen had a realization too.

She liked kissing Hud. It was undeniably pleasant. Nice. But that's all it was. There were no fireworks, no romance-novelesque sense of passion coursing through her veins. The kiss was ordinary. Mundane. Nothing special and certainly not earth shattering.

She was completely unprepared for her indifferent reaction. Hud must have mistaken the sense of wonder Reen imagined was across her face for a look of dreamy satisfaction because he still leaned close, holding her gaze, and Reen thought for sure he was about to kiss her again. Until the next guy in line gave a loud "*Ahem*. Let's go, Griffin."

"We'll talk later," Hud told Reen before giving her a leisurely wink and meandering off to join others.

As Reen turned, watching him walk away, she spotted Monica gazing, first at Reen, and then at Hud. Looking stricken, she wiped tears from her eyes as she hurried out of the building. Maureen flinched, having just witnessed the heartbreaking look of a woman in love who believed she'd just lost her man. Seeing Monica traumatized brought Reen no happiness or satisfaction. Not even a little. All she felt was a pervasive sense of regret.

The entire brief Hud-kissing experience left Reen staggered, more confused than ever. What the heck was going on with Monica? If she loved Hud, why break up with him?

And why on earth wasn't Reen over the moon about Hud's enthusiastic response to her?

With two more men still in line...make that three, as Drake took his place as last in line, Maureen had no time to ponder the peculiar happenings.

Chapter Nine

~<>~

THE NEXT TWO kisses went quickly, without incident, just as the others had before Hud took his turn. Glancing at the wall clock, Reen noted her shift was nearly over. Drake would be her final kiss. She hadn't expected him to buy a kiss from her after what happened when he brought her home from the opera a year ago. Of course, unlike that awkward moment they'd shared, this kiss was designed to be nothing more than a sociable peck on the cheek for charity.

So then why the butterflies in her stomach? Shaking it off, Reen assumed it was probably stress connected with Hud's kiss and the aftermath with poor Monica.

While Hud had surprised her by ignoring Millie's warning sign, she was sure the rule-respecting professor wouldn't. A friendly brush of lips against cheek from her pal was effortless and uncomplicated.

She glanced to the left to see Saffron give a little wave, smiling at Reen as Drake stepped into position. Reen offered her cousin a cheery wave in return. It was gratifying for Reen to know she was partly responsible for Saffron's joyful demeanor.

Shifting her attention, Reen looked into Drake's eyes and smiled. She was about to make some silly joke to her buddy but the words caught in her throat when she saw...*felt* the intensity of his gaze.

"The last time I tried this was a year ago," Drake said, as Reen wondered why, in all this time, she'd never noticed that his blue-gray eyes were so singularly striking. "I promised myself that would be the last time. But," he shrugged, "this is for a good cause, right?"

"Mmm-hmm." Reen's head bobbed up and down too quickly. "For the sick kids."

"Right. Just promise you won't duck this time, okay?" he teased while brushing a lock of hair from her eyes. "I doubt my ego could take it."

"Cross my heart," she made the motion while swallowing hard, "no ducking, Professor. Just go ahead and plant one right here," she instructed, tapping the center of her cheek.

Drake's beautiful white-toothed smile captured her attention as he came closer, cupping her face in his hands much the way Hud had done moments ago.

Reen opened her mouth to offer some clever quip, but nothing came out. Except a sigh. Her gaze skittered to Saffron once more, who stood there watching and smiling, and all but cheering them on.

Thud-boppa-thud...

Reen had no idea why her pulse raced. No clue why she felt all tingly inside...or why she was so incredibly aroused.

Instinct suddenly told her Drake was about to break the rules of the Kissing Police. An instant before her eyelids fluttered closed, Reen panicked. She couldn't do this. Kissing her pal, her good friend, would ruin everything. She considered jerking back, claiming she was suddenly sick and had to leave. Or maybe she could twist her head when he came in for the kiss, presenting her cheek as she'd showed him, instead of her lips.

No, that would be ultra-insulting after last year's ducking episode.

For heaven's sake, Maureen, get a grip, she chastised herself. *He's just closing in for a quick peck on the lips. That's all. No big deal...no big deal...no big—*

Drake whispered, "Happy Valentine's Day, Maureen." It was the last thing she heard before their lips connected and her head emptied of all those scrambled, panicky thoughts. Her only awareness was of Drake's lips on hers, his mouth opening while she willingly reciprocated.

It was the most perfect, remarkable kiss she'd ever experienced. Sweet, like perfectly ripe strawberries dipped in chocolate. Inviting, like the warmth of a small glass of port on a winter's night. Tender and sincere, yet zealous. Eager. Passionate. Romantic. Oh good God in heaven...*soooo* romantic...

Fireworks? No, those were pedestrian compared to what Reen experienced. It was as if the soft, gentle light of love had illuminated her entire being, radiating from her hair, her fingertips, her very core.

This, THIS, is the kiss she'd been waiting for her entire life.

The audible, unwelcome gasp emanating from the Kissing Police had Reen's and Drake's eyes popping open at the same time, commanding their attention.

"Professor Slattery, stop that at once!" Looking like a diminutive octogenarian dictator, Mildred marched over to the booth. "I expected more decorum from you, of all people! And Maureen Malone," she gave Reen the stink eye while waving a reprimanding finger, "shame on you, young lady! That's twice you disobeyed the rules."

Suitably chastened, Drake and Reen separated. With her gaze still locked on his, Reen spotted something she wasn't ready for. Without a doubt, the look in Drake's eyes was the *Holy cow, Reen's the one, the woman of my dreams!* look she'd yearned to see coming from Hud Griffin for so long.

Worse yet, she felt darned sure Drake must be observing the same look across her face.

As Mildred continued her harangue, Drake and Reen fully parted, with him taking two steps back and Reen retreating to the back of the small kissing booth. He looked as awestruck as she felt.

Drake's kiss acted like a key, unlocking the secret Reen had kept fully hidden even from her own conscious mind. The long concealed truth just exposed was one she'd continually rejected. Now her truth, her secret, reverberated until she feared everyone in the room might hear it.

Drake! It was Drake. It's always been Drake. He's the one.

In that moment, Reen's gaze slid once again to Saffron. It broke her heart to witness the shattered, accusatory look of betrayal on her cousin's face. And Reen couldn't blame her one bit.

Transferring her gaze back to Drake, Reen saw that he, too, had caught Saffron's heartbreaking expression.

"Oh no...this is terrible," Reen muttered, half covering her mouth with her fingertips. "Awful. Oh Drake..."

"Reen..." His voice was soft as he reached for her hand and she pulled it away.

"No...please." A rush of tears threatened to spill as she considered what had just happened. What had she done? First her blithe, unthinking actions had hurt Monica, and now Saffron. On top of that, she'd now lost Drake's friendship because things could never be the same between them after that epic kiss. Never, with a capital N.

Reen never meant to hurt anyone, not Drake, or Saffron, or even Monica who didn't even make the bottom of her list of favorite people. But what she'd meant to do and what actually happened were completely at odds. She'd been selfish and irresponsible, having fun while thinking only of her own gratification.

With Drake still there, his concerned gaze locked on her, Reen focused on him. "I need to go. I have to get out of here."

"Let me take you home," he offered, clasping her arm. "We need to talk."

"No." She yanked her arm away as if she'd been burned. "Please, just leave me alone. You need to get back to your date, Drake. Back to Saffron. Remember?"

Drake's eyes widened with realization. "Saffron..." He'd said the name as if he'd forgotten she was even there. With one last longing look at Reen, he turned, making the slow walk toward his date—who looked like she wanted to be anywhere but there. Reen echoed that sentiment. She had no doubt Drake didn't relish having to speak to Saffron after glimpsing her crestfallen appearance.

Determined not to start bawling in front of everyone at the Fling, Reen took a deep breath, retrieved her cane from the corner of the booth and hobble-clumped her way through the sizeable crowd, heading for the restroom as Sabrina came to the booth for her shift. Sabrina called after Reen but Maureen didn't stop or look back. She had very little time before the waterworks broke and she cried her eyes out.

Chapter Ten

~<>~

IN THE RESTROOM, Reen held back the impending onslaught of tears by alternating with deep breathing and splashing her face with cold water. She talked herself into being relatively calm and collected. With her pale complexion prone to blotchy patches of red when she cried, she didn't want anyone seeing that mess and worrying about her.

Since it was difficult for her to drive because of the damned boot and her aching tailbone, Laila and her husband had picked Reen up for the Fling. When she exited the restroom, ready to leave, her sister and Zak were still in the midst of all the activity. Laila manned the bakery prize table while it grew closer to the time of the drawing, and Zak worked his Sumerian Fitness Classes prize table. Everyone who'd purchased chances to win prizes was excited for the end of the evening drawings.

There was no way in hell Reen would spoil Laila and Zak's evening by asking them to leave the festivities early to take her home.

She was about to call a cab when she remembered her brother, Gard, had a late shift at the firehouse. When she saw him walking toward the exit, Reen snagged him by the arm, asking if he'd mind dropping her off at home since it was on the way. Everyone bought her excuse that she was leaving early because she'd overdone it by standing too long and sitting on hard surfaces because she forgot to bring her donut pillow. She told them she had a wonderful time but needed to get home so she could rest.

Gard paused on the way out to talk to their brother, Nevan. Reen dug out her all-you-can-eat crab dinner ticket from her tote bag, handing it to Nevan, telling him to use it or find someone who could. She'd just finished speaking when her eyes nearly popped out of her head as she spotted Hud walking toward her from one direction while Drake approached from another.

No. Just no.

She absolutely, positively didn't have it in her to talk to either of them after what happened at the kissing booth. Reen had to get out of there, pronto.

"Gard, could we leave now, please?" she'd asked her brother, tugging on his arm as he and Nevan spoke. "I'm sorry but I'm in too much pain to stand any longer. I don't want to cry in front of anyone." She hated using such a self-pitying excuse but lacked a better idea.

As she'd expected, Gard was happy to cooperate, whisking her out of the community center and to his vehicle.

~<>~

Finally, safely ensconced in Bekka House without another soul in sight, Reen wallowed in a whopper of an ugly cry as she peeled off her dress, yanked on a sweatshirt, and a pair of leggings with one leg cut off at the knee to accommodate her boot.

Each time she stopped the hiccupping sobs long enough to take a deep breath, she recalled the melancholy images of Monica and Saffron and a fresh flood of tears commenced.

How could she ever expunge the memory of Drake's kiss from her thoughts? The way he'd looked at her...how he made her heart dance.

Groaning aloud, she plopped down on the family room sofa. Forgetting about her fractured bottom, she'd dropped to the seat so fast, shards of pain shot through her tailbone, eliciting a brief howl of agony.

"Good! That's exactly what I deserve!" Ever faithful, Hazelnut was immediately at her side, howling in sympathetic harmony.

Incessantly babbling to herself, Reen turned on the TV, which did little to help. While there were usually never enough romance movies playing to satisfy her, several were on tonight, all of them sad, tragic, poignant tales of lost love.

Between fits of crying, Reen removed her Frankenstein boot, setting it atop the coffee table before her. One by one she ripped at the Valentine stickers with their mocking little messages of true love and adoration.

"You're my heart's desire," she read aloud before ripping the annoying sticker off. "My heart belongs to you." *Rip.* "True love forever." *Rip.* "To my one and only." *Rip.* "Be mine for all time." *Rip.* "Love you to the moon and back." *Rip.*

Rip, rip, rip, rip...

The puffy plastic stickers came off without too much trouble but the flat paper stickers stripped off in pieces. Digging under the paper with her fingernails and tearing the little bits of paper was both therapeutic and frustrating.

Within thirty minutes she'd lost interest in the boot, ignoring the sticky stuff she couldn't remove. Standing Frankie upright on the table, she reviewed her de-stickering job.

"It sucks. Just like everything else I did today."

Strapping the boot back on, Reen limped to the kitchen, rifling through cupboards, the refrigerator, and the freezer, hoping to find something to help soothe her nerves, knowing her chances were slim since she and Laila had overhauled the kitchen at Bekka House during their diet, replacing their favorites with healthy, reduced-calorie alternatives.

She remembered the all-you-can-eat Dungeness crab dinner she'd passed up at the Fling. Glancing at her heartwish ring, Reen snorted a laugh. "The way things are going I may as well just use my wish to magically transport the crab feast to me here."

Her twisted smile morphed into a puckered frown. "I don't deserve to indulge in a delicious crab feast. Inconsiderate people who carelessly ruin other people's lives aren't worthy of butter-drenched Dungeness crab."

Reen continued her search for anti-health food, sniveling, whimpering, and chattering indecipherably as she rummaged through bags, boxes, jars and cans. Her heart beat faster and fresh tears of gratitude sprouted when she pulled out a jar of—

"Nutella! Oh be still my heart!"

Her hopes were dashed when she unscrewed the lid only to find dark powder instead of lustrous, silky, chocolatey hazelnut goodness. Her shoulders slumped once she remembered she'd washed out the empty economy-sized jar about a year ago after digging around the insides with a butter knife to scrape up the last tantalizing vestiges of the chocolate-nut spread—and then she'd filled the jar with unsweetened cocoa powder.

"How fitting." Her lip curled into a sneer at the cruel discovery. "That's exactly what you deserve, Maureen Malone. A mouthful of bitter, sugarless cocoa."

Her life had turned upside down after her fiancé died, with Reen turning to copious amounts of food for comfort, resulting in a significant weight gain and bad food habits she had a difficult time breaking. Compulsive emotion-driven overeating had presented numerous problems, aside from her rapidly expanding waist.

She was so proud of herself for tackling her issues and controlling her fixation on food. She'd even reached the point where she'd become a weight loss counselor, offering guidance to others striving to lose weight. Becoming a popular counselor at the Tuned by Turner weight loss center gave her shriveled self-confidence a much-needed boost.

And now?

"I'm so ashamed," she confided to Hazelnut. "Haven't I learned anything? What's happened to my self-control? I know better than to turn to food for comfort. Seriously, Hazel, what the hell's wrong with me?" She pounded the kitchen counter as her vision blurred with a fresh round of self-pitying tears.

As always, her loving dog commiserated with her, doing her best to soothe Reen's chaotic emotions.

Seizing the jar filled with cocoa powder, Reen glared at it with such intensity she half expected the plastic to melt in her hands.

"The lack of Nutella is a sign," she decided aloud, squatting next to Hazelnut and wrapping her in a hug. "A sign that after all I've been through with rigid dieting, weight loss and maintenance, I need to find better ways to cope with my problems than feeding my fat face."

Feeling more lost than she had in a long time, Reen got to her feet, snatched a paper towel, and wiped her eyes and nose.

"That's it. No more crying." Through her volunteering experience she'd learned there was nothing as healing as reaching out to help someone else. "Nevan," she muttered, going to the cupboards and pulling out baking supplies and sheet pans, along with Laila's recipe book.

Her brother was having a tough time with the renovations for his burned out, smoke-damaged Nevan's Irish Pub. Their mother told Reen, "It's been one step forward and two steps back. Nevan's never been one to complain, so things must be especially discouraging if he opened up to me about it."

That was sad. Nevan was such a good guy, always ready and willing to help others. He'd always been a hard worker and didn't deserve to go through this.

Since Nevan was a fan of all things ginger, Reen hoped it might cheer him up if she stopped by tomorrow with a box of homemade gingery goodies.

"Who doesn't feel better with cookies and scones?" Reen asked Hazelnut as she got busy making Laila's recipes for spicy triple ginger cookies, and her bestselling ginger scones, both of them low-sugar and gluten-free. "Nobody, that's who."

Thinking about Nevan's considerable problems had Reen focusing on her heartwish ring. She held her hand out, watching the stone glisten in the kitchen's overhead lights. She still hadn't a clue about what she was supposed to wish for.

"Fine. I don't deserve a wish anyway."

She spent half the night baking. Her sister's recipes were so foolproof even an idiot in the kitchen like Reen could produce batches of guaranteed deliciousness as long as she followed Laila's detailed instructions.

She caught a sense of why Laila loved baking so much. It definitely helped Reen stop her sniveling and leave her pity party behind.

~<>~

The night flew by without Reen getting much sleep. At least she had a feeling of accomplishment by putting someone else's needs before hers. The cookies and scones turned out perfect. It was after nine in the morning when she turned her phone on again, spotting one voicemail and text message after another. It seemed everyone from her mother, to Hud and Drake, to Sabrina and Annalise, to Delaney and Laila—everyone—all of them, wanted to talk to her. The women were curious about what happened with Hud at the kissing booth. Apparently, he must have said something positive about Reen to his sisters afterwards.

"Great. Just great." Her head ached as she closed her eyes and groaned. "What's that saying, Hazelnut? *Be careful what you wish for*," she finished, answering her own question.

As she scrolled through messages she found Hud's text, asking if she wanted to get together for coffee at the café this morning so they could talk. "Talk? About what, Hud? Making Monica cry?" A growl clawed its way up and out of Reen's throat.

"Nope, sorry, no way Hudson." She remembered Sabrina telling her last night that her brother was leaving town today for a week to work on a renovation project in Rainspring Grove at one of the wineries.

Handy and mechanically inclined like Hud and Gard, Nevan was doing much of the pub's repair and restoration himself. What he hadn't counted on was the extent of damage caused by smoke, as well as charring of many of the structural wood beams. The historic brick building needed far more work than he'd originally estimated. Fortunately, Hud was a great help to Nevan, insisting on performing much of the work throughout the three-story building at half the price he would normally charge.

Glancing again at the time, Reen said, "Hopefully Hud's left town by now." With him gone, Reen felt safe paying a visit to Nevan to deliver her baked goods and lend him an ear. The pub was closed to the public so she didn't have to worry about any chance meetings.

Drake's voicemail message—all four of them—insisted they needed to talk about what happened last night. "Ha! Absolutely, positively not!"

The voicemail that broke her heart was from Saffron:

"How could you, Maureen? I bared my heart to you. I trusted you. I believed you when you said you wanted to help me win Drake. Yeah, right." Humorless laughter followed. "I saw the look of love you and Drake exchanged when you kissed. No one could miss it. It was unmistakable, even from across the room. He could barely even look me in the eye after that."

Reen dragged in a breath, expelling it in a pained sigh. Listening to Saffron's words was more painful than her broken bones. The tortured tone of her voice spilled over with hurt and betrayal.

"Tell me, Maureen," Saffron's voicemail continued, "did you two have fun laughing about me behind my back? *Project Drake?* Oh my God, I'm such a fool, mortified that I confessed my innermost feelings to you. Furious with myself for believing you honestly cared. Why, Maureen? Why? To get back at me for our differences in the past? Well congratulations..." The last of Saffron's raw message was garbled because she was crying.

Until hearing that melancholy message, Reen assumed there was no water left in her body because she'd cried it all out. Not so. Tears surged freely down her cheeks.

Unfortunately, the healing glow from all her baking last night had worn off.

She was close with all her sisters but she and Laila shared a special bond. Reen yearned to call her, opening up about everything that happened. She needed advice, sympathy, wise guidance.

"But I gave my word to Saffron," she told Hazelnut, who'd rested her head on Reen's knee, looking up at her with unconditional love, which only had Reen whimpering more.

"I promised I wouldn't tell my sisters about our conversation and what Saffron confided." As her dog's head tilted left and right, she pet her, thankful for having an attentive listener by her side.

"I've already made a huge mess of things. I'm not about to make the situation even worse by blabbing to Laila." This is one time Reen doubted Laila would understand, or have much sympathy for Saffron. They'd disliked each other for years, the same way it had been for Reen and Saffron until their heartfelt discussion yesterday.

Reen had a whole new respect for Saffron since their talk. She discovered she genuinely liked her cousin and wanted to know her better. She looked forward to them becoming good friends one day.

Breathing a monumental sigh, Reen could only imagine what Saffron thought of her now. How could they possibly salvage their newborn, fragile friendship after last night? Reen closed her eyes, trying to picture the two of them sitting down to talk as Reen apologized profusely for her actions. All she could envision was Saffron pushing Reen off a high ledge, or into the deep end of a pool, or out of a plane without a parachute.

If Reen told Laila what happened, her helpful, protective sister would probably take it upon herself to fix things by contacting Saffron to tell her it somehow wasn't Reen's fault. That would only provide Saffron with another well-deserved strike against Reen for breaking her word.

"But I really need to talk to someone about this, Hazelnut. I need solid advice about where to go from here. I can't do it by myself. Not now." She bent to wrap her arms around the dog, gently hugging her. "Not when my overtaxed brain feels like a big blob of scrambled eggs floating around inside my head."

She got up from the couch, straightened the family room, and picked up the umpteen used tissues she'd haphazardly tossed on the floor during her marathon crying jag. At least it was all contained to just one room. She'd crashed there after finishing her baking, sleeping on and off between bouts of blubbering.

In the midst of cleaning it dawned on her that today was Sunday. Drake wouldn't be at work and his kids wouldn't be at school. They'd be at home, a short drive from Bekka House.

She suspected Drake would come knocking on her door before long.

"Oh no. No, no, no, no." She covered her face with her hands. "Talking to Drake is the last thing I could cope with today."

Zipping to the bathroom as fast as she could hobble, Reen brushed her teeth, slapped water on her face, and combed her haphazard hair. She pulled on a clean sweater and jeans, pausing at the mirror before heading out.

Grimacing as she focused on her puffy, blotchy-red face, she griped, "I look like an alien." Swallowed by the bloat caused by her endless crying, her eyes looked miniscule. "A tiny-eyed alien with a big Rudolph nose." Briefly considering a makeup intervention, she realized her swollen features were beyond simple fixing and left the bathroom.

Gathering her purse and donut pillow, she stuffed them into her flowerchild tote bag. After adding the covered plastic boxes containing the ginger cookies and scones she'd baked for Nevan, she grabbed her cane and was on her way, hoping to make a clean getaway without running into Drake.

She welcomed the chance to talk to her brother and hear how his pub restoration was going. Hopefully it would help him to have a good listener, while reminding Reen that hers weren't the only problems worth consideration.

Chapter Eleven

~<>~

SAFELY ON THE road without a Drake sighting, Reen breathed a monolithic sigh of relief. While on her feet baking for hours had heightened her ankle and tailbone soreness, the time she'd spent in the kitchen gave her an opportunity to do some serious thinking. She'd already come to some important decisions.

Before leaving the house, she texted her mom to let her know she was under the weather and wouldn't be joining them for Sunday brunch. Today her family, except for Nevan who rarely took a break from his renovation project, was going to a popular Taiwanese dumpling house in Wisdom Harbor. Reen had looked forward to trying the new restaurant but suspected her blotchy, tiny-eyed alien face would instigate too much attention, inviting questions Reen wasn't prepared to address.

She parked downtown, feeling her spirits lift because of the sunny morning. Since the weather was so cooperative, she took a stroll along Ocean Charm Boulevard to help clear her mind. On the way to visit Ruthie Brone at String Me Along, Reen took a turn, heading for the dock to watch the sea lions jostling for position, cuddling, napping, barking and acting like a silly, loveable pack of dogs. If that didn't make her smile, nothing would.

Ten minutes later, a more relaxed Reen headed for the yarn shop. She wanted to deliver the cute blanket she'd made for Shannie, Ruthie's great-granddaughter. The little girl was no longer in her room at the hospital when Reen stopped by the other day. She prayed it was because of good news rather than bad.

Walking with her cane past the storefronts, she filled her lungs with clean, fresh ocean air. One of the many things she loved about living in the Pacific Northwest was the mild winter weather, except for those fluke Chicago-like days with cold, snow and ice, exactly like the one responsible for her slipping and falling on her big old gluteus maximus. Oregon winters usually provided soft rainfalls with gentle winds, resulting in lush foliage the rest of the year.

Today was one of those Pacific Northwest winter gems, a mid-February day offering blue skies, not a drop of rain in the forecast for the next few days, and moderate temps in the upper sixties. The walk helped her sort through the multitude of issues scratching at her mind.

Rather than walk past Griffin's Café, Reen crossed the road to walk on the other side of the street. She wasn't in the mood for lighthearted chitchat, or ready to bump in to anyone she knew. She couldn't keep dodging people forever but a day or two to clear her head would help.

The yarn shop was busy as always, with shoppers taking advantage of the last weekend of the Valentine's Day sale. As she hobbled in with the cumbersome Frankie on one leg and cane in hand, Reen spotted Ruthie hobbling toward her with her own cane, and a wide, welcoming smile on her crinkled face. She walked with a pronounced limp today and was more hunched over than usual. Only someone who knew Ruthie well could tell she was suffering, not that she ever said anything, but by the effectively concealed pain in her eyes.

Reen didn't know how old Ruthie was but since some of her great-grandchildren were young adults, she assumed she had to be at least eighty. Her thinning hair reminded Reen of the coily yarn hair she'd created for Ava's and Shannie's matching princess hats. Forever wearing her favorite rosy shade of lipstick, Ruthie rouged her cheeks with what looked like matching blush. Her eyebrows were penciled a good half-inch above her natural brows, giving her a perpetually surprised look.

She was one of Reen's all-time favorite people.

"There's my favorite knitter!" Ruthie greeted her, throwing an arm across Reen's shoulder and planting a kiss on her cheek. Reen resisted wiping off the colorful imprint of the lip-smack until she was out of Ruthie's sight.

"How's your arthritis?" Reen said at the same instant Ruthie asked, "How are those broken bones doing?" They laughed together, with Reen answering first. "I'm coming along fine. I couldn't help notice you're limping more today. Are you having a rough time?"

"Oh...I'm okay. This darned rheumatoid arthritis gets the better of me somedays but," she gave a dismissive wave, "you don't have to worry about me. I'm as strong as a horse." It was a phrase Reen heard Ruthie use multiple times.

A quick glance at Ruthie's twisted, gnarled fingers signaled the woman must be in great discomfort, but she never complained and always had a ready smile.

"I do wish I could still knit and crochet," Ruthie admitted, catching Reen's brief glance at her hands. "I miss that. I've tried but, believe me, a kindergartener could create a scarf that looks far better than anything these crooked old hands can produce. But you know what?" Her expression lit with a smile.

"What?" Reen asked, returning Ruthie's infectious grin.

"God never gives us more than we can handle." Ruthie added a confirming nod. "Of course," her frail elbow nudged Reen in the ribs, "sometimes I think the big guy upstairs might get overworked and make a few miscalculations." Her self-mocking laughter had a youthful ring to it. Again she waved a hand. "Aw, don't listen to me. I'm a very fortunate old woman. God has blessed me many times over and I have no reason to complain."

Reen was struck by the realization that Ruthie, with her crippled body and loss of the ability to enjoy the pastime she delighted in most, had many more reasons to feel sorry for herself than Reen did. Ruth Brone was a shining example of the kind of woman Reen hoped to become one day.

"You're a very special woman, Ruthie."

"You're just saying that so I'll let you know about upcoming sales before they're announced," she teased Reen.

"Darn it." Snapping her fingers, Reen tsked. "You caught on to my dastardly plan." Catching the strange, inquisitive expression across Ruthie's face, Reen asked, "What's wrong, do I have spinach in my teeth or something?"

"I was just wondering what happened to your lovely face, dear. An allergic reaction perhaps? Are you feeling all right?"

"Oh!" Reen completely forgot about her alien face. She should have worn one of her brimmed hats to shadow the consequences of her crying. "Yes, that's it, Ruthie, allergies," Reen lied. "Must have been something I ate last night at the Fling. I tried lots of different food samples. Blew up like a balloon." She puffed out her cheeks. *Whew!* Now she had the perfect excuse to give Nevan later when he noticed her blotchy mess of a face.

"Food allergies can be the devil. Glad you're okay. So what are you here for today?"

"Just popping in to say hello before I go to see Nevan at the pub."

"That poor boy works too hard." Ruthie shook her head. "Such a pity about the fire. I pray for him all the time. Let him know that, will you?"

"I will, Ruthie, thanks. He'll appreciate that. How's Shannie doing? I stopped by the hospital the other day to deliver another batch of hats to the kids and didn't see her there. They said she'd been sent home. I hope...is everything okay?"

"She's not doing very well, God bless her." Her eyes brimming with tears, she patted Reen's hand. "After her long battle with the leukemia it finally seemed she was headed for remission, but..." Ruthie's deep, shuddering breath ended on a desolate sigh.

Reen remembered the day Shannie tentatively approached her while Reen was on one of her volunteer shifts at the hospital. Looking up at Reen with her luminous brown eyes and a hopeful smile, the bald little girl asked if Reen could add some yarn hair to the next hat she'd made for her. "That way I can pretend I still have hair," she'd said with a smile devoid of self-pity. The girl's shy question broke Reen's heart. It was something she'd never forget, and it set her on a course to do the same for the rest of the children who'd lost their hair due to their cancer treatments.

"Do you remember little Ava Mitchell?" Ruthie asked.

"Shannon's best friend at the hospital." Reen nodded. "Sure. Ava's the one who asked me to make identical princess hats so she and Shannie could be twins. It was the first time I created the tightly coiled yarn hair. It turned out perfectly, thanks to your excellent instructions."

"Each time my grandson, Allan, brought me to visit Shannon at the hospital I'd watch her and Ava parading around like little fashion models wearing one of the lovely hats you made for them. Oh how she and Shannie loved playing princesses together."

"I'm happy to hear that. I'm sure it's really helpful for Shannie to have such a close friend there in the cancer ward. They always seem to be having a good time when I see them together in the activity area. How's Ava doing?"

Before Ruthie responded, Reen saw the unthinkable answer in the woman's eyes. She knew. And it bore a hole right through the center of her heart. "No..." was all Reen could say. "Oh...no..."

"Four days ago." Bobbing her head slowly, Ruthie continued, "It was after Ava lost her battle that Shannie's condition worsened. She was shattered, Reen, destroyed, to lose her friend. It...it was too much for her to understand and cope with."

"I can't even begin to imagine," Reen said honestly.

"Allan and his sweet wife, Linda, learned yesterday that the size of Shannon's tumors have increased considerably. She's at home now to be with her family before..." Ruthie's chin quivered. It was obvious she couldn't go on.

Heartbroken, Reen wanted to bury her head in her hands and sob. How could life be so cruel and unfair? Shannon was just beginning her life. And Ava? Reen still couldn't believe the child was gone. The only thing keeping Reen's grief-stricken emotions at bay was her need to be strong and supportive for Ruthie.

Gingerly, Reen took both of the old woman's hands, careful not to give Ruth's fingers more than a featherlight squeeze. "I wish, from the bottom of my heart that things were different. I'll keep Shannon in my prayers. Is there anything I can do for you and your family?"

Ruthie shook her head. "No, dear." Her smile was sad and sweet. "But thank you for your prayers, Shannie can never have too many of those. None of us will ever forget how instrumental you were in helping to keep our girl's spirits up during her illness. God bless you, Maureen."

"Me?" Taken aback, Reen touched her chest. "I didn't do anything."

"Ah, but you did. Last Christmas when things looked so bleak for Shannon, all of us Brones together were wearing your whimsical matching hats and sweaters—there was Santa and Mrs. Claus, the elves, and the reindeer. You brought such joy into a sad, frightening time for our family. It was impossible not to smile and laugh as we looked at each other in our festive, funny outfits. They say laughter is the best medicine and you kept us all, including Shannon, in the brightest of spirits with your thoughtful gifts."

Reen's eyes grew misty. "It means so much to hear something I did helped bring joy to your family at Christmas."

"You're on my great-granddaughter's list of favorite people. She loves your creations. The hats, sweaters, socks and scarves you've made for her are the talk of her school friends. They've helped Shannon feel less like an oddity after she lost her hair. It broke my heart when I heard the bullies at school were calling her baldy." Ruthie winced at the memory. "I'm delighted that my knitting and crochet student has surpassed her teacher. I'm so proud of you, Reen."

She gave Reen a kiss on her other cheek, most certainly leaving her with a matched set of bright rose lip prints. Reen didn't mind a bit.

"I'm a long way from surpassing you, Ruthie, but I appreciate your kind words. Before taking your class I could barely create three inches of adequate knitting without stabbing myself multiple times. My work was like a before picture." Reen laughed. "You taught me everything I know. It's because of you that I can make those hats and outfits for the children at the hospital."

Reen dug into her cavernous tote bag. "Which reminds me, could you give this to Shannon? It's a blanket with little cocker spaniels like her puppy, Lulu, all over it. It's small enough for her to snuggle under when she's reading or watching TV."

Accepting the wrapped package, Ruthie said, "She'll be thrilled to have a blanket featuring Lulu. Now she has a hat, socks, sweater and blanket, all featuring her puppy. Thank you, dear."

"My pleasure. I'll make a matching throw pillow for her bed next." The puppy blanket and pillow set seemed so trivial now. Maureen was determined to infuse the little pillow with love, hope, and all the adorable puppy cuteness she could manage, hoping it would help Shannon to smile, at least for a while, during the dark days ahead.

"You need to start charging for your work." Ruthie shook a gnarled finger at her. "You could have made a small fortune with all the yarn gifts you've given away. Lots of people can knit but few have your imagination and ingenuity."

"Thank you." She patted Ruthie's hand. "Maybe one day I'll set up a little business for myself. I'd be in seventh heaven doing what I love most for a fulltime job. But I can't accept payment for the creations I make for sick children. The delighted looks on their faces is so rewarding, Ruthie. It's all the payment I need."

Each time she saw a child's eyes go wide with joy when they received an item she'd designed especially for them, she had to keep herself from tearing up. They were so appreciative to have something personal and fun to take their minds off their illness, even for a little while. Taking money would taint that precious moment of happiness the act of giving provided.

"Don't forget about my offer for you to teach classes here at the store on a part-time basis, Maureen. You can make your own hours. I'm betting anyone familiar with your whimsical creations would flock to your classes. I-I may have to take time away from the store after..." her chin quivered again, "and I could use the help then."

The thought of Ruthie losing her great-granddaughter was crushing. "I've never taught anyone so I'm not sure if I'd make a good teacher, but you can always count on my help, Ruthie. Call whenever you need me and I'll be here. My love of spending time here at String Me Along is second only to my love of chocolate."

"I suspected as much." Ruthie chuckled. "How's that handsome young professor friend of yours doing? Shannie told me he and his twins delivered the hats you made after you fell."

"Drake's fine. It was a wonderful surprise to learn they'd delivered my hats to the kids."

"Nice boy, that Professor Slattery. Anyone can tell you're the apple of his eye."

Reen's face must have telegraphed her surprise because Ruthie gave a devilish chuckle.

"I can tell by the way he looks at you when he thinks you're not looking." She offered a conspirator's wink. "You know what?"

Reen couldn't help chuckling herself at Ruthie's attempt at matchmaking. "What?"

"I think he's the apple of your eye too."

Little did Ruthie know how spot on she was.

"Drake and I are just good friends," Reen said.

"Mmm-hmm, don't worry, I get it." Ruthie made a locking gesture at her lips. Apparently there was no fooling her.

Looking at the time on her phone, Reen said, "I have to run, Ruthie. See you soon, okay?"

"Of course. You take care of that allergy. I hope it clears up soon."

"Allergy?" She'd nearly forgotten about her alien face until Ruthie rested her cool hands on Reen's hot cheeks. "Oh, thanks, me too. Promise you'll take care of yourself. Don't push yourself too much, okay? You've worked hard for so many years, you've earned the right to kick back and relax."

They hugged each other and Reen was off to visit her brother.

Stepping outside the store, she was glad to be near her car because her ankle was throbbing. Her brain churned a mile a minute. It hadn't stopped since the Fling. After Ruthie's mention of him, Drake was foremost in her thoughts again—just behind the heartbreaking news of Shannie's decline, and the loss of poor little Ava.

Once out of sight of the yarn shop, she dug in her bag for a mirror and tissue, chuckling when she verified the bold pink lip imprints on each cheek. She wiped them off, talking to herself while unlocking her car door. After propping the donut pillow in place, she maneuvered into the car.

"Stop being all willy-nilly about Drake. Take a stand and act like a mature adult." Her shoulders sagged. Easier said than done. It was only right that she give Drake up...but she wondered...could she really be that self-sacrificing? That saintly? With the loving look across Drake's face after he'd kissed her at the forefront of Reen's mind, it took only a moment for the answer to become crystal clear.

"No. I can't. I won't. I'll have a talk with him, letting him know I have feelings for him." She frowned at the thought. "Feelings? No, too wishy-washy. I need to be more direct. I'll tell Drake I'm in love with him."

Then she'd sit down with Saffron, doing her best to explain and make amends, doing whatever it took to salvage their fragile friendship and regain Saffron's trust. She'd wait a couple days before contacting either of them, which should give her ample time to prepare what she wanted to say.

Before pulling into traffic Reen crossed her fingers. "If I'm a very lucky girl, I might, maybe, possibly, *please, please, please*, come out of this mess intact—with the man I love, as well as a repaired, solid relationship with my cousin."

Focusing on her renewed sense of hope and happy possibilities, she headed for her brother's pub.

Chapter Twelve

~<>~

"YOU'VE MADE tremendous progress since last week," Drake said, taking a long look around the inside of the building Nevan owned. The entire first floor had been relegated to his popular pub, although it no longer looked like an eating and drinking establishment. Drake wasn't well-versed in architecture or the building trades but it didn't take an expert to recognize top quality workmanship in everything Nevan and Hud had done.

"You think so?" Nevan scratched his head as his uncertain gaze followed Drake's. "Everywhere I look all I see is something else that has to be done."

Drake knew it must be daunting for Nevan when he studied the cavernous space that used to house polished dark wood booths, tables and chairs, and an ornately carved bar. Nevan had taken great pains to create an atmosphere similar to the generations-old family-oriented pubs he'd visited on his trips to Ireland. To have most of that destroyed must be damn tough.

"What you've accomplished is nothing short of amazing. What do you do, eat, drink and sleep here while you're working?"

"Pretty much," Nevan admitted. "This place is my life, you know? Some men have a wife and kids they're devoted to. I have a pub." Smiling along with Nevan, Drake nodded in acknowledgement.

"Seamus Malone, my grandfather, the Irish one on my father's side, used to say, 'You'll never plow a field by turning it over in your mind.' It's a good saying to remember when I'm feeling sorry for myself. So instead of whining and complaining about the sorry burned-out state of my pub, I'm plowing my field." Nevan's grin expanded. "My mother recently reminded me of the saying. I'm glad she did."

"Astrid's a wise woman," Drake noted.

"She's worried I'm not taking care of myself." Nevan thumbed toward the large cooler on the floor a few feet away. "That's filled with sandwiches, meatloaf, mashed potatoes—all my favorites...or so she thinks." Nevan shook his head, chuckling in quiet amusement.

"I thought you liked your mom's cooking. I've liked everything Astrid's made," Drake said honestly.

"I do." One shoulder hiked in a shrug. "As long as she sticks to her traditional Norwegian cooking or basic American dishes. I like most of her baking too. It's when she ventures beyond the norm into, say, Italian, Mexican, or Asian dishes, that we Malone siblings live in fear of a dinner invitation."

Drake winced. "That bad?"

"You have no idea." With a slow nod, Nevan said, "Never lie to your Norwegian mother, telling her you like something she makes because you don't want to hurt her feelings. Inside that chest," he pointed again, "sits frozen containers of Mom's Norwegian-style chili con carne made with her homemade smoked lamb sausage and rice instead of beans. Her Lillehammer-style lasagna made with Norwegian brown cheese in place of mozzarella and codfish balls instead of ground beef." Nevan cringed. "And lest we forget, there's Mom's infamous pickled herring mac and cheese."

"Whoa..." Drake couldn't help shuddering. Twice. "You're serious?"

"Unfortunately." Nevan's candid shudder mirrored Drake's. "Lesson learned."

"Can't say I've ever had—or want to have—the, um, pleasure of trying any of those meals." Unpuckering his sour expression, Drake picked up the large package leaning against the rough wood bench he sat on, setting it on his knees.

Slapping his hand against the package, he said, "Wish I could have brought you something as good as one of your Irish pork pies, the ones everyone in town's been craving since the fire. But since I'm lucky if I can scramble an egg, and toast a slice of bread without setting off the smoke alarm, I got you this instead."

"Presents? It's not my birthday." He took the package when Drake held it out to him, giving Drake a curious look as he felt its heft. "This weighs a ton. What is it, an andiron?" Nevan shimmied the jute twine from the brown paper wrapping, tearing into the paper.

"Careful," Drake cautioned.

"Ahh, something fragile, hmm?" Nevan took more care with the unwrapping. "Oh..." he said with a lengthy pause following the word. "It's a book." He glanced up at Drake. "A very *big* book." His lip curved into a semi-smile. "Well...thanks, Professor."

"Please," Drake patted the air, "try to contain your enthusiasm." Noticing the smirk Nevan tried in vain to hide, Drake promised, "This book is right up your alley. Go ahead," he gestured, "turn it over.

Nevan did, his eyes widening as he trailed a fingertip across the title of the thick coffee table book. "*A Pictorial History of Irish Pubs in Ireland and America*," he read aloud. His captivated expression told Drake he'd made the right choice.

Flipping through the pages, Nevan made one enthusiastic comment after another. "Wow! Very cool! These photos and illustrations are priceless. Drake, the book is perfect. I've been searching for something like this forever. Where did you find it?"

"At a thrift store, believe it or not."

"You?" Nevan's eyebrows hiked in amusement. "Don't tell me you caught the thrift-shopping bug from my mother and sisters."

"Hardly." Drake made a distinct denial gesture with his hands. "Reen saw an ad online for a new thrift store in Wisdom Harbor, near the university. She was still in the cast unable to drive when the shop had their grand opening. She pleaded with me to take her so she could spend untold hours burrowing through other people's discarded junk."

"I'll never understand how she can do that." Nevan shook his head. "I'd rather stick pins in my eyes."

"Tell me about it. But," Drake shrugged, "I was worried Reen might transform into that big-eyed thrift-shopper mode of hers and go crawling over some unstable mound of decrepit debris and hurt herself while searching for buried treasure, so I stayed in the store to keep an eye on her."

"Good call," Nevan said, "because I can see her doing exactly that."

"I had to yank her out of a few risky situations where overanxious rummagers were rifling through teetering stacks of junk and Reen, trying to balance with her crutches and rapidly filling tote bag, got shoved and almost fell face first into the jumble of rubbish. And then," Drake held his hands palms up in uncertainty, "rather than thank me, I was harshly reprimanded because she claimed I was responsible for making her lose the object she was reaching for to another shopper."

"Oh my God." As Nevan held his forehead, his genuine laughter was infectious. "I can *so* picture Reen doing that."

"Yeah, I've learned never to get between your sister and an object of her desire." Drake rolled his eyes skyward. "So I made myself scarce and let her fend for herself. Trying to get away from all the crazy shoppers elbowing each other in their quest to find a rare gem for pocket change, I moved to a corner of the store that looked relatively quiet and sane. It was the book area. Seems not many shoppers were bibliophiles like me so—"

"Bibli-what?"

"Bibliophile," Drake repeated. "Somebody who loves or collects books."

"Oh!" Nevan gave an *aha* nod. "Yeah, that's you to a T, Professor."

His tongue-in-cheek comment didn't bother Drake in the least. He knew it was all in fun. He'd been teased often enough for being an unapologetic egghead, or teacher nerd. The unofficial titles were accurate. Sure he had a cellphone, an iPad, and a Kindle but he readily admitted to being more old school, believing nothing could beat sitting for hours with his nose stuck in a good old fashioned print book—preferably nonfiction.

"Anyway, there were stacks of books," Drake motioned four feet up from the floor, "piled precariously, like they were about to topple if someone breathed too hard. I spotted this one," he tapped the Irish pub book, "obscured beneath a stack of travel books behind all the other stacks. You know what that indicated?"

"No," Nevan shook his head from side to side, "but I'm sure you're going to tell me."

"It meant I had to brave those stacks, getting myself encrusted with ancient dirt, dust and creeping crud, as I got on my hands and knees—*oh yes I did*—so I could extract this book," Drake slapped the book's cover, "for my pal, Nevan Malone." He waved a finger toward Nevan. "Once I'd wrested the tome from its decaying confines, I got to my feet, setting the book down for a nanosecond while I cleaned spiderwebs off my sport coat and—"

"You wore a sport coat to the thrift store?" Nevan offered a disbelieving look.

"Well yeah," Drake gave an affirmative nod, "I had a class to teach after I dropped Reen home. Here's—"

"Bet you were the only guy in there wearing a sport coat." Nevan snickered.

"I was the only guy in there, period." Drake grinned at him. "So, like I said, I set the book down for an instant and this single-minded woman barges through the crowd of shoppers," he gestured widely as he spoke, "and places her hands on *my* book." Drake jumped to his feet, recreating the scene.

"Quickly staking my claim by slapping my hand over the book," he clapped his hand on the book in Nevan's lap, "I informed her in no uncertain terms the book was mine. I'm the one," he clapped his chest twice, "who had singlehandedly braved the substantial trials and tribulations of mining the volume from the bottom of a musty, decaying stack of books. Do you know what this presumptuous woman had the audacity to say to me?"

"That possession is nine-tenths of the law?" Nevan guessed.

His forefinger jutting, Drake announced, "Exactly! Refusing to relinquish my find, the woman then had the nerve to tell me the book was hers unless I could prove what I said—that I had unearthed it, only setting it down momentarily while I de-spiderwebbed myself." Now pacing back and forth, Drake narrowed an eye. "Oh, Nevan, she looked so smug."

"So what did you do to get the book, a smash and grab?"

"I was this close to doing just that." Drake held his thumb and forefinger an inch apart. Standing in place and shaking off the tension of reliving the incident, he continued, "That's when your sister came to my rescue."

"Maureen?" Nevan looked dubious. "Don't tell me she bashed the book thief with one of her crutches. Reenie can get mighty testy when it comes to thrift shop discoveries."

"Nope. She used brains over brawn. You would have been proud of her." Drake's smile stretched wide as he remembered what occurred next.

"Hopping over with her crutches, her already full tote bag hanging from one shoulder, she says to the insistent woman, 'Oh you're so lucky to have such a thoughtful husband.' Looking at Reen like she was crazy, the woman, still clutching my book, frowned and said, 'He's not my husband.' I had to wonder myself what your sister was up to."

"With Maureen, one can never tell." Nevan fell into lighthearted laughter.

Back to setting the scene as he spoke, Drake said, "Your very clever sister says to the thieving woman, 'Oh, sorry, it's just that when I saw that man back there on his hands and knees digging that book out of the pile, and then saw you standing here with your hands on it, I naturally assumed you're the person he got the book for.'"

"Boomshakalaka!" Nevan held his hand high and Drake clapped it.

"Brilliant, huh?"

Nevan nodded in agreement.

"I wish you could have seen your sister in action, Nev. She provided just the proof the potential book thief needed. With an abundance of dramatic huffing and puffing, the nearly successful book bandit begrudgingly released the book. So it's thanks to my herculean efforts," Drake took a bow, "combined with your sister's shrewd thinking that you now hold in your possession this rare gem, your very own copy of *A Pictorial History of Irish Pubs in Ireland and America*. You're welcome." He made a sweeping bow.

Nevan applauded. "I appreciate your exceptional, heroic efforts, Drake. Looks like I owe you big time."

"After what I endured, you'll be in my debt the rest of your life," Drake teased.

"While I can never fully repay you for your ordeal, I can certainly make a dent in my debt to you." A mischievous grin spread across Nevan's face. Rising from his seat, he placed the heavy book down and walked a few feet. "Starting with this." He picked up the food-stuffed cooler and brought it to Drake, setting it at his feet.

"This, my heroic friend, is your hard-earned reward. Enjoy it with your children, and anyone else daring enough to sample my mother's creative cookery."

With his eye on the cooler, a swell of laughter burst out of Drake. "I can't possibly accept such a valued treasure." He gave Nevan a hearty pat on the back. "You're much too good a friend for me to take advantage of you. Your mom's right, you need to keep up your strength. So, while I appreciate your noble gesture, I insist you keep it all for yourself." He slid the cooler in Nevan's direction.

"Well if you change your mind, Drake, you know where you can find this."

"At the homeless shelter?"

Nevan's hand flew to his chest in mock horror. "I could never do that to our homeless population." After tossing Drake a wink, he asked, "So tell me, after making this great find," he patted his book, "has your opinion about thrift store shopping changed?"

Holding his thumb and finger an inch apart, Drake said, "Maybe this much." After pausing for effect, he added, "In all seriousness, yeah, I suppose I'd check out another few sales if they had books. It gave me kind of a rush to find a gem like this."

"No doubt." Nevan turned the book this way and that. "It looks almost brand new. Must have cost a fortune when it was new—and, boom, there it is." He pointed to the price printed inside the book jacket. "Eighty-five bucks. Whew! This is going to be great inspiration when I get to the design part of this overwhelming renovation project." Paging through the book Nevan brought several stunning photos to Drake's attention as they spoke, making Drake especially glad he'd waded through stacks of creeping crud and fought to get that book.

"On the way back to Bekka House, I got an earful of 'I told you so' from Reen as she jabbered endlessly about the countless merits of thrift-shopping." He chuckled remembering her unbridled enthusiasm that day. She called him over each time she made another discovery, proudly showing him some trinket as if she'd unearthed a stash of gold ingots. The two hours they spent at the shop got her mind off her ankle and tailbone, giving her a welcome respite from the pain.

"Yup," Nevan huffed a laugh, "that's Maureen all right."

"Your sister also had me stop at a neighborhood garage sale on the way home. I was like a zombie by the time I dropped her off and headed for the university.

"Well I appreciate all you went through," Nevan said, continuing to search through the book. "I'm already getting plenty of new ideas for the makeover, which will probably end up costing me a small fortune." His expression morphed into a mock frown. "I don't know if I should thank you or curse you, Slattery."

They spent a few moments flipping pages, admiring the artistry and detail of the various pubs, with Nevan pointing out features he especially liked.

"It seems you and my sister spend a lot of time together," Nevan said to him out of the blue, catching Drake off guard.

"Well...we're neighbors...and good friends," Drake said with as much indifference as possible, sensing it probably wasn't what his expression transmitted to Nevan. Reen had been on his mind almost constantly since that killer of a kiss they shared. They needed to talk but she'd been avoiding him.

"I saw it, you know," Nevan said, not looking up from the book as he continued looking through it.

"Saw what?" Drake felt his face heat. He knew damn well what Reen's brother meant.

"That lip-lock you and Maureen had at the kissing booth, you know, the kiss that sent Mildred Fophamer into a conniption fit." Nevan's lip curled into a wicked half-smile.

"Oh...that..." Drake cleared his throat.

"What's going on, Professor?"

Drake's huff of laughter held no humor. "Not a damn thing. So..." he said, curious about where this was heading, "are you planning to go into protective brother mode on me, Nev?"

"Naw, I was just curious." Nevan gave an offhand shrug. "I've known you had the hots for my sister for a long while."

Drake cursed beneath his breath. "So eloquently put." He expelled a noisy sigh. "That obvious?"

"Let's just say you're not as slick as you might have hoped." Nevan offered a playful smile.

"In other words, everybody knows." Drake had no doubt his cheeks were red. Nevan's head bobbed slowly in confirmation. "Aw hell."

"What's important is whether or not Reen feels the same way about you."

"Apparently not." Frustration shrouded Drake's mood. "She's been dodging me ever since the Fling. Won't answer my calls or texts. She won't even answer the door."

"I can picture Maureen sneaking around peeking through curtains and blinds to see if it's you on her doorstep." Nevan laughed. "She's not as slick as she likes to think she is either. At least that's one thing you have in common."

"The two of us need to sit down and talk because—"

Nevan's phone rang. When he saw the display he said, "Sorry, I need to take this. I won't be long." Drake nodded and paged through the book while Nevan answered the call.

"Hey, Red, everything still on schedule? Great, I'll be at the Portland airport tomorrow morning at eleven." He laughed at something Red said. "Oh yeah, no doubt. You'll be ready to crash after that fifteen hour flight from Dublin. Okay, buddy, see you tomorrow. Don't worry, I won't put you to work until the day after tomorrow." Chuckling again, he ended the call.

"You remember my cousin Red Devington?" he asked Drake.

"Saffron's brother? Sure. I've met him a couple times. Nice guy." His own mention of Saffron made him uncomfortable. It was a sticky situation. The last thing he wanted to do was hurt her but it seemed that's exactly what happened after he and Reen shared that kiss.

When he finally got her to agree to speak with him earlier this morning, his apology for his and Reen's unintentionally red-hot kiss topped his list of matters to discuss. Embarrassing his date and hurting her feelings was the last thing he'd intended. Telling Saffron he loved Reen—before he'd even had a chance to tell Reen herself, since she'd been avoiding him—was tough but he owed at least that much to Saffron. He hoped he'd succeeded in letting her down as gently as possible.

"Red's coming back from Ireland, lucky dog. Have you ever been there?"

"No, but it's on my bucket list."

"You have to go one day, Drake. It's well worth that godawful long flight. Red's leaving his investment banking job and opening a flower shop here in my building, right next door to the pub. He was never happy working for his father, Walter. Especially since Uncle Walter's the CEO and founder of Wisdom Harbor Bank," Nevan explained.

"That's quite a career change for your cousin."

"Yeah, pretty major. It's something Red's always wanted to do. He's got a green thumb and probably knows more about flowers than I do about beer and whiskey. He's calling it Cupid Central, or Cupid's Headquarters, something like that."

"Cupid..." Drake searched his memory. "Isn't that the name of his cat?"

"Yup," Nevan offered through lighthearted laughter.

"Well," returning Nevan's smile, Drake shrugged, "if that's Red's dream, then I say good for him. Any idea how long before the building's ready for your pub and his flower shop to open?"

"Your guess is as good as mine." Nevan's sigh conveyed his frustration. "Fingers crossed it'll be within the next six months. Until then, Red will be helping me with the renovation. He's really handy and knows his stuff."

"Will he continue working at the bank in the meantime?"

"No. He's already left. Red never wanted to be in that line of work, much to Uncle Walter's displeasure and disappointment. From the time Red was a kid, my uncle had been grooming him to follow in his footsteps."

"Just his son? What about Saffron and Lorraine?"

Nevan imparted a fleeting chuckle. "Walter Devington is old school, complete with old-fashioned sexist attitudes. He's trained his daughters to, *A*, marry well," Nevan counted on his fingers, "*B*, go into teaching, or *C*, become a nurse. Not a doctor, mind you, but a nurse."

Drake winced at the stereotyping. "Does your Aunt Colleen work?"

"Work?" There was that short-lived chuckle again. "Aunt Colleen's my late father Sean Malone's sister." Drake nodded in acknowledgement. "My dad was a hardworking, down to earth regular guy who came from a modest working class background—just like his sister. Unlike Dad, I doubt Aunt Colleen has ever worked a day in her life. She was smart enough to follow the number one criterion on my uncle's short list for women—to marry well."

"Which is why the Devington family resides in a mansion up on Beauregard Hill," Drake surmised.

"You got it. Oh but poor Aunt Colleen." Nevan manufactured a pout. "Beauregard Hill's a major step down from living in a

Manhattan high rise for her, you know, but as she's prone to say, quite often, she's used to suffering."

Drake laughed into his fist.

"I'm doing my aunt an injustice by telling you she doesn't work. On the contrary, her *job*," Nevan used air quotes, "is hosting dinners for dignitaries, attending charity events, smiling adoringly at her overbearing husband when he's giving speeches in public, and spending the rest of her time sitting in judgment of everyone else...especially her children. Colleen's a real throwback, just like her husband."

"Helps me understand those snide remarks I've heard from Reen and your sisters about the Devington side of the family."

"I'm telling you, Drake, it's a wonder Red, Saffron and Lorraine aren't hooked up to continuous antidepressant IV drips. I would be if I was in their shoes. Did I mention my aunt and uncle kicked Red out of the house?"

"What? No." Drake couldn't believe it. "Why?"

"Two reasons." Setting the massive book on the floor, Nevan crossed his arms over his chest. "First because he left his respectable banking position to come to work in the building owned by a member of the lowly working-class side of the family." Thumbing himself, Nevan joked, "That would be me in case you didn't guess. Being a florist is an unrefined job that's an utter embarrassment to the Devingtons."

"Wow. Second reason?"

Drake watched Nevan's head bob with a slow rhythm in response.

"Because Red came out to them before he left for his trip to Ireland."

"They kicked him out of the family home because he told them he's gay?"

"Uh-huh."

"Holy...I've heard of things like that happening in families but..." Drake shook his head in disbelief. "Did you know he was gay before he told you?"

"Not really but I'd always suspected he might be. Want to guess how my aunt and uncle gave Red the news that he's no longer welcome in their home?"

A variety of different scenarios flitted past Drake's mind. "I'm guessing it wasn't in a good way."

"Get this—they gave Red the heave-ho via text message," Nevan's eyebrow lifted, "while he was in Ireland on his two-week vacation."

"Ouch." Drake clapped his forehead in disbelief. "That's harsh. What's Red going to do? I've got room at the house if he needs a place to stay."

"Thanks, he'll be glad to hear you offered, but he'll be living here on the first floor at the far end of the building," Nevan motioned with his hand, "where there's no damage from the fire or smoke. It's the area where I have my apartment. He'll be just down the hall. Saffron and Lorraine had the unenviable job of gathering all their brother's belongings and having them delivered here via moving van."

"Unbelievable." Drake remembered Saffron telling him she and Red were close. This was just one more difficult thing for her to deal with, making Drake feel even worse. He liked Saffron very much, just not in the way she'd hoped he might. "Well at least we know Red will be a lot happier now."

"I think so. We'll see how happy Buster is about it."

"Your dog doesn't like Red?"

Nevan smiled. "Along with Red comes his cat, Cupid, and you know how Buster feels about cats."

"Ahh, that's right, he's not a fan. Where's Buster today anyway?"

"I leave him in the apartment when I'm out here working so he doesn't find his way into trouble and get hurt with all the tools, lumber and equipment strewn around. Last thing he needs is to step on a nail."

"Good idea."

"Soooo...speaking of Red reminds me of his sister, Saffron, which reminds me of you, which reminds me of Reen, which—"

Breathing a sigh, Drake held up his hand like a crossing guard. "Okay, okay, I get it. You want to know what happened."

Sitting back in his seat, Nevan crossed an ankle over his knee. "While I'm not in the habit of caring much one way or the other about people's love lives, I'll admit this whole shebang," he twirled his fingers, "has snagged my interest. After all, this involves not only my sister and my cousin, but also one of my best friends." He offered Drake a genuine smile. "How about a beer? It's a good way to loosen lips."

"Doesn't that sink ships?" Drake winked at him. "Sure, just one. I'm driving and have to pick up the kids from a friend's house so I don't want more than that."

"Gotcha." Nevan got to his feet. "You still prefer something malty to IPA?"

"If you have it," Drake told him.

"Hey." Spreading his arms wide, Nevan grinned. "What sort of pub owner would I be if I didn't have a variety of brews?" He walked to the other side of the room and Drake heard the sound or a refrigerator opening and closing.

"I wasn't sure if your refrigeration was still working or not."

"One side was knocked out but the small fridge is still operating. So, what the hell happened? Reen's been incommunicado. Nobody's seen or talked to her, other than Mom, who got a text from Maureen letting her know she was under the weather and wouldn't be joining the family for Sunday brunch."

Astrid might know about this? Good grief, that's all Drake needed to hear.

"It's all my fault," Drake began. "I should have stepped up to the plate..." His head tilted to the side. "Is that the right expression? You know how bad I am with football jargon."

Nevan snickered. "Yeah, and it's baseball, but go on."

"I should have told your sister a long time ago how I feel about her. I—"

"Which is?"

Drake growled out a breath. This wasn't going to be easy. "I'm in love with her. Have been for a long time, since she helped me and the kids after my ex left, and I was trying to be there for her after Bob died in that fall from the roof. He was my best friend." Drake gave a defenseless shrug. "I owed it to him to watch after his fiancée, but I never had any intention of falling in love with her. *That* I didn't owe to Bob."

"You say that like you feel guilty."

Drake's hand combed upwards through the back of his hair. "I do...I did...I don't know, Nev. Logically I know there's no reason to feel guilty. It's not like I was eyeing Maureen before he died, or when I was still married. We were all good friends together. Well, all of us except for Janet, who had little in common with any of us."

"Party girl," Nevan said.

"How stupid was I not to realize that before we got married and had kids?"

"You can't blame yourself, man. But you're right, you should have told Reen how you feel about her long before this."

"I'd planned to last year. It was the night I took her to the opera." Recalling the awkward incident made Drake wince, the same way he did each time it came to mind. "A friend gave me a pair of tickets he couldn't use. I knew Reen wasn't an opera fan but I thought the two of us getting dressed up for dinner and the opera might set the mood."

"I remember my mom and sisters gabbing about you and Reen going to the opera last year."

"She looked gorgeous, all decked out in this long greenish blue dress. She looked good enough to—" Remembering who he was talking to, Drake clamped his mouth shut.

"Uh...yeah, we don't want to go there." Nevan laughed. "So what happened? You chicken out?"

"Not exactly. I'd rehearsed what to say and do over and over again inside my head. I'd planned to tell her at her doorstep when I brought her home...after I kissed her."

"Are you saying you kissed and ran?" Nevan asked and Drake suspected he found this all rather amusing.

"The kiss never happened. Just before our lips touched, I told Reen she was beautiful. That's when your sister ducked."

"No!" Nevan's posture stiffened as he sat straight up. "Tell me she didn't." All signs of amusement were gone. "Holy shit, Drake, that's like the worst thing she could have done."

"Nope, not quite." Drake closed his eyes in a long blink. "Maureen finished by reminding me we're just friends and it would be weird for us to kiss. Like kissing one of her brothers." He gave Nevan a look he was sure telegraphed his frustration peppered with a hefty dose of long-lasting humiliation.

"Oh damn!" Nevan looked as pained as the recollection made Drake feel. "Damn, Drake."

"Uh-huh. Now you know why I never said anything to her after that."

"Well hell yeah." He looked like he'd eaten a lemon. "Wow, I had no idea."

"It took me a whole year to get up the nerve to try again."

"At the Fling," Nevan deduced.

"Up until the last minute I wasn't sure if I'd give her a peck on the cheek or a real kiss. I decided, *what the hell*, and went for the whole enchilada."

"And this time Reen definitely didn't duck."

"It was mindboggling, Nev. I saw it in her eyes. She felt the same way I did. I'm sure of it. And then, *bam*, she's hobbling out of there as fast as she could on that boot of hers."

"Because of Saffron? Red told me he heard a little about what had happened from her."

"Yeah. As soon as the kiss ended, Reen's gaze flew to where Saffron was standing and she reminded me I needed to go be with my date. When I looked across the room at Saffron I saw pain written all over her face. It killed me, Nev, made me feel like an imbecile. I like Saffron and wouldn't hurt her for the world, but I did. Terribly. I was too damn stupid to realize she had a thing for me."

"What are you going to do? Have you talked to Saffron yet?"

"Yeah, this morning. I tried talking to her last night but all she wanted was for me to take her home. She didn't say two words to me, just sniffled a lot, and then started crying when I took her to her door. She couldn't escape me fast enough. She finally answered my call this morning and I went to see her so we could iron things out."

"How'd it go?"

"Okay, I think. It was a good talk. Saffron was great about it. Very understanding. She said she realizes things like this happen. She's suspected for a long time that Reen and I had feelings for each other. But she said she specifically asked Reen about it and Reen denied it." Drake let out a lengthy sigh. "So now I don't know what the hell is going on with her, your sister, I mean. I can't believe I misread the look in her eyes after we kissed, Nevan."

"Tough situation."

"I don't expect you to offer any advice, especially since this has to do with your sister."

"While affairs of the heart aren't my strong suit, that doesn't mean I don't have any advice." Nevan's grin stretched across his face. "You're a good guy, Drake. You and my sister could have a good thing together if you both got your stubborn heads on straight."

Drake smirked. "Well, that was direct."

"I don't beat around the bush. First of all, are you positive you love Reen? Have you compared her and Saffron so you have an idea of who's better wife material for you?"

"Wife material?" Drake's laughter came out sounding nervous. "We're getting ahead of ourselves a little, aren't we?"

"Oh," Nevan answered, "so you're saying you're not thinking about marrying my sister, is that right?"

"Well, no, I didn't say that, I just—"

"You just want to have good time with Maureen for a while before going on to someone else when you get tired of her...like, maybe Saffron?"

Drake's back straightened. "Damn it, Nevan, come on, you know that's not what I meant. Of course I want to marry Reen. But it might be a good idea for her to admit she loves me too before we can even get close to that point."

"True. So, compare them for me. Saffron and Reen. Good points and bad."

"I don't have to do that because—"

"I'm waiting." Nevan crossed his arms over his chest, giving Drake a no-nonsense look.

"What I think about Maureen, huh? Sure, okay." Drake breathed a hefty sigh born of frustration. "I'll start by telling you she's a great kisser, and I thoroughly enjoyed that sizzling kiss we shared at the Fling." He closed his eyes in a long blink before continuing. "And that takes care of her good points."

"Whoa," Nevan winced, "that's pretty harsh, Professor."

"What can I say? Your sister drives me crazy. She's stubborn and pigheaded, which shouldn't surprise you. She lacks common sense and speaks and acts before thinking. She has little interest in learning anything outside her comfort zone. She's like a hoarder, obsessed with filling her house with other people's castoffs and endless tubs of yarn. Sometimes I think she has yarn for brains. She's got the self-confidence of a peanut. Is that enough for you? Because, believe me, I could go on."

"That's plenty. I get the picture. What about Saffron?"

"She's beautiful, that's a given. Unlike Reen, Saffron's sane and levelheaded. She's well-educated and intelligent. We share many of the same interests. She's kindhearted, and I think she'd be a great mom. Any man would be lucky to have her in his life. Seriously, I'd be crazy if I didn't want to marry Saffron, Nevan. She's perfect for me. Not a single negative comes to mind."

"Really? That's how you feel about them both?"

"That's exactly how I feel," Drake answered. "Which tells you I must be out of my mind because this logical list of plusses and minuses, all this rational thinking, doesn't mean a damn thing when you're crazy in love with someone. And that someone is Reen. You know how much doubt I have that your sister is the woman for me?" Nevan shook his head back and forth. "Zero." Drake made the sign with his thumb and finger. "And you know all those negatives I mentioned?"

"Yeah, that was quite a list," Nevan said with a chuckle.

"Right. Well each of those negatives are my positives too. Because I love your beautiful sister for exactly who she is. I wouldn't change a thing about her. I love her for every single one of her kooky seemingly brainless traits." Drake laughed. "I want to spend the rest of my life trying to figure her out...to understand how that haphazard brain of hers works. If I'm lucky, maybe I'll learn something about how to be a better human being, because there's no better person I know than your sister."

"I won't argue with you there. Maureen's got a big heart."

"I've seen her knitting until her fingers bleed so she can finish all her special projects for those sick kids in the hospital. She always puts everyone else before herself. I'm no fan of thrift store shopping but she's exactly like one of those rare, priceless gems your sisters and mom are always trying to discover. Reen's a diamond...just like the one I hope to put on her finger."

"Just as I thought," Nevan said with a slow nod. "You've got it bad, Professor. I have no doubt you love my sister. And you, my friend," he clapped Drake's back, "have my blessing."

Chapter Thirteen

~<>~

REEN PULLED into a parking space near the back entrance of Nevan's pub. A mirror check was necessary because she'd succumbed to a new avalanche of tears while she drove. The dire news about little Shannon, as well as what happened to Ava, was devastating. The mirror on the sun visor told Reen her blotchy face was beyond a simple touchup so she closed the mirror with a resigned sigh.

Unsure if Nevan was there, she wrote a note to leave with her baked goods in case she missed him. Tucking the note beneath the ribbon she'd used on the wrapping paper, Reen gathered her stuff, eager for the day she no longer had to cart around butt pillows and wear the cumbersome Frankenstein boot, and made her way to the door.

The door was propped open, probably to help with the still acrid smell of smoke permeating much of the wood inside. About to enter, she heard voices. Popping her head inside she glimpsed the backs of two men sitting together—Nevan and Drake.

Her heart stuttered at the sight of Drake. If she wasn't encumbered by Frankie, she might run to him, fall into his lap, throw her arms around him, and kiss him until she couldn't breathe.

Quietly setting the package of cookies and scones on a pile of stacked lumber, she turned to leave when she heard her name.

"What I think about Maureen, huh? Sure, okay." Reen could hear Drake sigh. "I'll start by telling you she's a great kisser, and I thoroughly enjoyed that sizzling kiss we shared at the Fling."

Clapping her hands over her mouth, Reen suppressed the giggle of joy threatening to burst forth. Oh how sweet! Drake was about to confide in Nevan that he loved her!

"And that takes care of her good points."

Reen frowned, sure she'd misheard Drake.

"Whoa, that's pretty harsh, Professor," she heard her brother comment.

"What can I say? Your sister drives me crazy. She's stubborn and pigheaded, which shouldn't surprise you. She lacks common sense and speaks and acts before thinking..."

As Reen listened to Drake's endless list of gripes about her, her jaw dangled in disbelief. Her heart stuttered again, for entirely different reasons.

Sucking in a deep breath, she heard her brother ask Drake, "What about Saffron?"

"She's beautiful, that's a given..."

When he finished with, "Seriously, I'd be crazy if I didn't want to marry Saffron, Nevan. She's perfect for me. Not a single negative comes to mind," Reen's knees buckled and she clutched the doorjamb. Everything hurt. It even hurt to breathe.

"Really? That's how you feel about them both?" her brother asked Drake.

"That's exactly how I feel."

"No... oh God, please no," Reen whispered through a matching set of fat tears. Backing away from the door, she cursed under her breath for the inability to run back to her car. Fresh tears obstructed her view as she clumped along. Once she got in her car she sat for a few minutes, taking deep breaths and talking herself into a calmer state before she started driving.

"I was so sure," she whispered as she drove back to Bekka House. "So sure..."

Once she got home she undressed, tossed her jeans and sweater on the bed, and threw on the same comfy sweatshirt and pair of leggings she'd worn last night during her cry-a-thon. The same wrinkled, dirty clothes she'd baked in and had slept in, that were now heaped in a corner on her bedroom floor.

Grumbling aloud, using curse words she'd never uttered before, she went into the kitchen in search of something 'medicinal' to take the edge off her emotional pain.

After scouring the kitchen last night, she knew chances of finding anything satisfying were slim. One hand snatched a paper towel to wipe across her teary, snotty face, while the other hand crawled into the deepest recesses of the corner cabinet, searching until her fingers landed on a crinkly bag. It had the feel and sound of something delectably crunchy and unhealthy. Hurriedly excavating the bag, her tiny alien eyes went as wide as they could when she saw it was a bag of Cheetos.

"Ha, fool me once," she said, remembering her disheartening non-Nutella discovery the night before. She removed the clip from the already opened bag to make sure it was the real deal inside before she got excited. It was. A nearly full bag.

"Cheetos!" she cried, holding the bag to her chest and crying harder. They were probably old and stale but she didn't care.

She was acting immature. Senseless, rash, foolish, inane, ridiculous. Downright laughable. Why not? After all, isn't that exactly what Drake thought of her?

"So, Mr. Bulgy Brain, you think you can purposely make me fall in love with you, kiss me like you mean it, then say contemptible things about me to my own brother? Is that what you think?" She slammed the kitchen cabinet door, startling Hazelnut who scampered for cover in another room.

"You want to tell my brother how much you despise me and adore another woman, hmm? You fake, you phony, you deceitful son-of-a-bitch rat bastard punk-ass!" She followed that with another off-color rant, haphazardly stitching phrases together that probably didn't even belong together, but it felt good. The sheer dirty, crude sound of it all was deliciously satisfying.

"Here I am all alone," Reen's arms stretched wide as she tearfully yelled, "where no one but my dog can hear me if I feel like swearing a blue streak." With that, she belted out the F-word, something she never did. It was exhilarating! "Drake would hate it if he heard me swearing," she said, irritated that the mere mention of his name was like a pin prick to her festive F-word balloon. "Because he's refined, polished and distinguished...and I'm not. But I don't care because..." she engaged in a giant sniffle, "because Drake doesn't love me anyway."

As soon as her brain transcribed the thought into words, Reen's sniveling morphed into an instant flood of tears, prompting her to concoct another inventive string of F-related-words, which helped stem her sobs. A moment later, her shoulders slumped. "Drake doesn't love me," she repeated so softly it was barely audible. Soul-crushing pain permeated her entire being.

"Fine, I don't care. I'm perfectly happy spending the rest of my life alone, growing old and gray with only Hazelnut at my side." Another rush of tears spilled down her cheeks. "Hazel?" Silence. "Hazelnut, where are you?" Nothing. Reen's shoulders drooped further. "Old, gray and alone, without even my trusty dog at my side," she amended.

Continuing her ceaseless grumbling and declarations of mostly nonsensical curse words, Reen set the bag of Cheetos on the counter to go in search of more junk. All she found was a nearly empty pint of her sister Kady's vegan chickpea and cashew *nice cream* in the freezer.

"Chickpea cashew? Good grief, Maureen...have you really sunk that low? Yes, dammit. Yes I have."

She ate the fake ice cream first, missing the silky mouthfeel of real ice cream, which she hadn't eaten since she'd dieted. After scraping the last vestiges of the quickly thawing ice cream substitute from the carton and licking every icky, beany remnant from the spoon, she began feeding her face with the Cheetos.

Cramming the last of the fatty, salty snack in her mouth she caught sight of the distinct orange coloration coating her fingers.

"Oh hell..." It had been so long since she'd eaten them, she forgot about Cheetos-fingers and how she'd learned to wear plastic gloves when eating them. The gluttonous way she'd been shoveling in mouthfuls of cheesy, crunchy goodness, she'd probably stained her lips too.

"So what? Who cares if a lonely old spinster has an orange mouth and fingers? No one. Not me. Certainly not Drake." She either engaged in a soul-deep sob, or a bleating goat had just entered the kitchen.

Panic zigzagged through her belly when she realized she'd finished anything worth snacking on. She certainly couldn't numb her mind on the refrigerator's contents—carrots, salad greens, or raw broccoli and cauliflower. She hadn't experienced a raging need for junky food like this in a long time and didn't like the power it had over her, making her feel like an addict in need of a drug fix.

Spying the bottles of Kahlua, Frangelico and Baileys in the corner of the kitchen counter brought a wistful smile to her lips. She headed for the sweet-flavored liqueurs, intent on drowning her strife with coffee liqueur, hazelnut liqueur, and whatever the heck the flavor of Baileys was.

Unfortunately, more than a smidgen of alcohol never sat well with her. Taking a wineglass from the cupboard, Reen poured a scant shot of each into the glass, drank it down, and smacked her lips.

She waited to see if it magically anesthetized her emotional pain. But all it did was make her stomach growl and cause some nausea.

Frustrated by her failure to soothe her emotional wounds with Cheetos, beany ice cream, or alcohol, Reen detected another round of sobbing welling up inside, ready to erupt like a volcano unless she could push it down by appeasing the demanding god of snotty bawling with copious amounts of—

"Chocolate!"

Remembering the big box of premium chocolates Saffron brought, she went to the cupboard where she'd stashed it. Before yanking the box from its confines, she frowned.

"No. How could I possibly justify selfishly using my cousin's thoughtful candy gift after what I did to her?"

She waited, counting to ten to keep herself from ripping into the chocolates.

"Oh the hell with it." Hazelnut finally reappeared, offering a soft bark, which Reen deciphered as her dog strongly encouraging her mistress to go forth and medicate with the chocolates without feeling guilty.

"Thank you, Hazelnut." Reen patted the dog before carrying the heart-shaped box to the family room, placing it front and center on the coffee table.

As her impatient dog sat close, singularly focused on the chocolates, ready to share in Reen's ill-deserved bounty, Reen sighed, giving Hazelnut a hug before rising from her seat.

"Sorry, Hazel, I love you too much to let you eat chocolate." She was proud of herself because, even in the midst of her ugly-cry-a-thon, she was a good, responsible, protective dog mommy. She gathered a few treats and toys for Hazelnut to enjoy while she prepared to stuff her own big fat chipmunk cheeks with unpardonably large amounts of chocolate.

It wasn't until Reen was nearly finished with the three-pound box of candy that she noted it was from Bunny's Chocolate Haven, the local chocolate shop owned by her and Laila's former employer, and arch nemesis, Bunny Turner.

Reen's eyes narrowed as she recalled Bunny, the mean, witchy woman who made her and Laila miserable when they worked as counselors at Tuned by Turner, Bunny's renowned, now defunct, weight loss center. After Bunny had caused Laila considerable strife, something inexplicable happened. Bony Bunny, who'd been about the same miniscule size as Monica Sharp, blew up like a balloon. It was the perfect comeuppance for a woman who was so nasty, unkind and insincere.

Reen remembered the night she and Drake were at Laila's place when Laila and former genie, Zak, were in dire trouble. They'd succeeded in conjuring the fearsome Inanna, an ancient Sumerian goddess, responsible for the spell that gave Bony Bunny Turner her well-deserved chunky comeuppance.

"Drake..." Reen whispered with a wistful smile, recalling with fondness how hard the two of them had worked together to save Zak and Laila. She'd suspected that Drake had feelings for her. If she'd only acted on it then, maybe they'd be happily together now.

With a heavy sigh, she gazed again at the heart-shaped box covered in lavender satin and tied with a purple grosgrain ribbon. Saffron had gone out of her way to choose a box of Reen's favorite type of chocolates, packaged in her favorite color.

And what had Reen done for her cousin in return? How had she thanked Saffron for trying to mend fences and make peace?

Pondering the response to that question had Reen sniveling and opening a second box of Kleenex because she'd already gone through the first.

"It's going to be okay, Saffron. He's all yours now. You're the woman Drake loves...n-not m-m-me." Her words came out wobbly as another torrent of tears engulfed her.

And so it went for the rest of the afternoon and into the evening, with ever faithful Hazelnut commiserating by accompanying Reen's wailing with her own tuneful howling.

So stuffed up she had to breathe through her mouth, Reen felt utterly defeated. "This just isn't working. I need someone I can confide in. Someone wise with sage advice. Someone I can depend on not to breathe a word of any of this to anyone else. Someone who—"

Half smiling, half weeping, she cried, "Of course!" picked up her phone and hit speed dial.

"M-m-mom?"

Chapter Fourteen

~<>~

REEN AND HER mother made a date to have a late breakfast. After hearing her daughter's tear-choked voice the night before, Astrid wanted to come right over but Reen asked her to wait. So much had happened, she needed some time alone to regroup. Fortunately, she wasn't scheduled to work at The Great Pretender until Tuesday.

Before Astrid arrived to pick her up, it took Reen forever to tidy the house, picking up haphazardly flung used tissues, and the sizeable collection of tiny brown pleated candy papers she'd tossed randomly during her tearful pity party.

Remembering her F-word barrage had her cringing. She'd tried convincing herself she'd been temporarily taken over by foul-mouthed aliens who believed she was one of their own when they spied her misshapen alien face.

Neither abundant cursing, syrupy liqueurs, nor any of the food she'd consumed helped to resolve her problems or make a dent in her demoralized disposition—which was no surprise at all because she knew better. She hoped a good long talk with her mom would help.

The one bright spot in her otherwise miserable night was when Reen woke briefly to the warm, spicy fragrance of her grandmother's *pepperkaker*. She knew from experience that meant the comforting spirit of her beloved late grandmother was near.

"Grandma Bekka..." the sleepy Reen acknowledged. "I wish you were here so I could talk to you."

Instantly, Bekka's heavily Norwegian accented voice whispered in Reen's ear, "I'm here, Reenie. You can talk to me anytime you need to. It's going to be all right, child. Have faith, little one."

Bekka, Astrid's mother, was one of three spirits who regularly visited Bekka House. The Malones weren't certain whether Grandma Bekka, her husband Jamie, and Varik's grandfather, Anders, were technically ghosts or angels. In any case, their presence was welcome and calming, which is why Reen thought of them as visiting rather than haunting.

Reen had scoffed at the stories of ghosts until she'd had her own unmistakable encounters. Since her grandmother's passing a few years ago, Reen and others in the house occasionally noticed the aroma of pepperkaker, Bekka's Norwegian ginger cookies, baking, without the oven being turned on. Sometimes there was also the faint, heaven-sent sound of Bekka's laughter tinkling throughout the house.

This time more than any other Reen hoped it was truly Grandma Bekka's positive message she'd heard, and not just her own wishful thinking.

Reen limped to the bathroom to get ready. The glimpse of her reflection was enough to frighten anyone. Her normally pale skin was a blotchy pink patchwork. The whites of her puffy, squinty eyes were now laced with vampire-red. Her unsightly appearance was offset by the seemingly indelible orangey ring circling her mouth.

After washing up, brushing her teeth, combing her hair and slathering on some industrial-strength blotch-begone Cheetos concealer, the improvement was negligible.

"There," she'd said, turning to Hazelnut after completing the makeup job she hoped would help normalize the remains of her ugly-cry face and snack attack. "What do you think? Better?"

The dog stared at Reen for a long moment before whimpering, ducking her head, and scurrying from the room. Reen broke into full laughter, which felt good after all that sinus-clogging crying. The mirror didn't lie, and neither did Hazelnut. Reen had troweled on enough foundation, concealer and powder to rival what morticians must do to make bloodless corpses look semi-alive.

That's how Reen felt this morning...semi-alive.

She hoped adding a slash of red lipstick and black eyeliner, neither of which she normally wore, would draw attention away from the hideousness. It didn't. The twin rounds of pink blush she added to her cheeks to help balance her jaw, chin and forehead blotches didn't fix things either. She still looked like hell—like a confused alien who was one third kabuki dancer, one third scary clown, and one third hooker.

If this were Halloween she'd win for best costume.

While working damage control on her face, she thought about the calls that came in last night. Two from Nevan and four from Drake. Both left voicemails telling Reen it was important they speak to her.

"Nope," she told her reflection, "I don't need a detailed word-for-word heart crushing account of how undesirable and unappealing I am, thank you very much."

When the doorbell rang, her eyes welled with tears. It would be a long while before her head's plumbing was operating normally again. Anything the least bit emotional made her nose burn and her eyes tear.

Leaning against the bathroom counter, Reen brushed away random specks of black from her cheeks which must have deposited there from using the out of date mascara and eyeliner that had been sitting in a drawer at Bekka House for who knows how long.

Apparently the eye makeup wasn't waterproof because the fresh crop of tears caused smeary raccoon eyes on top of everything else. To call her image scary would be too kind. Reen's head tilted as she gazed at herself. With the new addition of smeary black beneath her eyes, maybe she could claim she'd gone goth.

Shaking her head in defeat, she told her reflection, "Take a good look at yourself, Maureen Malone. No wonder Drake isn't attracted to you. No wonder he doesn't love you. You're not presentable enough to be a professor's wife, or the mother of his two adorable children."

The thought of Lilly and Kevin brought yet another batch of tears. She loved those kids. Being their stepmom would have been awesome. She guessed Saffron would have that honor now. Her cousin would make a fine parent, as well as a perfectly respectable professor's wife. Her chic mortician style would nicely complement Drake's tweed sport coats with the suede elbow patches.

The doorbell rang again, followed by knocking. Good grief, she'd been so enmeshed in her pity party she'd forgotten her mother was at the door.

"Be there in a minute, Mom!" she called out. Her mom had a key to Bekka House, as did everyone in their family, but Astrid avoided using it to maintain Reen's privacy while she was staying there. If she didn't get to the door and let her mother in soon, Astrid would be frantic, worrying something catastrophic had happened and she'd morph into full panicked-mom mode, which is the last thing Reen needed to cope with this morning.

Before heading for the door she put on a pair of enormous sunglasses she'd found in the back of another drawer. She hoped the oversized 1980s-era accessory would provide sufficient coverage.

A few minutes later, after pulling her mother into a sturdy hug, Reen loosened her grip and looped her arm through Astrid's, ushering her inside. "I'm really sorry to take you away from your weekly Coffee and Scones Crochet Circle this morning, Mom, but I—" She stopped abruptly, fearing she was about to cry again.

"It's okay, honey. Irma and Joselyn are both down with a nasty colds, so we called it off." Astrid smoothed back Reen's curls, which were a chaotic mess after Reen had run her Cheeto-y, chocolatey hands through her hair umpteen times while bawling. "What's wrong, sweetie? Everyone's worried about you because you haven't answered their calls or texts."

Plucking the oversized sunglasses from her daughter's face, Astrid's eyebrows pinched as she scrutinized Reen's extra-terrestrial visage.

"Oh dear..."

"I know." Reen nodded, fully aware her concealing efforts were a dismal failure. "I was up all night crying. The night before too. I tried fixing the results with makeup." She offered a diminutive shrug.

"I see..." Astrid studied her daughter's mottled face again. "Two straight nights of crying? My poor baby. What happened?" She went back to smoothing Reen's hair with her fingers. "Your hair feels greasy. Are you sick?"

"No. Yes. Well, not physically, anyway." She offered a humorless laugh while seizing the wool cloche hat from the table near the entrance and tugging it on her head. "I've made a terrible mess of things, Mom. I ended up hurting people I care about and I can't tell anyone about it because I gave my word to Saffron that I wouldn't," Reen babbled through tears.

"Your cousin?"

"Mmm-hmm. Then yesterday I received my well-deserved payback," she added, realizing the jarring sound of the sick moose call surrounding them was coming from her as she openly sobbed like a five-year-old. "But all my troubles pale next to the terrible news about Ruth Brone's great-granddaughter, Shannon, and her friend, little Ava Mitchell." Reen filled her mother in—as expected, the news made Astrid heartsick.

"I'm a terrible person, Mom. Selfish and self-centered. How can I feel sorry for myself when one child has lost her life, and another is quickly declining? I have no business having pity parties over anything as trivial as..." Her chin quivered as fresh tears gathered..

"Aw, shh, sweetie," Astrid held Reen close, patting her back. "Mama's here. Tell me all about it." Being comforted in her mother's arms was good medicine.

When Reen brushed away tears, her mother said her name in an odd voice.

"Maureen?" She took her daughter's hands, examining them. "Why are your fingers orange? And there's an orangey mustache above your lip. Were you finger painting or something?"

Even though full of angst, Reen couldn't help laughing. "I can't tell you here. I'm afraid someone might come over and I don't want to see anyone today. I just can't. Can we go out for breakfast somewhere?"

"Of course, honey. You want to go to Griffin's Café for your favorite? A Dutch baby pancake?"

Reen cringed at the thought of walking into the packed café looking the way she did. "That's the last place I want to go. I couldn't deal with all the questions."

"Sure...I understand. Did you have someplace in mind?"

Letting out the deep breath she'd sucked in, Reen said, "Tidal Wave Tavern."

"Really?" Holding her at arm's length now, Astrid winced. "On the outskirts of town? That place is so seedy. I thought you hated it."

"I do. That's why I want to go there," Reen explained. "It's the one place I can think of where no one we know will be on a Monday morning."

"You're probably right about that." Astrid chuckled. "Are they open this early?"

"They are. I checked online. They have a weekday morning special. Two pints of pilsner beer with a brat and egg sandwich on white toast, all for nine-ninety-eight." The aghast look across her mother's face had Reen laughing again.

Quickly composing herself, Astrid smiled. "Sounds so much better than the eggs benedict, Dutch baby pancakes, three-cheese omelets, chicken-apple sausage, and thick-sliced bacon Annalise serves for weekday breakfasts at the café." Her smile was wide and genuine. "If Tidal Wave Tavern is where you want to go, honey, then that's where we'll go." Astrid slipped Reen's camouflaging sunglasses back in place and tugged the brim of her hat down more before they headed out the door.

~<>~

"And so that's it. Now you know everything," Reen said, sipping from the world's worst coffee—even worse than Drake's—while sitting in a highbacked vinyl booth with sticky seats. She was thankful for the dark interior lighting so her kabuki-clown-hooker face was in the shadows. It also helped that she couldn't see what sort of gunk might be lurking around on the sticky seat. She'd probably have to throw away her butt pillow after this. Even the thin carpet seemed greasy. And the smell? The tavern was permeated with *eau de stale beer*.

Curling her lip in disdain, Reen groaned. "Thanks for agreeing to come here, Mom. I'm really sorry about this."

"Nonsense. Any time I get to spend with my daughter is quality time, regardless of the surroundings. It's really quite...charming." Astrid gave a nonchalant gesture, sipping her coffee with a near imperceptible shudder.

Tidal Wave Tavern was like a step back in time—maybe to the 1950s, which is how far back the nudie calendar hanging behind the bar dated. It was the sort of calendar you might see in the back of a car mechanic's shop.

The musty vibe of the place, with its walls full of rusty thumbtacks, tacked on ads, postcards, photos, and small pinup girl calendars, all curled from decades of age and shiny from the molecules of grease in the air, reminded Reen of a depressing film noir, one of those gloomy black and white movies where people sat at the bar drinking and crying in their beer. One of those films where women with slit-to-the-thigh skirts and cigarettes dangling from their lacquered lips wound themselves around men at the bar.

The 50s were probably the last time the booth backs and seats had been covered...or cleaned. This wasn't a place where high school or college kids would have hung out back then, unless they were members of a motorcycle gang.

"I won't say a word to anyone about what happened with Saffron," Astrid promised. "I completely understand your predicament and the importance of discretion."

"You were the only one I could call," Reen told her honestly.

"I'm surprised and brokenhearted for you regarding Drake, sweetheart."

"Thanks, Mom. This is one of those times when a girl needs her mom and no one else will do."

Astrid clasped Reen's hand. "That's just how I felt about your Grandma Bekka. I still miss my mother so much." Her eyes watered. "I'm glad you called me, Maureen. I'm always here for you. There's nothing you can't tell me."

Astrid absently moved the greasy pile of hash browns around on the plate with her fork while Reen did the same with hers. The odd-textured clump of scrambled eggs was obviously instant. The only thing remotely edible might have been the buttered toast, except for the neon-yellow non-butter substance topping it that had a peculiar taste and smell.

"I know what happened the last two days must be upsetting but I doubt it's as bad as you think."

Shaking her head in disagreement, Reen grumbled in response.

"It may take some time but once you and Saffron talk, she'll understand," her mom assured. "It's not like you set out to purposely sabotage her. And it's not your fault Drake ignored the *kissing police*," Astrid said, hanging air quotes around Millie's title. "I doubt you or Drake had that intimate kiss in mind when he stepped up to the booth. It just happened."

Reen thought about the unexpected kiss and its consequences throughout the night, coming to the same conclusion as her mom. "I think you're right. From what he said to Nevan about it, Drake was surprised the kiss was so good."

"Your sisters and I think Drake's been harboring feelings for you for a long time."

"I suspected the same." Reen's head bobbed slowly in accord. "I just didn't want to admit to it. I was content with us being platonic friends. Drake's a good man. I know he'd never purposely do something to hurt Saffron, or me. We just accidentally let ourselves get carried away at the kissing booth." Reen huffed a laugh. "Funny, here I thought it was true love, and to Drake it was nothing more than an unexpectedly good kiss with his hat-knitting neighbor."

"Do you think Drake knew anything about your talk with Saffron?"

"I'm not sure. And I don't know if Drake told Saffron how he feels about her yet."

"For all you know, Maureen, Drake may have thought of Saturday night as nothing more than a casual, friendly date with Saffron." Astrid offered a sympathetic smile. "Perhaps you misheard the conversation between Drake and Nevan."

"I appreciate you trying to play devil's advocate, Mom, but trust me, I heard everything loud and clear. My eyes might be swollen almost shut but my ears are fine." She smiled. "Now I know exactly what Drake thinks of me." Breathing a sigh, Reen offered a tired smile. "And how he feels about Saffron." Groaning, she rubbed her forehead.

"Ooh…maybe you don't want to do that, honey."

"Do what?"

"Rub your face like that. It's pushing around all that gunky makeup and your face is starting to look like an impressionist painting." Astrid covered her mouth and laughed. "I'm sorry. I don't mean to laugh, it's just..." She looked at Reen again, visibly swallowing another laugh.

Reen dug the mirror out of her tote, looked at herself and had to choose between crying or laughing. She chose the second.

"I should have cut some eye holes in a paper bag and pulled that over my head instead of this hat." She tugged it down further.

"I'm sure your face will look fine by tomorrow," Astrid comforted. "Do you think you should tell Drake how you feel about him? It might make a difference."

Reen went back to pushing the food around on her plate as she considered her mother's suggestion. "I never admitted my feelings for Drake to anyone, including myself, because I was afraid."

"Of what?"

"That I'd lose the wonderful relationship I've had with him and his children. We were almost like a family. I'd risk losing that if I'd told him how I feel. Things would have become awkward and uncomfortable. I had everything a woman could hope for in a good solid relationship—everything except for romance."

"And sex," Astrid reminded her, making Reen's eyes flash wide before she laughed.

"Mom!"

"What?" Gazing at Reen over the rim of her mug, Astrid shrugged. "It's true, isn't it?"

"Well yes but—"

"But nothing." Astrid floofed Reen's objections away with a wave of her hand.

"I was also afraid I couldn't measure up to Drake."

"What?" Astrid's features twisted. "Now you're being just plain silly."

"Not according to what Drake told Nevan." She gave her mother a hard glance when Astrid opened her mouth to speak again. "I know you're going to say I shouldn't belittle myself, but I'm not. I'm just being factual, Mom. I know I'm intelligent but I'm nowhere near as brainy as Saffron or Drake."

"So? What does that have to do with anything? Since when do people need to have matching IQs to be a couple? I'd like to see Drake try to knit one of those complicated character hats you make for the kids in the hospital. You have your strong points, Maureen, and Drake has his, just as you both have your weak points. That's how healthy relationships work."

"Yes but don't you see? Saffron really is perfect for him. They have so much in common, opera, classic literature, theater, and those godawful boring documentary films and lectures they both adore." Reen rolled her eyes skyward. "All I have in common with Drake is..."

She thought for a long moment, unable to come up with any shared interests except one. "Humor," she finally said. "We enjoy making each other laugh." Lifting her hands, she let them slap against the tabletop in frustration. "Big deal. Horsing around together isn't enough of a foundation for a relationship."

"No lulls in the conversation, plenty of laughter, enjoying activities and eating out together, and his children love you. That's more than many couples ever have together. Just because you don't have multiple degrees or like listening to dry as sand lectures about...what was that last one he took you to?"

Her lip curling in disdain, Reen said, "You mean 'Marx, Nietzsche and Hegel's Logic of Essence'? Or perhaps you're thinking of the university lecture we attended two months ago, 'World Economic History before the Industrial Revolution'?"

Struggling to keep a straight face, her mother quickly lost the battle. "You actually sat through those?"

"Yup." Reen nodded slowly as she remembered. "Drake was enthralled. His assessment included phrases such as *rich with substance and entirely captivating*, which was slightly," Reen held her thumb and fingers an inch apart, "different from my opinion that they were rich with mind-numbing sleep motivation."

Astrid wrinkled her nose. "I'm afraid I'd have to side with you on that, honey."

"Saffron understands and appreciates all that scholarly stuff. The two of them could sit and discuss whoever's logic of essence all night and not tire of it."

"Probably," Astrid agreed. "But the fact you're not a fan of tedious lectures or documentaries doesn't mean you and Drake have little in common. Opposites attract, remember?"

"Mom..." Reen tried hard not to appear as frustrated as she felt. "It doesn't matter. Drake loves Saffron, not me. I heard it with my own ears." She tugged on them. "So case closed." Propping her elbow on the tabletop, she sighed and rested her forehead in her hand, catching herself from ending up with her chin clunking against the table when her elbow started a slow glide along the greasy surface. "If only I hadn't ducked when he brought me home from the opera. I might have had a chance with him then."

"That's exactly what you should tell Drake. It could make all the difference."

"No." Sitting straight in her seat, Reen shook her head with resolve. "I can't. I won't. I'd be stabbing Saffron in the back if I told Drake how I feel—especially now that he's thinking about marrying her." Reen recalled how earnest Saffron during their conversation. She'd never seen her cousin so animated, so excited. Saffron Devington was the dictionary image of a woman in love.

Determined to do the right thing, Reen vowed, "I won't tell Drake I love him. I'll continue treating him like a good friend and nothing more. That's the way it has to be."

"My poor baby." Her expression brimming with sympathy, Astrid reached across the table, touching her daughter's cheek.

When Astrid took her hand from her daughter's face, Reen caught her surreptitiously wiping her fingers with her napkin. Once she got home she'd find a paint scraper and clean all the glop off her face.

"As for Hudson," Astrid said, "it's unfortunate Monica saw his reaction when he kissed you, but that's not your fault either. Since everyone knows you've had a thing for him, it's no wonder Hud knew too and capitalized on it."

"And here I thought I'd done such a good job of keeping my feelings secret."

"Um...no." Astrid chuckled. "Who knows, maybe Hud was trying to make Monica jealous. Or maybe he found himself genuinely attracted to you and it was a pleasant surprise for him."

"That's the weird thing." Reen's sigh was monumental. "All this time I honestly thought I was crazy about him, but now?" She shook her head back and forth. "Why, Mom? I keep wondering if it's because I only wanted what I couldn't have. If that's true, that makes me pretty damn shallow, and about as mature as a thirteen-year-old."

"Sometimes," Astrid patted Reen's hand, "there's simply no explaining affairs of the heart. The good news is that Hud appears to be strongly attracted to you. Maybe you should explore that further. You might develop real feelings for him."

"Even though Monica's not my favorite person, I couldn't do that to her, not after I saw the way she looked at Hud Saturday night." Closing her eyes, Reen could easily picture Monica's heartbreaking expression of devastation.

Lifting her hand, Reen turned it, watching as the heartwish ring generated a faint glow in the dim room. "Last night I thought about the ring and how I might be able to use it to fix this whole mess. But I don't have a clue how to put all the puzzle pieces into one concise wish that would make everyone happy." She took a bite of toast, wrinkling her nose when she remembered why she'd left it on her plate.

"Don't agonize over your wish. Trust me, when the time is right, your heart will know what to wish for. As difficult as everything seems now, it will all work out. You'll feel better in a few days."

No, she'd never feel better about losing Drake. But she couldn't have her nurturing mother worrying about her. "I'm sure you're right," she fibbed. "I'm really glad I called you last night." She fought off a round of tears. "I love you."

"I love you too, Maureen, more than you'll ever know. I'm glad I could be of some help. That's what moms are for." Winking, she took Reen's hand, bringing it to her lips and kissing it.

The stone in Reen's heartwish ring glowed.

"I have a feeling that glow means all will be well and you'll be making your wish soon."

"You can sit anywhere you want," came a man's brusque voice. It sounded like the same man who spoke to Reen and Astrid when they'd arrived earlier. With fading tattoos all over his wrinkly arms, the scruffy guy in a grimy t-shirt and grubby jeans looked sixty-ish.

Reen felt a substantial wobble as someone slid into place in the booth seat behind her.

"You want the usual, Nancy?" the man asked.

"Naw, I'm gonna get fancy today and get me the Monday special, Smokey Cat." The woman's gravelly voice sounded like that of a longtime smoker. "You can bring both pints over at the same time." Her laugh came out like a cackle.

At the term Smokey Cat, Astrid and Reen exchanged smiles, silently mouthing the words. Reen wasn't sure if that was the guy's name or another special on the menu.

She was about to continue her discussion with her mom when she heard a familiar voice.

"Mom do you really think you should be drinking beer this early in the morning? You need to take care of yourself. Remember what the doctor said."

Reen's eyes bugged. If she hadn't been sitting on her donut pillow she would have slid down against the back of the seat to hide. Grabbing her phone from her purse she sent a quick text to her mother with MONICA, in all caps.

Chapter Fifteen

~<>~

ASTRID'S EYES widened too. She'd been facing the people who were seated behind them but she and Monica had never met so she didn't recognize her by sight when the two women walked in.

"Get off my back, Monica. Fuck the doctor, and you too if you don't stop trying to keep me from having a little fun and happiness in life," Nancy said. "I deserve it, you know. I've sacrificed my entire life for you and Murphy, that no good brother of yours."

Doubting her eyes or her mother's could grow any bigger, Reen put her finger to her lips in a shushing motion and Astrid nodded.

"Mom, please, you're going to embarrass me," Monica pleaded.

"In here? In front of Smokey Cat?" Another cackle. "He don't give two shits about what you and me got to say, baby doll. Hey, Smokey Cat," Nancy called out, making Reen and Astrid cringe. Reen imagined Monica cringing even more.

Astrid dug into her purse, withdrawing a pen and small spiral notepad. She motioned to the paper, then to each other. Having no doubt Monica would recognize her voice if she heard it, Reen nodded in agreement.

"Yeah, what?" Smokey Cat responded. Reen saw him walking toward their booth, a beer in each hand with foam sliding down the sides of the cloudy glass mugs.

"You don't care what me and my daughter talk about in here, do you, hun?"

"Is that a serious question?" Smokey Cat hacked a dry coughing laugh. "Why should I care what you two broads are yacking about?"

Reen heard the sound of two glasses hitting the wooden tabletop. "Here's your beer, beautiful."

"See?" Nancy said to Monica. "He don't care." There was silence for a moment after which Reen heard an *ahhh* coming from Nancy. "That's good stuff."

"Sure you don't want nothing, Monica?" Smokey Cat asked.

"No thanks, my stomach's a little off today."

"Want me to see if I can scrounge up a tea bag for you?"

"That would be nice. Thanks, I appreciate it."

Astrid was busy writing. *Monica must be a regular if Mr. Cat knows her by name.* When Reen read her mother's note, she silently chuckled at the *Mr. Cat* reference. Glancing around the dingy room, Reen decided Tidal Wave Tavern certainly didn't seem like the sort of establishment Monica would frequent.

"I'm glad you asked me for breakfast, and here at my favorite stomping grounds too. You don't do that a lot no more. But you're not fooling me, Monica. I know you'd rather come to my pal Smokey's place, waaay far from your ritzy neighborhood, than risk having your hoity-toity friends see me walking into your fancy-ass apartment building 'cause you're embarrassed of me."

There was semi-quiet for a moment as the sound of Nancy slurping beer could be heard. "Unless you tell 'em I'm your cleaning lady, of course." Nancy snorted a laugh.

"I'm only embarrassed when you show up drunk, crying, and asking my neighbors for money," Monica said. "Which is what happened the last time you came over unannounced. I was mortified, Mom."

"Mortified, shmortified." Reen pictured Nancy's hand casually waving through the air in a mocking gesture. "Speaking of money, you got the dough I asked for? I'm running short. I need it for groceries and rent or they'll kick me out."

The sound of exasperation traveled over the top of the booth with Monica's sigh. "Mom, that's not true. You know I pay for your rent and buy your groceries. You should have plenty of spending money left for other essentials."

"I don't like that rabbit food you buy me. I ain't like you, trying to look like a skeleton. I want real food, like mac and cheese, potato chips, Cheetos, Oreos, Butterfingers, and ice cream."

Hearing Nancy's Cheetos remark, Reen tried to hide her telltale fingers until her mother's eyebrow hiked in realization and they exchanged smiles. Reen lifted her shoulders in resignation. She'd avoided mentioning yesterday's snack binge.

"A skeleton? Really, Mom? All during my childhood you called me a big galoot, a fat cow, a clumsy oaf."

"You were getting fat. I was trying to motivate you. Looks like it worked. You're welcome."

"Here ya go," Smokey Cat said. "Found a tin back in the kitchen with a few tea bags. It's been around for a while. Hope it's still fresh."

"I'm sure it's fine. Thank you." Reen and Astrid watched Smokey Cat walk back to the bar. Monica continued in a subdued voice, "I've looked back at my photos, Mom. I might have been slightly chubby, but I was never fat...never the big, bulky way you made me feel about myself. And now..." Monica's chuckle sounded tired and worn out, "now you're faulting me for being too thin. Looks like I just can't win with you."

"Don't blame me for your lifelong diet problems. I never told you to starve yourself so you look like a bag of bones, did I? What do you do, puke out what you eat to look like that?"

There was a stretch of silence before Monica admitted, "For years I did, yes. The therapist who helped me with the bulimia told me I had BDD, body dysmorphic disorder, because I saw myself as being fat when I wasn't. I still have trouble...but I'm much better now."

Amazed, Reen scribbled across the paper, *I had no idea!* Astrid's expression showed her own surprise.

"You're *better*?" Nancy's laughter was clearly mocking. "You say that like you actually had something wrong with you instead of some phony, made-up celebrity-type disease. Most head-doctors are crackpots. They tell you a bunch of hooey, then charge you big bucks for it. You don't need no fancy medical names or initials for your diet problems. You were fat, then you got skinny. Period." Nancy guffawed. "You shoulda come to me. I could have straightened you out for a lot less money than that crackpot probably charged you."

"I've spent my life trying to please you, trying to get an ounce of praise, approval, or appreciation from my mother." There was a long pause before Monica added, "I'm still trying. But nothing I do is ever good enough for you."

Hearing Monica nearly broke Reen's heart. Both Reen and Laila had dealt with weight problems, including the phenomenon of still seeing themselves as being heavy after they'd reached their weight goals. The sisters knew firsthand how difficult it was to be an overweight woman in a thin-obsessed world.

A major difference between them and Monica's situation is that Reen and Laila had their family's love, understanding and encouragement as they battled their compulsive overeating issues. Their mother couldn't have been more supportive as her daughters struggled to lose the excess weight. Shutting her eyes, Reen tried in vain to erase the mental images of her binge-eating episode yesterday. She was ashamed for her pitiful lack of self-control.

"Oh for shit's sake, stop exaggerating," Nancy said, annoyance coloring her tone. "You've always been a drama queen, Monica, always trying to be the center of attention."

Reen shuddered. It was almost as if Nancy was describing the way Reen had been behaving the last two days, whining and complaining about her assorted trials and tribulations.

"You're in your twenties," Nancy said. "Time you got your shit together and stopped feeling sorry for yourself."

"I'm thirty-three, Mom."

"Well, there you go, see? You're old enough to know better."

Tsking, Astrid muttered "For heaven's sake," while Reen made abrupt shushing motions at her lips. Monica would die of embarrassment if she had any idea they were seated in the next booth and could hear their conversation.

"As for the rabbit food," Nancy continued, "I wouldn't even feed that crap to my dogs or cats."

"Please don't tell me you brought in more cats and dogs after we talked about that," Monica said. "Mom, you're not supposed to have any pets in that building. If the new landlords find out—"

"Yadda, yadda, yadda," Nancy said. "I told ya, stop telling me what to do. Just give me a few hundred to tide me over. I can make do with that."

"A few hundred? I want to do everything I can to help you, Mom, but I'm not made of money. I've been having trouble meeting my own living expenses lately."

"Oh puhleez. Don't give me that poormouth song and dance. You've got plenty of money. You live in the fanciest part of town."

"The real estate market's been slow for quite a while. Sales are few and far between. My roommate, Saffron, and I share the rent and expenses for our apartment. We were able to rent it for next to nothing because the real estate company we work for owns the building and is turning it into condos. We have a reduced rent agreement with Wotring Realtors allowing them to show our apartment to prospective buyers whenever they need to while the renovations are being done."

Reen drew a surprised "O" face on the paper, turning it to her mother. She could tell her mother was just as taken aback by Monica's admission.

"Saffron? Devington?" Nancy asked. "The one whose family lives in that mansion on Beauregard Hill?" Monica must have nodded because Nancy went on with a smirk in her voice, "The Devingtons are filthy rich."

"What does that have to do with me?" Monica asked. "I'm not a Devington. I'd never dream of poormouthing to my best friend. Saffron has enough problems of her own to deal with."

"She's got a snooty attitude," Nancy claimed. "Remember that time I met her when I came to your swanky digs to see you? I could tell the bitch didn't like me."

Gee, I wonder why, Reen quickly scrawled, turning the pad to Astrid, who nodded in agreement.

"I know Saffron can come across somewhat irritable or standoffish but it's not intentional. She has to deal with her demanding family and they really stress her out. Saffron's a good person, Mom. She lives solely on her own income, not off her family's money. She keeps what she needs to make ends meet and gives most of the rest to charitable causes and people in need."

Clearly as surprised as Reen at the information, Astrid gave an approving nod.

"People in need? She never gave me nothing. She sounds like an idiot," Nancy said. "If I had all that Devington dough at my fingertips, you can better believe I'd know how to spend it. I could give her lessons."

"I'm sure you could, Mother." Reen could hear the impatience in Monica's voice. "I admire Saffron for her determination to be an independent woman who makes it on her own, rather than using her family name."

"When she could be living like a queen. Baaaah."

"The last thing Saffron would ever do is ask her family for money, and I don't blame her. She manages fine on her own. Like me...as long as you don't drain me of the rest of my savings, that is."

"Don't try to fool me, baby doll. What about those designer duds you wear, and that expensive jewelry? I been around. I know how much that stuff costs."

"I buy it all secondhand, Mom."

"Bullshit." Nancy must have taken a drink because her beer mug thudded against the tabletop.

"It's true. I drive into Portland and shop at estate sales or at Goodwill for clothes. The jewelry is all costume and secondhand too."

Both Reen and Astrid grabbed for the notepad at the same time, with Reen being successful and jotting, *OMG, I can't believe it!!!!!* Astrid scribbled just below that, *Me too!!*

"Why go into Portland? There's plenty of garage sales around here, and a perfectly good Salvation Army store a mile away. My neck of the woods ain't highbrow enough for you?"

Monica heaved a weighty sigh. "I can't shop thrift in Glassfloat Bay, someone might recognize me. Wotring Realtors is a high profile company that expects their agents to maintain a certain image. My broker would be embarrassed and furious if I was spotted shopping for secondhand clothes. How would that reflect on Randall Wotring and his business? When I get the clothes home I take out my sewing machine and fix them up so they look new and updated so I can maintain a professional appearance."

"Since you're saving all that dough on where you live and what you wear, you should have plenty of extra cash to give your poor mother instead of being so stingy."

There was no need for Astrid and Reen to exchange notes this time. They shared sympathetic expressions. Reen wouldn't guess in a million years that Monica lived this way. Reen, her sisters and mother loved to shop thrift, and didn't care who knew it. She'd never pegged Monica for someone who shopped anything but high-end retail. She always looked so perfectly put together.

"What are you spending all the money on, Mom? You always wear the same two or three outfits, and you still live in the same shabby apartment where Murphy and I grew up. The neighborhood's even worse now with all the crime and drugs in plain sight. I've been trying to get you to move from there but you won't listen."

"I told you, I like it there. Nobody bothers me. I got friends there. Good friends."

"Your drug addict friends you mean?" Silence dragged on until, in a disappointed tone, Monica said, "Oh Mom...please tell me you're not using drugs again. Or spending all the money I give you at the liquor store."

"Drugs? I told ya before, I been clean for months. And I'm sober. Well," *cackle, cackle, cackle*, "practically. I have a few beers and a little whiskey now and then, to help with my rheumatism. I need the dough 'cause I need some new clothes, just like you said. Mine are falling apart they're so old. See?"

"Fine. I'll take you shopping and you can pick out whatever you need."

"I don't need you to hold my hand." Nancy's tone grew harsher. "I'm a big girl, Monica. I just want the money. What's a matter...you don't trust me to spend it on clothes? You think I'm lying? That's a hell of a way to treat your mother after I spent my life sacrificing for you."

"I wish you'd stop saying that." Monica's voice was weary and nearly inaudible. "The only ones who did any sacrificing were me and Murphy...ever since we were kids. Ring a bell?"

Reen and her mother exchanged another round of stunned expressions.

"Bah...I don't know what you're talking about. I gave up my life to take care of you and your lousy, ungrateful brother. I wanted to be an actress, and I could have too, if I hadn't been stuck with you two snot-nosed kids after your father hightailed it out of there with that barfly tramp of his. You should be thankful I gave up my dreams for you instead of sitting across from me acting all high and mighty like the Queen of Sheba, talking down your nose to me."

The sound of Nancy drinking her beer was followed by a loud *ahhh*. "I had the looks too," she went on. "Ask anybody. I was a sexpot. You got me to thank for your looks and those double-D boobs of yours."

Reen sagged in her seat, remembering how she and Laila had mocked Monica behind her back for having implants. It was one more thing Reen added to her list of reasons why she should feel ashamed.

"Murphy and I were like the parents, taking care of you and Dad when you were both falling down drunk. You embarrassed us so much in front of our friends that they all stopped coming over. Murphy and I had to do janitorial work in the apartment building so the landlord would allow us to stay because you never paid the rent."

"There ain't nothing wrong with working hard and toughening up, missy. It did you good. Look at you now, with all your fancy clothes and that high-priced address you don't want me coming to visit. Everything you got is thanks to me, for teaching you how to look out for yourself."

Reen slid the notepad toward her, writing, *Poor Monica!* Her eyebrows knitting, Astrid nodded. Reen couldn't believe how quickly her longtime animosity toward Monica had evaporated. She regretted being so smallminded and judgmental.

"How do you do that?" Monica asked.

"Do what?"

"Put that spin of yours on everything. Whenever we talk about the past you come out with this absurd fairytale of yours, Mom. Our homelife was radically different from your version. If Murphy and I hadn't gathered bottles and containers, returning them to stores for cash when we were preteens we would have starved because you and Dad drank away his paycheck each week before he took off with Jasmine. We had to quit high school to work fulltime so we could pay off the bill collectors and not have to live on the street. Does any of that sound familiar?"

Once more, Reen and Astrid exchanged astonished looks. *Monica quit school?* Reen wrote. She and Astrid shook their heads in disbelief. Never in her wildest dreams did Reen expect to hear anything like this.

"Me, me, me, that's all I ever hear from you," Nancy said. "Seems you've always got something to complain about whenever I see you. Don't forget that if it weren't for me, the woman who gave birth to you, you wouldn't be here. You wouldn't be selling million dollar houses and living the life of Riley with all your snooty, rich friends. You should get down on your knees, thanking me. Like it or not, I'm your mother and I deserve respect."

"You two want anything else?" Smokey Cat asked Reen and Astrid, wiping the tabletop with a wet, soiled rag. Reen was tempted to shush him so she wouldn't miss any of what was going on in the next booth. Without saying anything, Astrid smiled, held up her coffee cup and nodded, gesturing also to Reen's.

"More coffee coming up." He finally left the table.

With a quick glance to Astrid, Reen indulged in a teary smile. Thanks to her loving family and good friends, she had little to complain about. Her life was good. Wonderful, in fact, even with the current crop of problems facing her. She had *so* much to be thankful for.

"Respect? Thanking you?" From the distorted nearly unrecognizable sound of Monica's voice, Reen imagined her pretty face looking twisted and full of incredulity.

"When parents don't care enough about their children to stay clean and sober," Monica continued, "when they beat their kids black and blue for no reason, ignore them for days on end, disappear for days, leaving their two, frightened, underaged kids alone to wonder whether their alcoholic, drug-addicted parents are alive or dead, that's a problem—not an example of how to gain a child's respect or thanks."

There was silence for a minute or two before they heard Monica's soft, drained voice again. Reen thought it sounded like she may have been crying.

"Regardless of everything you've done, I love you, Mom...but I don't respect you."

"I love you too, baby doll," Nancy said. "Parents aren't perfect. We make mistakes like maybe getting addicted to drugs or alcohol. But that's not our fault. Raising kids ain't easy, Monica. Maybe one day you'll have a kid and find that out for yourself, then you'll understand and you'll feel guilty for treating me without no respect."

"Oh I understand." Monica sniffed, then blew her nose a moment later. "I understand you and my father chose to shove coke up your nose or a needle in your arm, getting high every day instead of choosing to parent your children. Instead of worrying about feeding or housing your babies—your children who never chose or asked to be born."

Coffee sloshing into their cups drew Reen and Astrid's attention away from the conversation. "Here's your coffees and your check, lemme know if there's anything else you want."

"Thank you," Astrid said softly, obviously as eager as Reen to get back to focusing on the sad tale unfolding in the next booth. *This is hard for me to hear*, Astrid wrote. Reen nodded in agreement. When she looked up from the paper into her mother's eyes she saw tears welling there. Reen reached for her hand and squeezed it.

I'm so thankful you're my mom, Reen wrote. *I love you so much*. Reen wiped at her teary eyes, smudging her paper napkin with black from her non-waterproof makeup. *Love you too, sweetheart*, Astrid replied.

A single mother after their firefighter dad died saving children in a school fire, Astrid raised all six of her children on her own while holding down a job to make ends meet. Reen couldn't recall her mom ever complaining about her situation. And God knows she never blamed any of her children.

It was such a blessing when she and Tore Thorkelson found each other and fell in love a few short years ago.

"How about you?" Smokey Cat asked Nancy and Monica. "Anything else?"

"We're good, thanks," Monica answered while almost at the same instant Nancy said, "Gimme another pint, Smokey." The sound of Monica's frustrated tsk was evident.

After some time passed, Nancy said, "Look, I did my best. I tried. No one teaches you how to be a parent. I know I coulda done better. I'm sorry your father and me didn't take care of you two better. Believe me, this ain't the life I pictured for myself when I was a kid. You gotta know one thing, Monica. I always loved you and Murphy. I still do." That was followed by the sound of Nancy's sniffling.

"Oh hell..." Monica muttered barely loud enough for Reen to hear. "Don't cry, Mom. I don't want us to argue. I want for us to be on good terms. It—it's especially important now."

Reen felt the highbacked booth wobble again. It must have been Monica sliding into the seat to sit next to her mother. Reen was incredibly thankful her back was to them, concealing her from Monica's view. There was silence for a few moments, except for what sounded like both of them sniffling and crying.

"I wanted to see you today," Monica said, her voice filled with emotion, "because I have something important to tell you."

"Yeah? What?"

"For one thing, I broke up with Hud a few days ago."

"Who's Hud?"

"The man I told I was seeing. Hudson Griffin."

"You go out with so many guys it's hard to keep up. He cheat on you? They all end up doin' that sooner or later. Always with somebody younger than you."

"No, nothing like that. Hud's a good man. He owns his own contracting business."

"A good man?" Nancy snorted laughter. "There ain't no such thing. Contactor, huh? Blue collar guy?" Monica must have given a confirming nod because Nancy said, "Interesting. You always had your sights set on finding a rich corporate dude in a three-piece suit. I'm surprised you lowered yourself to be seen on the arm of a guy who works with his hands for a living."

"I met Hud when he worked on a remodeling project for a duplex I was selling," Monica told her mother. "Once I got to know him I realized it's not a man's job or bank account that makes him special, it's his heart. Hud's got a big one. I love him, Mom. Really love him."

Again, Reen remembered Monica's forlorn look Saturday night after Hud left the kissing booth. No wonder she'd looked so lost.

"If he's so peachy, why'd you give him the boot?"

"I broke things off because I—I'm sick, Mom."

"I don't get it...he's afraid of germs or something?"

"No, I..." Reen heard the sound of Monica's trembly sigh. "I have cancer, Mom. Stage four. There's a mass the size of a honeydew melon next to my right ovary. The last test results show the cancer has spread to my lungs."

Reen's hand flew to her chest. In the brief silence that followed, her eyes widened in horror. The sensation of shock and disbelief was almost palpable. Her mother mirrored her shaken expression.

Stunned, Reen and Astrid grasped hands across the table as tears rolled down their cheeks. There wasn't enough time or paper for either of them to jot down all their feelings at this moment. Paper was unnecessary because their hearts were communicating.

"I don't like talking about sickness. It's depressing. Let's talk about something else, huh, baby doll?"

Reen was half tempted to tear off her Frankenstein boot, walk over to their booth and slap Nancy upside the head with it.

"Mom, you need to pay attention. This is important. I've met with my attorney and he's helping me draw up my will so you'll be taken care of after...after I'm gone."

"Where you going?"

Her eyebrows knitting, Reen was sure something must be wrong with Nancy mentally. Perhaps due to all the alcohol and drugs over the years. Astrid tapped her temple, concurring with Reen's assessment.

A long silence ensued. When Monica spoke again, her voice cracked. "Please, Mom, try to focus on what I'm saying. I'm trying to tell you that I'm dying. Two years ago the surgery, chemo and radiation put me into remission for a while. Last year it all came back, more aggressive than before."

The poor thing's been battling this for two years! Astrid wrote, shaking her head with compassion. Reen had no idea. It explained why Monica was so irritable during the real estate transaction when Laila bought the bakery.

"The treatments aren't working anymore. It's increasingly difficult to control the pain. It's almost unbearable at times. I have trouble keeping food down. That's one of the reasons I've lost so much weight." It sounded like Monica sucked in a deep breath then and blew it out. "I don't have a lot of time left. Probably no more than a month at best. The doctors expect the cancer to spread to my other organs quickly. They'll stop all treatment then."

"Well that's a real downer."

"Yes, Mom...yes it is."

Reen recalled that Monica had worked with Saffron steadily over the last couple years. It wasn't until recently that she'd taken any time off work, as far as Reen knew. She must have been in a great deal of discomfort and yet she never let on. No one had ever mentioned that Monica had complained. The woman was strong, brave and determined. No wonder Monica's patience sometimes grew short and she came across harsh at times.

While Monica was doing her best to hold her head high, Reen was busy being snarky, judgmental, and sarcastic. She'd jumped to false conclusions about Monica, convinced she was faking illness at the café, being dramatic to gain Hud's sympathy. That was no act.

"That's why I broke things off with Hudson," Monica told her mother. "I haven't told him about the cancer. It's not fair for him to take care of me as I'm dying, or for him to watch me die. It's not like I'm his wife, I'm just his girlfriend."

"True, no one wants to be around somebody who's dying," Nancy agreed in a calm, nonchalant manner. "Ugh, talking about dying is creepy. Whoa, look at my arms. I got goosebumps!"

Astrid made a disgusted face as she grabbed the notepad. *I'm so tempted to go to that poor girl and pull her into my arms for a big hug,* she wrote. *And then give her mother a swift kick in the ass.* Reen nodded in agreement, taking the paper and adding, *Monica needs a mother...but not that one.*

"Saffron's been such a wonderful friend," Monica said. "She's the only one I've told about my illness. She's known about it for the past two years. I asked her to keep it in confidence. The last thing I want is for people to feel sorry for me or worry about me. Saffron's made arrangements to get me into an excellent hospice when the time comes. She's been volunteering there for years and assured me they'd take good care of me."

All the information was so profoundly sad. Reen and Astrid just sat there blankly staring at each other as they openly wept. Once again, words were unnecessary as their hearts spoke to each other.

"Saffron—" Reen heard the sound of discreet crying coming from Monica. "Saffron promised she'll stay by my side until the end. She said she doesn't want me to die alone—that no one should. Do you see now what I mean about her being a good friend and kindhearted person? I don't know what I'd do without her."

Reen realized that must be why Saffron kept mentioning that life was too short and precious not to repair their often faltering relationship. She was so right. Reen sent up a soundless prayer of thanks that Monica had a true, loving friend like Saffron at her side now when she needed it most.

"Talk is cheap," Nancy responded. "Maybe Saffron'll stick around and maybe she won't. Guess you'll find out. Just make sure your lawyer makes your will foolproof so your brother don't try to take nothing away from me. He's young, he can work. I'm too sick and disabled to work."

There was an abundance of exasperation in Monica's lengthy sigh. "You're not disabled, Mom, or too sick to work. You just don't want to get a job, that's all. You've always been perfectly happy to live off me and Murphy."

"That ain't true. I had me plenty of jobs. Worked my knuckles to the bone tryin' to keep a roof over our heads and food on the table."

"No, Mom, you didn't. That's another of your fairytales. You were fired from each of those jobs within a matter of weeks to months for misconduct related to drugs and or alcohol. Like when you were a server and got caught sipping from drinks you were bringing to customers."

Reen curled her lip in revulsion and Astrid mirrored the expression.

"I'll tell you something, missy, it ain't my fault I was an addict. It never would have happened if your father wasn't a drunk. It's because of him I got started on meth, you know. That son of a bitch is the reason my teeth are rotting."

"I told you I'd pay for you to get your teeth fixed, or get dentures. I can take out a loan."

"I don't like dentists. It's like paying some guy to torture you. I'd rather deal with meth mouth." Nancy's familiar cackle rang out again. "Anyway, tell your lawyer to make the will tamperproof so I don't get screwed."

Monica's sigh was audible. "Don't worry," she assured Nancy, "everything will be taken care of. Whatever's left in my savings account will be yours. I've worked extra hard the last couple of years to build my savings for you in case I didn't make it. You'll be fine."

"I hope so. You do something different with your hair? The color's off and I never seen you wear it up like that before."

"I've lost a lot of hair from the cancer treatments. I had to buy a couple of wigs." After a moment, Monica added in a faint voice, "Does it look okay, Mom? Does it look like a wig to you?"

Reen's heart went out to Monica. The poor thing sounded so vulnerable...like a little lost child eager for her mother's approval.

"It looks okay, baby, just different from usual. I suppose you're gonna tell me you got that at a garage sale too." The sound of Nancy snickering was evident.

"No, they were retail. Saffron bought them for me as a surprise. I have her to thank for having two different looks as I undergo this last round of chemo."

"Chemo...yeah...so," it sounded like Nancy slapped the table then, "let's get back to me for a change. Are you gonna give me some spending money today or what?"

Reen watched as Astrid gripped the tabletop until she was white-knuckled. Nancy Sharp was unbelievable. Incredibly selfish and uncaring. How could she be so cold and indifferent when her daughter tells her something so devastating?

"I can only give you thirty dollars today, Mom."

"Thirty bucks! You kidding me? What the hell is that supposed to cover? That'll be gone by tomorrow."

"Tomorrow? You need to try hard to manage your money—to make it last longer," Monica said. "I've told you before I'd be glad to sit with you and show you how to do some simple budgeting."

Nancy made a raspberry sound. "Boring," came her singsong voice.

"It might be boring but you need to learn how to budget because I'm limited now as to how much cash I can give you."

Monica had thoroughly impressed Reen with her cool, calm, collected manner while conversing with this awful woman.

"I've had some heavy expenses related to the cancer treatments and—"

"Tell your doctor to prescribe generic meds. It's cheaper. If it's that close to the end for you, maybe you can just stop the treatments now to keep more money in your bank account. Maybe you can spare fifty bucks today?"

Fidgeting in her seat, Astrid fumed, grabbing the notepad and pen. *I'm THISCLOSE*, she wrote, *to punching that woman's lights out*. Before handing the paper to Reen, she added about a dozen exclamation marks, dotting them so hard she poked holes through the paper. Reen knew her anti-violence mom must be furious to even jokingly mention something like that.

"I'm sorry, I just don't have it, Mom. I've got enough to pay for our breakfast and to give you thirty dollars. That's it."

"Well I'll just have to suffer, I guess," Nancy said. "But what else is new? That's all I've done...suffer and sacrifice. And who cares? Nobody, that's who."

"I know you really believe that," Monica said. "I don't think I've ever heard you say you were truly happy. Not once. If I had one wish, Mom, I'd use it to make you happy and well."

"Well ain't that nice. I appreciate that, Monica. But I got an even easier way to make me happy. Hey Smokey Cat," her voice rose, "bring me one more beer for the road! See?" *Cackle.* "Instant happiness." Reen heard the sound of fingers snapping. "Just like that."

Reen could picture Nancy turning back to Monica when she heard, "You got enough to pay for another brew for your ma, don't you, baby doll?"

"Sure, Mom...sure."

"That's a good girl. I love you, babe. You know that, don't you?"

"I know, Mom." It was quiet for a couple of minutes before Monica added, "Mom?"

"Yeah, baby?"

"I-I'm scared."

Closing her eyes as she sucked in a sharp breath, Reen felt an acute sensation of heartbreak and sympathy for a woman she barely knew—and had never been fond of—and another woman she'd never even met. One glance at her mother told Reen that Astrid shared in her sympathy.

"It's okay. Don't you worry, baby. I'm always here for you, Monica. You're mama's always here for you no matter what. You remember that."

"I will, Mom...I will."

Nancy seemed to slip in and out of lucidity. Thank God the woman had the presence of mind to offer a few kind, supportive words at that critical moment.

Reen doubted she'd ever be able to think of Monica Sharp again without imagining her wearing a superhero cape, proudly flapping with the breeze. Reen only wished she'd made the opportunity to get to know this remarkable woman better—instead of having judged her so unkindly. Hopefully there was still time.

Reen and Astrid stayed hidden in their high-back booth until Monica and Nancy paid their bill and left about fifteen minutes later.

Reen's head was splitting, partially from endless hours of crying, and partly because of the gargantuan headache she'd developed listening to Nancy Sharp whine, moan and complain to her dying daughter.

"Okay, they just drove off," Astrid said, straining her neck to see out the tavern's murky window. "We can leave now. I don't know about you, honey, but I can't wait to get out of this place." She rubbed her arms briskly.

"Me too." Reen started her careful scoot along the booth's seat.

"I'll carry your tote bag and donut pillow for you," her mom offered.

Once Reen maneuvered her way to the edge of the grimy booth, she used her cane to help her get up. The first thing she did when standing was to pull her mother into a hug, squeezing her and relishing Astrid's firm, reciprocating embrace. They stood together like that for a long while, both of them weeping.

As they walked to Astrid's car, Reen said, "I appreciate you, Mom, and everything you've done for us six kids all these years. I've never been more aware or thankful until what we just witnessed."

"Thank you, sweetheart."

Reen may have made a terrible mess of things, hurting people along the way, but no matter how critical the chaos, or how severely feelings had been hurt because of her actions, she had the precious gift of time to make things right again.

Monica didn't have that same luxury.

Sitting in her mother's car and staring at the beautiful pastel blue of the sky with its fluffy marshmallow clouds, Reen's attention was captured by the warmth around her finger. She looked down to see the stone of the heartwish ring gently glowing.

From this moment forward, Reen vowed she'd no longer waste time feeling sorry for herself. No more wallowing in guilt. No more spending precious time engaging in mean-spirited thoughts about other people. Instead, she'd use her time wisely, constructively...with a little help from her heartwish ring.

Chapter Sixteen

~<>~

THE NEXT MORNING, with only a faint peachy-hued shadow remaining on her face and hands, and her eyes nearly normal sized, Reen no longer looked alienesque. She just looked like she had a cold or allergies, which is the explanation she decided to use at work for her puffy eyes and drippy nose.

While getting dressed, her gaze fell on the collection of objects on her dresser. She smiled each time she spotted them. They were part of a personalized healing kit lovingly put together by her modern-day flower child sister, Kady, before she left for her seminar in Seattle.

There was a clear quartz crystal, a small amethyst cluster no bigger than the tip of her thumb, a package of lavender-patchouli incense sticks, and a flash drive filled with lyrical chanting and dolphin music. All designed to soothe, de-stress, and hasten Reen's healing.

The rest of Kady's thoughtful kit was in the kitchen. It included three petite glass jars, each containing a different healing tea blend Kady had concocted, and the refrigerator held her sister's special coconut oil-based salve, which she'd infused with natural pain relieving ingredients. As soon as Kady found out about Reen's injuries she got busy formulating the customized new-agey care package. Her little sister was a wee bit woo-woo but Reen adored her.

Half an hour later at the bakery, as Reen sat with Laila enjoying an early morning cup of coffee and maple bacon scones, Laila sniffed the air.

"You really smell good. What is that?" Getting closer, she sniffed again.

Unable to resist having some fun with her sister, Reen truthfully answered, "My butt," which earned Reen a deserved whap to her upper arm.

"Uh, no, I don't think so," Laila said. "Seriously, what's that fragrance?"

"I already told you. My butt." She watched Laila narrow one eye. "Technically." Reen offered an impish grin. "It's the healing salve Kady made for me. She put lavender essential oil, chamomile flowers, eucalyptus, and all sorts of other stuff I can't remember in it. She even made the cutest tiny recipe card with all the ingredients. I rubbed it all over my ankle and my butt."

"The recipe card?" Laila asked, tongue in cheek, before adding, "So, does it help?"

"I'm not sure but it's a great conversation starter." She and Laila laughed. "Actually, it does help with the pain somewhat. Kady called me last night." It was one of the only calls Reen had answered in the last two days. Talking to Kady usually had a calming, upbeat effect on her. She'd needed a mood elevator after overhearing Monica's conversation. "She'll be back from Seattle this weekend and setting everything in motion to get her bookshop running."

Laila tapped the tabletop and grinned. "I'll bet you fifty bucks she'll have tarot cards and a crystal ball there."

"Well, duh." Reen made a silly face. "Is there sand in the desert? Are there peanuts in Snickers? Do we each have at least three different dress sizes in our closets? Is there—"

"Okay, okay, I get the idea." Pushing the air, Laila laughed. "We teased her unmercifully about her fortune telling and psychic abilities when she was a kid but it's downright unnerving how accurate Kady's predictions can be."

"I know!" Before she left for her Seattle trip, Kady told Reen her aura had positive vibrations. She was convinced a powerful, positive surprise was coming Reen's way soon—something life changing. She saw it during a tarot card reading she'd done for Reen.

So much for her sister's mystical abilities. Kady's prediction came only days before the roof fell in on Reen's life, which, actually *was* life changing, but not at all positive.

Reen's musing was interrupted by Laila's gasp.

"Maureen Malone," Laila pointed an accusatory finger, "you were eating Cheetos!"

She'd almost forgotten about the remaining traces of orange but Reen should have known her eagle-eyed dieting partner would spot the telltale remnants of her dietary debacle. Reen and Laila had eaten enough of the cheesy snack together over the years to recognize the hard to remove signs of Cheetos consumption, even after the orange had faded to peach.

Opening her mouth to deny her snack attack, Reen broke into laughter instead. "Busted."

"What happened?"

"Nothing," Reen lied with a casual shrug. "I came across them in the back of a cabinet and they got the better of me."

Folding her arms over her chest, Laila elevated her chin. "Well...if you don't want tell me..." Her wounded look was accompanied by a sniff.

Reen sagged in her seat. "I can't talk about it now, Laila. I promise, I'll tell you everything soon."

"Everything?" Laila frowned. "That sounds like multiple things. Is that why no one's been able to reach you since Saturday?" Reen gave an affirmative nod. "Whatever it is, you know you can tell me. I'll be glad to help if I can."

"I know. Thanks. Don't worry about me, I'm okay. I just need to work some things out."

"Regarding your heartwish?"

"Yes," Reen quickly answered over the rim of her coffee cup. It was easier than going into a detailed explanation. Plus, she needed to speak to Saffron and Drake before she could say anything to Laila.

Laila's expression shifted noticeably as she studied Reen's face. "Oh, Reenie," she said, clasping Reen's shoulder, "you don't have allergies. You've been crying."

"Please, Laila." Reen sucked in a deep breath, vowing not to let the waterworks start again. She hadn't cried since leaving Tidal Wave Tavern yesterday. "Not now. If I start talking about it I'll start crying all over again and go back to looking like an extraterrestrial."

Scrunching her face, Laila laughed. "What?"

Reen managed a smile. "Like I said, I'm fine. I just need some time. You'll understand after we talk." She hoped Laila would, because the last thing she wanted was to hurt her sister's feelings.

"Okay..." Laila nodded, "okay." Still nursing a look of concern, she headed back to the bakery's kitchen.

"Close call," Reen muttered to herself as she popped the last of the scone into her mouth.

With her head buried in work-related details in the bakery's office behind the storefront, the hours flew by. Last night Laila had texted her to stay at home and relax today but Reen needed to get out of the house, away from engulfing thoughts about choosing her heartwish. At work, Reen had little time to ponder her personal problems, which was the way she wanted it.

"Tuesday already," she muttered, glancing up at the schedule Laila had made for the staff. Ignoring Reen's protests, she'd put Reen on light duty and short days, warning her to stick to paperwork and forget about lifting heavy trays of baked goods until she was fully healed. Her desk job at TGP had nothing to do with helping out in the kitchen but Reen enjoyed getting involved in Laila's baking process, assisting her sister and the bake staff wherever she could.

Two covered plastic bins on the floor in the corner of her office held the Valentine decorations the staff had removed from display after the holiday. Momentarily distracted by the boxes, Reen allowed her thoughts to travel back to Saturday's events and all that followed.

"So many changes in just three days," she said, forcing her attention back to number crunching.

Ten minutes later, Laila called out to her sister as Reen plodded through the financials. When Reen looked up, she observed Laila's cautioning expression as her sister tapped her wrist where a watch would be.

"It's one-thirty. You were supposed to leave at noon today, remember?"

"I know but I just want to finish up the—"

"Get your broken butt, shattered ankle, and puffy Cheetos face out of here, Maureen," Laila interrupted. "Now!"

There was no use arguing with her protective sister. Reen saluted Laila, offering a crisp, "Yes ma'am!"

She smiled when she stepped outside. It was another dry, sunny February day at the Oregon coast.

Filling her lungs with fresh air as she walked to her car, she felt thankful for the many blessings in her life. "It feels good to be alive," she noted aloud. There were so many more positives than negatives. With Monica's grim future in mind, Reen reminded herself that, while things were still a mess, it was only temporary. She'd slog through it all and survive.

"Maureen, wait up!"

At the sound of the voice behind her, Reen froze in place on the sidewalk. "Hud..." she murmured. "Oh hell..." She could hear him jogging to catch up to her. A moment later he was at her side.

"You're a hard one to reach." Hud gave her a bright, generous smile. "Didn't you get my texts and voicemails?"

"I did...I'm sorry, Hud, I just—"

"You're not going to make me beg to take you out for that cup of coffee, are you? Because," he thumbed his chest, "Hudson Griffin never begs." Full of charm, he winked at Reen as she looked up at him, attempting a smile.

Remembering what Sabrina told her Saturday, Reen said, "I thought you were working out of town." She wished she'd listened to Laila and had left work earlier. She wasn't ready for this, even though she knew it was a very necessary talk.

"I was just about to leave. We had to postpone construction because all the materials hadn't arrived on the jobsite. I'm headed for my truck as we speak." He motioned ahead and Reen followed where he pointed, catching sight of his Griffin of All Trades vehicle parked just down the street.

"Keeping tabs on me, hmm?" His teasing tone was light and carefree.

Oh good grief. "No, I—"

He looped his thumbs in the pockets of his jeans. The guy was appealing, devastatingly handsome, but any romantic interest Reen might have had in him previously had dissolved.

"I'll be in Rainspring Grove for a week or two. We're working on an expansion project at one of the wineries. From the plans I've seen, the place should be quite an attraction when it's finished."

"Sounds nice. That's beautiful country with all the velvety green hills and valleys." Feeling her pulse thumping fast in her ears, Reen willed herself to calm down. Talking to Hud was on her to-do list, but toward the bottom. She wasn't prepared for this accidental encounter.

"Well," Reen said with her best adios smile, "have a good drive, Hud. I hope all goes well with your job. Good seeing you." She picked up her pace. Sadly, the speed with which she clumped along ensured a caterpillar could keep up, so Hud had zero trouble.

"I won't be home this weekend but I should be back next Friday. Beachstreet Brazilian Steakhouse just opened in Wisdom Harbor. Supposed to be great. Heard of it?"

He obviously wasn't taking the hint. "I saw an ad for it." Reen envisioned blue electrical current emanating from her eyes as she tried beaming telepathic rays at him, urging him not to ask her for a date. *Please don't ask...please don't ask...*

"I'd really like to take you there for dinner, Reen."

Her shoulders sagged. Clearly she wasn't gifted with her sister Kady's woo-woo gene.

"It's about time we got to know each other better," he went on. "Friday, Saturday, Sunday," Hud shrugged, "whatever works best for you."

"Hud, I'm sorry, but..." Stopping in place, she closed her eyes, drawing in a deep breath. When she opened her eyes Hud's happy-go-lucky expression had converted to wary.

"Well I'll be damned. You're turning me down, aren't you?" Reen answered with an apologetic smile. "Why, Reen? I thought you—"

She touched his arm. "Because you belong with Monica," she told him without hesitation. "Thank you for the invitation, Hud, but we both know your heart's with Monica."

Hud's eyebrows pinched. "Apparently you haven't heard. We're no longer seeing each other."

"I heard." Reen nodded. "I think you're a great guy, Hud. I value our friendship and—"

"Aw, come on. The friend speech twice in the matter of two weeks?" Clapping his hand against his chest, fingers spread wide, he groaned. "What the hell. You've got to be kidding me. The next thing I know, you'll be telling me I have a great personality." He rolled his eyes.

"Well," she offered a one-sided shrug, "it's true. You do." In her pathetic attempt to lighten the situation, Reen felt the corners of her mouth quiver as she tried to smile. If she hadn't been so nervous she wouldn't have made the stupid mistake of calling him a good friend while he was asking her out. Hadn't she learned anything from her embarrassing blunder with Drake last year? The last thing she wanted was to have her unintentionally callous remark salt Hud's still fresh wound.

"I don't get it. I thought you had a thing for me, especially after that house-on-fire kiss we shared at the Fling." His hand plowed through his hair as he chortled a laugh. "Wow, just goes to show you, you can never figure out a woman."

"I'm sorry. Really. The kiss was great. You're right, I did have a thing for you," she admitted. It was probably the most difficult thing she'd confessed to a guy since that time in third grade when she told Marty Maston she liked him and he ridiculed her in front of the whole class. But she needed to put her own feelings on the back burner now and do her best to soothe Hud's injured ego.

It was weird that she felt the need to soothe the ego of one of the hottest, most eligible bachelors in Glassfloat Bay. However, gorgeous or not, she'd just stomped on his ego a few days after he'd been summarily dumped by Monica.

"At least I thought I did," she went on. "And why not? You're a real catch, Hud." Issuing the compliment, she smiled up at him, without him returning her smile. "But" her shoulders hiked into a contrite shrug, "sometimes things happen when we least expect it. Unplanned, inexplicable things."

"Yeah...tell me about it." Hud's previously cheerful expression was toast.

"I know you still have strong feelings for Monica and—"

"What?" He looked at her like she was crazy. "Do I look like I'm wearing a loser t-shirt with *I'm pining for Monica Sharp* across the front?" He gestured over his chest with his hand. "I don't know where you're getting your information, Reen. Scratch that, you probably got it from one of my sisters, but you're wrong." He jabbed a finger toward her. "And so are they. Monica and I are over. Done. I don't want anything to do with her. She's made it abundantly clear she feels the same way."

Hud looked downright angry. Or was it hurt? Most likely half and half. "You have feelings for Monica," Reen repeated, keeping her tone gentle. Wrapping her arm around his waist as they walked, she felt him stiffen against her touch. "And I'm sure Monica has feelings for you. You love each other and belong together."

"Oh for chrissakes," he muttered beneath his breath. "I don't know if you're trying to play therapist or fortune teller, Maureen, but neither's working." Hud stopped walking long enough to nail her with an accusatory look. "When I stopped to ask you out I hadn't counted on being on the receiving end of your motherly concern. Trust me, that's not what a man expects from a woman he just invited to dinner. You don't know anything about what happened between me and Monica—"

"I know she chose to end the relationship and told you she wanted to be friends," Reen swiftly interjected, intent on doing everything possible to get the two of them back together—for whatever short time Monica had left. "I'm sure Monica regrets it, Hud. You should give her a call or go see her and tell her how you feel about her. Let her know you want to make things work. Maybe you'll—"

"And maybe you should mind your own damn business, Reen." He sped ahead.

"Hud, wait! Please!" With her boot slowing her down, catching up to him took a lot of resolve. She grabbed his sleeve, yanking until he turned to her. She had to make him listen. It truly *was* a matter of life and death.

His narrowed gaze fell to her hand on his arm. Frustration was evident in his sigh. "I'm late, Maureen. I've got to go." Hud jerked his arm from her grasp.

"Listen to me for just a minute. *Please*," she pleaded. "You need to go to Monica. You'll never forgive yourself if you don't."

"What?!" His incredulous expression told her he thought she was nuts. That's okay. She could deal with him thinking she was a crackpot as long as she got through to him.

"She loves you, Hud. I know she does. And she needs you. *Hud...Monica needs you!*"

Reen hated being vague with him but she didn't know how else to handle it. She was on the verge of telling him about Monica's cancer and critical prognosis, but Monica would be mortified if she knew Reen had overheard the conversation with Nancy. The only other way Reen could know Monica had cancer was through Saffron, and Reen wouldn't risk having Monica think Saffron had disclosed such private, personal information when Monica had specifically asked her not to share it with anyone.

Still gawking at her with a quizzical expression conveying his doubts about her sanity, Hud said, "Seriously, what the hell, Reen? I never figured you for being such a busybody. A pushy, screwball one at that. I gotta go."

She clasped his sleeve again. "Monica needs you, Hud. You need to go to her."

"Dammit, Maureen..." Irritably shrugging her hand from his sleeve again, he nailed her with an exasperated look, demanding, "Why do you keep saying Monica needs me? Did she tell you that?"

"No, I...I have a strong feeling." Reen supposed she sounded absurd but it didn't matter. A sudden, inexplicable sense of urgency told her it was imperative that she get through to Hud...*now*. "Look, Hud, I don't care if you think I'm screwy or a busybody, I just need to make you listen. Please, you need to hear me. Go to Monica. She needs you, right now. I-I feel it deep inside." Reen clutched her gut.

Hud barked a surly laugh. "And here I thought that psychic crap was your sister Kady's shtick. See you around, Reen." He shoved his hands in his pockets and headed for his truck, just a few yards away.

She stood there for a moment, watching him get into the vehicle, clearly grumbling to himself as he got situated. "Well, that didn't go well," she chastised herself. With her car less than a block away, she kept walking. "Note to self—you can cross therapist and consultant off your list of possible career goals."

She would have to be an idiot not to know she had no damn business interfering with Hud and Monica. But she longed to help. Even when Reen was blindly convinced Hud was *The One* for her, it was in-your-face obvious how much he and Monica cared for each other. She'd simply chosen to ignore it.

If only Hud realized he and Monica were missing the opportunity to spend time being close before cancer robbed her—and him—of her life. It was beyond heartbreaking.

Reen's car was parked close to String Me Along. Her pace came to a halt in front of the store as she studied the shop's winter-themed window display, smiling when she spotted the bluebird scene she'd created for Ruthie while still in her cast. The older woman had a great fondness for the birds.

Fashioned from knitted and crocheted objects, the tableau was in calming shades of blue, gray, and white. Two colossal wooden knitting needles and a pair of wood crochet hooks were crisscrossed over the width of the window.

Reen had constructed the sizeable 3-D bluebird using knitted and crocheted elements. It was her own design and she was pleased with how well it turned out. The bird, which had a pair of pearl-gray worms dangling from its beak, was perched on a white-knit-covered branch, simulating snow. She'd crafted the loopy, stringy bird's nest from dozens of strings of yarn that she'd later stiffened with white glue. The nest showcased three open-mouthed baby birds waiting to be fed.

Ruthie's handwritten calligraphy on a large card near the corner of the window read, *The Bluebird of Happiness: with thanks to Maureen Malone for her exquisite creativity and her generous heart.*

Reen's hand flew to her chest. "Oh my gosh." Touched by Ruthie's kind tribute, and the fact that she thought enough of Reen's work to use it as the main focus of her shop's display, had happy tears sprouting to her eyes.

Revisiting her bluebird scene reminded her of her motivation for creating it. She'd explained to Ruthie that the scene represented the preciousness of life, young and old. In crafting it, Reen had attempted to express how much joy Ruthie and String Me Along had brought not only to Reen, but to generations of knitters and crocheters.

The baby birds represented the hundreds of yarn workers, hungry to learn from Ruthie, while the Bluebird of Happiness itself represented Ruthie and the infinite delight she'd spread through her wonderful, patient lessons, and her shop's ever-evolving inventory.

Reen remembered how Ruthie's face seemed to light from within upon seeing her gift and hearing Reen's explanation. She'd thanked Reen profusely, promising she'd treasure the gift always.

Deciding to thank Ruthie for displaying her bluebird scene so beautifully, Reen reached for the door handle, turning and pushing to open it. It didn't budge. It was only then that she noticed the store's closed sign hanging through the door's glass.

It was unusual for the shop to be closed this early on a weekday. Perhaps Ruthie was short of help, or had an in-depth class to teach, or... Taking a deep breath, Reen willed her sudden dark thoughts away and stopped surmising.

Focusing on the display again, she was glad she'd stopped by. Viewing the hope-filled scene was like plugging herself into a USB port to recharge. The softly warming band of metal around her finger, and its gently glowing stone at the center, reinforced the sensation. It was almost as if the ring, or perhaps it was her heart, spoke to her.

Touched by a renewed sense of inspiration, Reen now had the impetus she needed to set her heartwish in motion.

Chapter Seventeen

~<>~

REEN COULD HAVE left Bekka House and gone back to her own place as soon as she got out of the cast and had Frankie strapped on her leg. But she felt more at home here. The large, nearly century-old structure was left to Reen's family after her Norwegian grandmother, Rebekka Eriksen, passed away. The family loved Bekka, her warm, welcoming house, and the property's lovely location near the sea. The trio of loveable ghosts who haunted it were the icing on the cake.

Reen knelt at the foot of the vintage aluminum Christmas tree. She'd turned on the rotating color wheel, watching it glimmer across the quirky collection of ornaments. Releasing a contented sigh, she smiled, feeling at ease for the first time in days.

"This is it, Hazelnut." Reen's fingers gently raked through the dog's fur. "The perfect spot to make my heartwish." Her mother and sisters were right, she didn't need to agonize about the right wish to make. All at once it came to her, telling Reen what her heart already knew.

She could almost feel her heart swell with joy when the multifaceted wish made itself clear. Her wish would be made from a place of love in her heart, rather than a place of hurt, sadness or, worse, bitterness.

A sense of tranquility enveloped Reen as she made her preparations. "It's the perfect wish. The only one I could possibly make," she muttered while plumping a large floor pillow, then topping it with her donut pillow.

The family room of Bekka House was the heart of the home. There were so many wonderful memories and so much love between these walls, Reen felt as if she were cocooned in generations of affection.

She'd left her phone buried in her purse all day and hadn't heard the texts or voicemail alerts that arrived. A quick glance now told Reen all she needed to know.

Her mother texted, saying she'd talked to Nevan and needed to speak to Reen about Drake. Nevan texted, saying *he* needed to talk to Reen about Drake. And Drake texted, saying they really needed to talk. Finally, there was a text from Saffron, telling Reen they needed to talk.

"Nope, nope, nope, and nope." She already knew what they all had to say. She'd deal with it all. Eventually. Silencing her phone by setting it on airplane mode, she tossed it onto the couch several feet away. "They'll all have to wait until I'm finished crafting my very special heartwish."

When the teakettle whistled, Reen, with Hazelnut at her heels, headed for the kitchen to make herself a pot of tea, using equal portions of the three healing tea blends Kady had formulated. Her little sister had created this with love, expressly for Reen, which told her it would be a perfect accompaniment to her wish making process. She added a small dollop from the jar of local, raw Pacific Northwest honey Kady had included.

Wafting the warm, aromatic air from the pot of herbal tea toward her, Reen closed her eyes, breathing in deeply. "Mmm, smells heavenly." Swathed in the woodsy, wildflower scents of tea, honey, and Kady's healing balm had a calming, meditative effect.

Back in the family room she dragged the coffee table close to the silver tree, setting her pot of tea and one of Grandma Bekka's favorite china teacup and saucer sets in the center. Next to those, Reen positioned her laptop along with additional elements of Kady's lovingly prepared healing kit: the clear quartz crystal, small amethyst cluster, package of lavender-patchouli incense sticks, and the flash drive filled with lyrical chanting and dolphin music Kady had created.

As the soothing music played, Reen lit a stick of incense before surveying the scene she'd staged. Deciding everything was perfect for her wish-making, Reen indulged in a satisfied smile.

She watched as her curious dog slanted her head this way and that while melodic harmonies of ocean waves, chattering dolphins, tweeting birds, chanting humans, and unfamiliar musical instruments chimed through the air.

Nibbling a fingernail, Reen gave her carefully crafted scene a final look. "Hmm...something's missing..."

Snapping her fingers, Reen headed for her bedroom where she withdrew a small photograph from her nightstand drawer.

Positioning the photo to rest in the trench between the rows of keys on her laptop's keyboard, Reen gazed at it for a long moment with a heartfelt smile.

The picture of Reen, Drake, Lilly and Kevin was taken at last year's Jazz Festival in the Park, on the university's campus in Wisdom Harbor. A vendor offering face-painting for the children took it with a Polaroid camera after the twins' faces were decorated with vibrant, glittery designs. They stood smiling with Reen and Drake behind them, hands on the children's shoulders, and leaning their heads together as they beamed grins at the photographer.

Reen remembered the day well. It was one of her favorite photos. Her phone was full of pictures of Drake and his kids but this one was special. The four of them looked like a happy family having the best time ever—which is exactly what that autumn day had been like. Also, this photo was the only one Reen had with Drake that she could hold in her hand.

"You'll need to be brave, Hazel." The last couple of times Reen was present during a heartwish, the one for Laila, then the one for Gard, glowing blue light sparked from the ring, filling the room.

"So don't get scared, okay, sweetie?" She ruffed Hazelnut's fur as the dog sat unfazed. Before continuing, she poured herself a cup of Kady's tea, taking a few sips. It was flavorful, soothing, and helped to strengthen her resolve.

Reen sat on the pillow with Hazelnut's head resting in her lap. "My pre-wish preliminaries need to come first," she told the indifferent dog while positioning her laptop so she could see the screen clearly. The open document displayed the notes she'd made to remind herself of the points she needed to address before making the heartwish itself.

Closing her eyes, Reen focused on a mental image of Saffron. Addressing the universe, as Kady would say, she spoke softly, with conviction. "I'm sorry it's taken us so long to get to know each other, Saffron. I want us to become better friends. I believe in time we will. I'm ashamed of myself for judging you so harshly. Monica is so fortunate to have you in her life. I deeply regret the pain it caused you when Drake and I kissed. I want you to be happy with the man you love, Saffron. I will never do anything to prevent that and will always be in your corner."

After opening her eyes and expelling a clearing breath, Reen gazed at the laptop's screen again, reading what she wrote. She breathed a lengthy sigh.

"Drake," she began, her attention shifting to the photograph, "you've been a great friend to me. We've had tremendous fun together, and we've shared some critical events. You were with me when Laila's life turned upside down because she found a genie in a bottle." A slow smile took hold as Reen recalled the remarkable adventure and how wonderful Drake had been through it all.

"You're a good man, Drake, and a wonderful father. My mom and sisters wondered if I was afraid to admit I had feelings for you because I thought it might be a betrayal to Bob, my late fiancé and your best friend." She went on with a wistful smile. "My guilt was for an entirely different reason."

Pausing, her eyelids fluttered closed and she inhaled deeply before taking another fortifying sip of tea. "My guilty, shameful secret, Drake, is that I worked hard to suppress my significant attraction to you while you were still married to Janet and I was engaged to Bob." She winced recalling how guilt-ridden she'd felt at the time.

"In fact," Reen's gaze floated to the alternating colors highlighting the aluminum tree, "I think I was in love with you then." She looked skyward, vowing to be more honest with herself. "I don't think it, I know it. I was basically lusting after you in my heart. Do you have any idea how ashamed I am about that, Drake? It was a betrayal to Bob, a kind, wonderful man, and to Janet, who was my friend at the time, even though she turned out to be a skanky viper."

Gathering her thoughts, she regarded the sparkling silver tree again, finding the changing colors meditative.

"Last year when you tried to kiss me after the opera, I was thrilled. I'd spotted signs of your interest in me, but it was amazing to have it confirmed that night. You looked so handsome. I watched your face draw near, your lips mere inches from mine and then...all I could think of was infidelity. So I ducked."

Reen breathed a wobbly sigh of frustration before finishing the tea in her cup and pouring another. "Silly, I know, because there was never any cheating involved. We were both free by then but still..." She ran her fingertip over the photograph. "I never should have ducked. Everything would be different now if only I hadn't acted so colossally stupid that night." With a resigned sigh, she added, "I don't want to dwell on what might have been. If I get caught up in what-ifs, I'll never get through this." Pausing, she sipped from her tea, silently reading her notes and willing herself not to get weepy.

"This talking to the universe thing is more difficult than I thought."

She focused on the sweet, spicy fragrance of the lavender-patchouli incense wafting through the air, and the melodic sounds of dolphins surrounding her. Her gaze fell on the sweet little Norwegian boy and girl ornaments hanging on the tree, which held special significance to Delaney and Varik—the Viking her sister had dreamed of her entire life before he showed up on her doorstep in person. Remembering their unlikely romance made her smile.

"I think I conjured up my supposed crush on Hud as a coverup so no one would suspect I had feelings for you, Drake. I did such a good job, I even had myself believing it." Reen laughed gently. "I acted surprised when people said they knew I had a crush on Hud but, in truth, I wanted everyone to know so they wouldn't focus on matchmaking for you and me."

She sipped from the herbal tea, appreciating its ginger essence, while glimpsing her laptop screen, scrolling through her notes.

"I'm speaking from my heart to yours right now, Drake. You deserve all the best in life. So does Saffron. I can't imagine two people better suited to one another. I have no doubt whatsoever that she'll be a wonderful wife and terrific stepmom. Be happy always, you two. You have my sincerest blessings and heartfelt best wishes."

Experiencing the familiar sting of approaching tears, Reen took a deep breath and fanned her eyes.

"My darling, hunky-dorky professor, you are my sweetheart, my dearest love. Drake Slattery, I'll love you until the day I die." Smiling, she closed her eyes. "Though I'll forever carry that love in my heart, it'll be tucked in a far corner where even I will have trouble finding it. From this day forward I'll be your good, platonic friend, always there whenever you, Saffron, or your children need me. Amen."

Reen wasn't sure why she said *amen*. She hadn't said a prayer, and the word wasn't in her notes. It just felt right.

With a gentle, introspective chuckle, she concluded, "Maybe it was a prayer after all."

Her heartwish prominent in her thoughts, Reen took time finishing her second cup of tea, grateful for her little sister's kind, caring heart.

"Okay, Hazelnut, this is it. Time to make my heartwish." The metal band around her finger grew comfortably warm, while the heartwish stone glowed.

"I'm not wishing for a man in my life, or for love. If it's meant to be, I'll find it on my own. My wish is multilayered, involving more than one person. Since it's the wish my heart needs to make, I think that's all right." She looked toward heaven. "Dearest Grandma Bekka, please help guide me to make this wish in such a way that it's certain to be granted."

As she rested her hand against her heart, the stone's glow encompassed her. Following a silent prayer, Reen uttered some of the most important words she'd ever speak.

"As I make this wish, my heart and soul make it as well. It is my truest, deepest heartwish." If she hadn't witnessed previous heartwishes, she might have been unnerved by the light radiating from her ring but she expected it.

"First, I wish for vibrant, healthful life to be restored to Monica Sharp. My wish is for a full recovery, complete healing, with all traces of cancer eradicated so she will go on to live a long, happy life surrounded by those she loves, and who love her, including Hudson Griffin."

Reen felt vibration in her hand as an arc of blue-white light darted from her ring like a mighty spark of electricity to the knitted angel ornament she'd made for the family's silver tree. Hazelnut, who'd been sound asleep through Reen's lengthy discourse, woke up, her eyes popping wide as she scrambled to her feet, focusing on the rays of blue light surrounding Reen's angel ornament.

"It's okay, Hazel, don't worry." She hugged her dog who seemed more fascinated than fearful. "I think that's my confirmation the wish was accepted."

"The second part of my heartwish," the streak of blue light expanded as she spoke, now surrounding an angel ornament Astrid had crocheted for her children, "is for the profound spiritual, emotional and physical healing of Nancy Sharp, Monica's mother, so they can enjoy a healthy, loving, mother-daughter relationship from this point forward."

Preparing to make the final part of her wish, Reen noticed she and Hazelnut were cocooned in a bubble of gentle blue light. Surprisingly, Hazel seemed to comfortably accept it.

"The third and final part of my wish, is for little Shannon Brone, Ruthie's great-granddaughter." She looked up as rays of blue enveloped her knitted cocker spaniel dangling from the tree, the one that looked like Shannie's puppy, Lulu. "I ask that all traces of cancer are forever eliminated, and that she will go on to live a long, happy, healthy life."

Reen yearned to make her heartwish cover all children everywhere battling cancer and other diseases, but she knew that wasn't possible. Her inner knowing had already made it clear that she was pushing things by including Shannon's healing along with Monica's and Nancy's.

With the final portion of Reen's multifaceted wish complete, the entire family room became bathed in the inviting blue-white light. Reen and Hazelnut sat silently, staring at the magical, mystical magnificence of it all, before turning to each other, with Hazelnut giving a soft bark followed by a generous lick to Reen's face.

"Thanks, Hazel. I think we did a good job too."

One of many amazing factors for Reen during the wish making process was realizing her heartwish ring seemed to identify each wish in advance as the blue glow highlighted the ornaments most related to Reen's thoughts.

The fragrance of Bekka's *pepperkaker* filled the area, causing Hazelnut to lick her lips while sniffing the air. Reen had felt her grandmother's presence during the entire process.

"Thanks for your help, Grandma. Until now, I've made such an awful mess of things. I hope I did everything right. I wish I could know for sure whether or not all three parts of my heartwish have been granted."

At that precise moment, Reen's phone, the one she'd placed on airplane mode so she wouldn't be bothered, nearly exploded with one alert after another for voicemails, texts, and new calls just arriving.

"Wow...well I guess I'm about to find out," she said, an instant before someone started pounding on her front door.

Chapter Eighteen

~<>~

REEN WASN'T SURE what to do next. Should she answer the phone or the door? Had she succeeded, or had she unintentionally whipped up some disaster? Whoever was at the door was ringing the bell now as well as knocking. Persistently. Still dazed by the lightshow a few minutes ago, Hazelnut offered a belated bark as she headed for the door, dutifully alerting Reen of...something.

"All righty, the door it is." Sucking in a fortifying breath, Reen hoped whoever was on the other side had a smile rather a scowl.

Opening the door, she barely had time for it to register that she was looking into the eyes of a man wearing a knitted pink Viking hat with two ivory-colored horns and pair of long yellow yarn braids before she was grabbed hard against his chest and thoroughly kissed.

No doubt about it—that was Drake's kiss. Even after experiencing it only once, it was instantly recognizable.

Sinking into the exquisiteness of his kiss, Reen heard herself whimper in his arms. Dear God, this is what she wanted. This, *THIS* was her unexpressed heartwish—the one she'd purposely avoided making because she knew he was in love with Saffron.

Saffron!

The reminder sobered Reen enough to give Drake a forceful push away from her.

"Drake Slattery, what the hell?" Her shallow panting and thundering heartbeat failed to instill the accusatory question with as much vehemence as she'd intended.

"Nice to see you too, Maureen. Since you've been unreachable since Saturday, I thought maybe you'd moved to Timbuktu." His chuckle sounded frustrated. When Reen opened her mouth to respond, he held up his hand. "Please, do me a favor and keep quiet so I can have my say."

"I will not!" She backed away as he stepped closer. "What are you doing here? If that Viking hat is supposed to soften me up so I forget what you said about me, it's not going to work," she lied, thinking he looked absolutely adorable and it was quite clever of him to show up on her doorstep wearing the silly thing.

"It's on loan from Lilly." He held the braids out to the sides. "What do you think? Totally me, right?"

Determined not to smile at his endearing playfulness, Reen continued her harangue. "What on earth will Saffron think if she finds out you barged in here forcing a kiss on me?"

"She'll think I'm madly in love with you. And like me, she'll think you're a stubborn little idiot."

"Idiot? Oh yeah? Well—" She stopped abruptly, her mouth snapping closed when the rest of his words finally sank in. "In love?" If she had a mirror she'd probably glimpse a pair of huge anime eyes looking back at her. A smidgen of her icy rage began to thaw...but then her brain summoned up Drake's mean, cruel, brutal conversation with Nevan.

Nope, uh-uh. Regardless of his lovability quotient, she wasn't about to let Drake Slattery make a fool of her.

"What are you talking about?" she demanded, fists planted at her hips. "With my own ears I overheard you tell my brother you love Saffron—that you all but despise me." Her eyes narrowed.

"If you'd answered your mother's calls and texts, or your brother's, or mine, you would have learned you'd only heard a portion of that conversation. If Astrid hadn't called me I wouldn't have known what happened."

"My mother called you?"

With a slow nod, Drake confirmed, "Right after she spoke to Nevan and he told her about our talk. The three of us have been trying to reach you ever since, but you've been avoiding us."

"I've been busy, getting ready to make my heartwish," she informed him. "Which I just did before you arrived."

"Ah," Drake's arms folded over his chest, "so I must have been your wish then." His devilish smile was bracketed by the pair of yellow yarn braids. "I was, wasn't I?"

"No, Professor Giant Ego, my heartwish had nothing to do with you."

"Really?" Leaning one hand against the doorjamb, he looked unconvinced. And incredibly enticing. "And yet, *voila*, here I am, right after you made your wish." His expression shifted from skeptical to smug as he gestured wide.

"Pure coincidence," Reen insisted.

"Is that so? Then what did you wish for, hmm?" Drake bent the ivory-knitted horns back and forth as he spoke, accompanying the action with a confident grin.

Refusing to smile, which was more difficult by the minute, Reen paused before responding. She wanted to keep the wish to herself. Whether it worked or not, she didn't want to cause Monica any embarrassment, or to take credit for her healing. She wanted to do something kind and unselfish. Something pure. If she boasted about it she'd only be looking for praise and admiration. She couldn't imagine heartwishes were meant to work that way.

"Something personal and private," she finally told Drake, who continued playing with the Viking hat. "Will you please take that thing off." She motioned to his pink headgear. "How am I supposed to have a serious conversation with you when you look—"

"Irresistible? Adorable?" he offered helpfully. "Or maybe the word you're looking for is kissable." One eyebrow shot up in a beguiling manner.

Reen decided his dazzling smile should come with a *Caution: Danger of Succumbing to Adorability* warning.

She assured him, "That's not what I was going to say," even though she was thinking it. Eager to change the subject, she kept her expression somber. "Why did my mother call you?"

"She wanted to confirm what Nevan told her." He slipped the Viking cap from his head, placing it on the small table near the door. Reen was kind of sorry to see it go. Glancing up at the top of his head she spotted his dark hair spiking in some spots and flattened in others. Even hat-hair looked appealing on Drake.

Resisting the temptation to smooth his haphazard hair with her fingers, she focused on his lying, two-faced explanation instead.

"If you had stayed there," Drake continued, "snooping on Nevan and me a few minutes longer," his expression had a distinct *gotcha* feel to it, "you would have heard me tell your brother—"

"That I drive you crazy? Yeah, I already know that. That I'm stubborn, pigheaded, have no common sense, and speak before thinking? Go ahead and deny it, Drake, I dare you."

"Nope, all that's true but—"

Reen's startled gasp was accompanied by a strangled, "What?!" Flailing an outstretched finger at him she pushed against his chest. "I can't believe you actually admitted it! You also said I'm a hoarder, obsessed with useless junk. Then you said—"

"Wow..." Drake gazed at her with astonishment. "And here I thought your genie brother-in-law, Zak, was the only one in the family with a photographic memory. If you'd just keep quiet long enough for me to explain—"

"Explain what? That you also said I have yarn for brains and the self-confidence of a peanut? Sound familiar, Romeo?" Not allowing Drake to get a word in edgewise, she added, "Then came all the things you love about Saffron. Mmm-hmm," her head bobbed like it was on a tightly-wound spring, "I heard every word." Reen crossed her arms over her chest, jutting her chin toward the ceiling.

"I said lots of nice things about Saffron, all of which are true. Then I said—"

Spreading her fingers wide, she held her hand in front of his face. "I. Don't. Care. I already heard everything I need to hear. You're just trying to make it up to me because you got caught, that's all. It's obvious that you—"

"Stop, just stop!" His features drawing into a scowl, he stepped toward Reen, clapping his hand over her mouth. "There, you see? It's just like I told your brother, you make me crazy! You have a penchant for that." Reen tried grumbling a fiery response but Drake practically yelled, "For God's sake, will you please just keep quiet for five minutes and stop jumping to conclusions?"

Looking up into his eyes, his beautiful blue-gray eyes that looked all serious and stormy, Reen nodded. She figured she may as well hear him out, if for no other reason than to watch the big phony stand there, squirming, as he tried to cover his tracks with a flimsy veil of lies.

Slipping his hand from her mouth, Drake finger-combed his flattened hat-hair, his voice softening as he told her, "You would have heard me tell your brother that when you're crazy in love with someone, like I am with you, nothing else matters. I told Nevan I love his beautiful sister for exactly who she is. I wouldn't change a thing about you, Reen. I told him I love you for all of your kooky seemingly brainless traits."

"You did?" Her voice came out like one of Hazelnut's squeaky mouse toys.

"I did." Gently cupping her face with his hands, he brought his lips to hers, kissing her the way he did in her dreams. It was like she'd won the lottery, which was mindboggling because, as much as she longed for Drake to love her, this wasn't even part of her heartwish.

"I love you, Maureen," Drake reaffirmed once their lips parted, leaving her with the blissful knowledge that she'd never grow tired of hearing him repeat those words. "And I know you love me too, so don't try to deny it. It's high time we stopped playing games with each other. We're best friends, and always will be, but that's not enough for me."

"I love you too, Drake. I have for a long time." Tugging his head down, she dotted little kisses all over his face, as far as she could reach. He reciprocated by holding her in a loving embrace. It felt so natural, so perfect, to be in Drake's arms. This is where she belonged.

"So what are we going to do about it?" Drake released her, holding Reen at arm's length.

Beyond eager to have this long overdue conversation with the man she loved—and who loved her—Reen's mouth popped open to offer her best, most joy-worthy suggestions...until she remembered her cousin.

"What about Saffron?" she asked, angst building as she ran her fingers through her hair. "She's crazy about you, Drake, and I've already hurt her so much."

"It's going to be okay. Saffron and I met over coffee and had a long talk. If you check your phone you'll find a message from her too. She wants you to know she was upset and overreacted when she left you the first voicemail. She knows you'd never purposely try to hurt her."

"Really? You're sure?" Happy tears gathered in Reen's eyes.

"Positive. I explained everything to her." He brushed a single tear from her cheek with his thumb. "I was completely honest...told her I love you. She said she'd always suspected we had feelings for each other. When I apologized for the kiss at the Fling, which was inappropriate with her being my date, she surprised me by breaking into a big grin. She called our kiss a clear case of spontaneous combustion." Drake laughed. "She had that right."

Reen felt a colossal pressure lifting. "I would never, *ever*, intentionally hurt my cousin."

"She knows that." Drake smoothed Reen's hair back with his fingers. "No one who knows you would believe you're capable of something so mean. Kooky? Hell yes." He laughed as Reen opened her mouth to protest and he shushed her with a swift kiss. "Cruel or unkind? Never." A lengthier kiss this time. "Saffron told me about her visit to see you on Saturday, when she confessed to you that she had feelings for me."

"She did? Poor thing...she must be devastated." Reen nibbled her bottom lip.

"Not so much." Drake let out a cheery pop of laughter. "Apparently I'm already like yesterday's cold mashed potatoes."

Reen's head tilted in confusion. "Huh?"

"Does the name Calder Maythorne mean anything to you?"

"Sure, he's—"

"The guy your cousin's been crushing on for more than a decade. After seeing her at the Fling he looked her up, found out she was working Sunday, and stopped by the real estate office that morning. He asked her out, which means your formerly heartbroken cousin is now in seventh heaven." Drake's relieved smile was a mile wide.

"Wow, that's fabulous! I'm so happy for Saffron." Reen clasped his hand. "She deserves every bit of happiness she can get. However..." She cupped his face, reaching on her tiptoes to give him a sweet kiss.

"However?"

"Calder Maythorne is no Drake Slattery," Reen let him know. "I'd say Saffron got the raw end of the deal. I'm happy because now I get to keep my darling, hunky-dorky professor all to myself." She rested her head against his heart, relishing in the clean, crisp smell of his aftershave and the hard cushion of his chest muscles beneath his sweater.

"There's that hunky-dorky expression of yours again." His eyebrow arched in question. "What exactly does that mean?"

"You've probably heard my mom say *hunky-dory*. It's a favorite phrase of hers, meaning everything's peachy. Well, with you in mind, I sort of," she offered a coy shrug, "altered the saying to fit you better."

His tentative expression told Reen he was still clueless. "You know..." Reen batted her eyelashes at him, "hunky as in tall, dark and handsome."

"That I like." Drake held her close.

"And dorky as in brainy intellectual bookworm," she finished, her hand gesturing from his head to his toes. "Hunky-dorky!"

Frowning, he held her at arm's length again. "You're telling me that's a good thing?"

"Uh-huh. The best." She loved the way he looked at her, the way he smiled. The teasing sparkle in his eyes. So adorable. So charming. So tantalizingly hers.

"Come on," she took him by the hand, "let's sit down. I'll make us a fresh pot of my sister Kady's herbal tea." She laughed when Drake wrinkled his nose. "Or some coffee. We've got so much to talk about."

"Great idea, but first," he remained in place, holding both her hands and offering another killer smile, "you can admit it now. You made your heartwish about me. About us. Didn't you? Go ahead and confess, I promise I won't tease you about it...too much." He gave Reen a playful wink. "I'm sad to say you wasted your wish though, because I've been in love with you for eons. Any magic between us has been there for a long time, without us owing our love to an ancient Viking ring."

Indulging in a dreamy sigh, Reen said, "That was beautiful, but honest, Drake, my heartwish wasn't about you."

"Well if your wish wasn't about us getting together, then what or who—"

Drake's question was interrupted by the doorbell and knocking at the door.

Smiling up at Drake before she answered the door, Reen told him, "I want to keep the heartwish to myself for now. I promise to tell you about it one day, okay?"

As Drake opened his mouth to respond, his eyes and Reen's went wide as they heard, "Maureen, it's Hud. Let me in, I've got to talk to you." The knocking became insistent.

With a slow, deliberate turn toward Reen, Drake stared at her. "Hud?" It was part question, part accusation. "You wished for Hud Griffin?" His expression was all kinds of wounded and a few shades of angry.

"No, Drake, I—"

"Reen? I know you're there, I can hear you talking. Open the door, please. It's important."

Her heart thudding, Reen opened the door, angling her head in curiosity. "Hud? I thought you left for Rainspring Gr—" Before she could finish her sentence, Hud grabbed her into an embrace, practically forcing the air out of her lungs and startling the heck out of her. It was the second time in less than an hour that she'd been yanked into a lung-deflating clinch.

"I love you, Maureen Malone," Hud said into her hair, doing a partial rocking motion as he continued holding her in his arms.

"Damn. It *was* Hud," Drake said, sounding none too happy about it and huffing a humorless laugh. "Naturally. I should have known."

Placing a hand over Drake's arm as Hud finally released her, Reen shook her head. "No, Drake, it wasn't..." She breathed a full-blown sigh as Drake crossed his arms over his chest, nursing a mighty scowl. "Now who's jumping to conclusions?" She looked at him with what she felt sure was the same mask of frustration she'd seen on his face earlier when he accused her of not listening to him.

Tsking, she focused on Hud. "Hud, what are you doing here?" she asked, truly clueless. "What's this all about? Come in," she ushered him with her hand, "Drake and I were just about to have some tea or coffee."

"I'm here to thank you for being a busy body, Reen." Hud's laughter was gentle. "I can only stay a few minutes, I'm on an errand and have to get back soon. After we talked earlier I got in my truck, heading for Rainspring Grove." Hud looked at Drake and grinned. "Maureen really ticked me off."

"Did she now?" Drake asked, looking like he'd just sucked a lemon.

"Big time, sticking her nose into my personal business and pestering me."

"Pestering?" Drake shot another biting look at Reen. "She wanted you to go out with her?"

"What?" Scrunching his features, Hud looked at him like he was crazy. "No, she turned me down cold. Reen was badgering me to go to Monica, to get her back."

Drake's arms uncrossed. "Oh." He gave Rene a sheepish look and, with a slow nod, she narrowed an I-told-you-so eye at him.

"Thank God you did, Maureen." Hud expelled a deep breath with a whoosh. "While driving I kept turning what you said over in my mind," his finger twirled around his head, "especially about me needing to go to Monica. You said I'd never forgive myself if I didn't go right away. Remember?"

Reen nodded. "I do."

"How did you know, Reen? How could you possibly have known?"

Her eyebrows knitted in puzzlement. "Know what?"

"I was halfway to Rainspring Grove when I turned around, heading back. I drove straight to Monica's apartment. Saffron was there. I got there just after she'd called 9-1-1." Turning sheet white as he spoke, a sheen of tears glistened in Hud's eyes. "Monica had collapsed. Her heart stopped beating."

Both Reen and Drake gasped.

"I performed CPR until the med team got there. Her heart stopped and started three times before they arrived, and then again in the ambulance."

"Oh my God." Reen's hand flew to her throat.

Echoing Reen's words, Drake was just as stunned.

"Moments before the paramedics arrived Monica briefly regained consciousness. She gave me the biggest smile, Reen, and then she cried, telling me she loved me. Asking me to forgive her. Forgive her...can you imagine?" His eyes closed tight and Reen spotted tears rolling down his cheeks. It was an odd sight for a man like Hud.

"At the hospital," Hud continued, swiping a hand over his eyes, "in the ER, I met her oncologist. He spoke to me and Saffron as the medical team worked on Monica. Did you know she had stage four cancer?" Without waiting for an answer, he went on, "I had no idea. She kept it from me...from everyone, Saffron told me. The doctor said there wasn't any hope. Monica was in the end stages and would die, probably within the hour. We were allowed in to say our final goodbyes."

The expression on Hud's face changed, the color returning to his cheeks and his demeanor brightening. "My God...I'll never forget what happened next. Not for the rest of my life."

Drake rested his hand on Hud's shoulder. "What happened?"

With a faraway look in his eyes, Hud said, "We were losing her, my sweet, beautiful Monica. Her breaths became shallow...so thin we could barely detect them. I told her I'd love her forever and then it happened. The blue light." Hud's hands gestured wide, his fingers spread open like a magician making a grand *poof* motion.

"It flooded the entire room, bleeding out into the hall. The machines she was hooked up to went crazy, buzzing and beeping. I wondered, did she die and am I seeing her soul depart?" He shook his head as if to clear it. "I know it sounds nuts but, you should have seen that light. It was almost as if Monica was lit up from the inside. Saffron and I just stood there, our jaws dropping as we watched. The nurses and doctors were shouting and moving around lightning fast."

Drake turned, giving Reen a loving look when he heard Hud's detailed description. He'd been present during Laila and Zak's heartwish and had seen that same light, so Reen was sure Drake knew what had happened.

"I still have trouble believing it. One minute Monica was at death's door and the next...she opened her eyes, sat up and smiled. When Saffron and I moved in close, Monica pulled us both into a hug, telling us she loved us. We were shooed away as the doctor and the staff checked her out. All her vital signs were perfectly normal. Do you hear? *Normal*!"

Covering her face with her hands, Reen broke into tears. Her heartwish had worked! It worked! She felt Drake's arm wrap around her shoulder.

"Her doc said they need to run a battery of tests but as far as he could tell, Monica is healthy, growing more vibrant by the minute." His hand plowed through his hair. "Isn't that crazy? The doc's face was like a big blank sheet of paper. Totally dazed, shocked." Hud took Reen's hands in his, placing a kiss on her knuckles.

"Maureen, if it hadn't been for you I would have been two hours away from Glassfloat Bay when Monica went into cardiac arrest. Saffron's never performed CPR and didn't know how to do it. My sweet Monica would have died before the paramedics arrived."

Finding it impossible to speak, Reen squeezed her eyes shut tight, drawing in a long wobbly breath as she realized her heartwish wouldn't have worked if Hud hadn't arrived exactly when he did.

Though the magic of the heartwish ring was powerful, it couldn't bring the dead back to life. Reen would forever be grateful to the powers that be for having her heartwish timed with such amazing precision.

"I-I don't even know what to say," Hud continued, "other than thank you, Reen, for saving Monica's life as well as my own because I couldn't live if I lost her. You were right—we're meant to be together."

With another deep breath, she smiled. "Hud, are you sure you won't come in for a while? You look like you could use a rest."

"She's right, Hud," Drake agreed. "A cup of coffee or maybe a glass of wine or something."

Hud shook his head. "Thanks but I'm fine. In fact, I've never felt so fine." He managed a broad grin. "I had to stop by to thank you, Reen, on my way to pick up Nancy, Monica's mother." Reen's eyebrows shot up at the news.

"She lives on the other side of town. I haven't met her yet. Listen to this, she called Monica's cell the instant the blue light saturated the hospital room. Can you believe that? Like mother's intuition or something. Saffron answered the phone. Nancy told her there was a beautiful blue light surrounding her, and it seemed to tell her she needed to call her daughter immediately. She was worried and wanted to let Monica know she loved her." Hud scratched his head. "She saw the light the same time we did! Like something out of a sci-fi movie."

Hud's words touched Reen's heart in the best possible way.

"When Saffron filled her in on what happened, Nancy asked if I could come pick her up and take her to the hospital. She said she wants to meet the man Monica loves, so she could thank me in person for saving her daughter's life."

"That's wonderful, Hud." Happy tears sprouted in Reen's eyes. "Oh, this means it's all going to be all right," she muttered her inner thoughts aloud. "It worked. All of it worked."

"What worked?" Hud asked.

"The magic of love and wishes from the heart," Drake answered, giving Reen a secret smile.

Hud gave a thoughtful nod. "I wish you could have seen how happy Monica was when she heard why her mother called. Saffron told me they've had some difficult times."

"I have a feeling that's about to change," Reen said.

"I think so too. Glancing at the time on his phone, Hud told them, "I've got to go. I don't want to keep my future mother-in-law waiting."

Chapter Nineteen

~<>~

"HOW COULD I possibly not love you, Maureen Malone?" Drake said once Hud left. "Your wish must have been for Monica, which makes you the sweetest, kindest, least selfish person I've ever known, especially considering the woman's not exactly your favorite person."

With all that had happened, Reen's thoughts were a whirlwind. "I'm no saint, Drake, believe me." She gave a wry smile. "I've learned so much the past few days, about Monica and Saffron, as well as about myself." Looking up into his eyes, she shrugged. "Maybe about myself most of all."

Before Reen could form another coherent thought, Drake lifted her up into his arms, kissing her profoundly. Wrapping her arms around his neck, she sank into the deliciousness of his kiss until it dawned on her that he was holding not only her weight but the weight of her heavy Frankie boot too.

"Drake, you need to put me down. You'll break your back!" She squirmed, trying to get down, but he held her firmly in place.

Heading for the family room, he proudly advised, "In case you didn't already know, my enviable *hunky-dorky* classification signifies I'm far stronger than I may appear."

"Is that so?"

"Indubitably." He brushed a kiss across her lips, making her wonder why they'd wasted so much precious time being platonic friends when they could have been enjoying closeness like this all along...as well as certain other benefits.

"You mean like objects you see in the car mirror may be closer than they appear?" Reen teased before showering kisses along his jawline.

"Exactly." His brow furrowing as he shifted her weight in his arms, Drake admitted, "Although I do believe the considerable bulk of your Frankenstein boot may currently be causing the collapse of several vertebrae."

Reen gasped aloud. "Put me down!" She twisted in his arms again.

"You should probably avoid all that wiggling."

She stilled. "Sorry, I didn't mean to make it worse."

"Not because it makes you heavier—which it does—I mean because all your wiggling's making me hot."

Paying attention to the room's comfort level, she said, "You're right, it is kind of warm in here. I can turn down the heat."

With one eyebrow vaulting, Drake locked eyes with her. "Not that kind of hot."

"Oh." Her smile spread once she realized what he meant. "*Oh!*" The way he gazed at her sent a warm, tingly quiver coursing through her.

Gently setting her on the sofa, he asked, "Where's your butt pillow?" Before Reen could answer, he spotted it on the floor and retrieved it. Then he noticed all the details she'd set up for making her heartwish.

"It looks like you were practicing voodoo in here, except for the absence of little dolls with pins jabbed in them." He sniffed the air, picked up the now cool pot of tea, and smelled that too, screwing his expression. "Smells like voodoo too."

Reen laughed. "It's my attempt at setting the scene for my heartwish. I got most of the stuff from Kady. Careful not to tease me too much or I'll get out my Drake voodoo doll and pin you right in the—"

"You plugged in the tree's color wheel too," he said, unfazed by her mischievous threat.

Looking in the tree's direction, she'd forgotten it was still on. "I didn't have time to turn it off before you came banging on my door." The corner of her lip curled in a playful smile. "I'm not in a hurry though. I love watching as the colors revolve."

Bending in front of the coffee table with his hands on his knees, Drake surveyed her handiwork before picking up the photo of the two of them with his twins from her laptop's keyboard. A warm smile crossed his face. "I remember this." He looked up at Reen. "What a great day we had together. You know what Lilly told me at dinner that evening?"

"Hopefully that she had a wonderful time. I sure did."

"She asked if you and I can get married so we can be a real family." The loving way he gazed at her with his charismatic smile was almost poetic.

Deeply moved, Reen touched her cheeks as they grew warm. "She did?" It was a major statement for a child to make to her father. Reen had always suspected Drake's kids honestly cared for her. This sweet confirmation was so gratifying.

Nodding, he told her, "Kevin seconded Lilly's suggestion, which is monumental considering he never agrees with anything his sister says." Drake and Reen laughed together because nothing could be more true.

"That makes me so happy." Reen sank into a delighted sigh. "I think you already know how I feel about Lilly and Kevin."

"And me too?" His expression reminded her of a hopeful little boy, making her adore him even more.

"And you too. What did you tell the kids when they asked?"

"That we cared very much about each other and were almost like a family right now. Then I was honest, telling them I didn't know what might occur in the future, but that I would be happy if it happened one day."

"Sounds like the perfect answer to me."

Almost as perfect as Drake dropping to one knee and proposing to me, right here, right now.

Rebuffing her wayward thoughts, Reen silently chastised herself for being impatient and greedy. Knowing Drake loved her was enough. She was happy. Truly.

"Good, because, as you know, I can sometimes get too teacher-ish when talking to the kids."

"You mean like when you told Lilly about the Viking woman in the opera," she motioned to invisible horns on her head, "who was heartbroken because her boyfriend died and—"

"That's Brunhilde."

"Right, and she commits suicide by throwing herself on his funeral pyre so she could be with him in death." She gave an impish smile. "Teacher-ish like that?"

"Um...yeah. Like that." Chuckling, Drake nodded slowly. "You see? This is just one of the reasons I need you in my life. You help keep my teacher-ish-ness in check."

"Hmm...I must have missed English class the day *teacher-ish-ness* was in the vocabulary list."

Removing the photograph from her laptop's keyboard must have awakened the screen because she saw Drake studying it as he squatted there.

"Oh! No, don't look at that." Reen flailed a finger toward him, grunting while attempting to get off her trusty donut pillow and rise from the too-cushy couch. The document on her laptop held her innermost feelings and wasn't meant for anyone else's eyes.

"Why not?" His gaze didn't waver from the screen.

"Those are personal reminder notes I made for my wish. Private stuff." With a shooing motion, she added, "Just look away, Drake."

There was a sparkle in his eye. "If this is so private perhaps you shouldn't leave it on display here in the middle of the family room for anyone to read."

"Well if you hadn't charged in the way you did, Mr. Smarty Pants—" Reen blustered, doing her best not to give in to rising laughter. By the time she'd risen from the sofa and made it to the coffee table to stand behind him, it was clear Drake had read much of what she'd typed.

"Reen..."

"What?" Her voice was nearly inaudible.

"You love me that much?" He looked dumbfounded as he read through the section about him and Saffron. "Enough to let me go so I could be happy with Saffron because you thought I loved her." Gazing up at her, he added, "Even after all the hurtful out-of-context things you overheard while you were snooping, you still had my happiness foremost in mind."

Reen stood at his side, her thumbs looped in the pockets of her jeans. "Snooping is such a disagreeable word. I prefer to think of it as," she dangled finger quotes, "*accidentally eavesdropping.*" Bending, she snaked her arms around his neck and shoulders. "And yes, I love you that much, Drake Slattery. And more. So much more."

"You could have used your heartwish to make me love you, and to find someone else for Saffron, but your wish wasn't even remotely self-centered." He scrolled through the document, his finger trailing over a particular paragraph. "There's not a damn thing here in your wish that benefits you, Maureen. Everything you wished for is to help make positive changes in the lives of others." He gazed up at her, admiration in his eyes. "Do you know how special that makes you?"

Feeling awkward and embarrassed, she wrinkled her nose. "Thanks but I'm really not comfortable with that, Drake. I'm sure anyone else armed with the same information I had would have made a similar wish instead of something self-serving. I never intended for anyone to know what I wished for, not you and not my family."

Drake looked at her like she was crazy. "You honestly think you could keep something this important from your mother and sisters? There's no way the fierce, loving, protective Malone women would let you keep your wish private, Maureen. They'd harass you until you fessed up. Then they'd celebrate your unselfish decision."

"With cake and heaps of buttercream frosting?" Reen joked, trying to break the discomfiture of the praising going on. But Drake wasn't laughing at her frivolity. His expression remained sincere and solemn. Reflecting on what he'd said, Reen realized he was spot on about her family and she smiled. "Okay, you're right about Mom and my sisters. I'd be the same way if one of them was the wish-maker. The thing is, I wanted to privately, anonymously, do something good and selfless for a change and—"

"For a change?" Eyeing her like she was irrational, he said, "You must have a terribly skewed opinion of yourself. As long as I've known you, Reen, you've been intent on helping others. Always putting yourself last, making sure everyone else is doing well before you see to yourself. Look at what you've done for the kids at the hospital alone. That's only one small facet of all you do for others."

Reen felt her cheeks grow warm with an odd mixture of embarrassment and joy—joy that this is the kind of woman Drake believed she was. It filled her heart with gratitude that the man she loved thought of her in such a positive light. She only hoped she could measure up to his faith in her.

She'd always had a difficult time accepting compliments. Her default mode was to crack a few jokes and laugh off the adulation. Before opening her mouth to make a silly pun, she realized it would not only belittle her heartwish, but also make a mockery of all the wonderful things Drake had just told her. Regardless of how awkward it felt to accept a compliment graciously, it was important that she respond appropriately. Swallowing hard, she shifted her gaze away from Drake to the teapot near the laptop, trying to choose the right words.

"This is hard. I don't even know what to say." She fidgeted in place before lifting her gaze to his. "The best I can come up with is simple but it's direct from my heart. Thank you, Drake. The praise you gave me was beautiful and I'll never forget it."

"Not nearly as beautiful as you or your charitable heart." Drake went back to reading her notes. "Your wish for Shannon Brone, I get. She's a classmate of Lilly and Kevin's and you know her well, but..." Clearly puzzled, he shifted his focus from the laptop's screen to Reen. "I didn't think you even liked Monica Sharp, yet you used your wish to save her. And her mother—you've never even met her, have you? There must be an interesting story behind your wish."

In all the commotion she'd almost forgot about little Shannie. She prayed that portion of her wish was as successful as the parts about Monica and Nancy.

"There is. Definitely. I'll tell you about it all...as long as you promise to save all your praise and compliments for my eulogy when I'm ninety-nine-years-old and expire from an accidental-on-purpose chocolate overdose while knitting my bazillionth afghan." She fell into an easy smile, with Drake responding in kind.

"That sounds reasonable." Their gazes locked, and Drake's heated look melted her insides. "I like thinking of you as a cute little old lady, still addicted to chocolate and your knitting. I can't think of anything I'd enjoy more than sitting beside you in our twin rockers when we're old and gray."

When we're old and gray. That sounded positive...like Drake could be contemplating a long-term commitment.

"Oops," he snapped his fingers, "I almost forgot."

She watched as he pulled out his phone and started texting.

"Seriously? Now? What's wrong, I'm not interesting enough?" Reen teased. "In case you didn't know, Professor, texting while sitting next to the woman you've just professed to love isn't very good boyfriend etiquette."

Continuing to text, Drake gave her a quick sideways glance. "I'm letting Astrid know everything's okay. She made me swear I'd let her know how things turned out after I came to see you." He hit send.

"My mom knows you're here with me now?"

"Yup."

"Well that means she'll be—" The rest of her statement was interrupted by rapid knocking at the front door of Bekka House.

"That would be your mom," Drake said with a twinkle in his eye.

"Of course. She's probably been waiting in a car parked outside, or maybe in the bushes until she got your text."

"In the car." Nodding, he thumbed toward the front door.

Reen's eyes popped. "Seriously?"

"She insisted. Stay here, I'll get it."

When he opened the door, Astrid stepped in, closing it behind her. Their whispering went on for a small eternity. She was able to see them from where she sat but, as much as she tried, she couldn't make out anything they said, until...

"Wait...everybody?" Drake's strangled voice sounded an octave higher than usual, kind of like a squeak toy. "But I thought it was just going to be you and the kids."

Straining to hear their stealthy, mostly whispered conversation, Reen heard her mother say, "It'll be just fine, Drake. After all, you're used to having an audience. It will be just like you speaking in front of one of your classes." Which didn't make any sense at all to Reen.

"Hello, Mom!" Reen called out.

"Hold on, Maureen," Astrid told her, "I'm still grilling the professor."

Reen laughed at that.

"Ready?" Astrid asked Drake, her phone in hand.

Reen watched Drake's hand shoot up, raking through his hair as he answered, "I...uh...yeah, I guess so."

"Ready for what? What are you two up to?" Reen asked, getting up from the sofa.

"Shhh, patience, my dear, patience." Astrid held up a finger, motioning for Reen to wait while she appeared to send a text. Five minutes later, the doorbell rang, accompanied by a chorus of rambunctious voices that included the sound of her sisters jabbering away.

"Were they all waiting out there in their cars too?" Reen asked, dumbfounded.

"Of course not, dear," Astrid answered. "Everyone was at Drake's house, watching the kids and making their preparations."

"Everyone? Preparations for what?" Reen asked.

Disregarding her daughter's question, Astrid turned, clutched the doorknob and opened the door. "Come on in, everybody, it's open," she called, while taking Drake by the elbow and steering him into the kitchen.

Hurrying to the coffee table, Reen closed her laptop, tidying up before her mother or sisters spotted the portions of the wish-making preparations she needed to conceal. She hobbled around, stuffing things in drawers, behind pillows and beneath the sofa cushions.

The cacophony of voices she'd heard moments before now floated through the air, trailing from the front door to the kitchen. Reen watched as Zak, Laila and their twins, followed by Varik, Delaney, and baby Rebekka came into the house. Next came Annalise, then Nevan, with Gard and Sabrina close behind.

Chattering with each other, their arms were full. The guys were equipped with beer, wine and other libations, except for Nevan, who carried a large foil-covered platter.

Her eyebrows arrowing down, Reen's thoughts whirred until they landed on the only plausible explanation... *Ooh, I'll bet somebody is pregnant and this is a surprise announcement party!* But then, she wondered, why wasn't she in on the secret?

"Hey, isn't anybody going to say hello?" Reen called to the gathering in the kitchen as she finished the last of her neatening in the family room.

"Me! Hi sweetie!"

Returning her attention to the front door, Reen was pleasantly surprised to see her youngest sister, Kady, bringing up the rear, along with Drake's kids, Lilly and Kevin, and Sabrina and Gard's son, Harry. The newest addition to the Slattery family, Knitten the kitten, was cradled like a baby doll in Lilly's arms.

"Kady, you're back!" Clumping over to her sister, Reen draped an arm over Kady's shoulder.

"Hi Miss Reen!" Lilly said. "Bye Miss Reen."

"Wait!" Reen called as they started to run off. Looking full of mischief, Lilly and the boys strolled up to Reen. Reen smiled, asking them quietly, "Say...do you little munchkins know what's going on? Come on, you can tell me."

"We can't say anything." Lilly set Knitten on the floor, watching as Hazelnut ventured close, ever so slowly, sniffing the air as she approached the kitten, following the curious little guy as he explored the family room with an eye on the silver tree. Uttering a low growl, Hazelnut seemed to warn Knitten away from any idea of leaping on the metal branches.

"Hazelnut's not going to eat Knitten, is she?" Lilly asked.

Reen smiled at the question. "No, honey, they'll be fine together. They just need to get acquainted." They watched as the dog and kitten romped around together, then rested on the floor with the frisky kitten climbing all over a very patient Hazelnut. "See?" Reen said to Lilly. "They'll be inseparable." Placing her hand on her knees, getting down closer to the kids' level, Reen cleared her throat.

"So, tell me, what's going on, kids?"

"Miss Astrid said we have to lock our lips and throw away the key," Lilly answered, making the motion. "Otherwise we won't get any ice cream later." She and the boys clearly relished demonstrating with exaggerated motions that they were unable to open their mouths. Clapping their hands over their mouths the trio engaged in a chorus of giggles.

"But..." Reen tried but Lilly had taken her brother and Harry by the hand and the trio ran toward the kitchen.

Giggle...giggle...giggle...

"They're so cute," Kady said, snapping Reen's attention back to her sister.

"I thought you were still at the seminar."

"The last lecture was early this morning," Kady explained. "When I talked to Mom earlier she filled me in, so I checked out of my hotel and headed back from Seattle because I didn't want to miss this."

"I don't understand." Reen's eyebrows knitted. "Miss what? What's all the secrecy? Is somebody having a baby? Or, oh my gosh, Kady, it's about your bookstore, isn't it?"

"No, actually, Reenie, it's—"

"Kathleen Doolan Malone!" Astrid's voice boomed from the kitchen. "Hush!"

"Oops, sorry." Making the same locking motion over her lips that Lilly had, Kady gave a shy smile.

"Come on, seriously, what the heck's going on here? Somebody? Anybody? Drake?"

"Hi sugarpuss!"

Reen looked from Kady, who headed for the kitchen to join the others, to see her stepdad crossing the threshold and closing the front door behind him.

"Tore? Wow, they dragged you into whatever this is too, huh? Maybe you can tell me what's going on."

"Well, it's—"

"In the kitchen, Tore," Astrid directed before Reen could get anything out of him. "Did you remember to bring the bag?"

Tore looked down at what appeared to be a garment bag slung across his arm. "Got it," he answered.

"Good. Put it in the half-bath," Astrid instructed. "Drake will be right there."

That really had Maureen confused. "Aw, come on, Mom," Reen said. "What are you up to?"

"Just stay there, Maureen, we'll be there in a minute."

Reen's grumble was purposely audible. "Um, you know," she cleared her voice loudly, "I'm kind of feeling like that time when I was eight and everybody was playing red rover on the playground and I was the last one to get picked. Or...or like that time stuck-up Jory Sattler invited everybody to her birthday party at Burger King except for me and nose-picker Nina."

Her heartfelt declaration went ignored by everyone but Hazelnut, who cuddled against her leg. "Aw, I knew I could count on you, sweetie pie," Reen said, bending to pat the dog. But then Hazelnut's nose started working overtime, sniffing the air, redolent with mouthwatering aromas. Offering Reen a brief, apologetic glance, she scampered off with her new friend Knitten at her heels to join the others.

"Et tu, Hazel?" Reen whined as her best pal abandoned her.

Everyone in the kitchen seemed to be talking at once, all in hushed tones. The only distinct thing Reen could decipher was the periodic pop of laughter from her brothers and the other men, as well as the clattering of dishes and silverware.

Moments later, everyone emerged from the kitchen, filing into the family room. Astrid and Tore stood in front of a built-in bookcase, while the rest formed a semicircle in the room, leaving Reen at the center. The three young children shared wide, scheming smiles. As a matter of fact, so did everyone else. The only person not in the room was Drake.

Reen was impressed by how still and quiet the kids were, with Lilly instructing the boys where and how to stand. As the three children stood, arms straight at her sides, like soldiers at attention, Lilly asked, "Is this okay, Miss Astrid?"

"Perfect." Astrid offered a kind, approving smile.

"I guess it's time to get this show on the road, Drake," Nevan called, rubbing his hands together briskly.

Through a mile-wide grin, Gard added, "Let's go, Professor, time's a wastin.'"

"Aw, don't gang up on the poor man," Kady said. "You'll disturb his aura." Calling to him, she advised, "Just take a few, deep, cleansing breaths, Drake. You'll feel better. Your chakras might need clearing too, all except for your fourth chakra, the heart chakra. I can tell that's wide open."

Drake called from the half-bath, "Is that a good thing?"

"Absolutely." Kady waved away any doubt. "I'm sure you can feel the energy of your heart chakra since it's obviously full of love, compassion, forgiveness, and acceptance."

"You can feel all that, right, Drake?" Zak called to him in a teasing tone.

"Yeah, sure...of course," Drake answered, obviously clueless.

"Drake might have multiple degrees in eighty subjects, but I doubt any of them was a Master's Degree of Woo-woo," Gard joked.

"Come on, this is getting silly," Reen noted. "Why are you keeping me in the dark? Who's pregnant? Or who got some great news? Or who—"

"Patience, dear," Astrid said. "Stop jabbering and stand right where you are." With a simple alerting gesture, Astrid and the rest of her family backed up, leaving Maureen standing alone.

"I feel like there should be a spotlight shining on me," Reen joked. "If you're looking for a little song and dance, sorry, that's not my area of expertise, especially while I'm wearing this thing." She slapped the top of her boot. "Maybe you'd all like to watch me knit a hat?" She laughed, feeling more clueless and jittery by the second.

"Time to get your butt out here, Professor," Nevan called, "and join my sister in the spotlight."

"They make it sound like you're going to come out here and start tap dancing," Reen called to Drake, frowning. "You haven't been taking dance lessons, have you?" The idea tickled her insides and she held back laughter.

"Hardly," came Drake's anemic-sounding voice. "But I'd rather tap dance in front of everybody than..."

Silence.

"Than what, for heaven's sake?" Reen flapped her arms in frustration, letting them slap at her sides. "What?!"

"Quit stalling and get the show on the road, Drake," Nevan needled him again.

"Now?" came Drake's voice.

"Yes, now, dear," Astrid told him.

"It's your turn to shine, buddy." Shoving his hands into his pockets, Nevan rocked on his heels. "If you make it out of this alive, that is."

"I dunno...I wouldn't bet on it," Gard said with a conspiratorial wink.

"I'm just glad it's not me," Varik joked.

"You and me both," Tore agreed, giving Varik a companionable slap on the back.

"You have a warrior's soul, Drake," Zak added with his deep Mediterranean accent. "To do this in front of everyone takes intestines," As mild chuckling spread across the room, Gard leaned over and whispered in his brother-in-law's ear. "Ah." Zak nodded. "*Guts*," he corrected himself with a broad smile. He still had trouble with modern American idioms.

The men all laughed, only to receive *The Look* from Astrid.

"Boys," she chastised her sons, sons-in-law, and husband. That curdling look of hers accompanied by that single word was all it took.

A sudden chill sent a shiver through Reen. Something major was about to happen. She could feel it in her bones. Glancing up, she saw Drake exiting the half-bath, walking toward her with an intensely serious expression. He wore a dinner jacket and carried a single red rose.

Reen's heart skipped a beat. "Oh my God..."

"Ooh, Daddy, you look so handsome!" Lilly said. "Like Prince Charming!"

When Drake reached Reen, he got down on one knee, handing the rose to her and eliciting her delighted gasp of surprise.

"Oh my God..." Reen repeated. "Drake, what are you doing?"

As he reached into his pocket he gave her a crooked grin. "Unless I'm doing it wrong, you should have a pretty good idea." Withdrawing a ring box, all he got to say was, "Maureen," before...

"Wait! Stop!" Astrid cried, and all eyes were on her.

Chapter Twenty

~<>~

"MOM!" A HORRIFIED Reen yelled, her heart thundering.

Scrambling to get something out of her large tote bag, Astrid pulled out her favorite accessory—her vintage Kodak Instamatic.

"Okay, hold that pose for a minute." *Click.* "Perfect."

"Seriously, Astrid?" Drake said, his voice strained.

"Sorry." Smiling, Astrid told Drake, "But you two will thank me later." Gesturing for Drake to proceed, she finished, "You can go ahead now, Professor."

With a cavernous woosh of breath, his voice dripped with sarcasm as he replied, "Thanks very much."

Click...click...click...

Still positioned on one knee, he offered Reen a crooked smile. "Maybe I should just give in and have your mother text everyone we know to come over and watch my proposal performance."

"I wouldn't make jokes like that unless you're prepared for Astrid's fingers to start flying across her phone inviting all of Glassfloat Bay," Tore advised, demonstrating with his fingers flitting through the air.

Reen watched the color drain from Drake's face.

"You-you haven't," Drake said, "...have you, Astrid?"

"Me?" Looking shocked, Astrid clapped her hand high on her chest. "Why...I wouldn't dream of doing such a thing."

The guys started joking about Astrid's comment until Reen chastised, "You guys! Come on, this is supposed to be a solemn, romantic, memorable occasion for me."

Smiling, Tore nodded to Drake. "You just pretend we're not here and go right ahead, Drake."

"Or, you could try clicking your heels together three times," Nevan suggested, "and wishing to hell you weren't here." That comment elicited laughter from all, and playful arm punches from his sisters Delaney and Laila.

"Hey..." Drake glanced around the room. "Give me a break so I can get through this before I lose my nerve, huh?"

All it took was Astrid making a zipping gesture across her lips for everyone to be quiet.

Giving Astrid a nod of thanks, Drake focused his attention on Reen. "I'm going to do my best to be brief," he vowed, "but you know how wordy I can get, so we'll see how that goes." His halfhearted pledge was met by a few groans.

"Boys..." Astrid cautioned.

"Anyway," Drake continued, "while I may be somewhat verbose, I do promise not to be teacher-ish."

Everyone laughed when Kevin made a dramatic hand-swipe across his forehead, saying, "Whew!"

Still on bended knee, Drake surveyed the room full of family and friends. Reen saw him swallow hard and caught a glimpse of the deer-in-the-headlights look in his eyes. She hadn't realized until that moment how nervous Drake must be, proposing in front of an audience. Growing up in the Malone clan, she was used to a lack of privacy and an affectionate bunch of well-meaning people forever sticking their noses in each other's business. But this was new for Drake, who'd grown up an only child with no aunts, uncles, grandparents or cousins. She remembered his parents had been quiet and reserved.

Reen bent down low. Tenderly stroking his cheek she spoke quietly. "See all the people in this room? Everyone talking about this...about us?" Drake nodded. "Well I don't. As far as I'm concerned, it's just you and me here. This special moment is ours...it belongs to us and no one else."

"No whispering aloud," Nevan teased. "We want to hear everything." Light laughter spread through the room.

Reen gave Drake's free hand a gentle squeeze. "Go ahead, Drake."

He gazed into her eyes for a long moment before a smile took hold. Visibly calmer, he kissed her forehead. "Maureen Malone, at this moment, you're the only person in the world...in *my* world."

After another gentle caress to his cheek, Reen straightened to a standing position.

Taking a deep breath, Drake opened the ring box, revealing a white-gold band with a center diamond, bordered on either side by a row of alternating amethysts and diamonds. The ring was unique and stunning.

Looking from the ring to Drake's eyes, she could feel the depth of his loving gaze clear to her soul.

"This was my mother's ring, and my grandmother's before that. I had it altered to include your favorite purple stones. If my parents were still alive I know they'd bless our union and want you to wear our family ring. They knew how much I love you, Reen. In fact, they'd encouraged me to do this a long time ago."

The familiar sting of tears rose to Reen's eyes and she detected a sort of stereo sniffling from her mom and the other women as they listened to Drake.

"I love you, Maureen, and I want to spend the rest of my life with you...because it will probably take me that long to figure you out...and to find you among the floor-to-ceiling piles of yarn and other people's discards."

Reen made a vain attempt not to laugh, while listening to the faint sounds of supporting laughter around her.

"You're the kindest, most generous, loving person I know, Reen. It's been killing me pretending to be nothing more than your friend, when what I longed for was to make you mine forever, enjoying the rest of our lives together. Marry me, Reen, and make me the happiest man on the planet." Drake held the ring to Reen's finger, giving her a hopeful look.

Along with the omnipresent clicks of Astrid's camera, Reen heard a chorused "Awwww," throughout the family room.

Without a speck of hesitation, she joyfully exclaimed, "Yes!" as he slid the ring on her finger.

Click...click...click.

Rounds of congratulatory cheering chorused throughout the room.

"You've made me so happy, Drake. I never really imagined this day would come." Spilling with teary, elated laughter, Reen felt on top of the world. "You know what this means, don't you?"

"What?"

"This," Reen gestured around the room, "is going to be your life from now on. Sure you still want to go through with it?"

Getting to his feet, Drake took her into his arms, swinging her around. "More than ever."

Holding each other, they kissed and whispered endearments. Once Drake set Reen on her feet, everyone gathered close, hugging the newly engaged couple.

Kevin turned to Lilly. "Was that it?" He lifted his hands in question. "Did Daddy propose to Miss Reen?"

"Mmm-hmm, just like Prince Charming and Cinderella," Lilly answered with a dreamy sigh. "Except Miss Reen's wearing a big boot instead of a glass slipper." That had Maureen and everyone else chuckling.

"That means they're gonna get married!" Harry announced, excitedly elbowing Kevin and Lilly repeatedly. The three of them giggled together, shouting out, "Yay!" and jumping up and down in place.

Click...click...click.

Lilly and Kevin ran to their dad and Reen, wrapping themselves around the couple's legs and hugging them tight. Clearly not wanting to be left out, Hazelnut and Knitten joined them, rubbing up against their family. In an instant, the four humans and their adoring pets were enveloped in gentle rays of blue-white light emanating from the stone of Reen's heartwish ring.

A hushed awe cloaked the family room until Hazelnut let out a muffled woof and Knitten offered the loudest meow they'd heard the little kitten make so far.

"Wow! Look at the light!" Kevin waved his hands over the ring. "Cool! What is that?"

"That's the light of love," Drake replied. He and Reen smiled at the children and each other with recognition and understanding.

"Huh..." Reen held her hand aloft, watching the light radiating. "And I didn't even have to make a heartwish."

"Because we make our own magic," Drake assured.

The pleasing fragrance of pepperkaker and cherry pipe tobacco floated around them. Already familiar with Bekka House's trio of ethereal Norwegian visitors consisting of Reen's late grandparents, and Varik's late grandfather, Drake smiled with a sense of awe and gratification.

"Thanks for that aromatic welcome to the family," he addressed the hospitable spirits. "Rebekka and Jamie Eriksen, and Anders Jenssen, you have my word I'll do my best to be a good husband to Maureen."

"I think they already know that," Astrid said with a bright, teary smile.

"I knew our friendly ghosts would be happy for us," Reen said. "How could they not love you, Professor?"

Once the smell of the spicy ginger cookies and tobacco faded and the blue light evaporated, Drake faced his fiancée, taking her hands in his and lowering his head to rest against her forehead.

"I feel like I've waited my whole life for this moment, Reen. The two of us standing close, openly enjoying the pleasure of each other's company without pretending we're nothing more than pals."

"I second that," Reen assured him, admiring her beautiful engagement ring.

"And I never thought that godawful long proposal would be over. Can we eat now?" Nevan cracked, earning buddy-laughs from the other men and looks of rebuke from the women.

"I second that." Gard raised his hand.

"Yeah," Varik snickered, "what happened to being brief, Professor?"

Visibly confused, Zak clapped his hips. "Briefs?" to which Nevan barked a laugh just before Varik leaned close, explaining the multiple meanings of the word to his brother-in-law.

"Watch out guys," Tore warned, "Astrid's about to bore a hole through you with *The Look*."

"They never grow up, do they?" Laila tsked...then covered her mouth to conceal her own laughter.

"I wouldn't blame you if you decided to back out now," Reen told Drake, "because, trust me, once you're part of the Malones this sort of thing will be a regular occurrence. Your life will never be the same."

Drake looked at his new fiancée, then at Tore and Astrid, his future in-laws, and finally at everyone else gathered together. "I wouldn't have it any other way. Lilly, Kevin and I look forward to being a permanent part of the gargantuan Malone clan. Right, kids?"

"Right!" the twins chorused, jumping in place.

"Are you going to be our mommy now, Miss Reen?" Lilly wiped at happy tears with the palms of her hands.

"Sure she will," Kevin answered with conviction.

"Yeah, just like how Gard is my dad now after he and my mom got married," Harry added.

"Technically, I'll be your stepmom," Reen confirmed, squatting to get down to the twins' level, "loving you both just as much as if I gave birth to you. But I'll never try to take the place of your mommy. Janet will always be your mom."

"Our mother makes us call her Janet," Lilly told Reen, which broke her heart to hear, "so we want to call you Mom and Mommy. Please say yes. Please, please, please!" Lilly bounced in place. "We love you, Miss Reen."

"Me and Lilly decided a long time ago when we were kids that we want *you* to be our mom if you and Dad got married," Kevin told Reen.

"Oh, my goodness." Reen clapped her chest. Blissfully overcome, she couldn't imagine being any happier. This was everything she wanted. The four of them together as a real family. She sent up a silent prayer of gratitude for her many blessings.

"Yes!" she enthusiastically responded. "Absolutely. I love the sound of that. You can call me Mom, Mommy, Mommy-Reen, or whatever makes you happy. Come here, you two cuties, and let me give you a great big future-mommy hug."

Astrid came to Reen's side. "You see, sweetheart?" she whispered to her daughter. "Didn't Mama tell you everything would be hunky-dory?" Cupping Drake's face with her hands, Astrid smiled at him, then kissed him on both cheeks. "You did good, Professor. Welcome to the family, Drake."

"Thanks, Astrid."

"I'm starving!" Kevin said, cradling his belly. "Can we eat now? *Fiiiinally?*"

"Absolutely." Astrid mussed his hair. "It's time to celebrate!" She directed everyone back to the kitchen to ready the edibles and libations they brought, then asked the guys to set up the folding table and chairs in the family room, and light the gas fireplace for ambience.

"There's enough food to feed the whole town," Astrid assured as she headed for the kitchen. Looking back over her shoulder, she winked at Drake. "But don't worry, son, I promise I didn't invite them all too." With a tinkling of laughter, she disappeared into the kitchen.

Drake's smile stretched ear to ear. "Your mom's a very special lady. I think she really likes me. Did you hear how she called me *son*?"

The encouraged look on his face warmed Reen's heart. "I certainly did. As far as Mom's concerned, you're already a Malone. Believe me, that's a high compliment. Sooo...how did my mom know you were proposing today?"

Shrugging, Drake confirmed Reen's suspicions, "I may have let it slip when we were talking. As soon as she started telling me her plans for this," he twirled a finger meant to include everyone there at Bekka House, "I knew I'd made a mistake. I told her I could never propose in front of everyone and," another shrug, "well, you know the rest." He gave her a sheepish smile.

Sabrina, Annalise, and Reen's three sisters set down platters of food in the family room, then hurried over to Reen and Drake, where they practically squeezed the life out of them with congratulatory hugs, kisses and mile-a-minute happy talk.

"It's like you handed me my *Delaney's Diary* column for next week all wrapped up pretty and tied with a bow," Delaney told Reen. "My readers will love it."

"Why am I not surprised that your sister's private life is soon to become fodder for your readers?" Annalise teased.

"Hmm..." Laila tapped her cheek, "could it be because that's what Delaney always does?" she mused.

"Oops..." Delaney gave an impish shrug. "Guilty as charged," she replied, covering her mouth to camouflage her laughter.

Having long ago become resigned to Delaney's family-related news scoops, Reen said, "All I ask is that you remember Drake's new to all this. Please don't write anything that might make the professor's students laugh at him."

"Too late. They already do anyway," Drake admitted through a chuckle. "So I wouldn't worry about it. I've read your blog and books, Delaney, and really enjoy them. I trust you not to write anything that will embarrass me," his eyebrow hiked, "or Maureen."

Wrapping an arm around Drake's waist, Delaney rested her head against his arm, "You're going to make a great brother-in-law."

"Did you wish for Drake?" Kady whispered in Reen's ear. "I promise not to tell."

Reen believed Kady. Her little sister was almost childlike in her honesty and kindness. However, Reen was honestly able to reply that her wish hadn't involved Drake.

"No. Honestly, Kady, the wish kind of made itself known, just the way Grandma Bekka always told us it worked."

Overhearing Reen, Laila asked, "You already made your wish? What did you wish for?" The women were all fixated on Reen, awaiting her next words.

"I really want to keep it private for now." In answer to their exasperated eye-rolling expressions, she added, "I'm not trying to be cagey, honest. I promise to tell you when the time is right, okay?"

"Oooh..." Delaney's eyes opened wide. "This sounds deliciously cryptic. I can't wait to hear."

Reen was glad for the interruption when they were joined by the men, who set drinks and food on the long folding table.

Drake sniffed the air, gleefully pointing to a platter. "Your world famous Irish pork pie!" he said to Nevan. "My favorite food."

"Since you're going to be my brother-in-law," Nevan hiked a shoulder, "I figured it's the least I could do to help ease some of the Malone-family shock factor."

Glancing down the length of the table, Gard asked, "Where are the plates?"

"Watch out, Drake," Sabrina warned, eyeing her husband. "Making Nevan's pork pie disappear like magic," she snapped her fingers, "is Gard's super power."

"Sabrina's right. You," Nevan pointed at his brother, "are only allowed one normal-person-sized serving."

"Normal size?" Gard made a show of scratching his head. "I don't even know what that means."

"Obviously," Nevan continued, "which means you don't get the honors of cutting into the pie because we all know how big your slice would be."

The Norwegian accent of Delaney's husband, Varik, came next as he stepped up to the table. "You can trust me to slice it."

A hearty "Ha!" popped out of Delaney's mouth.

"I'm the fair and impartial father figure here," Tore guaranteed. "I'll do it," he insisted, his accent thicker than his cousin Varik's.

"Don't believe him," Astrid shouted from the kitchen.

"Ouch." Tore clapped his chest. "She knows me too well."

"Stand aside, boys." Annalise authoritatively shooed them away. "I don't trust a single one of you rabid pork pie addicts." Removing the foil from the six-inch high, flaky lard-crusted pie, to a chorused tune of *ahhhhs* from the men, she proceeded to slice the chilled meat pie into even, sensible-sized slabs.

Leaning toward Drake, Nevan cupped his hand at the side of his mouth, whispering, "I made another smaller one for you and Reen. I left it at your house in your refrigerator."

"Thanks...future bro-in-law." Clapping him on the shoulder, Drake tossed Nevan a grateful smile.

"While the guys are glomming down pork pie, ladies, I've got six flavors of scones in the kitchen," Laila chimed in. "Including a batch of vegan scones just for you, Kady." Her sister clapped with anticipation. "And a brand new scone flavor in honor of Drake and Reen that I'm calling Engagement Scones. They have a chocolate-hazelnut ganache filling wrapped around hazelnut marzipan. They're dotted with chopped hazelnuts and drizzled with chocolate-hazelnut icing." Laila's proud smile was followed by, "There may be some Frangelico liqueur involved too."

Her luscious description had Reen salivating. "Please tell me they're part of your lower calorie line."

"Oh *hell* no!" Laila's brisk snap of laughter rang through the room. "I'm good, but not *that* good. These have approximately eighty thousand calories each, and they're worth it. Anyway, there's no dieting allowed at your engagement party."

"I brought a pan of smoky maple-sugar bacon crackers," Annalise told them to a resounding chorus of *Yum!* "And my four-cheese macaroni and cheese casserole with potato chip crumb topping." A resounding *Mmmm!* was the reaction.

"I made five-alarm chili con carne with black beans and all the fixings," Delaney said, again to a positive chorus.

"And I brought ginger-mint kombucha-mushroom tea, carrot-mango leather, and a bowl of kale crisps seasoned with soy paste and nutritional yeast. We'll have a real feast!" Kady happily added to the concealed chagrin of her sisters. Kady's concoctions were known more for their calming and healing properties than their appealing taste. Her heart was in the right place but...

"Thanks, that sounds wonderful, Kady," Reen lied, patting her sister's arm.

"Wow, all the food sounds great," Drake said. "How long have you all been working on this?"

"Yeah," Reen said, "How could you even know we'd be getting engaged—I sure didn't."

"Kady told us she had a premonition," Delaney said.

"I got this tingly feeling about you, Reenie, so I did a tarot card reading," Kady explained. "I followed that with a crystal ball reading, and ended doing an astrological chart. It was no surprise to see that your stars were perfectly aligned." Her smile lit up her pretty face. "I told Mom about it first. She said she already knew it was going to happen soon, even without a premonition."

"We started things rolling," Astrid said, joining the women in the family room, "so we could be ready whenever you two slowpokes finally realized you were meant for each other. And," she spread her arms wide, "*voila!*"

"It's almost like I had nothing to with any of this proposal stuff," Drake joked.

"Don't worry, you'll get used to it eventually, Professor," Astrid told him with a good-natured wink before returning to the kitchen. "I could use some help getting the rest of the food ready," she called over her shoulder. Still happily chatting, the women followed Astrid.

Tore lit the gas fireplace so the women could gather in front of the fire to eat. The guys settled at the far end of the cavernous room on the recliners and cushy chairs in front of the TV, drinking beer and eating pork pie while dissecting the mistakes made by football coaches over the past year. Soon, a fevered discussion of why Portland, Oregon didn't have their own NFL team dominated their conversation.

Reen and Drake were left standing together in the family room while everyone else bustled around.

Hugging her close, Drake spoke in a sexy tone. "Alone at last." She spotted the gleam in his eye as he glanced left and right, adding, "Sort of." The way he looked as he lowered his head to hers was sheer magic, making anticipation dance through Reen's system. His kiss was even more magical than her imagination. Drake kissed her so completely it nearly curled her toes.

Draping his arm around Reen's shoulder, he noted, "It's been a day of surprises...one after the other. I'm glad all the surprises are ov—"

Interrupted by the doorbell, Drake's happy demeanor drooped.

"No..." Sporting a frown, he groaned like one of his six-year-olds. "Aw come on, seriously?"

Reen couldn't help laughing at her fiancé's obvious case of frustration.

"All I have to say is that better not be Hud coming back to give you another hug."

Chapter Twenty-One

~<>~

ASTRID POPPED OUT of the kitchen, lifting her hands with a shrug. "We've run out of Malones as far as I know, so I have no idea who's been hiding in the bushes. I'll get it." Wiping her hands with a dishtowel, she headed for the front door. Opening it, she turned to her daughter with a bright smile. "It's for you, Maureen."

"Of course it is," Drake said, walking with Reen to the door.

Once she spotted the visitors, Reen's eye's popped wide. There stood her cousin Saffron, Monica Sharp, Hud, and another woman who Reen suspected must be Nancy, Monica's mother.

"Maureen!" Monica called, running toward Reen and wrapping her into a straitjacket-tight hug, as if they'd been bosom-buddies for years. "Oh Reen, thank you, *thank you*! You saved my life. Whatever it was you said to Hud, and for whatever reason, you brought him to me and he brought me back from the brink. Literally! One minute I was at Death's door, and the next, there was this heavenly blue-white light surrounding me—and everything changed." Releasing her grip, Monica asked, "Can you ever forgive me?"

Taken aback, Reen took a moment to get her thoughts in line. She gave Astrid, still at the door, a quick glance and received a knowing look of love in return.

"I'm so proud of you, honey," Astrid said softly, kissing Reen's cheek. "I love you more than you can know." Without Reen having uttered a word, by Monica's description of the events, Reen had no doubt her mother knew what she'd wished for.

"Forgive you for what?" Reen asked returning her attention to the woman standing before her with healthy pink cheeks, bright eyes and a face that no longer looked ashen or sunken. She was the picture of health. "There's nothing to forgive."

"I've been so unkind to you, and you never deserved it. I was going through a terribly difficult time dealing with stage four cancer, although that's no excuse for my rudeness to you and Laila when she was buying the bakery."

At the sound of her name, Laila stepped out of the kitchen, dishtowel in hand.

"I hope you and Laila can forgive me for being so awful," Monica finished.

"Of course," Reen said, hoping Monica's cancer was fully eradicated. "I'm sorry you had to go through that. It must have been so stressful and frightening."

"Cancer? I'm so sorry, Monica," Laila said, and Reen could tell by the expression on her sister's face that she meant it wholeheartedly. "What are they doing for it, chemo, radiation?"

"It's gone!" Monica told Laila, downright gleefully. "Poof! Like magic. I can hardly believe it. Just like that," she snapped her fingers, "all traces of it disappeared. The doctors can't understand it."

Laila turned to her sister, locking eyes on Reen with a look of wonder on her face.

"A few minutes later," Hud interjected, "Monica's doctors just seemed to accept it, as if she'd never even had the cancer. Swear to God, it was the weirdest thing I've ever seen."

"I've never been one to believe in miracles but..." A tear trickled down Monica's cheek. "I've been truly blessed."

"How wonderful." Reen brimmed with happiness at the success of her heartwish. "I appreciate your apology and hope all your difficulties are far behind you now."

"I believe they are." Monica beamed a radiant smile. "Let's start from scratch, Reen, hmm?"

"Definitely." She nodded in agreement. "With coffee one day soon."

"I second that," Saffron chimed in.

"And some of Laila's scones," Monica added, turning to Laila with a smile. "I've been dying to try them."

"Sounds perfect," Reen said, with Laila nodding her agreement. Turning to her mom, Reen introduced Astrid to Monica.

After the introduction, Monica turned, clasping the other woman by the wrist and tugging her forward. "This is my mother, Nancy Sharp."

One look at the woman was all Reen needed to confirm that her Nancy-portion of the heartwish had worked too. Nancy was an attractive woman, an older more weathered version of her daughter, with a ready smile and warmth in her eyes. Reen was certain this wasn't what she would have seen if she'd met Nancy at The Tidal Wave Tavern the other day.

"It's a pleasure to meet you," Nancy said, partially covering her mouth as she spoke, most likely to conceal her bad teeth Reen assumed, remembering overhearing Nancy and Monica talking about it. "Thank you for whatever it was you said to Hud to make him come to Monica when he did." She patted Hud's chest. Looking proud and immensely happy, Hud had his arms around Nancy and Monica, tugging them close. "He was there to give Monica CPR when her heart stopped. Because of you, Reen, Hud was able to save my little girl's life."

Reen saw tears brimming in the woman's eyes. Tears of love, which made Reen's heart swell with gladness. Clasping Nancy's hands, Reen told her, "I'm delighted to meet you, and so very glad everything has turned out so well." More introductions were made as everyone filed out of the kitchen and into the family room, carrying food and drink, setting them on the large folding table the guys had set up.

"Just how much food did you all bring?" an amazed Drake asked, watching platter after platter exit the kitchen.

"This is just for starters," Astrid answered. "Tons more still in the kitchen," she added, heading for the family room with a covered bowl.

Taking Reen by the elbow, Laila led her away from the others. "I know what you did," she whispered to Reen, kissing her on the cheek. "I love you so much, sis."

Willing herself not to cry, Reen smiled. "Love you too."

"Can I help with the food?" Nancy asked.

"You don't have to ask twice. Let me put you right to work," Astrid teased, looping arms with the woman and ushering her into the kitchen. "There's a big pan of fudgy triple chocolate brownies that need to be cut and placed on a serving platter."

"You're making my mouth water," Nancy told Astrid as the pair disappeared into the kitchen.

"Looks like we intruded on a party," Monica noted. "Whoa...I just realized Drake's wearing a tux. We should be going. We just wanted to stop by and thank you."

"It's an unexpected party," Reen told her. "Mom found out Drake was planning to propose today," she showed Monica her engagement ring, "so she whipped up this shindig without me having a clue. And you're not intruding at all. It seems you have plenty to celebrate yourself. Please stay. There's more than enough food. The Malones have no concept of portion control."

Catching Hud's curious gaze, Drake glanced down, brushing the lapels of his tux. "The monkey suit was Astrid's idea," he explained. "She thought it would make the proposal more," he hung air quotes, "Romantic." For effect, he followed that with an exaggerated roll of his eyes.

"She was right," Reen said. "It did."

One corner of Hud's lip quirked. "You look damned uncomfortable."

"I am, thanks."

"You're welcome."

"I'd say Monica's hero deserves a big slab of Nevan's Pork Pie." Drake clapped Hud on the back, leading him to the growing food spread.

"Only a fool would turn down that offer," Hudson said, following Drake.

"Your ring is gorgeous, Reen. Congratulations!" Monica said. "We can stay but not for too long. Mom's decided to check herself into Wisdom Harbor Hospital's rehab facility for a few months." Monica's eyes glistened with tears. "She, um...she's had some addiction problems and wants to get better. Anyway," she swiped a tear from her cheek, "we've got her stuff in Hud's truck and he's driving us there. Mom needs to be there by six o'clock."

"Perfect. That'll give you enough time to sample the six different flavors of scones that Laila brought."

Before Monica could respond, Saffron said, "Yum! I'm in." She grabbed Reen into a firm hug. "I just want you to know you and I are good, Reen. Drake and I had a long talk and everything's fine." Her smile was full and genuine. "Congratulations. I know you and Drake will be very happy. You belong together. I've always believed that. I'm just glad you finally admitted it to yourself." She winked.

"You and me both," Reen agreed.

While they spoke, Monica joined her mother and the others in the kitchen. When she was out of earshot, Saffron said, "I didn't tell you about Monica having cancer before because she didn't want anyone to know. She's been fighting it for the past two years. We almost lost her, Reen. If it weren't for you we would have. But something astonishing happened, something miraculous. It seems she's completely cancer free now."

"I'm really happy for her." Reen smoothed her hand over Saffron's arm.

Saffron's gaze lowered to Reen's hands, one of which was adorned by her engagement ring and the other with the heartwish ring. "Your engagement ring is stunning. And this one," Saffron tapped Reen's heartwish ring, "I've heard a lot about over the years. It's the heartwish ring, right?" The ring gave off a distinct glow, startling Saffron.

"That-that's the same blue-white light we saw in Monica's hospital room." Wide-eyed, she stared at Reen. "My God, Reen...it was you, wasn't it?" Her hand clasped Reen's tightly, with the ring's gentle blue glow showing through their fingers. "You wished Monica healthy, didn't you? But," Saffron's eyebrows knitted in confusion, "how could you possibly know? This is incredible. I've got to tell Monica." She turned toward the kitchen but when she attempted to slip her hands from Reen's, Reen held tight.

"Please don't." Placing a finger to her lips, Reen smiled at her cousin. "One day I'll tell you about it, but please...don't say anything to Monica or anyone else. I don't want any credit for this. That's not why I did it."

"Okay." Saffron's eyes welled with tears. "I won't. I promise." She grabbed Reen so tightly against her, Reen felt it clear to her spine. "I'm so ashamed for misjudging you, Maureen."

"We're guilty of misjudging each other." Reen held Saffron at arm's length and smiled. "But that's all in the past. I look forward to you, me and Monica getting to know each other better." Reen drew her cousin into another embrace, kissing her cheek. "Come on," she guided Saffron toward the growing display of food being arranged in the family room, "we have some scone sampling to do."

Before they reached the food table, the doorbell rang. "You have got to be kidding me," Drake muttered. "Come on." He grabbed

Reen by the hand, leading her to the door. "We both know it's going to be for you."

Chapter Twenty-Two

~<>~

REEN NEVER EXPECTED to see Ruthie Brone, her great-granddaughter, Shannie, and Shannon's parents, Linda and Allan Brone, all boasting bright-eyed smiles when Drake opened the door, ushering them inside.

"What a wonderful surprise!" Reen said, watching as Ruthie's grandson maneuvered his wheelchair-bound grandmother over the threshold and into the house. She'd seen Ruthie using canes and a walker, depending on the severity of her pain and stiffness, but this was the first time she'd seen her in a wheelchair.

Shannon gave Reen a hug around her legs. An instant later she let go and twirled in place, giggling merrily. Then she started hopping around like a bunny.

"Look at me, Miss Reen! See what I can do?" She concluded her performance by running around the living room, then plopping to the floor to cuddle with Hazelnut and Knitten, who'd come to investigate.

"Be careful, sweetheart," Linda cautioned.

"Let her be, honey." Allan drew his wife into a side-hug. "She'll be fine."

It was the first time Reen had seen the previously frail little girl being active, much less running and jumping. This indicated the final portion of her heartwish had succeeded. Seeing Shannie sporting the Lulu puppy hat and sweater she'd knitted for her warmed her heart.

"Wow, look at you, Shannie!" Reen turned her attention from the lively Shannon to her family, who looked euphoric.

311

"Can you believe it?" Linda asked. Ivory complected with white-blonde hair, she had ice-blue eyes. "We just came from the doctor. An instant after he'd told us the cancer was growing again, the room filled with pastel blue light." Linda spread her hands and arms in a wide circle. "Needless to say, we were all stunned."

"The doctor's face paled as he glanced again at the test results," Allan said. "He was practically speechless when all of Shannie's test results were negative."

"As if the cancer had never been there," Linda went on as tears ran freely down her cheeks. Drake grabbed a couple tissues from the nearby half-bath, offering them to Linda who dabbed her eyes and nose. He handed a couple to Ruthie who was crying too.

"Believe me, these are the happiest tears a mother could ever shed. Our little girl is alive and well—*well*, Maureen!" Linda clasped Reen's arm, squeezing tight. "Not just in remission—the cancer is gone! Vanished. I don't know how that's possible but..." she started crying all over again, "it's a miracle."

"A miracle," Ruthie repeated.

Drake tugged Reen to his side, whispering to her, "And you're my little miracle worker."

Allan drew his wife closer. "We're headed out for a celebration dinner and wanted to stop by to share our happy news with you, as well as invite you to join us, because you've been such an important part of our little girl's path to healing."

"Thank you. " She took one of Allan's hands and one of Linda's, offering a congratulatory squeeze. "You must be positively elated. Come in and stay a while, please. We'd love to have you join us for a joint celebratory meal. We've got wall to wall food," Reen gestured to all the edibles lining the family room, "and—"

"And wall to wall people," Ruthie noted. "Oh...and I just noticed Drake is wearing a tuxedo."

Glancing first at Drake's formal wear, then at each other, both Linda and Allan looked sheepish. "Sorry, we never even realized," Allan said. "I'm afraid we're imposing on a special occasion."

"Nonsense," Reen insisted. "Your amazing news about Shannon gives us even more reason to celebrate."

"What are you celebrating?" Linda gazed around the area bustling with people.

Holding out her left hand, Reen told them, "Drake and I just got engaged!"

"Congratulations!" the three adults said in unison.

"My future wicked mother-in-law," Drake joked in a purposely amplified voice, "forced me to propose in front of the entire Malone clan—in a tux."

"I heard that, Drake," Astrid called in a teasing voice from the kitchen, following that with greetings to the Brones. Everyone else offered their greetings as well, pointing out food and drink as well as places to sit. Shannie was happily playing with the cat, dog, and the other three kids.

Allan wheeled his grandmother into the family room.

"See? What did I tell you?" Ruthie said to Reen. There was a distinct sparkle in the old woman's eyes as she gazed up at Reen. "I knew you two would end up together sooner or later. Heck," she gave an insightful wave, "everybody knew it except for you, Reenie." She exchanged knowing glances with Linda and Allan.

"And maybe me," Drake said, eyeing Reen before shifting his smile to Ruthie.

"Well it all turned out in the end, didn't it?" Ruthie's aged face spread into a wrinkly grin. "We have a present for you," she informed Reen, patting her hand. "Now we can call it an engagement present."

"You brought me a gift?" This day teemed with one surprise after another.

"A thank you gift," Ruthie confirmed. "Allan, dear, could you bring me closer to the silver tree? I swear, that decades-old tree has a magical vibe to it." She pointed the way and Allan wheeled her close. "You have the color wheel going. Perfect!" she said with the surprised delight of a child. Shannie echoed her great-grandmother's sentiments when she and Lilly skipped into the room with Hazelnut and Knitten at their heels.

"What can I get you to drink?" Nevan asked them. "Coffee, tea, cocoa, beer, wine, those sticky-sweet syrupy liqueurs women like, you name it, we've probably got it."

"You're such a sexist." Reen chuckled.

"And we've got mountains of food," Gard reminded them. "Including my brother's Irish Pork Pie. That snagged Allan's attention and he was off to grab a piece of meat pie and bottle of porter.

"Scones?" Laila stopped by with a variety-filled platter of her baked goods and some small paper plates.

Swallowing a bite of Laila's new Engagement Scone, Linda said, "Divine! Definitely better than the restaurant we were going to."

"Ruthie!" Kady bent to give the woman a kiss on the cheek. "I haven't seen you in forever. I brought a big container of the special healing tea you like, along with some raw manuka honey to sweeten it...something told me you might be here today." She winked at the old woman.

"Your psychic abilities never fail to amaze," Ruthie said. "I'd love a cup, dear." Offering a warm smile, she patted Kady's hand. "It sounds like just the healing elixir I need. Maybe if I drink enough of it it'll get me out of this contraption." Ruthie tapped the arms of her wheelchair.

"It's delicious," Monica's mother, Nancy, said, lifting her own mug. "Love the ginger in it. This is my second cup."

"I'll be happy to make a batch for you," Kady told Nancy.

"Thanks. That would be wonderful. As Ruth said, it's great healing elixir." With a smile, she walked past them and took a seat.

Kady studied Ruthie's wheelchair. Squatting at her side, she asked, "Are you still able to stand and walk a bit, or do you need to stay in the chair all the time now?"

"Her rheumatologist said she can be up and around as much as she's able, but not to overdo it," Linda replied.

"He said moderate activity is good for me," Ruthie added. "I'm determined to spend as little time in this contraption as possible."

"Good. I'm going to make a special healing meditation video for you that you can play on your phone, tablet or laptop. It'll have soothing ocean wave sounds with dolphins, relaxing harp music in the background, and some specific healing phrases that I'll record for you. The video part will be soft colors swirling and slowly flipping."

"That sounds lovely," Ruthie said. "I'm amazed you can do all of that."

"I think you'll find it very relaxing and therapeutic. I'll prepare a big jar of my special, healing tea too, the blend that includes the hibiscus and fennel that you enjoy, and some vegan snacks that I'll make according to autoimmune protocol recipes for your rheumatoid arthritis. Soon you'll be needing that chair less and less. I can bring everything over late tomorrow afternoon if that works for you."

"Well yes but I feel awful having you go through so much trouble for me," Ruthie objected.

"Trouble?" Kady's features scrunched. "You?" Rising to her feet, she told her, "You've done so much for all of us, Ruthie. It's time we gave back to you."

"What a sweet thing to say. I was so happy to hear you'll be co-owner of Bubble Tide Books. Tomorrow we'll have a nice chat and you can tell me all about it."

"I look forward to it." After planting another gentle kiss on the woman's cheek, Kady headed back to the kitchen to fix Ruthie's cup of tea.

"She's such a kind, darling girl." Giving Reen a pointed look, Ruthie added, "Just like her sister. Maureen, you've gone out of your way to bring happiness to our little Shannie during her cancer battle. And you've done the same for so many other children at the hospital."

"Grandma Ruthie is right," Linda agreed. "When dark times loomed for the Brone family, your whimsical knitted and crocheted items helped us smile and laugh when we thought it was no longer possible."

"You'll never know," Allan said, joining them again, "how needed and healing that sense of mirth was for us."

Astrid gingerly pinched her daughter's cheek. "My Reen is a very special young woman, isn't she?"

"One in a million," Drake agreed.

Reen started to fidget. "No, I'm not...I..." She wasn't used to having a ton of adulation heaped on her.

In tune with her unease, Drake held Reen close to his side, giving her a supportive hug, whispering in her ear, "Hang in there, you're going to be fine, sweetheart."

Hearing her fiancé call her *sweetheart* calmed Reen, reminding her of the years of joy ahead for her and Drake.

"I want to tell you about my decision," Ruthie told Reen. "As you can see," she struck the arms of the wheelchair with the heels of her palms, "the rheumatoid arthritis decided to bully its way into my life and has me stuck in this darned thing. Which," she waved a determined finger, "will only be temporary...especially with Kady's help. That said," she uttered a sigh, "it's time that I step back from running my beloved String Me Along."

Sorry to hear that, Reen wondered if Ruthie's deterioration was why she found the store closed when she stopped by.

"You, more than anyone, know how I feel about my shop, Reen. God knows I love all my kids, grandkids and great-grandkids but not a one of the Brones is interested in taking over the family business. Allan, Linda and Shannon are the only family still living here in Glassfloat Bay, the rest have all moved out of town. Truth be told, I doubt any of the Brones even knows what to do with a pair of knitting needles, other than to jab someone with them." She gleefully gestured in demonstration.

While Ruthie laughed at her own joke, Reen remembered her granddaughter-in-law, Linda, had zero interest in anything yarn related.

"What can I say?" Linda's cheeks colored while she smiled, nodding in resignation. "I'm afraid Grandma Ruthie is right. For some reason Allan doesn't take kindly to being a voodoo doll stand-in." With a quick teasing glance at her husband, Linda took another bite of scone.

"So," Ruthie went on, "I've decided to sell String Me Along."

Reen couldn't help the gasp escaping her lips at Ruthie's news. "What? Oh no!" Her voice came out louder than she'd intended, capturing the attention of others in the family room.

"Oh wow..." Drake muttered.

"Honey?" Astrid asked her daughter as she set a charcuterie board on the coffee table.

"What happened?" Delaney asked, placing a ramekin of Greek olives on the table. "What's wrong?"

"I'm fine. It's Ruthie." As curious family and friends gathered around, Reen repeated Ruthie's decision about selling. They understood Reen's angst, knowing String Me Along was Ruth Brone's lifeblood...as well as Maureen's impossible dream.

Kady returned, serving the tea to Ruthie, then tilting her head as if listening to something far off. Touching her fingers to her temples, she closed her eyes for a moment.

Elbowing Gard, Nevan said, "Shhhh...our little sister's having one of her woo-woo moments." Gard snicked a quiet laugh in return.

Astrid tsked. "Not now, boys..." she warned.

Turning to Reen, Kady gave a reassuring smile. "Don't worry, it's all good," she told her sister. "I'm receiving nothing but positive vibes about whatever is going on here." She made circle motions with her hands.

"Kady is right. There's nothing for anyone to be sad about," Ruthie assured. "This is a time for joy." Rather than appearing mournful, Reen noted Ruthie's aged face looked more serene and youthful as her smile expanded.

"Joyful," Ruthie continued, "because I'm selling my yarn shop to the one person I can trust to love it as much as I have for the last fifty years." Her eyes glittered as she turned her attention to Reen. "My dear Reen, that person is you. Along with the shop comes all the inventory. All the yarn, equipment, everything. It includes the building itself too, along with my apartment there. I'm moving in with Allan, Linda and Shannon. They have a great big house with plenty of extra room for me so I won't be in the way too much."

"You could never be in the way, Grandma," Allan assured her with a kiss to her cheek. "Sometimes I think my grandmother loves her yarn shop more than she loves any of us," he claimed with a teasing smile. "When Grandma Ruth came to us with her idea, we had a family meeting. All the Brones readily agreed with her plan."

Reen's head swam with the news. It was an honor, but Reen could no more afford to purchase the yarn shop than she could afford one of the mansions on Beauregard Hill. The dismal thought had her shoulders slumping.

"That sounds like a good thing, Reen," Hud noted, sidling next to Monica. "Don't look so gloomy."

"He's right," Drake said. "This is what you've always wanted. Your dream, Reen."

"What did I tell you?" Kady said.

"Reen, we believe you have the knowledge, the creativity, and, most important, the heart to keep String Me Along operating successfully for another fifty years," Linda said.

"I'm betting you love it just as much as I do," Ruthie said. "I know you'll take care of it, nurture it, and make it bigger and better than it's ever been. So, what do you say? I promise to make you an offer you can't refuse." Ruthie winked.

"Oh Ruthie, Allan, Linda, I'm honored that you've chosen me to take over the business." She turned her attention solely to Ruthie. "Ruthie, you've taught me all I know. I've told you before that you truly have the patience of a saint. But..." Reen drew in a deep, wobbly breath.

"I can't possibly afford to purchase String Me Along, or the upkeep and daily operations of the store and the building. I wish I could. But," her slumping shoulders lifted in a shrug, "I can't. I'm sorry to disappoint you."

Arms folded across their chests, Nevan and Gard shot a knowing glance at Kady, who continued standing there with the same serene smile.

The idea of losing the shop forever was crushing to Reen. If no one wanted to buy it, what would happen? Maybe it would be gutted and become a fast food place, or a videogame venue, or any number of other non-yarn-related retail spaces.

"I can take out a second mortgage on my house," Drake quickly offered.

Grasping his hand, Reen said, "Thank you, Drake, but I can't allow you to do that." She took a deep breath. "I could make payments," she told Ruthie, "but I doubt I'd qualify for a business loan."

"I have some money put away," Astrid started, "and I could—"

"You're finally in a position, Mom," Reen interrupted, "where you can travel to all those places you've wanted to see around the world but had to put on hold while you raised us six kids by yourself. I insist you use that money for yourself. You deserve it. I want to see oodles of photographs that you and Tore take while traveling all over with your trusty little Kodak camera."

"My family is loaded," Saffron proposed. "I can ask my parents for—"

Fully aware of how volatile Saffron's relationship was with her wealthy but difficult parents, Reen cut in, "Thank you so much, but there's no way I'd let you be obligated to your mother and father on my behalf."

"If Ruth will agree to give me the real estate listing," Monica said, "I'll give you my full portion of the commission. That should help."

Reen found Monica's offer especially touching. "That's such a kind offer, Monica, but I can't have you do all the work without any compensation."

"I'm sure we can all put our heads together and come up with something," Nevan offered.

"Varik and I are doing fine—I can give you the royalties from my Delaney's Diary books," Delaney added.

"I'll keep the building in top repair," Hud told Reen, "making any needed improvements without any charge."

"Count me in. Whatever it takes," Hud's sister, Annalise said, with their sister, Sabrina, voicing her agreement.

As everyone added their kind, giving suggestions, fat tears rolled down Reen's cheeks. She felt so blessed...so loved. "Thank you all, from the bottom of my heart, but..." Her chin quivering, she had to pause.

Drake looked to the Brones. "Can you give Reen a couple of days to think this over? It's a big financial decision." He turned to Reen. "I'm sure we can figure something out together." He looked around the room where everyone was gathered. "Maybe we could all chip in, buy it together, and put it in Reen's name." His suggestion was met by nodding and chorused agreement.

God she loved this man.

Ruthie's expression morphed into the strangest ear to ear grin. She almost looked elfish. Allan and Linda followed suit. It was weird watching the three of them grinning when Reen felt so demoralized.

"Nope," Ruthie answered Drake without hesitation. "Maureen doesn't get any extra time. I need a decision today. Right now." She tapped the watch on her wrist. Reen thought Ruthie's almost mocking demeanor was oddly inappropriate considering the circumstances.

"Well I...I understand..." Reen answered. "In that case, I'm truly sorry to say—"

"Why don't you have a look at the purchase price before you give me your final answer, Reenie?"

"It really doesn't matter, Ruthie, because—"

"Maureen," Allan interjected. "Just look at it." He removed a folded document from his jacket pocket, presenting it to Reen. With an encouraging nod, he turned it over to her.

Determined not to cry any more than she already had in front of everyone, Reen took the papers, opening them to see a real estate contract fully prepared with a sales price of—

"One dollar!" Reen's head snapped up. She looked from one Brone to the other before her gobsmacked gaze landed on Drake. Returning to the contract, she read aloud, "This sales price is exclusively for Maureen Malone." She looked up again, her expression twisting as she tried to absorb what was happening. "I don't understand. This must be a typo. It says you want to sell the shop—the entire building and its contents—to me for just a dollar?"

"Of course, you can make payments if you can't afford it. For less than ten cents a month you can have it paid off in a year," Ruthie cracked, promptly dissipating the tension Reen felt.

Tears obscured Reen's vision. This was another instance of a dream come true for her, without her even including it in her heartwish.

This was the happiest day of her life.

"This is the happiest day of our lives," Ruthie said as if she had a direct line to Reen's brain and had heard her thoughts. "We were hoping we could make it your happiest day too."

"Told you so," Kady said with combined pride and gladness.

Turning to Drake, Reen gazed into his eyes, and he into hers, exchanging knowing thoughts about Reen's heartwishes.

"Tick-tock," Ruthie teased, tapping again on the watch at her wrist. Without a doubt she was having a ball with all of this. "Time's running out. You going to accept, Reenie, or not?"

"Yes! Oh my God, yes, Ruthie. But...but are you sure? I mean...just a dollar? How? Why?" she sputtered. The concept was simply too foreign for her to believe.

"Absolutely, positively," Allan assured. "Grandma wanted to just give it to you, but selling it for a dollar makes it a binding legal contract here in the state of Oregon."

"Since he's an attorney," Linda said, "Allan has all the particulars already worked out. You gave our family the gift of healing laughter when we felt sure we'd never be able to smile again, Maureen. That's invaluable. Your whimsical knitting projects made our little girl smile when she was too sick to even eat. You'll never know how precious a gift that was for us."

"Wow...I honestly don't know what to say." Reen didn't even try to hold back the flood of joyful tears.

Snaking his arm around her waist, Drake tugged Reen close to his side, kissing her temple. "I believe the elusive word you're looking for, sweetheart, is *yes*."

"Yes!" Unabashedly bawling and laughing at the same time, Reen told them, "I, Maureen Margaret Malone, soon to be Slattery, do hereby absolutely, positively accept your unbelievably kind and generous offer." She went to Ruthie's wheelchair, giving the woman a loving hug. "Thank you so much. I promise I will never let you down."

A host of congratulatory offerings from everyone nearly bounced off the walls.

"There is one condition." Ruthie lifted a bent finger. "It's not mandatory but I'd be pleased if you'd considered it."

"Anything, Ruthie."

"The name of the shop, String Me Along, I'd love for you to keep it for as long as I'm still around."

"Perfect. I was going to ask if I could keep the name. I've always loved it."

"Wonderful!" Ruthie beamed.

"I do have a favor to ask of you in return, Ruthie."

"Whatever you need." She nodded, taking Reen's hand in her fragile fingers and giving it a gentle squeeze.

"Promise me you'll keep involved with the shop as often as you're able. Maybe teach some classes that wouldn't require you to use your hands very much. I want you to be an integral part of my dream business, Ruthie. To help guide me as I do my best to step into your shoes because I don't want to mess anything up."

"Excellent idea." Kady gave her sister a big, knowing smile.

"Nothing would make me happier," Ruthie assured Reen. "I want to be..." she paused for the right word. "Relevant. Needed. As I get older I worry about feeling useless and ineffectual." She beckoned with gnarled fingers and Reen bent low so Ruthie could wrap her arms around her, kissing her cheek and no doubt leaving an indelible pink imprint there. "I'll always help in any way I can. That should help keep me alive and kicking for a good long while."

That, of course, was Reen's master plan. She wanted to keep Ruthie happy and healthy for as long as possible.

"You all know what time it is, don't you?" Nevan asked. Without waiting for replies, he made a broad gesture, encompassing the room. "Time to eat!"

"As soon as Maureen signs the real estate transaction papers," Allan said, taking a pen from his pocket, holding it aloft and waving it.

"Hold that pose right there, Allan," Astrid told him. A moment later, camera in hand, she snapped a picture. "Okay, now one of you accepting the document," she instructed Reen. *Click.* "All done." Astrid smiled. "You can go ahead now."

After signing, while everyone was busy mounding food on their plates, Reen spotted Shannon, bristling with good health and so full of life, running down the flight of stairs to the playroom along with Hazelnut, Knitten and the other children. When the energetic little girl ran back upstairs because she'd forgotten something, Reen's heart swelled with joy.

Drake came to Reen's side, taking her hand as they watched Shannie together. "I know how much this means to you. You look like you're about ready to explode with happiness."

"I am. Just look at her, Drake. Isn't that the best thing you've ever seen?"

"Definitely sensational...but not the best." Turning Reen to face him, he kissed her. "The best thing is right here in my arms. I love you, Maureen." He kissed her again. "I must have already said that to you a thousand times today but I'll never grow tired of the words my heart needs to tell you, over and over again."

Reen had no idea Drake could be so romantic. "I love you too, Drake. So much. If this is all a dream, I hope I never wake up. Just imagine, me, Maureen Malone Slattery," she couldn't help letting out a squeal of delight, "in my very own yarn shop, spending my days helping people learn how to knit and crochet, and surrounding myself with every conceivable kind of yarn and knitting needles and crochet hooks and patterns and how-to-books and—"

"Whoa," Drake laughed, "sounds like you'll need a bigger shop."

"You forget, Professor, I've got the whole building, which includes Ruthie's old apartment. I've seen it and it's huge!" Closing her eyes, Reen indulged in a satisfied sigh. "Come on, Professor Hunky-Dorky, let's get something to eat. The quicker we do that, the quicker they'll all leave and we can have the house to ourselves." Looking up at him she gave him her best devilish look, waggling her eyebrows.

His eyes wide with expectation, Drake grabbed Reen's hand, racing into the family room.

Chapter Twenty-Three

~<>~

HOURS LATER, after the remains of their impromptu engagement party had been cleaned up, Reen breathed a full, tuneful sigh. Although incredibly happy and ecstatic, the overabundance of joy had tired her to the point of exhaustion.

One by one friends and family members had departed, with Astrid and Tore the last to leave, taking Lilly and Kevin with them for their promised ice cream treat. They were keeping the kids overnight so Drake and Reen could have some time to themselves after the chaotic day of magical surprises.

"I swear," Drake vowed after they closed the front door for the last time, "I'm half-tempted to hang a do not disturb sign outside." He wrapped his arm around Reen's shoulder, nuzzling her neck. "I thought they'd never leave. Now...where were we before half the town stopped by and your persistent mother forced me to propose to you in front of everyone?"

"Regrets?" Reen asked, toying with his fancy bowtie.

"Yes," he said, pausing long enough that Reen's pulse skipped. "I regret having to wear this monkey suit...again, at your mother's insistence."

"You've had a crash course in the willful nature of your future mother-in-law today," Reen teased.

"She's quite a persuasive woman."

"Tell me about it." Reen snickered, then figured she'd be wise to do a little damage control in case Drake got the wrong idea. "But she's definitely not a monster-in-law. I promise."

"I know." Nailing her with a perceptive glance, he added, "I also know without a doubt where you get your headstrong personality." Chuckling, he stuck two fingers in his shirt collar, trying to loosen it. "Damn, I hate wearing these things."

"But you look incredibly debonair in your tux. Just think of all those fabulous photos we'll have of you looking so charming. We'll show our grandchildren when we tell them the story of how Grandpa Hunky-Dorky proposed to Grandma Knitter." Reen gave Drake another onceover. "You really do look devastatingly handsome in a tux, Professor."

"You think so, hmm?" With a pointed look, he added, "Just wait until you see me out of it." He stopped his collar tugging long enough to waggle his eyebrows at her the same suggestive way she'd done to him earlier.

Together they walked, well, Reen hobbled, to the sofa where they sat next to each other, with Hazelnut leaping up on the cushion next to Drake.

"You know you're not supposed to be up here, Hazelnut," Reen reprimanded, not sounding at all resolute. She was too happy to muster her disciplinary voice. Sensing her mistress's dilemma, the dog remained exactly where she'd planted herself, looking as cute as possible while shining up to her future papa.

"I can't believe we're finally alone," Drake said in the sexiest voice she'd ever heard her best buddy utter. "Well," he shot the dog a glance, "almost."

"Aw, poor Hazel. She looks kind of forlorn, don't you think?" Reen asked.

"The dog looks like she always looks," Drake noted after a cursory glance. "Like a dog."

"I think she misses Knitten. Let's give Hazel a bone and put her in the other room so she can look out the window...and you and I can have some romantic fiancé-fiancée time together." Reen's fingers tiptoed up from Drake's knee to his chest, stopping at his heart. "Sound good?" she asked, in her most evocative tone.

"Good?" Reen watched the pupils of Drake's eyes dilate as she listened to his low, throaty chuckle. "Oh, baby, that sounds superb." He kissed the pulse point inside her wrist and edged closer. "You and me, finally enjoying the benefits we should have been savoring for a long time." Leaning in for a kiss, Hazelnut beat him to the punch, plopping between them and slurping their faces like they were lollipops.

Clearly aghast, Drake made an *eeew* face.

Reen failed at her attempt not to laugh at the hilarious sight.

"Apparently dog spit is something I'll have to get used to." He shuddered as he looked left and right for something to wipe the wetness from his face, finally settling on the back of his hand.

"Yes it is, because you're Hazel's daddy now," Reen advised, resorting to the babytalk she used for her darling pet as she tussled the fur on Hazelnut's ears and neck. "She wants to show that she loves you, isn't that right sweetie pie?"

With a side glance, Drake asked, "Which one of us is *sweetie pie*, me or the big fur baby here that's expertly manipulating my fiancée?"

"You're both my sweetie pies, of course," Reen answered, drawing them into a three-way hug.

Mumbling something unintelligible, Drake muffled a laugh. "Remember when you asked me earlier if I have any regrets?"

"Drake!" Reen gave his arm a good-humored slap.

Still chuckling, he said, "Point me to where you keep the furry sweetie pie's bones so you and I can get down to...business." There was no mistaking the amorous look in his eyes.

Once Hazelnut was happily gnawing on her new bone, cloistered away in another room, Reen cuddled close to Drake, resting her head on his chest. Glancing down at her hand, she held it aloft, engaging in a tuneful sigh. I love this ring so much, Drake. And I love being your fiancée." Her gaze traveled from the ring to her Frankie boot, which she hoped would be gone before her wedding.

Her wedding!

Her head popped back up, hitting the bottom of Drake's chin. "Ow!"

"Drake!" She hadn't meant it to come out as if she'd cried "Fire!" but it did, causing Hazelnut to bark in the other room. The day had been such a whirlwind, Reen hadn't really had a chance for all the good news to fully sink in yet.

Alarmed, Drake bolted upright in his seat. "What is it? What's wrong?"

"Nothing! Not a single solitary thing. We're getting married, Drake! Married! I can hardly believe it. I'm so excited." Propping her elbow on the back of a sofa cushion, she rested her chin on her fist. "Let's talk about it."

"You want to talk? Now?" His voice sounded strangled but his spirited laughter was full, round and genuine as his hand snaked up inside her sweater. "I'm definitely not in a discussion kind of mood."

"Yeah...me neither." Reen worked to remove his bow tie.. "But I was kind of wondering..."

Drake sighed. "Hmm?"

"About where we're going to live. I'm going to sell my house. It's way too small for the four of us. We should live in your house. I love that place and all the work you've done there. And then we can make a sort of passion pit room upstairs in—"

Skewing his expression, Drake barked a surprised laugh. "A *what?*"

"You know, like a private, sexy hideaway just for us," Reen explained, seeing it clearly inside her head.

"A passion pit, huh? Where did you come up with that?"

Shrugging, Reen told him, "It's an expression I've heard Kady use."

Drake rolled his eyes. "I'm very fond of Kady, but your *flower child slash hippie*" he hung air quotes around the term, "little sister's somehow stuck in the 1960s. Not quite sure how that throwback happened."

"Kady is special. And adorable. Anyway, our special getaway spot," Reen continued without missing a beat, "would be upstairs in one of the rooms in the apartment above String Me Along."

"Why just one room? Why not wire the entire apartment for hot sex?" He gave her a wolfish grin. "I can think of all kinds of accessories we could use to decorate." She could swear his eyes twinkled as he smiled. "Zak told me all about the sex toys he and Laila bought from Provocative Pleasures."

"Ha! You can wipe that anticipatory grin right off your face, Professor, because we won't be going there. Ever. Laila couldn't have been more mortified when he took her there."

"The way Zak tells it, Laila drove him there."

Reen narrowed one eye at her chuckling fiancé. Drake was enjoying this way too much. "That's only because Zak was still a genie then and couldn't legally drive himself and—" Listening to her own implausible explanation had Reen half growling and half laughing. "This is ridiculous. Why are we even talking about this?"

"Passion pit," Drake offered the helpful reminder.

"Oh yeah..." It felt a wee bit early in their brand spanking new fiancé-fiancée relationship to have a discussion about sex toys. Drawing her bottom lip through her teeth, Reen turned her attention to the silver tree and its diverse collection of ornaments. "I'll have to get busy knitting our likenesses into a pair of ornaments, with you wearing your tux, and a Viking hat, and carrying thick academic volumes," she mused aloud, deftly shifting the conversation. "Mine will have me holding tiny skeins of yarn and a box of chocolates." The cuteness of her idea made her giggle.

"Well that's one way to change the subject." Following her lead, Drake smiled and turned his attention to the tree Reen still gazed at. "But I like the idea of miniature Professor and Mrs. Hunky-Dorky ornaments."

"I'll make little Kevin, Lilly, Hazelnut and Knitten ornaments too. The entire Hunky-Dorky family."

Drake leaned close and kissed her temple.

Touching the spot he'd kissed, Reen smiled. "What was that for?"

"Just because I love you."

"Ohhhhh..." She melted against him. "I love you too. So much."

The sofa cushion they shared was their favorite spot in Bekka House. They'd sat together there umpteen times as buddies, watching a family movie with his kids, or just shooting the breeze. Reen remembered fantasizing about snuggling close to him like this each time Drake drifted into professor mode. She'd struggle to stay alert as he regaled her with academic-themed theories regarding topics he found utterly fascinating...and she found dry as dust.

She remembered sitting through his tedious professorial discussion about the perceived historical significance of the island of Atlantis, whether it ever actually existed, and its most plausible location. The topic sounded interesting, until he delved into all the hypotheses, conjectures, speculations and everything else that made her wish she had a couple of toothpicks to keep her eyelids propped open.

On the other hand, Drake always managed to stay alert...well, at least he stayed awake, when Reen told him at length about the latest knitted hat pattern she'd created; or how she'd unearthed a 1940s era ceramic salt and pepper shaker set at the bottom of a spiderweb-covered pile of *junque* at a garage sale. And he patiently listened as she complained about her exaggerated love of chocolate and how it got the best of her and the scale sometimes. All topics of conversation she realized were of zero interest to Professor Slattery.

No doubt about it, they were a perfect match.

As they sat now, fingers entwined and heads resting together, mindlessly gazing at the decades-old metal Christmas tree, Reen breathed another contented sigh. After a long, exceedingly eventful day it was finally just her and Drake, fiancé and fiancée, friend and buddy, soon to be lover and lover, future Mr. and Mrs. The wonderful notion tickled her.

"Did all of this really happen, Drake? My heartwishes coming true, the yarn shop, and...holy cow, Drake, are we really engaged?"

"Mmm-hmm." Drake held her in his arms, kissing her soundly. Oh how she treasured the feel of being this close to the man she loved. "Today, my beautiful fiancée," he told her, kissing her forehead, "we took the first steps into our new life together. Our new *lifetime* together."

Happy from the top of her head to the tips of her toes, Reen couldn't remember engaging in as many dreamy sighs as she had today. "What you said was poetic, Drake." She caressed his cheek. "It seems there's a lot more going on in there," she tapped his head, "than endless facts and figures."

Quiet for a long moment, Drake had a faraway look in his eyes.

"What are you thinking about?" Taking his hand, she nestled it against her heart.

"Inanna...last year," he said. "Remember her?"

"Are you serious?" Reen's expression twisted at the peculiar and reference. "How could I possibly forget being visited by a Sumerian goddess who filled Laila's dining room with roaring thunder and cracks of lightning as we all sat around the table?"

"Don't forget her pet lion, Ninazu," Drake reminded her.

"Hardly." A sudden jolt of recollection made Reen shudder.

"Inanna of Sumer. Queen of Heaven, goddess of love and war—"

"Careful Drake," Reen interrupted, "you don't want to summon her and her lion again."

"Definitely not."

"If it wasn't for Inanna," Reen remembered, "Zak would still be imprisoned in that genie bottle for all eternity."

"Very true. I did some exhaustive research about her while we were working to save Zak," he said absently, that distant look still clouding his eyes.

Reen immediately recognized that data-filled look. Good grief...Professor Slattery was on the verge of getting all teacher-ish on her. Now, of all times!

"Inanna was a Mesopotamian goddess associated with love, beauty, sensuality, sex and fertility, as well as war, justice and political power. I find that unanticipated combination of unrelated attributes remarkable, don't you?" Reen nodded because she figured she should. "She was originally worshiped in Aratta and Sumer as Inanna," Drake continued. "Interestingly, the Akkadians, Babylonians and Assyrians later worshipped her as Ishtar..."

His gaze fixed on the hypnotic color rotation of the silver Christmas tree as he spoke, her brilliant history-loving fiancé rambled on about Inanna, Greeks, Phoenicians, Aphrodite, and other stuff Reen imagined must have been somehow related.

Muffling an oncoming yawn, she blinked because her eyes were glazing over. If she didn't do something fast, she'd fall asleep and Drake wouldn't even know it because he'd just keep jabbering on, lost in his captivating world of education.

She turned his face toward hers and placed a hand on his kneecap, applying enough pressure to draw his attention away from the facts and details written on the blackboard of his mind.

"Drake...sweetheart?"

"Hmm?"

"I love you, so, so much. All that information is positively fascinating," she lied, "but...please tell me you're not about to go into one of your ungodly lengthy professor-ish discussions right now. I think we were about to engage in something a bit less professor-ish and slightly more...shall we say, exploratory...if you know what I mean." She made her eyebrows bounce to, hopefully, give him the message.

She watched as Drake's preoccupied expression converted to one of realization and he offered her a dazzling smile. A moment later he fell into laughter. "I'm sorry, Reen. Really." Holding her face, he planted a promising kiss on her mouth. "I get carried away with the allure of history sometimes. I think about one thing that leads to another and...well, you know." Looking sheepish, he chuckled again.

"Mmm-hmm, I know." She kissed his chin. "I just want to know, briefly—remember, the keyword is *briefly*—what on earth made you think of Inanna as we're sitting here now?"

"I was thinking about her appearance last year. Before she vanished with a blinding flash of light, Inanna conferred her blessings and sang a chant to the gods, asking that Laila and Zak, as well as the two of us be kept safe and protected for all our days. Remember what she said just before that?"

Reen didn't have to think long. She'd thought of Inanna's odd words and prediction often, wondering what the goddess meant.

"I do. She told us the coming year would be life changing for us both. She said your soul mate is a woman you've already met. Then she turned to me, lifted an eyebrow, and gave a low, throaty laugh, saying, 'Well...that's interesting.' When we asked her what she meant, she became cryptic and said, 'Some things are best left unexplained.'"

"I'd say we finally understand what that was all about." Reen gave a slow nod of agreement. "So," Drake shrugged, "that's what made me think of her...and get caught up in one of my orations." His laughter was full and rich. One of the things Reen loved about Drake was his ready ability to laugh at himself.

Her smile grew wide. "Ouch..." she winced. "It hurts when I smile. I think I've used up my smile-muscle quotient for the next month."

"A month sounds just about right," Drake said.

"For what?" She toyed with his shirt studs, slipping her fingers between them, connecting to the warmth of his bare chest beneath.

"For us to get married. How about the first day of spring? You've always said you didn't care about having a big wedding, but if you do, we can wait until—"

"No!" Reen shook her head emphatically. "I don't want to wait a second longer than absolutely necessary to become Mrs. Professor Hunky-Dorky. The first day of spring is perfect. We can have the ceremony right here, in front of the tree, with our family and close friends. Kevin can be our ring bearer and Lilly will be the flower girl."

"I love it...and I love your naïveté."

Reen scrunched her face in confusion.

"You don't honestly expect Bekka House not to be jampacked once Astrid hears about our *little* wedding, do you?"

She didn't have to think about it for more than a moment. "Naïveté was an apropos word," she agreed. "According to the bone doc, I should be out of the boot by the middle of March." She wrapped her arms around his neck. "Professor, I love you so much it hurts." They leaned close for another impassioned kiss. "Ow." She puffed out her bottom lip. "See?"

"You're right. It is puffy. You know why?"

"Only if you can tell me without a lengthy scientific explanation." Her smile broadened.

Kissing her pouty lip, he said, "Because you're paying the price and being punished for making me wait so long for you."

"Is that so?" She teased him back.

"Unequivocally. In fact, recently gathered statistics substantiate the—"

Reen burst out laughing. "Oh my God, we're going to have so much fun together, Professor. Long after we're old and gray and both of us grow absentminded." She jerked her head toward him. "Of course, you're already ahead of me as far as being absentminded goes."

"Huh? As far as what goes?" he asked, a teasing gleam in his eye.

"Just promise you won't ever forget that I love you, okay?"

"My heart will always remember, even if my brain doesn't. But just to be on the safe side, I'll make a note of it in the margins of my academic journals so I'm reminded each time I open my books, which is several times a day."

"Perfect. I'll knit a cover for your journal. Just think, Drake, we can spend our weekends haunting garage sales so we can look for—"

Now it was Drake's turn to laugh. "It's going to be a great life, Reen, as we have fun making each other crazy."

"Will I have to go to operas, ballets, and lectures?"

"Only if you make me go to garage sales and thrift stores."

"In that case, I guess I'll have to brush up on Brunhilde, Swan Lake, and the rise and fall of the Mayan civilization," Reen said, wrinkling her nose.

"And I'll have to practice my bartering skills." Mirroring her silly expression, he added, "I'm sure I can find a suitable book to guide me in the matter of what might be fitting offers to make sure we can secure mounds of other people's useless, discarded junk."

Gazing into each other's eyes, they embraced and kissed.

"My darling Maureen-Malone-soon-to-be-Slattery, promise me you'll never change. I adore you just the way you are."

"And I adore you, and your, no *our*, wonderful children, and our dog Hazelnut, and our kitty-cat Knitten, and all of our upcoming secondhand shopping trips, and—"

Drake silenced his fiancée with a kiss so stunning it rendered her speechless.

"Hmm," he observed, "I'll have to do more of that."

"Often."

"Would my fiancée like to know what else I'm thinking about now?" Drake mused with a teasing expression, gently lowering Reen on the sofa cushions.

"That depends on how much talking is involved."

"Don't you want to spend some quality time now discussing all the upcoming wild, crazy, wonderful times we'll enjoy together on our decades-long journey to old age?" Drake's fingers found their way beneath her top, smoothing their way from her waist up to her front-clasp bra, which he skillfully unfastened. The warmth of hand exploring her cool, bare skin was exquisite. His perfectly promising kiss created a delicious tickle low down in her belly.

"I thought perhaps we could discuss Brunhilde's involvement with Bugs Bunny," he teased, his voice low and thick with passion.

Heady from the breathtaking kiss and anticipation of what was to come, Reen answered, "Oh, I don't think so." Threading her fingers through Drake's hair as his tongue teased her lips, she added, "I'd much rather have you educate me on the detailed theories of the birds and the bees. Strictly using show and tell, of course."

"I believe that can be arranged." Drake's smile lit his face as he finger-combed her hair, locking gazes with her. "Oh my sweet Maureen...if you only knew how precious you are to me."

When their lips met this time, the area surrounding them flooded with blue-white light.

Once it dissipated, Drake gazed lovingly at Reen. "And so," he said, "begins the wonderful lifelong journey of two people deeply in love, on our way to that matching pair of rocking chairs."

At that point, the professor ceased his talking...and proceeded with several hours of show and tell.

~<>~

Thank you so much for choosing to read The Knitter's Heartwish. I hope you got as much enjoyment out of the story as I did writing it. Creating and getting to know each of the six Malone siblings and their mom, Astrid, has been satisfying and rewarding for me...well, except when one of them wakes me up at 3:00 a.m. to let me know they disagree with something I had them think, say, or do.

In the Heartwishes books I've created the sort of loving, close-knit, caring, and supportive family and friends that I wished I'd had growing up. For me, one of the best perks of being a writer is creating fictional worlds, populating them with a large cast of characters, then "living" in that world for hours on end as I tell their stories. Being so thoroughly immersed in a fictional world I've created, the pretend people and their hangouts soon seem to become real. My favorite part is getting to hang out with everybody.

I can't imagine not writing. I write to make myself and my readers happy, which means you're very important to me and I appreciate you! If you enjoyed this book I'd be delighted if you left a positive review or rating on the site where you purchased it. Your review can be long or short, or even just a star rating.

Good reviews tell me that readers enjoy my books, which helps encourage me to continue writing. They help new readers make decisions about whether or not to read my books. Reviews also help my books to be seen so they don't get lost in a site's complicated algorithms. The more reviews a book gets, the better chance it has of readers finding it. You can also help other readers find this book by recommending it to your friends.

As you can probably tell, I'd be exceedingly happy if you left a positive review for my book. Thank you!

I really enjoy connecting with my readers. Visit DaisyDexterDobbs.com[1] to sign up for my newsletter and mailing list to get notifications for my new book releases, contests, and more.

You can also find me here:

Facebook: DaisyDexterDobbs[2]

Instagram: DaisyDexterDobbs[3]

TikTok: @daisydexterdobbs[4]

Twitter: DaisyDDobbs[5]

Goodreads: daisydexterdobbs[6]

Email: DaisyDexterDobbs@gmail.com

Thanks again!

—*Daisy Dexter Dobbs*

~<>~

1. https://www.daisydexterdobbs.com/contact.html

2. https://www.facebook.com/daisydexterdobbs/

3. https://www.instagram.com/daisydexterdobbs/

4. https://www.tiktok.com/@daisydexterdobbs

5. https://twitter.com/DaisyDDobbs

6. https://www.goodreads.com/daisydexterdobbs

Don't miss out!

Visit the website below and you can sign up to receive emails whenever Daisy Dexter Dobbs publishes a new book. There's no charge and no obligation.

https://books2read.com/r/B-A-MIIB-NPUWB

Also by Daisy Dexter Dobbs

Heartwishes
The Viking's Heartwish
The Genie's Heartwish
The Firefighter's Heartwish
The Knitter's Heartwish
The Nymph's Heartwish
The Psychic's Heartwish

Watch for more at www.DaisyDexterDobbs.com.

About the Author

Long dedicated to providing the magic of escapism through her books, Daisy Dexter Dobbs started writing happily-ever-after stories when she was five, often reading them aloud to her guests, using a toilet plunger as a microphone.

Today, Daisy's books transport readers on wondrous voyages of the imagination. Infused with positivity, hope, joy, humor, friendships, family, and romance, her stories often include a touch of magic and fantasy—and always a happily ever after.

Daisy has ghostwritten speeches for politicians; been an art director; a weight loss counselor; mayor's executive secretary; a Realtor; travel agent; editor; she even worked as a butcher's meat wrapper, quitting on the spot when she saw a big eyeball coming toward her on the conveyor. Having worked at more than 40 different jobs provides Daisy with a bottomless pit of...questionable experience she draws from for her books.

A Chicago native now residing in the Pacific Northwest, Daisy is happily married to her soul mate, the man who is the inspiration for every hero she creates. They have a wonderful daughter, son-in-law, and rescue granddog. Happily for her family and friends, Daisy no longer feels the need to use a bathroom plunger as a microphone when entertaining guests.

Read more at www.DaisyDexterDobbs.com.

Lightning Source UK Ltd.
Milton Keynes UK
UKHW010638130922
408795UK00001B/117